·C

GRISHIN

Also by Hans Herlin

THE LAST SPRING IN PARIS

SOLO RUN

WHICH WAY THE WIND

COMMEMORATIONS

GRISHIN

Hans Herlin

Translated by J. MAXWELL BROWNJOHN

DOUBLEDAY & COMPANY, INC.,

GARDEN CITY, NEW YORK

1987

Library of Congress Cataloging in Publication Data

Herlin, Hans, 1925–
 Grishin.

 Translation of: Grishin.
 1. Lenin, Vladimir Il'ich, 1870–1924—Fiction.
I. Title.
PT2668.E748G713 1987   833'.914   86–29072
ISBN 0-385-23696-4

for my wife

Contents

"There is no present or future—only the past,
happening over and over again—now."

EUGENE O'NEILL, *A Moon for the Misbegotten*

PART ONE

March–June 1918

•1•

Russia began out there, less than five hundred yards away. From the window where he was standing Grishin could see the Finnish sentries on the nearer bank of the small river that marked the frontier. They were Sissits, ski troops in long sheepskin coats and tall fur caps. Both men were visible as a pair of dark shapes crisply defined by the log fire they had lit to keep the cold at bay. Grishin could not make out the bridge beyond them or the Red Guards on the Russian bank.

Snow had fallen in the last two days, after a spell of cold, dry weather. It was springtime snow, as frail and pale in color as the lambs that were born at this season of the year. Reflected by this white blanket, moonlight suffused the darkened room and cast a glow over its walls, which were painted white.

Grishin stood quite still, like a man holding his breath, but there was no tension in his stillness. It seemed as natural to him as the watchful immobility of a wild animal.

He remained just as motionless when a door in the main house opened and a woman emerged. Wrapping a voluminous shawl around her shoulders, she set off along the covered walkway that led to the guest annex. Four hours by car from Petrograd, the country mansion came complete with spacious grounds and several lakes. It was one of several properties owned by the woman's father, who had traded in caviar before the Revolution.

The walkway was carpeted with windblown snow. The woman sank in knee-deep in places, but the drifts only slowed her a little, never brought her to a stop. How strong she is, Grishin thought, remembering her sturdy, broad-hipped body and firm breasts.

Lydia Vydina knocked at the door, stamped the snow off her boots and removed the shawl. When she came and stood behind him, the night air that clung to her struck chill on the nape of his neck.

He still didn't move, but went on gazing in the direction of the frontier. She laid her hand lightly on his shoulder. There was more diffidence in the gesture than intimacy.

"You'd never ask, would you, however much you wanted to know?" Her tone was as diffident as the touch on his shoulder. "The message came through," she said at last.

Grishin slowly turned in a single, fluent movement, with the lithe grace of an athlete in full command of every muscle. The moonlight flooding in through the window made his skin look paler than it really was. His lean, stern face became deceptively placid and gentle when he smiled, but his eyes never lost their keen intensity.

He still said nothing, and she began to wonder if he had heard her at all, even though this was the moment he must have been waiting for ever since his arrival ten days earlier.

"Your guide, Spogis, is on his way."

"So it's tonight." He ran his fingers through his sleek, dark hair. "When will he get here?"

Grishin's voice was soft and deep. He had a way of lingering over his words that sometimes rendered them almost unintelligible.

Only once before had she heard the same sort of husky drawl, and that was while nursing at a field hospital during the war. The voice had belonged to a soldier with a bullet wound in the throat.

She lit the kerosene lamp beside the bed, which occupied most of the little room. "Would you mind drawing the curtains?"

"When?" he repeated.

"He's bringing a family from Moscow. Have you ever known a Russian train to be punctual? We've plenty of time."

There was no clock in the room. The calendar on the wall beside the door showed the date as March 8, not March 21, which it really was. The Bolsheviks had formally abolished the old Russian calendar in February—it was thirteen days behind the Western one —but Lydia Vydina, being the daughter of a bourgeois and the widow of a czarist officer, refused to acknowledge any of their post-Revolutionary innovations.

"How will they get to the border?" Grishin asked.

"Spogis will take them from Sortavala to the river—by sleigh, probably, in view of the snow. They won't be here till after eleven.

That's when the Russian sentries are relieved, and the guard commander is a friend."

"How well do you know this Latvian?"

"Spogis? Your people trust him. Mr. Hall trusts him. He has helped nearly forty men and women to escape, most of them in the last two months. They've stepped up their reign of terror. It's easier to intimidate people than win them over."

Lydia Vydina had evolved her own vocabulary to describe current events. "They" were the Bolsheviks, the Red revolutionaries who had ruled Russia since the previous October. "Once upon a time" or "in the old days" referred to the period prior to March 1917, when Czar Nicholas had abdicated.

"How did you get into this business?" he asked. "Did James Hall recruit you?"

"It isn't fashionable for Russian women to float around the house looking decorative, not these days. Besides, the money helps me to keep up the estate."

"Has Hall ever been here?"

"My family got to know him when he was attached to the British Embassy at St. Petersburg." She refused to call it Petrograd, Grishin noted. "He came here several times, usually in winter. He's a good skater in spite of his weight. Since they seized power he's been using this place to spirit certain people out of Russia. 'The Window,' he calls it."

Grishin thought of the file Colvin had prepared for him in London. In January the new Soviet government had granted the Finns their independence and undertaken to withdraw all Russian troops, but Red Guards and Finnish militiamen were still fighting fiercely in the south of the country. The main Helsingfors-Petrograd railroad line had been cut, hence the necessity to make his way to Moscow by the more northerly route.

"Perhaps you'd like to have a word with the couple from Moscow when they get here?" He wasn't listening, Lydia could tell. She raised her voice a little. "The husband's a goldsmith. They closed his business down. Jewelers are social parasites, and parasites must be exterminated."

"These border crossings," he said, "—have they always gone without a hitch?"

"Of course, why shouldn't they? Mr. Hall provides the refugees with passports and travel permits. Spogis escorts them to the frontier for him."

"Are they interrogated once they're across?"

"Yes, by an Englishman who comes here for the purpose."

"And then?"

"Then, if they've been clever enough to smuggle some of their money abroad, they settle wherever it happens to be. The others head for a country where they know the language, usually France. It doesn't really matter, though. Russians are never genuinely happy abroad. They're out of their natural element."

She shot him an inquiring glance—his Russian was faultless—but he refused to take the bait. She said, "It's getting cold in here." Kneeling down beside the stove, which was faced with Dutch tiles, she raked the ashes and put some more wood on.

"Why hasn't Hall sneaked your parents out?"

"You don't know my father. They told him he could keep one suit of clothes, and what did he choose? A frock coat—I ask you! He lives by selling off what little he has left, bit by bit."

The fire, which had almost gone out, blazed up again.

"He refuses to leave the country. He's even taken a job with the so-called house committee, which graciously permits him and my mother to occupy one room in their own home. He's responsible for seeing that the tenants' papers are in order."

"Survival is a great incentive."

"Either he doesn't grasp what's happening, or it's his professional mentality. The caviar merchants of Astrakhan have always made and lost fortunes overnight. It costs the earth to lay sturgeon nets. There are innumerable stretches of water in the Volga delta, and no one can ever be sure where the fish will choose to spawn. You can be rich one year and ruined the next. My father probably thinks the Red fish have spawned in the wrong stretch of river, but that next year all will be well again."

She put some more wood on the fire and shut the little door. Then she went over to the cupboard.

"You must eat something before you go."

"Don't bother."

"You'll regret it if you don't. These days the Russians live on millet gruel and government proclamations."

"Just some tea, then."

She took out some cups and saucers of fine Russian china,

together with a silver teapot and sugar bowl. Grishin watched her
set the table. Something about the ceremonious way she did this
irritated him, as if she were conjuring up memories of her former
life—a life spent amid antique furniture, valuable paintings, rare
old books—and he found it hard to imagine such an existence. Her
father he could picture far more easily: an old man trudging
through the slush-filled streets with a newspaper-wrapped bundle
under his arm, on his way to sell or barter some last little objet d'art
—a figure in a threadbare frock coat too thin for the time of year
and shoes that had barely lasted the winter.

Grishin could sympathize with a man like that. He too had made
and lost fortunes in his life, though the money was usually spent
before he laid hands on it. He had married twice and parted from
both wives with little regret. The very thought of a permanent
home and a well-ordered life made his feet itch. Those who set
store by such things had been bred to them; he had not, and they
defied his understanding. The idea that tomorrow might be a
repetition of today was entirely alien to him. He had led a rootless
existence all his adult life, changing his name as often as his abode,
and had no intention of doing otherwise. Why else would he have
accepted Colvin's assignment—why else would he be here now?

It relieved him that the waiting was over. While Lydia Vydina
was making tea, he laid out the clothes he intended to put on
before he left. Their acquisition was the product of a sudden
impulse. Unbeknown to Colvin, he had bought the entire outfit in
Whitechapel Road. London's East End differed little from a Moscow slum, not least because it had long been a hideaway for
Russian immigrants of every description.

London . . . Grishin wondered where Colvin was at this moment. It was two hours earlier in England, so he would probably
still be at his desk in that anonymous building in Pall Mall. Colvin's
office, with its faded Axminster carpet, lay at the end of a long,
gloomy passage. His collection of firearms, some of them mounted
on the walls and others displayed in glass-fronted cabinets, made it
look like the lair of some shady arms dealer.

Major Colvin himself, a man with sandy hair and alert, foxy eyes
set very close together, reinforced this impression. Nobody knew
what regiment he'd served with, just as nobody even knew his first
name. Grishin had never been sure whether it was a fad, a love of

secrecy for its own sake, or a useful form of camouflage that Colvin, being head of the British Secret Service and one of the Empire's most powerful men, should have chosen to operate from a shabby back room in Pall Mall.

Had the weather turned colder in London too, and had Colvin felt the change in his missing leg?

"Odd, isn't it, getting twinges in a nonexistent foot?" Colvin had asked. It was unlike him to mention such a thing, and Grishin had been puzzled by his introductory remark that evening. He'd brought him a present from Belgium: a Model 1900 Luger 06 9-mm Parabellum—a weapon rare enough to tickle the fancy of any true connoisseur.

Grishin had been away on a Service assignment behind the German lines in Belgium, building up an escape route for British fliers shot down over enemy-held territory, when Colvin recalled him. More than that, he'd had him picked up by plane from behind the German lines and flown back across the Channel. A car had been waiting at the airfield to take him straight to Pall Mall.

"I'd like to try the gun out." Colvin had dismantled it with relish, expatiating on its design and provenance as if nothing else mattered in the world. "Let's drive down to Clapham—that is, unless you object. There are people who don't like being driven by a one-legged man."

Colvin didn't speak again until he was behind the wheel of his specially modified Napier and heading south across the Thames for the firing range where his agents underwent their small arms training. He drove at breakneck speed.

"Would you go to Russia for us?"

Why the interrogative, Grishin wondered. Normally, Colvin would simply have briefed him on his assignment.

"This job, Blade—it's different. That's why I'm giving you the option. Your objective would be inside the Kremlin itself."

"My objective?"

The Napier's tires screamed as Colvin slalomed around another tight bend.

"Marvelous, the way they modified the controls, don't you think? Really marvelous." The Napier sped on. Then Colvin said, "Strictly between the two of us, would you tell me your real name?"

"John Blade."

"Yes, I know. So it says in your personal file."

Grishin made no comment.

"There are rumors, you see. For whatever reason, you're said to have concealed your true origins when you joined us. According to the said rumors, you're anything but an Englishman. A Greek, a Pole—even a Russian. You get my point? If you *were* a Russian, this job might put a strain on your loyalty. You might become emotionally involved."

Grishin had never heard Colvin talk that way. He normally issued assignments, supervised their preparation, and specified the precautions to be observed. A notice on his office door read: "Be bloody, bold, and resolute, but don't be *too* bloody bold!" That was his only general rule. The modus operandi of an assignment he left to the individual agent. Personal feelings didn't come into it, still less ethics. Emotions, conscience, scruples—what part of an agent's anatomy would harbor abstractions like those? No such organ existed. Not in men like Colvin. Nor, for that matter, in Grishin himself.

"Leave it at that," Grishin said. "Leave it at John Blade, the way it's always been."

"Very well, Blade. Would you be prepared to go to Moscow and kill a man for us?"

"What man in Moscow?"

"Let's get to Clapham first, and give me time to work out a couple of details. After all, it isn't every day the Service plans an assassination."

Grishin recalled the glint of amusement in Colvin's foxy eyes as he added, "Roman emperors were seldom murdered by unknown enemies. It was their nearest and dearest who stood the best chance of killing them . . ."

"You're miles away . . ."

Lydia Vydina: the present.

The luxuriant hair that framed her face was dark and curly. Her eyes, under their strong, thick eyebrows, had the slightly blurred look of the shortsighted. She was no longer facing him across the table, with its blue Catherinian china, silver teapot, and sugar bowl. She had turned the wick of the kerosene lamp down, so the room was in semidarkness. Grishin watched her pick up her shawl and drape it over the icon in the niche at the head of the bed.

Then she proceeded to undress. Hurriedly, as if they were a disguise whose touch on her body she couldn't endure a moment longer, she stripped off her dress and underclothes. When she was naked, she carefully readjusted the shawl to ensure that the icon was completely hidden.

She had done the same thing the first night. Russian tradition prescribed that a woman about to commit adultery should cover the icon first. Grishin had made no comment, feigning ignorance of what the action signified, but tonight he was suddenly overcome with irritation at the sight of her naked on her knees before the veiled icon.

Her husband, a captain in the czarist army, had been dead eight months or more, murdered by the men of his own mutinous company at Aleksandrovska. They had taken their bayonets and pinned him to the door of a shed beside the railroad station where a train was waiting to transport them to the front. That was what Grishin saw as he looked at the woman's naked body: the sun beating down on a station in the dusty steppe; starving, rebellious soldiers in ragged uniforms and worn-out boots or tattered foot cloths; and a crucified figure bleeding from countless wounds.

When Lydia Vydina had told him of her husband's death, lying naked in his arms, she did so as hurriedly as she had just undressed —as if she yearned to rid her soul of some intolerable burden.

"Come to bed. What are you waiting for?"

Her breasts were heavy but firm. The amulet suspended from a chain around her neck nestled invisibly between them as she knelt there on the bed, head framed by a corona of tousled curls, legs doubled up beneath her sturdy body, eyes fixed on his face.

He strode to the bed and leaned across her. She clutched his arm when she saw what he intended to do.

"No, please, you mustn't!"

He thrust her aside and tugged the shawl off the icon.

"No! Please don't!" She vainly tried to wrest the shawl away, then gave up and covered her eyes with both hands.

"Your husband's dead," he said. "He's been dead for months."

"You wouldn't understand!"

"A widow isn't committing adultery when she sleeps with another man."

Hesitantly, she lowered her hands. She glanced at the icon, a soot-stained Madonna in a broad silver frame, then turned and gave him a searching stare.

"It's just a superstition," he said, more gently. He let the shawl slip through his fingers to the floor.

She didn't ask the question even then, but later, while lying beneath him and caressing the scars on his back, she gave him the same look of mute inquiry. Lydia knew that the welts were no ordinary scars, but a pair of Cyrillic characters—a C and a K— burned into the skin beneath his left shoulder blade with a branding iron.

She'd seen photographs of other men whose backs were similarly disfigured. The letters stood for *Sibirsky kotorshnik,* and those who bore them had been recaptured after escaping from a Siberian prison camp.

"How did you know that?" she asked, still brushing the scars with her fingertips.

"How did I know what?"

"About the icon."

"Icons," he replied calmly, "are my reason for visiting Moscow."

"So you said, but why are you really going?"

He didn't answer, but his expression changed. The grim intensity and ferocity of it made her feel as if she were looking into a face as scarred as the skin beneath her fingers. Then his smile returned, restoring its unblemished tranquillity.

She raised her head and glanced at the icon in the niche, then looked away in a hurry. The Virgin's eyes were disturbingly lifelike.

Grishin surveyed the bridge, the river and its snow-encrusted banks. Mist was rising from the water. The trees and undergrowth on the Finnish side had been cleared, whereas the far bank was densely wooded to the water's edge. The small expanse of open ground at the other end of the bridge was lit by the flames of a log fire.

The Sissits had removed the barbed-wire barrier from their end of the bridge and returned to the warmth of their own log fire. Judging by the boyish faces visible between their fur caps and the collars of their thick sheepskin coats, neither sentry could have been more than eighteen.

I'm going home . . . That was what Grishin told himself, but he felt he was going into exile quite as genuinely as the Muscovite jeweler and his wife, who had crossed the bridge in the opposite direction a few minutes earlier. The moonlight showed up their footprints in the otherwise untrodden snow. They had, he saw, kept precisely to the middle of the bridge.

He discarded the remains of the cigarette he'd rolled from the pungent tobacco he carried in a leather pouch inside his shirt, which was no better than the coarse Ukrainian makhorka that was all he could expect to find on the other side of the border. He had changed into the secondhand outfit he'd acquired in London: soft Tatar boots, black trousers, a woolen shirt, a three-quarter-length, high-buttoned jacket, and the dark cloth cap that was almost a revolutionary's status symbol.

He picked up his duffel bag and settled it on his shoulder. Then he turned to the woman beside him.

"You'd better go back now."

"Yes, of course. Spogis will be expecting you." Lydia Vydina was holding the shawl tightly across her body with both hands. Her lips were white with cold. She took a step toward him, but he merely settled the bag more comfortably on his shoulder. There was such finality in the gesture that she abandoned all thought of kissing him good-bye.

He set off, only to pause once more.

"Where's the frontier?"

"What do you mean?"

"Where does Russia start?"

"I've never thought about it. In the middle of the bridge, I suppose."

"Go back now. Thanks for the packet of tea."

He was already beginning to forget her face and her name, she thought. By the time he reached the other side, he would have forgotten her body as well.

Grishin kept to the middle of the bridge, doing his best to tread in the others' footprints. His Tatar boots, with their soft leather uppers and flat soles, were unsuited to snowy weather. He walked with an almost imperceptible limp. He'd broken his right ankle at the age of thirteen, when a conductor had thrown him out of a speeding freight car, and the fracture had never been properly set. His foot still ached to this day.

At the other end of the bridge his path was barred by a pair of timber trestles. An elderly, bearded Red Guard opened them just far enough for him to squeeze through the gap. The man's threadbare greatcoat was almost as ancient as the rifle slung from his shoulder. Beyond the barricade Grishin saw a machine gun with an ammunition belt dangling below its tarpaulin cover.

The Red Guard waved him toward the log fire, which had melted the snow for a few feet around.

"Over there, comrade. Move!"

A little farther away, a few yards inland from the riverbank, Grishin saw a log cabin with one lighted window and smoke trickling from the chimney. A horse-drawn sleigh stood outside the door, but there was no sign of Spogis, the Latvian courier.

"Papers, comrade."

The second Red Guard, who was warming himself at the fire, wore a greatcoat as threadbare as the first, but his bright red arm band looked new. The long flaps of his sheepskin cap stood away from his head like a pair of outsize ears. Looking at his broad cheekbones, hollow cheeks, and small, slanting eyes, Grishin sensed that he was a man capable of enduring extreme hardship. He could read his face as clearly as if they both sprang from the same stock.

He handed over his passport and special entry permit. Both documents, which had been provided by Colvin and endorsed by the Soviet authorities in London, guaranteed the British citizen Hugh Thomas "right of free passage to Moscow."

The Red Guard with the gaunt Tatar features held the papers up to the light as if studying them closely. Then he handed them back and spat on the ground.

"Another foreigner," he said contemptuously. "All foreigners are spies!"

The older man, who had just returned with an armful of firewood, chuckled. "You'll soon learn to read, Timur. Every village will have electricity, every village its own school—Comrade Lenin has given his word. Say what you like about the Revolution, brother, but Lenin's promises appeal to me."

"Save your breath." The man called Timur spat again, this time into the heart of the fire. "Search his bag—thoroughly." He stepped aside as if it would be beneath his dignity to do so himself.

Grishin swung the bag off his shoulder and put it on the ground. Beside the fire stood a makeshift table—four stakes driven into the ground with an old door on top. The bearded man emptied the bag and spread out the contents: clean underwear, a spare shirt, a pair of shoes, several bars of soap, shaving things, one packet each of tobacco and tea. There was no money in the bag, and Grishin had little cash on him apart from one half of a forty-ruble bill, the other half of which was supposed to be in the Latvian's possession. The last item to come to light was a small, labeled bottle. The Red Guard put this aside.

"Aha!" he said. "No medicines. Medicines may not be imported." He shot a triumphant glance at his comrade, seeking approbation.

Grishin waited. He wondered why Spogis hadn't appeared yet, but he wasn't really worried. His senses merely absorbed and evaluated each sound with heightened attention: the crackle of blazing logs, the gurgle of river water, the muffled stamping of hoofs from the horse harnessed to the sleigh. Then he heard a door creak open, saw a widening shaft of light and, outlined against it, two figures emerging from the log cabin.

One was a tall, powerfully built man in a voluminous coat that brushed the tops of his boots—Spogis, from the description he'd been given. The other man was slim and a head shorter. They exchanged a few words and shook hands. Then the smaller man hurried over to the fire.

"Mr. Thomas?" he said, addressing Grishin. "Welcome to Soviet Russia." He turned to the bearded Red Guard with the self-assured arrogance of a superior addressing a subordinate. "Who told you to search him?"

The newcomer was a clean-shaven man of around forty, with thin lips and a thin, pointed nose. His head was bare, and his sleek hair encased his head like a second skin. The cloth from which his uniform was tailored bore no resemblance to that of the Red Guards' shabby greatcoats. Grishin detected the darker patches that showed where his former insignia and badges of rank—those of a czarist officer—had been removed.

"You may proceed," he told Grishin, gesturing to the sleigh.

"Your friend is waiting for you. I wish you a safe journey." His voice was as bland as his expression.

Grishin had stowed his belongings in the bag, medicine bottle included, and was about to shoulder it again when the gaunt-faced Red Guard stepped forward.

"Comrade officer," he said. "aren't you going to examine his papers?"

"That won't be necessary."

"It's better to be sure. Don't you intend to have him searched?"

"I told you, it's unnecessary—are you deaf? We were warned to expect this man by our representative in London, Commissar Litvinov himself. He's a welcome visitor, comrade soldier. Let him pass."

"A commissar in London means nothing to me. All foreigners are spies. If you won't search him, comrade officer, I will." The man's voice was coldly contemptuous, almost insolent. He had temporarily lost all respect for his comrade officer's rank. Ignoring him, he turned to Grishin.

"Leave that bag where it is and come here."

Grishin complied. He even cooperated by raising his arms. Timur had a deft and nimble pair of hands—Grishin scarcely felt them run over his body. He was so convinced that the man would discover the knife secreted in his left boot, he was almost disappointed when it passed unnoticed.

Timur concluded his search. Then, as if he had divined Grishin's thoughts, he stooped in one swift movement and plucked the knife from its hiding place. His expression remained dispassionate, devoid of triumph. What Grishin found far more interesting was the officer's reaction—the sudden look of concern and disquiet on a face that had been so bland until a moment before.

Timur scrutinized the weapon in his hand. More of a dagger than a knife, with a long, sharp, tapering blade and a reindeer-bone handle, it was a *puukklo* such as Finnish hunters used. Grishin had found it in the hallway of Lydia Vydina's house, hanging on the wall with others of its kind.

"A handsome knife." Timur held it by the tip of the blade.

Grishin smiled. "Useful, too."

The elderly Red Guard chuckled derisively. "Useful, he calls it! Where are you going to find the meat to cut with it, foreigner?" The chuckle became a guffaw. His shoulders shook. Drawing a big wooden spoon from the leg of one of his worn-out felt boots, he flourished it in Grishin's face. *"That's* useful! If you're lucky you'll find a railroad station, and if you're even luckier there'll be a soup kitchen there. Soup you'll be given, but no spoon, so how will you eat it? You'll go hungry in Russia without a spoon, comrade foreigner!"

"That's enough!" said the renegade czarist officer. "Let me see that thing."

But Timur took no notice. Instead he proffered the knife to Grishin handle first. "A handsome knife indeed."

"Thanks." Grishin took the *puukklo* and replaced it in his boot.

The bearded Red Guard was still chuckling. "You'll go hungry in Russia," he repeated, "you mark my words!"

Timur looked Grishin in the eye. "Some men carry spoons, others carry knives." He aimed another jet of saliva at the fire. "That's right, isn't it, foreigner?"

Grishin felt the cold penetrate the thin soles of his boots as he trudged across the snow-covered ground to the sleigh. He'd bought them in Whitechapel Road for purely sentimental reasons, because they'd been so glowingly recommended by the old Russian storekeeper with his patriarchal beard and grimy caftan: "Look, *barin,* genuine Tatar boots! You won't find better this side of Kazan, believe me. You see? They fit you perfectly. They must have been waiting for you to come along . . ."

The sleigh was a high-backed two-seater, the horse an emaciated nag with a shaggy coat. Spogis was just relieving the horse of its feed bag. The animal's withers barely came up to the Latvian's chest. His big, round face had the fresh coloring that goes with red hair and the plump cheeks of a well-nourished child. Grishin surmised that he and the officer—who had retired from the scene—had been drinking together in the warmth of the guardhouse.

Grishin settled himself in the sleigh with his bag on the floor in front of him. Spogis sat down alongside and picked up the reins, which his thick fur gloves made it hard for him to hold. As the sleigh turned, Grishin caught a final glimpse of the blazing fire and the two Red Guards beside it, staring after them.

"Those Red Russian swine!" Spogis growled. "They're a bunch of animals . . . Comfortable? Warm enough? You've certainly traveled a long way just to see animals like them!"

"Haven't you forgotten something?" Grishin said.

"Of course." Spogis reined in until his gloved hands rested against his barrel chest. The sleigh glided to a halt. "You want to be on the safe side. Better safe than sorry, eh?" He had to remove a glove in order to reach inside his coat and produce the other half of the forty-ruble bill. His hand was red and fleshy, like his face, and moist with perspiration.

Grishin overcame his faint repugnance sufficiently to take the scrap of paper and hold it up against his own half of the bill, which Colvin had given him in London. The moonlight was bright enough to disclose that the two halves fitted perfectly. He hadn't expected anything else.

The runners glided over the snow with a ceaseless, muffled hiss. The narrow track wound its way through a dense forest of birch trees whose branches drooped low under their burden of fresh snow. Conversation between the two men had lapsed, killed off by Grishin's persistent silence.

Spogis had told him that the journey to Sortavala station, where he was to board a train, would take them over an hour. He used the time to take stock of the situation.

Something about the way things had gone at the border made him uneasy, but he was too old a hand to jump to any premature conclusions. His uneasiness might simply stem from the fact that it had been Colvin's idea, not his own, to cross the border at this particular point and in this particular manner. He recalled how Colvin had finally divulged the details of the plan while trying out the Luger at the Clapham firing range.

"A fortunate coincidence has cropped up," he had said. "The kind of luck you dream of but are seldom blessed with."

According to Colvin, the new masters of Russia had discovered a veritable Aladdin's cave in the Kremlin when they took possession of it. Sumptuous robes worn by former patriarchs and czars, ancient icons, jewel-encrusted reliquaries, gold and silver chalices —all had been gathering dust for centuries in the crypts of the various Kremlin churches.

"Their value? Inestimable. Who could put a price on such things?"

Grishin had said nothing. He wondered why Colvin was telling him all this.

"Be patient, Blade, I'm coming to the point. The Bolsheviks are in dire financial straits. They have a man here in London, their first accredited envoy, Litvinov. He's known among his comrades as 'Breadbasket'—that's because he's been so good at filling the Party's coffers in the past. Anyway, Litvinov was instructed to sound out various London auction houses to see if any of them might be interested in appraising the Kremlin treasures on the spot and auctioning them abroad later on. Litvinov conducted his inquiries with the utmost discretion, of course, but you can't keep a thing like that secret forever. Once we got wind of it, it wasn't too hard to bring pressure to bear on the relevant auction house and persuade the directors to let *us* provide an expert for the trip to Moscow."

Grishin had looked dubious, but he still said nothing.

"It'll simplify matters a lot if you can travel to Moscow openly. You'll have access to the Kremlin itself, that's the prime advantage. As Hugh Thomas of Christie's, you'll be welcomed there with open arms. The plan's pure gold, I tell you. I'm handing it to you on a plate."

It might have been this last assertion, more than anything else, that had aroused Grishin's skepticism. He didn't believe that anything had ever been handed him on a plate, least of all gold. He knew from personal experience how hard it was to dig that metal out of the frozen ground, but he had no intention of saying so to Colvin or anyone else.

"It's the best solution, believe me. The Cheka are very efficient at eliminating their own people in their own country. How well equipped they are to deal with threats from abroad we don't know. Hall's information on the subject is still scanty."

"Jim Hall? In Moscow?"

"I thought that would please you. Yes, he's been installed there for several months now. He'll be your local controller."

That had put a better complexion on things, but Grishin didn't feel obliged to admit it.

"Hall will provide you with money and information and anything else you need. You can use the consulate's cipher. I know you like to handle things your own way, so the arrangements you make with Hall will be entirely up to you—with one exception. London reserves the right to determine exactly when the plan is put into effect. Go to Moscow and make all the requisite preparations, but wait for a go-ahead from me."

"I still haven't heard you mention a name."

"Can't you hazard a guess? We'd barely heard of the man till a year ago, I admit. The Germans seem to have gauged his importance far sooner." Colvin paused to let off several shots at a human silhouette. A cluster of bullet holes appeared in the region of the dummy's heart. "Fits the hand like a glove, this Luger. Beautifully balanced, too. Like to try it?"

"I already did."

"German Intelligence had assembled a fat file on the gentleman in question long before we even knew how to spell his name. They'd had their eye on him for years—they even established contact with him. We now know they sneaked him millions of marks from the German imperial treasury—him, a notorious revolutionary—to help swell the Bolsheviks' party funds. Why? Because the goddamned Huns saw farther than we did—because they took the man seriously and believed him when he promised to pull Russia out of the war against them if the Bolsheviks came to power. They listened to him while we shut our ears. When America entered the war, everyone thought it was the beginning of the end for Germany. What on earth could the Huns do to counteract it? What indeed! Look at the dates: America declares war on April 7 last year. Two days later, on April 9, Easter Monday, the Germans put our man and thirty-two of his confederates aboard that now world-famous sealed train and spirit them back to Russia via Sweden—like plague-infected rats . . .

"The rest is history, isn't it? A long, hot summer, a Red October, a hard winter, and hey presto! Cast your mind back to last November. Remember what London audiences were lining up to see? Not *Cabiria* or *The Clansman* or *Secrets of New York*—no, the season's real cinematographic hits were newsreels of the October Revolution in St. Petersburg and Moscow. People clapped and cheered and jumped to their feet whenever our man appeared on the screen: a short, stoutish, balding man—rather unprepossessing, if the truth be told . . ."

It was unlike Colvin to speak at such length. Grishin felt more surprised than ever.

"Even dyed-in-the-wool capitalists developed a soft spot for our man and his revolution. Does the name Fleming mean anything to you—Lloyd Fleming of Fleming's Bank in Lombard Street?"

Grishin shrugged.

"The Russians and the Germans concluded an armistice at the beginning of January, but they hadn't yet signed a peace treaty. London still cherished hopes of saving the day. Why not lend the Bolsheviks some money, why not supply the Red Guards with arms and military advisers in return for an undertaking that Russia would reenter the war against Germany? Why not gamble on Red —for the moment, at least?

"Our prime minister loves a gamble, and Lloyd Fleming seemed the ideal man for the job. He could be sent to Russia as a special envoy. One more detail, Blade—one small but vital piece in the jigsaw puzzle: A dozen years earlier, Fleming Senior had lent an obscure political agitator named Vladimir Ilyich Ulyanov the sum of one thousand pounds so that he could rent a hall in London and hold a party congress there. His IOU was still in the old man's possession, but he'd never pressed for repayment. That meant his son could go to Moscow armed with a curious gift in the shape of a yellowing scrap of paper. It provided an excellent entrée, not only for himself but for Britain."

Grishin had shown interest for the first time. "Is he still there?"

"Oh yes, he's been left in Moscow to negotiate and show goodwill, but the climate here has changed. Our government has adopted a harder line. Now that the Russians have actually signed the Brest-Litovsk treaty with the Germans and their allies, the great awakening has begun. How to hold the Red tide in check, that's the big question now.

"All of a sudden, our masters remembered the Service and yours truly. No need to spell the situation out—no need even to mention a name. Colvin will *know* what's expected of him . . .

"But you, Blade—you'd like me to spell it out, wouldn't you? Very well. Only one man engineered the Russian Revolution, so there's only one man in Russia worth killing: Lenin himself." Colvin smiled sardonically. "Will you take the job?"

"You assumed that from the outset."

"Think you can pull it off?"

"You seem to think so."

"What about you?"

"Anything's possible."

"If things go wrong, we never so much as discussed the subject, understand?"

"Perfectly."

"Then the job's yours."

Well over a thousand miles from the Clapham firing range, from London, from England, from Colvin and the shadowy figures behind him, Grishin let his thoughts return to himself and the present.

Listening to the hiss of the runners and the labored breathing of the horse, he recalled the salient features of the scene at the border: Spogis's protracted session in the guardhouse, the way he and the officer had shaken hands, the officer's reaction to the sight of his knife. Last but not least, Spogis's outburst of rage at the Red Guards: *Those Red Russian swine!* In retrospect, it struck a suspiciously false note. The Latvians had suffered more at the hands of the czarist regime than any other ethnic group. The Czar's Cossack regiments had slaughtered them in droves, so why should Spogis view the Bolsheviks with such hostility?

The nearness of the man was getting on Grishin's nerves, becoming more and more distasteful to him. He squeezed into the corner of the seat, with the sole result that the Latvian spread himself still more. From time to time he produced a liquor bottle from the recesses of his fur coat and swigged at it.

"How much farther?" Grishin asked.

"If only this nag had a decent turn of speed we'd be there by now. Those Red bastards don't even feed their animals properly . . . Never mind, though. Another fifteen minutes and you'll be comfortably installed in a first-class car with a glass of good, strong tea at your elbow."

"Will you be coming too?"

"Not first-class, maybe, but I'm certainly not staying here. I like Moscow—I like cities in general. The country gets me down. You've no idea how glad I am whenever one of these trips is behind me."

The birchwoods had thinned, Grishin noticed, and isolated outcrops of red granite jutted from the snow. Now and then he glimpsed an expanse of water shimmering through the trees. Sortavala was a small town at the northern end of Lake Ladoga.

"Is the station outside the town?"

"Eh?"

The bulky figure beside him straightened up with a jerk. Spogis seemed in urgent need of another pull at his bottle. His hand disappeared inside his coat but emerged empty. He urged the scrawny horse into a faster trot, using the end of the reins as a whip.

"Outside town, yes."

Grishin clung to the side of the sleigh for support as Spogis turned off the track and steered the sleigh along a rough path leading straight into the woods. Before long he caught sight of some lights ahead. They looked like the windows of a row of small, squat shacks. The one on the right had a flat roof and a tall chimney from which smoke was rising into the air.

"Pull up!"

Instead of complying, Spogis lashed the horse's rump even harder. Grishin leaned across and wrested the reins from his grasp.

"Hey, what are you doing?"

Grishin reined in hard. The hiss of the runners ceased. Then the sudden silence was broken by a sound like the heavy breathing of some monstrous animal: *whoff . . . whoff . . . whoff . . . whoff . . . whoff . . .*

"What the devil?"

"Stop here. Just for a moment." Grishin spoke in a low voice, but there was nothing unexceptional about his tone.

"Why? We're nearly there."

"I know."

Grishin threw back the fur rug and climbed out. He realized then that the lights at the edge of the wood, which he'd taken to be the windows of some peasant cottages, belonged to a railroad train. The three cars were coupled to a wood-burning locomotive: the panting beast. Its smokestack was slowly, rhythmically emitting puffs of pale smoke. All that could be seen of the station was a snow-covered roof and a few telegraph poles.

The car immediately behind the locomotive was painted blue to indicate first-class—"soft-class," as the Russians called it. The other two were green, or third-class. In front of the windows' yellow rectangles Grishin could discern the figures of some men in ankle-length greatcoats and fur caps. There were six of them silently pacing up and down, two to each car, all with rifles slung from their shoulders.

Spogis stared at Grishin, glassy-eyed. "What the devil have we stopped for?"

Grishin walked to a tree a few yards away. With his back to the Latvian, he pretended to unbutton his fly.

Spogis began to laugh, uneasily at first, then more and more unrestrainedly. He was even drunker than Grishin had thought.

"Why didn't you say so right away? I'll join you, my friend. All men are equal with their flies open. Pissers of the world, unite!"

Grishin could have killed him for that alone.

Had he already come to the conclusion that there was no alternative? Though reputed to kill without compunction in the service of the Service, he had never lost his awareness of what it meant to destroy a fellow creature—never forgotten the moment when he first saw a human being done to death. He'd been only nine years old when the Cossack captain forced him to watch . . .

Grishin continued to survey the deserted station, the train, the patrolling sentries, and listen to the locomotive's heavy breathing.

Sortavala station should have been swarming with poorly clad townsfolk toting bundles and sacks filled with food for which they had scoured the countryside, storming the doors of the train, wrenching them open, squeezing into the cars, perching astride the buffers, scrambling onto the roofs. But there was nothing of the kind to be seen. Discounting the locomotive, everything was deathly still.

Grishin's thoughts raced on. If he deviated from Colvin's plan, his best bet might be to head north. He had a second set of papers sewn into the lining of his jacket. His only other assets comprised a little over two hundred rubles, the two halves of the forty-ruble bill, and the scrawny little horse, which he might be able to sell or barter. On the other hand, he was lightly built, and some of these scrawny little Russian horses had surprising powers of endurance. His final consideration, and the one he liked best, was that he would be dependent on nobody but himself.

"What's the matter, my friend, sprung a leak?"

Grishin bent over, ostensibly to button his fly, actually to withdraw the knife from his boot. He turned around with the blade held flat against his thigh.

"Come on," Spogis called impatiently. "What are you waiting for?"

Grishin said, "I hope the train's heated." You've double-crossed me, he thought. I don't know why, Spogis, but you're a traitor.

"Of course! There'll be a nice warm stove in the car—and a steaming samovar. All for you, my friend. You'll be as snug as a bedbug."

Grishin looked at the round face and clear eyes. There were beads of sweat on the forehead beneath the tilted fur cap.

"You must feel like a stove yourself in that coat of yours," he said. There was no point in waiting till the Latvian turned his back —the fur-lined coat and high collar would protect him. The only vulnerable spot was the pale patch of skin where his coat and the jacket beneath it left his throat exposed.

Grishin was unconscious of the disarming smile on his lips at that moment. When he raised the knife, he did so swiftly and without hesitation.

Spogis must have seen the knife, for all Grishin's speed, but he didn't react. It never occurred to him that he was in mortal danger. He felt so secure in his thick fur coat, his big, warm-blooded body, his vodka-induced sense of well-being. Besides, he was a giant of a man who could have killed Grishin with his bare hands.

It might also have been the smile on Grishin's face that allayed his suspicions. By the time he began to wonder what it meant, it was too late.

•2•

Lloyd Fleming should have been thoroughly inured to Lena Valentinova's capacity for doing unexpected and incongruous things. Their very first encounter had been an education in itself.

It dated back to January, when Fleming, a fluent Russian-speaker who had managed the Moscow branch of his family bank for several years, arrived in Petrograd to take up his duties as the British government's special envoy to Bolshevik Russia. His train, which pulled into Petrograd's Finnish Station three hours late, was so thickly coated with ice that the doors had frozen shut. While waiting for them to be pried open, he'd scraped a peephole in the frost flowers on his window and peered out at the dimly lit platform. A woman was standing there, her slender form swathed in a long gray greatcoat gathered at the waist by a leather belt. That, together with her gray fur cap, identified her as a volunteer member of the 1st Petrograd Women's Battalion. At that time she was still Lena Muranova, wife of a Hero of the Revolution.

"*Dobro poshalovach,*" she'd said. "Welcome, comrade banker. I've been assigned to look after you."

Then she walked up to him and—with a "May I?"—blew experimentally on the sleek fur collar of his overcoat. "Genuine sable, no?"

He hadn't known what to say, suddenly embarrassed to be wearing such an opulent garment.

She'd laughed. "No need to look sheepish. A taste for the good things of life isn't exclusive to capitalists."

Yes, Lena was full of surprises, so he shouldn't have been so taken aback by her question last night.

"Will you come with me when I go to get my Easter cake blessed?"

Fleming was startled. Where in Red Moscow could she have found the flour and other ingredients, let alone a priest to bless the finished product? Above all, why should she—Lena Valentinova, a Bolshevik—subscribe to a tradition from the days of yore?

"I want to see if my luck will hold this year." He'd simply stared at her uncomprehendingly, so she went on, "You bake a cake, buy a candle, stick it in the cake, light it, get the cake blessed, and make your way home. If you get there before the candle goes out, you'll be lucky for the rest of the year."

"You genuinely believe in that sort of thing?"

"You English are so prosaic."

He shrugged. "All right. When shall we meet and where?"

"Yelizaveta Maria, tomorrow morning at six. It's the only Mass. The workers have to be at work by seven."

"On Easter Sunday?"

"Shame on you, comrade banker! Haven't you read the Party's proclamation? 'Easter means higher output and no absenteeism!' The masses must be cured of their addiction to food and drink, dyed eggs and Easter cakes . . ."

Easter was earlier than usual this year, and Easter Sunday fell on March 31. Spring had begun ten days ago, according to the calendar, but no Muscovites had yet removed the inner frames of their double windows, and until that happened nobody felt that spring had really come. The morning was a cold one, with temperatures around the freezing mark. It had snowed during the night, and an icy north wind was sweeping across the great plain in which Moscow lay.

It was 5 A.M. and still dark. The *izvostchik,* the cabby who had promised to call for Fleming in return for a handsome tip the night before, failed to show up. After waiting a few minutes, he set off for Kuznetsky Most on foot in the hope of finding a droshky there.

Kuznetsky Most and the adjoining streets—Lubyanka Sofika, Tverskaya, Petrovka—had boasted the finest stores in Moscow, but a number of them were now completely devastated and gutted. Of the remainder, whether or not their windows had been smashed and their façades pitted by shellfire, most had closed down.

It was the fighting in Petrograd that had stolen the headlines. Everyone knew about the storming of the Winter Palace, the bombardment of the city by the cruiser *Aurora,* the looting and summary executions. In reality, Moscow had witnessed a series of far bloodier battles amounting to a six-day war. Thousands had died in the bitter street fighting between the Reds and the Whites, and it was in this part of the city, with its banks and luxury stores, that the Bolshevik artillery had done its most effective work. The Kuznetsky Most branch of Fleming's Bank was a ruin.

Lloyd Fleming eventually found a cabby dozing on his box at the end of Petrovka. The man demanded a horrendous fare. When Fleming tried to beat him down, he merely laughed.

"We've had a revolution, *gospodin,* didn't you know? What's the point of a revolution if it doesn't put more money in your pocket?"

Their route took them to a district in the northwest of the city not far from Warsaw—formerly Alexander—Station. Moscow's racetrack lay west of them, and Fleming noticed that the jockeys and their mounts were already out exercising in spite of the early hour. Visible in the gloom beyond the oval racetrack was another expanse of open ground flanked by the huts of a military installation. The Lettish Rifles were quartered there. A band practice must have been in progress, because the gusty wind carried snatches of music to Fleming's ears.

Regardless of the fare he was charging, the cabby pulled up at the mouth of a narrow street a couple of hundred yards short of his destination.

"This is as far as your rubles will take you, *gospodin.*"

He might have been deterred by the state of the street, which was badly potholed and slushy with melting snow. On the other hand, some sixth sense might have alerted him to the possibility of trouble.

At the far end of the street, with its rows of squalid-looking houses, Fleming made out the onion dome of the church and the high brick wall enclosing the convent of Yelizaveta Maria itself. He didn't see the demonstrators till he was almost there. They were standing outside the main entrance but making no attempt to stop people going in. They brandished their banners and placards rather halfheartedly as Fleming walked past.

Somewhere in the city, it occurred to Fleming, hundreds of women must be busy daubing thousands of feet of red bunting with an endless succession of slogans. But why were the demon-

strators here, of all places? Yelizaveta Maria bore no comparison
with other, more illustrious convents and monasteries. Apart from
the convent proper, where the nuns had lived, and a modest
church little bigger than a chapel, all it comprised was an infirmary
and an orphanage. Furthermore, it was situated in one of Moscow's poorest working-class neighborhoods. Once the nuns had
been evicted, the People's Commissariat for Education had requisitioned the premises as a reception center for waifs and strays of
both sexes.

There were millions of these war orphans throughout Russia,
most of them in Moscow, where size guaranteed anonymity.
Some were loners, but others banded together into organized
gangs that robbed, killed, and terrorized whole districts. Lena
Valentinova had been put in charge of the former convent when
she was discharged from her women's volunteer battalion and
transferred to the new Russian capital from Petrograd in company
with various government departments.

There was a courtyard inside the main gate, and the church,
with its slender belfry, stood opposite. People were crowding
around the door as if bread were to be distributed inside, not
blessed. Fleming noticed, as he hurried past them, that they all
carried little cloth-wrapped bundles.

The nave was in darkness save for the flickering candles in the
Easter cakes arrayed before the reliquaries and icons. It was as
though the clock of history had been turned back. Lena Valentinova, who had been waiting for him just inside the door, was
wearing a black lace shawl over her head. All he could see of her
face were her high cheekbones and big, dark eyes.

"I wasn't sure you really meant it."

"Christ is risen," she said in a low voice. The traditional Easter
greeting seemed to come quite naturally to her. Like everyone else,
she was carrying a bundle wrapped in a white napkin. "You're
late."

"It took me ages to find a droshky. Is that your cake?"

"Yes. Come along, Mass will be starting any minute."

"Did you bake it yourself?"

"Yes, believe it or not. It's made with real flour, thanks to our
friend and benefactor Mr. Crabbin, who also supplied the raisins
and almonds. I got the receipe from the former Mother Superior."

The people in front of them were shuffling along the right-hand aisle toward an elongated box resembling a coffin. It was lined with gold-embroidered cloth, and in it lay a lifesize figure of Christ. This being a poor congregation, the figure was only made of painted cardboard.

The men and women filing past this effigy crossed themselves in the sixfold Orthodox fashion, bent over the coffin, and kissed the cardboard Christ's feet, hands, and head.

Although Lena Valentinova neither crossed herself nor bestowed any kisses on the cardboard figure, it seemed to Fleming that she bore her bundle off to one of the side altars with no less reverence than the others. Kneeling down, she unwrapped her cake, stuck a candle in it, and lit the wick. There were cakes everywhere, all adorned with burning candles. Most of them looked plain and unappetizing, but Lena's was a genuine Easter cake in the shape of a little lamb dusted with icing sugar.

Somewhere an organ began to play. A priest appeared, followed by two altar boys carrying incense and holy water. The entire congregation kneeled to receive his blessing.

Fleming, feeling thoroughly ill at ease, allowed his thoughts to stray. He thought of Crabbin, who had provided the makings of Lena's Easter cake—Arnold J. Crabbin, a wealthy American philanthropist so smitten with revolutionary fervor that he had founded an organization called Aid for Russian Children and funded it with a personal contribution of one million dollars. Fleming and he shared the same Moscow apartment house.

Fleming's daydreams were dispelled by the murmur of the congregation. The bearded priest—attired in a dirty, crumpled layman's suit because wearing a cassock in public would have exposed him to abusive remarks or physical violence—had completed his tour. He returned to the high altar and disappeared through the painted doors. The organ music died away.

Lena Valentinova picked up her Easter cake, shielding the flame with her hand. Their progress to the door of the church was slow, as though delayed by a bottleneck of some kind. When they eventually got there, Fleming saw why: The courtyard had been invaded by demonstrators. There were far more of them than before. They waved banners and shouted at the faithful as they emerged, their rhythmical cries sounding almost like an ecclesiastical litany. "Opium . . . opium . . . opium," they chanted. "Religion is opium . . ."

Some students were holding a grotesque, diabolical-looking effigy aloft. Not simply cut out of cardboard, it was a skillfully
fashioned papier-mâché figure with crimson horns, glaring eyes,
sharp fangs, clawlike hands, and a blood-red loincloth around its
waist.

Several women crossed themselves at the sight. There was no
physical harassment or jostling. When the students set fire to their
travesty of Christ and flames leaped into the air, the churchgoers
merely grew more silent and the demonstrators chanted louder.

Lena Valentinova's sole concern was to shield the flame of her
candle. They were crossing the courtyard to the main building
when a sudden gust of wind blew it out. It was Fleming who looked
dismayed. Lena herself appeared unmoved.

"It doesn't matter," she said. "I'll cheat a bit and light it again
when we get inside."

Fleming refrained from looking back at the demonstrators and
their sacrilegious scarecrow, which was now blazing fiercely and
disintegrating into fiery fragments. They reached the entrance to
the former convent. Fleming held the door open and followed
Lena into the lofty hallway, which had been stripped of all its
religious appurtenances. They were about to set off down the
corridor that led to Lena's office when a voice stopped them in
their tracks.

"One moment, comrade."

The early visitor was standing beside a tall window opposite the
entrance. He didn't walk over to them, just stayed where he was.
Fleming registered the black leather jacket, black breeches, and
riding boots. The red stars on the stranger's lapels and the holstered Mauser on his hip dispelled any remaining doubts Fleming
might have had that he was looking at a commissar of the Cheka—
the Special Commission for the combating of counterrevolution
and sabotage.

The man indicated Lena's cake. "I see you keep up the old
traditions, Comrade Muranova." His face was smooth and round,
almost effeminate, but the gray eyes were hard as granite.

"Valentinova," she amended. "I've reverted to my maiden
name."

"The new era has its advantages, eh?" The gray eyes transferred
their gaze to Fleming. "Wonderfully convenient, our new divorce
laws. All it takes is a visit to the registry office and a declaration by

one partner that he or she finds it impossible to go on living with the other. Far simpler than your English system, Mr. Fleming, don't you agree?"

Lena spoke before Fleming could reply. "Mr. Fleming, permit me to introduce Commissar Peters—Yury Peters. Like all Cheka commissars, he can't resist parading his omniscience." She turned to Peters. "Or should I say sham omniscience, Yury?"

"Excellent results can be obtained with either, comrade."

Peters, who had kept both hands behind his back during this exchange, extended his left hand. Fleming shook it awkwardly.

"I'm sorry," said Peters, "my right hand is pretty useless." He produced it from behind his back and held it out for inspection—a misshapen claw with stiff, half-closed fingers. The skin was mauve and shiny, like grafted tissue. Peters' face remained impassive.

"I don't know what your plans were, Mr. Fleming," he said, "but I've been sent to fetch you. Felix Edmundovich—Comrade Dzerzhinsky—has expressed a wish to see you at your earliest convenience."

He turned back to the window, as if that said it all, and gazed out at the convent garden.

"Had you noticed, Comrade Valentinova? The first snowdrops are in flower."

It was a silent trip back to the city. Peters had seated himself beside Fleming in the back of the car, a requisitioned Rolls-Royce with a Cheka driver at the wheel.

They passed the racetrack again. The horses and riders were still at their morning workout. Fleming wondered how the animals had managed to survive last year's revolutionary turmoil and the rigors of the intervening winter. Only last week a young elephant had died of pneumonia at Moscow Zoo because there wasn't enough coal available to heat the elephant house. The meat, three whole tons of it, had been distributed to the working population.

So where did the horses get their fodder from? How did the Soviet authorities explain to the masses that the Moscow racing season would open "as usual" on this very day, Easter Sunday, or that they had licensed the publication of a racing journal and authorized a bookmakers' syndicate to take bets?

What was one to make of such inconsistencies? Could it be that the Bolsheviks themselves, Lenin included, didn't know what they were playing at? Fleming tended to wash his hands of such questions. Even after three months in Petrograd and Moscow, he still found the situation baffling.

The official with whom Fleming had always got on best, and the one from whom he had always secured the readiest hearing and the most assistance, was the very man he was on his way to see: the dreaded boss of the Cheka.

Dzerzhinsky, whose forty-five years made him ten years Lenin's junior, had originally set his sights on the post of commissar for economic affairs. Lenin, however, had earmarked him for a job he considered more important still. "The security of the Revolution is at stake," Dzerzhinsky was told. "Filling empty bellies is of secondary importance, Felix Edmundovich. If the success or failure of our cause has to hang by a thread, I'd sooner it was a strong one—a wolf's hair. I need a wolf who'll keep my Russian sheep in their Soviet pen."

That was how Dzerzhinsky, a revolutionary of Polish extraction and a man who shared many of Lenin's traits, not least his taste for irony, had become head of the Cheka.

Was it Dzerzhinsky's sense of irony that had prompted him, when looking around Moscow in search of premises for his Cheka headquarters, to settle on the building that had once housed Russia's biggest life insurance company? And what of the Rolls that was taking Fleming there now? He was well aware that it had belonged to none other than the last ambassador to the Russian imperial court, Sir George Buchanan, whose contempt for the Red revolutionaries was notorious, and who was rumored in Moscow to have inspired a recent London *Times* lead article entitled "Bullets Are the Only Cure for Bolsheviks!"

Situated at the end of a long corridor, Dzerzhinsky's sixth-floor office was a spacious room with lofty windows commanding a panoramic view of downtown Moscow and the Kremlin. Its only furnishings, apart from a photograph of Lenin on the wall, were a desk and three chairs.

When Fleming walked in, he was still recovering from the sight of Spogis's corpse. Yury Peters had conducted him down to the cellar without a word and there it was, reposing in a crate on slabs of ice. If Fleming expected Dzerzhinsky to mention the macabre confrontation, he was wrong. Dzerzhinsky, lounging behind his desk, made no immediate reference to it.

A man in a long, belted Russian smock was bending over the Cheka boss, trimming his pointed black beard.

"I hope you won't mind if he finishes me off?" Dzerzhinsky gestured to one of the chairs in front of his desk. "Long hair and beards are out of vogue since the Revolution. This growth of mine is almost incompatible with true revolutionary sentiments."

Dzerzhinsky surveyed Fleming across the desk. He had oddly contrasting eyes. One was big, bright, dark, and watchful; the other, paler and less vivid, was veiled by a drooping lid. Fleming recalled a remark someone had made to him on the subject: "He's got God in one eye and the Devil in the other."

"You've settled in nicely, I hear. Is everything to your satisfaction?"

"Thank you, yes. Why not come to the point?"

"All in good time. I gather you've spoken with Krasin. Your bank's losses are to be made good. As a capitalist, you should be pleased."

"Krasin mooted the possibility, but he still needs Lenin's approval. It's always the same old story—neither yes nor no. For instance, I've spent days trying to trace Lenin's whereabouts. Is he still at the Hotel Metropole, or the National, or the House of Soviets, or has he already moved into his offices at the Kremlin? Anyone would think it was a state secret."

"Any special reason for your curiosity?"

"Naturally. I came here to do a job. I sometimes doubt if I'll ever get anywhere."

"You're dealing with Russians, don't forget. All my adopted fellow countrymen understand is *nichevo*. If you want a Russian to jump onto a chair, the least you must do is tell him to jump onto a table. You've only to look at the meal this barber's making of my beard."

He waved the man away impatiently, and the clicking of scissors ceased. Dzerzhinsky ran a hand over his beard. He had slender hands—an ascetic's hands, Fleming thought. They looked as if they'd never come into contact with anything but pen and paper.

"I apologize for intruding on your Easter," Dzerzhinsky said when they were alone. "I hope you enjoyed the drive, at least. A superb car, that Rolls—Comrade Lenin allocated it to me person-

ally. Vladimir Ilyich is an expert judge of human nature. He knows
that the finest cure for the temptations of public office is to satisfy
them."

"An interesting topic for discussion—some other time."

"Quite so." Dzerzhinsky pulled a slim folder toward him. "I had
a good reason for inviting you here today, unfortunately, as you'll
soon appreciate. We don't deal in coincidences in this building, so
it was no coincidence that you were escorted here by Commissar
Peters. Did you notice his right hand? The bullet that shattered it
was meant for Comrade Lenin." The oddly dissimilar eyes came to
rest on Fleming once more, one of them alert, the other seemingly
absent and contemplative.

"An attempt on Lenin's life? That's the first I've heard of it."

"It happened three months ago, at Petrograd on January 1. He'd
just been addressing a Red Guard assembly. On the way back to
the seat of government at Smolny his car had to cross the Simeon-
ovsky Bridge. The snow was deep, so it was traveling quite slowly.
Rahya, one of Comrade Lenin's Finnish bodyguards, was driving,
Lenin himself sitting in the back with Yury Peters. When shots were
fired at the car, Peters had the presence of mind to throw himself
on top of Comrade Lenin and pin him down. One of the bullets
shattered his hand. Naturally, we didn't publicize the incident."

"Who fired the shots?"

Dzerzhinsky frowned and shook his head. "The would-be assassin has never been identified. Personally, I've always rejected
the theory that the operation was planned and executed by you
British."

"That's something, at least."

"Times change, though. Who knows what London's present
policy may be?"

"I still don't understand what you're driving at."

"You saw that carcass downstairs. I apologize for its condition,
by the way—we didn't find it for four days. The temperature
hadn't risen much above freezing, fortunately, but it took another
three days to get it here. Did you recognize the man?"

Fleming hesitated. He would have to tread carefully. Jim Hall
had, in fact, introduced Spogis to him on one occasion. The British
consulate obtained its food supplies by train from Archangel, and
the Latvian had been responsible for supervising their transporta-
tion.

"Yes, but I know very little about him."

"Until your consul general was recalled, Spogis acted as his chauffeur-bodyguard—a kind of maid of all work. He drove his wife to the hairdresser, his children to school, et cetera." Dzerzhinsky paused. "However, Mr. Hall entrusted him with other work as well. Spogis used to escort certain people to Finland on his behalf—people not enamored of life in our peasants' and workers' paradise. The clerks in our passport offices are all-powerful these days. Some of them help for the sake of helping, others are avaricious and take bribes . . ."

"If you're insinuating that Jim Hall—"

"I'm merely telling you that he succeeded in organizing a secret escape route across the Finnish border at a place he called 'the Window.' You really didn't know?"

"How do *you* know, if it's so secret?"

Dzerzhinsky ignored the question. "Mr. Hall relieves me of a minor chore—he skims off the scum of our society. That's why we've never intervened. All that matters to us is to keep a check on *who* leaves the country."

"In case they take their Rolls-Royces with them?"

"To ensure that they leave the proletariat's property behind—yes, that too. But to revert to Spogis. He was a greedy man. He hit on the idea of selling forged passports and travel documents himself, which was how he came to our notice. We pulled him in, twisted his arm a little, and came to a mutually profitable arrangement: we allowed him to remain in business provided he gave us advance notice of those who were to be sneaked out through 'the Window.' More important still, he supplied us with particulars of those who were to be sneaked *in.*"

"Very thorough of you," Fleming said noncommittally. "Have you informed the British consulate?"

"Spogis is a week overdue. Mr. Hall knows that, just as I'm sure he knows who crossed the border that night, traveling east: a man called Thomas—Hugh Thomas. Ever heard of him?"

"It's a very ordinary name."

"Hugh Thomas is an employee of Christie's, an expert on icons and other religious knickknacks. We knew that he was on his way here—we'd authorized his trip. Unfortunately for them, your people made a mistake, one of those silly little oversights—"

"*My* people?"

It was a feeble protest, and Dzerzhinsky brushed it aside. All the urbanity had left his face. "We happen to know that Mr. Thomas is still in England. He hasn't turned up at his office, naturally, nor has he shown his face in London. He's lying low—or rather, being kept out of sight, but not sufficiently well. That, of course, poses certain questions. What kind of expert have you really sent us? Above all, why go to such lengths?"

Fleming shrugged to convey that Dzerzhinsky's point was lost on him, but he couldn't quell his mounting uneasiness.

"The Cheka's task is a difficult one, Mr. Fleming. We have no files, no records from the past. The Czar's secret police bequeathed us nothing but ashes. Imagine trying to run an organization dedicated to the suppression of counterrevolution without a file in the place! However, starting from scratch does have certain advantages as well. It enables one to concentrate on the present and gives one time to ponder things. For instance, how one man can contrive to be in two different places at once . . .

"When Spogis told us he'd been instructed to wait for Mr. Thomas at the border on the night of the twenty-third, we thought it might be informative to have a chat with the impostor, whoever he may be. Just a quiet chat, like the one we're having now."

"Hardly a chat," said Fleming. "You're doing all the talking."

Dzerzhinsky eyed him coolly across the desk. He took a sheet of paper from the slim buff folder and proceeded to read aloud. It was a report from the officer in charge of the Russian frontier post on the night in question. Although the room was cold, Fleming felt his cheeks begin to burn as he listened to the report and feverishly debated its implications. What was he becoming involved in? Who in London was behind this mysterious affair, and why had Hall never mentioned it to him?

Dzerzhinsky replaced the sheet in the folder. Resting his hand on it, he leaned forward as though eager to observe the effect of his words.

"Remarkable, isn't it? Here we have a man, ostensibly an art expert, who's willing and able to liquidate a casual acquaintance in cold blood. He can't have known of Spogis's dual role, yet he killed him to be on the safe side, presumably because something had aroused his suspicions. Oh yes, he's an expert sure enough . . ." Dzerzhinsky paused. "You've no idea what London is up to?"

Fleming said nothing.

"You saw that Latvian—alive, I mean. Spogis was as strong as an ox and extremely shrewd, yet someone took him unawares and killed him. The autopsy revealed no signs of a struggle, and the wound in the throat indicates that the killer knew how to handle a knife. That description I just read you—does it ring a bell?"

One little phrase from Dzerzhinsky's report had lodged in Fleming's mind: *A sharp face,* the guard commander had written, *like a knife blade.*

"No," he said, "I can't say it does." But he was lying. The words had triggered a recollection: lunch at the Savoy with Colvin, who had nodded to a man at a neighboring table.

"This file," Dzerzhinsky said, tapping the folder with his forefinger, "—I don't want it to grow too fat."

Fleming shook his head bemusedly. "Why are you telling *me* all this?"

"You're a banker," Dzerzhinsky retorted with sudden vehemence, "—a capitalist. You belong to the world of high finance, Fleming, where money and politics are inseparable. Somebody always finances the gun—or the knife."

"I thought you were above such flights of fancy," Fleming said, but he couldn't get the thought of Colvin out of his head. Did the Secret Service have a finger in this pie?

Dzerzhinsky glanced at Lenin's photograph. "The British would be ill advised to imagine that this is an opportune moment to make some kind of move against us—they'd only be playing into our hands. We're weak, to be sure—we can hardly persuade the workers to pick up a hammer, let alone a rifle—but any form of outside intervention would unite us."

"Nobody's contemplating any such thing."

"According to one rumor, you may even be planning to land troops on our soil."

"It's only a rumor, as you rightly say."

"Perhaps your government thinks there's a simpler way of overthrowing the regime."

"I'll have a talk with Jim Hall. If there's anything I think you should know, Commissar, I'll tell you."

Dzerzhinsky pushed back his chair and stood up. Fleming rose too. The room had grown darker, he noticed. Big snowflakes were drifting past the windows.

Dzerzhinsky accompanied him to the door. "You aren't a Catholic, I suppose, being an Englishman?"

"Being a Bolshevik, are you?"

"Most Poles are Catholics, that's why they know what Easter signifies." Dzerzhinsky's voice became soft and lilting again. "But Easter is the season of *pesach,* the Hebrew Passover. The Jews, a sect like us Bolsheviks, were in Egypt when the festival originated —defenseless, surrounded by enemies. In despair, they asked their Lenin what to do. There was only one way to protect their families, he told them. They must take newborn lambs, slaughter them, and daub the blood on their doors. Seeing that blood-red sign, the angel of death would spare the firstborn of any house that bore it and pass by—hence *pesach,* the Passover.

"If necessary, Mr. Fleming, we shall safeguard our house by butchering every lamb in existence, and being in Russia we'll do so without a qualm. Don't forget that in Russian 'red' also means 'beautiful.' Have a talk with Mr. Hall. Tell him anything you like, but be sure to tell him this: Never set a dog on a wolf."

●

"You know the statue of Gogol in Arbatskaya Square?" Fleming said. "They've gone and stuck a red flag in his hand. Gogol brandishing a red flag, I ask you!"

He was sitting in Jim Hall's office on the second floor of the British consulate, already feeling better because he could do the talking while someone else listened. He'd been holding forth on any subject that came into his head with the exception of his real reason for being there.

All he needed at present was to drink in the cozy atmosphere of this room with its lofty windows and molded ceiling, the familiarity of its English furniture, and the proximity of the man behind the desk, his reassuringly imperturbable manner and tacit tokens of attention: a little nod here, a cocked eyebrow there. Jim Hall was only thirty, or ten years younger than himself, but his corpulent figure and leisurely demeanor gave an older, almost paternal impression. Fleming had temporarily banished the thought that Hall, apart from being the British Vice-consul, was Colvin's representative in Moscow.

It had taken him over half an hour to cover the distance from the Lubyanka on foot, and when he came to Arbatskaya Square—the

British consulate was situated in one of the streets leading off it—
he'd been startled to see the red flag in Gogol's bronze hand. The
sight of it only intensified his desire to hear English spoken. He
strode on even faster, eager for the company of "Big Jim" Hall.

Outside the former Yusupov mansion that now housed the consulate, some thirty men and women had been lined up in front of
the tall, spiked railings. Patiently braving the cold, they tucked their
chins into their collars and marked time on the snowy sidewalk,
greeting Fleming with despondent, resentful stares when he strode
past them into the consulate.

Hall's voice broke in on his reverie. "May I offer you something?" he said. "Some tea, perhaps?"

"Anything, as long as it isn't Russian *chai.*"

Hall gripped the arms of his chair, hauled himself to his feet, and
lumbered over to some double doors whose white paintwork was
elegantly embellished with gilding. Opening them a few inches, he
ordered tea for two and returned to his desk. He moved with
surprising agility for a man of his bulk.

"You look as if you've lost a bit of weight," Fleming said.

"I have, I regret to say."

"Worried about something?"

"Nice of you to notice. I wish everyone showed as much concern for my welfare."

Fleming half turned in his chair and indicated the windows
overlooking the street. The wind was blowing the snow almost
horizontally past them. "Those people out there, are they waiting
for visas?"

"Yes. A sad sight, but one becomes inured to it." Hall squeezed
back into his chair. "I think that's what the Bolshies bank on."

Hall's allusion to the Bolsheviks jogged Fleming's memory. He
recalled the purpose of his visit, and the thought revived the disquiet that had impelled him to undertake it. He couldn't restrain
himself any longer.

"Something happened on the Finnish border, Jim, at a place you
apparently call 'the Window.' What's it all about?"

At that moment a secretary entered with the tea, and Hall
calmly made room for the tray by pushing some folders and newspapers aside.

"Thank you, Miss Cale. I'll be mother."

Fleming waited impatiently for the secretary to close the double doors behind her. Then he got it off his chest: his visit to Yelizaveta Maria, the unheralded appearance of Yury Peters, the ride in the Rolls, the corpse in the cellar, his conversation in Dzerzhinsky's office. Hall, who scarcely said a word throughout this recital, greeted it with a poker face that reminded Fleming of his true function in Moscow.

"Damn," he said casually, "Spogis took care of our food supplies. He was the only one who managed to ensure that the stuff actually got here. He'll be hard to replace."

"But somebody cut his throat, Jim, and it wasn't Hugh Thomas of Christie's. Who was it? One of Colvin's agents? Colvin sent him, didn't he?"

Hall sidestepped the question. "Look, Lloyd, you read the reports I compile for you. On the Western Front, the Germans have gained more ground in a week than they did in the previous four years—eight thousand square miles of it. They're advancing like a steamroller—they're threatening Amiens and shelling Paris. The British alone have lost four thousand men killed and ninety thousand prisoners, and all because these goddamned Reds aren't attacking the Huns in the rear. How much longer do you intend to negotiate with the bastards and get nowhere?"

"I never knew you were such a Russophobe, Jim. These things take time. However, there's a rapprochement under way. Krasin proposes we sign a trade agreement."

"He's offered the Yanks one too."

"So much the better."

"And the Germans."

Fleming's jaw dropped. "You must be mistaken."

"I'm not. Negotiations with the Germans will open in the very near future. To demonstrate how much importance they attach to them, the Bolsheviks have agreed to welcome a German ambassador here, and guess who it is? Their old adversary—the man who outsmarted them at the peace conference: Baron Wilhelm von Mirbach."

"Are you sure?" Fleming asked in a strangled voice.

"A couple of hundred workmen are busy refurbishing the German embassy."

"A German ambassador in Moscow?" Fleming sounded unconvinced. "Anti-German sentiment is stronger here than anywhere else in Russia. You won't catch a Moscow orchestra playing Bach or Beethoven, even today. The Muscovites loathe the Germans."

"Personal likes and dislikes mean nothing to the Bolshies, Lloyd —they don't lose any sleep over the individual. It's 'the masses' that count, and Lenin holds them in the palm of his hand."

"Do I take it you're voicing London's latest line?"

Hall sidestepped again. "What infuriates me is the halo he's assumed—Lenin, I mean. He presides in the Kremlin like a living god. The so-called masses worship him, find excuses for him, forgive him all their disappointments. If they need a whipping boy for the regime's excesses and inefficiencies, they pick on someone like Dzerzhinsky."

Hall searched impatiently for something on his desk. He leafed through a stack of papers and fished out a blue envelope of the kind that emanated from the consulate's cipher room.

"I was going to have this delivered to you by hand, but nobody answered when we called Crabbin's number. It's personal."

Fleming pocketed the cable unopened.

"So it was Yury Peters who picked you up and showed you the body?"

"Yes. Did you know he was wounded during an attempt on Lenin's life?"

"What kind of questions did he ask you?"

"Dzerzhinsky asked the questions."

"Mm, I might have guessed. I don't know anything like enough about the Cheka, Lloyd. As a competitor, I'm bound to say it's remarkable what that devious Pole has managed to build up in such a short space of time. The Cheka is the one Bolshevik machine that runs like clockwork." Hall frowned. "Believe me, I genuinely trusted Spogis. It never once crossed my mind that he might be a police informer. He sneaked forty-odd people out of the country, and the Bolshies sat back and let it happen. They pulled the wool over my eyes good and proper."

"What precisely does Peters do?"

"He's head of Section Nine. That makes him responsible for the personal safety of the Party leaders."

Fleming sipped his tea, "Surely London wouldn't go to the lengths of planning an attempt on Lenin's life?"

Hall said nothing.

"Well, Jim?"

"I didn't take that as a question. Was it one?"

"I deserve to be told. This business affects us both."

"Not exactly. When London wants its official position represented, that's up to Lloyd Fleming, Esquire. Any other time, *I* have to stick *my* neck out."

"Look, Jim. Most of Dzerzhinsky's rigmarole was lost on me, but the one thing I did hoist in was a warning to you: 'Tell him not to set a dog on a wolf.' Those words haunted me all the way here. Who is this man with a face like a knife?"

"You really want me to tell you?"

"Do you know him?"

"We've worked together, yes."

"Where?"

"Various places." Hall heaved a sigh. "I'll have to get off a signal to London—tell them what happened at the border. Colvin will have a blue fit."

Fleming remembered the folder on Dzerzhinsky's desk. "If you never suspected this Latvian, as you say, why did the agent? Would he really have killed him on the strength of a vague suspicion?"

"It wasn't so vague, was it, as things turned out?"

It was futile to go on pumping Hall, Fleming realized, and anyway, he wasn't sure he wanted to. That way he could preserve an illusion of a world in which men like Colvin and his agents were merely chimeras that vanished in the light of day. All he said was, "Think he'll make it to Moscow?"

"Very probably."

"But I gather he was coming here officially. Now he'll be dependent on his own resources."

"He's an experienced man, not a raw recruit."

Fleming glanced at Hall sharply. He felt he was being excluded from something. "Sounds as if you admire him, or would that be going too far?"

"There are plenty of good agents. His strong suit is staying power. He's no daredevil. The ones with stamina are better. They live longer, too."

"Will he contact you in spite of this incident?"

For the first time, Hall lost his air of imperturbability. He seemed at a loss. "No idea. From his point of view, I'm rat bait now."

"My sympathies, Jim. I must be going. Thanks for the tea."

"You've hardly touched it. Miss Cale will be hurt—it's genuine Ceylon."

Fleming patted the blue envelope in his breast pocket. "Thanks for the cable, too. I assume it's from my wife?"

Hall said nothing. Fleming knew that his affair with Lena Valentinova was no secret. Echoes of it had even reached London.

"I suppose you haven't been instructed to spy on us?"

"No, Lloyd, even the Service hasn't sunk that low yet. You might be a trifle more discreet, though. There are those in London who think the lady may be exerting too much of an influence on you."

"Meaning what, exactly?"

"Meaning that since you met her your views have become— well, faintly tinged with pink, let's say. Lena Valentinova's a Bolshevik, a Party member. She also sits on one of those special tribunals the Reds have set up in place of regular courts."

"Is that what they're saying in London? We never discuss such things. I don't even know where she stands, politically."

"You asked me and I told you."

"Thanks anyway. Now let's drop the subject, shall we? Incidentally, may I phone her from here?"

"Of course. Give Miss Cale the number and she'll get it for you. I'll call her."

He had no need to. At that moment Miss Cale burst into the room—or rather, hobbled. Her ankle-length skirt, buttoned up the side, was too tight for rapid locomotion.

"Quick, Mr. Hall, look out of the window!"

Hall took some time to extricate himself from his chair, so Fleming got there first. When he opened the window and looked down, Miss Cale's dramatic entrance seemed more mystifying than ever. Perfect peace and quiet reigned below.

"Don't you see?" Miss Cale said over his shoulder. "They've all gone, just like that."

She was right. The men and women who had been waiting outside in the cold had disappeared. Stationed in front of the iron railings were Red Guards in long gray greatcoats and gray fur caps. They didn't move, just stood there, two on either side of the gateway, with rifles slung and bayonets fixed. Fleming spotted another four beneath the trees across the way. At the end of the street, where it met Arbatskaya Square, stood an armored car.

Snow was still falling, but it hadn't settled, and the wet cobblestones gave off a steely light.

Miss Cale broke the silence. "The soldiers are supposed to be there for our protection. A commissar waltzed in and informed the chargé d'affaires of the new arrangement. He couldn't guarantee our safety otherwise, so he said."

"No need to be alarmed, Miss Cale. Mr. Fleming would like to telephone someone. He'll go with you and give you the number."

●

Lena Valentinova was already waiting for him outside the three-storied mansion he shared with Arnold Crabbin. All seemed in order when they entered the top-floor apartment, but Fleming soon saw that the premises had been searched in his absence.

The intruders had left traces of their handiwork, as if anxious to ensure that it would not pass unnoticed. They had removed some books from a shelf and left them on the table in front of the fireplace, failed to close a wardrobe door, and transferred a vase of flowers from the windowsill to the top of Fleming's safe. The most blatant clue was a pair of gray gloves he'd never seen before, "accidentally" left behind on his desk.

Lena reacted just as she had that morning in the entrance hall of the convent: without surprise, annoyance, or apprehension. She seemed to accept the whole thing as a matter of course.

"At least they didn't make a mess."

That was just the trouble. Fleming would have been less perturbed to find the apartment in chaos. Was it another warning from Dzerzhinsky—a warning to steer clear of the man sent by London?

But whatever Dzerzhinsky might think, no connection existed—or would ever exist—between that man and himself. They belonged to two different worlds.

3

Grishin peered at the eastern horizon, searching for any hint of dawn. Sunrise was still some while off, but he didn't want to miss the moment.

Moscow, Russia's new capital, lay to the south. The darkness there was so complete that one could be forgiven for doubting the city's existence and wondering whether the muddy, rutted road led anywhere at all.

Moscow . . . On the one hand Grishin burned with expectancy and a fierce desire to reach his destination; on the other he was close to exhaustion, edgy and apprehensive.

The peasant seated beside him on the box of the two-wheeled cart did little to raise his spirits. Whenever he wasn't chewing sunflower seeds from the little pouch on his chest, he sang the melancholy songs of his homeland in a mournful, reedy voice. A broad-faced Ukrainian farmer, he had fled with his family from the advancing German troops—"between two harvests," as he put it.

Now that he had finally settled fifteen miles north of Moscow, it was his practice to take his wares—vegetables, eggs, and a hen or two—to Vindau market on the northern outskirts of the city. He and Grishin had set off at 3 A.M. for the Yaroslavl-Moscow highroad, which the torrential rain of recent days had transformed into a quagmire.

Grishin had reached the farmstead only the previous night, after a journey lasting nearly three weeks. For the first few days he had simply ridden north, compelled to make repeated detours by the lakes and waterways that abounded on the Russo-Finnish border. His most sensible course, while still near the Finnish frontier, would really have been to get in touch with Colvin and work out a new plan of campaign, but not even hunger had reconciled him to that idea. He had always found it easier to obey instinct than reason.

On the fourth day he had turned east, knowing that this would bring him to a railroad track. He would have preferred to avoid railroad stations, but he had no choice. To him and the millions of refugees now roaming Russia—uprooted families, demobilized soldiers, deserters, homeless children—stations afforded the only hope of obtaining a bowl of soup or, failing that, some hot water with which to brew tea. The Red Guard at the border had been right. In the buffet of the first station Grishin came to, a miserable shack where the soup smelled even more repulsive than the wretches lining up for it, he'd been obliged to surrender his cap as a pledge of good faith before someone would lend him a spoon.

He had tried to sell the horse to sundry farmers en route, but without success. A horsemeat butcher made him an offer at the Easter fair in Konosha, but he'd grown so attached to the beast that he turned it loose instead. In any case, he needed no money for rail fares. One of the Bolsheviks' revolutionary innovations had been to proclaim the right of free travel for all, a noble gesture fraught with disastrous economic consequences.

Having eventually reached Vologda, Grishin continued his journey by boat, first on the river of the same name, then down the Volga itself. When still some hours from Moscow, he boarded another train.

Although no one had yet found fault with the papers that had been sewn into his jacket, documents identifying him as Yevgeny Grigory, he felt nervous about showing them to any more officials. Accordingly, he had left the train when it halted in open countryside some fifteen miles short of the capital, planning to enter by a more circuitous route. It transpired at the local village that many of its peasants regularly went to Moscow to sell their produce in the city's markets, and that was how Grishin had met up with the man from the Ukraine.

> *Alas, my fertile Ukraine,*
> *you gave the Germans your bread*
> *and now go hungry yourself . . .*

Now that the eastern sky had begun to pale, the peasant stopped singing. It was going to be a gray, sunless day. On the horizon Grishin could discern the jagged outlines of the city: factory smokestacks jutting from a sea of flat-roofed buildings, and, like the antithesis of all that soot-stained ugliness, the green and blue onion domes of innumerable churches. So Moscow was still there after all . . .

On the left of the road lay a cemetery, on the right an expanse of open ground strewn with black specks. All at once the specks came to life and the air was filled with the harsh cries of awakening ravens. They rose from their overnight nesting places, thousands upon thousands of them, and flapped off in the direction of the city.

The peasant at Grishin's side pointed to them. "If it wasn't for those scavengers, the Muscovites would drown in their own filth."

Another sound mingled with the croaking of the ravens, not dissimilar and no less hideous: the strident wail of countless factory sirens. The road ran downhill and narrowed as it passed beneath a railroad bridge. A freight train made up of grimy cattle cars had halted at a signal, and armed Red Guards were standing on the footboards.

"Bandits!" The peasant spat out a mouthful of half-chewed sunflower seeds. "They're picking the countryside clean, confiscating anything they can lay hands on, the stinking Red swine!"

The entire trip had been punctuated with similar remarks. The peasant sold his produce in Moscow because it fetched twenty times more there than in the country, but he detested the city.

"They think they've had a hard winter." He laughed maliciously. "Wait till summer comes, Yevgeny Grigory—then they'll really know what it is to go short. They'll be smoking their own shit, you mark my words!"

The road was deserted no longer. Other horse-drawn vehicles were heading for the suburbs, interspersed with men and women pulling handcarts. Perhaps because he was looking down on them from above, Grishin got the impression that they were thinner and less robust than the countryfolk he'd encountered so far. It wasn't fully light yet, and their faces looked wan and drawn in the gloom.

"There must be a streetcar somewhere," Grishin said.

"We'll be at Vindau station in a minute. You'll find a stop there."

Grishin sighted the station a couple of hundred yards away. Several tracks converged on it, and one of the platforms was occupied by a train that bore no resemblance to the grimy cattle cars on the bridge. The locomotive was coupled to some blue first-class cars with lighted windows.

They drove past a side entrance and into a spacious forecourt. A streetcar emerged from one of the adjoining roads, squealing as it rounded the bend, and came to a stop. Innumerable passengers emerged and streamed across the forecourt to the station's main entrance.

"Drop me here, would you?"

The peasant reined in. Grishin picked up the bag at his feet and prepared to jump down, but the Ukrainian suddenly gripped his arm.

"Better not get out here, Yevgeny."

Not far from the cart was a heap of cobblestones and beside it a massive tar boiler. The road menders hadn't turned up for work yet, but a fire was already burning under the boiler, and clustered around it were a dozen or so urchins dressed in rags. None could have been more than twelve, Grishin estimated, but their firelit faces looked far older: they were somber and hollow-eyed.

"Watch out for that bunch. If there's one thing to beware of here, it's street thieves."

Grishin climbed down and slung the bag over his shoulder. "Thanks for the lift. You sang well."

The peasant picked up the reins. "Keep an eye on that bag of yours. Even if there's nothing much in it, they may think there is. They'd cut your heart out, believe me. God protect you in Moscow."

Grishin identified the station buffet by a dim lamp over the door. The sight of it whetted his appetite, but he was deterred by the thought of the stuffy atmosphere inside. He removed the pouch from around his neck, took out a cigarette paper, shook the last of his tobacco onto it, and rolled himself a cigarette to dull his pangs of hunger. As he lit it, he became aware that the children had sidled up to him, staring. Watching him just as intently, but a few feet away from the rest, was a girl with big blue eyes and an odd-shaped mouth. The lower lip was little more than a thin line, the upper lip abnormally full.

"Hey, you!"

The boy who'd spoken was bigger and stronger than his companions. His face was black with woodsmoke and grime, but a scar stood out white beneath his left eye. His outstretched hand clearly indicated what he wanted.

"One more puff," Grishin said calmly.

"You heard me!"

Knives had appeared in the youngsters' hands. They gathered around their leader as though silently conferring.

"All right," said scarface. "One more puff, but I'm warning you!"

Grishin warily raised the smoldering cigarette to his lips. Never taking his eyes off the boy, he inhaled a lungful of smoke.

"Vera?" called a woman's voice. "Vera, the police!"

Two open cars came racing into the forecourt and screeched to a halt. A dozen green-uniformed policemen alighted and fanned out fast.

The scarfaced boy hesitated, but only for an instant. Then he snatched the cigarette from Grishin's fingers and took off with the whole gang at his heels. They split up after a few yards and sprinted in all directions. The blue-eyed girl hadn't moved. A young woman was standing beside her with one hand resting on her shoulder.

"Stoy! Stoy! Stoy!"

The policemen's shouts were followed by a shot, then another shot. Two of the boys staggered and fell headlong. The rest ran on without so much as a backward glance.

There was no reaction from the passersby. None of them uttered an exclamation or paused to stare; they simply hurried on. The girl and the woman stood immobile. They were quite alike in spite of the difference in age. The woman had the same blue eyes. Her fair hair was combed back and gathered into a bun on the nape of her neck. She looked at Grishin nervously.

"Did they try to rob you?"

Grishin didn't reply at once. He was watching the policemen who were bending over the two boys. One of them had been hit in the leg, but he made no sound as they carried him to the nearest car. The other made no sound either, but not because he was too proud to show pain. He was dead.

"Were they trying to rob you?" the woman repeated.

"Rob me? No, we were sharing a cigarette, that's all."

She stared at him, surprised at first, then with relief. "Most people are scared of the street children."

"Is that why they hunt them like rabbits?"

The policemen drove off with their human cargo. It was only then that Grishin realized how tense he'd been. He relaxed, partly because of the woman's friendly manner.

She was wearing a black three-quarter-length coat with red piping and epaulettes of the same color, and the legs of her baggy breeches were tucked into boots. It was a railroad conductor's uniform.

"Are you really a conductor?" He guessed her to be twenty-five at most.

"Senior conductor," she said proudly. "Why shouldn't I be?"

"I always thought senior conductors were dignified-looking gentlemen with side whiskers."

"Where were you during the Revolution, asleep in bed?"

"I must have been." Grishin recalled the first-class cars with the lighted windows. "Did you just get in?"

"Yes, in the nick of time, too—eh, Vera?" She patted the girl's shoulder. "What about you? You aren't from Moscow, are you?"

"No." A crowded streetcar pulled away from the stop in the station forecourt. The passengers had overflowed the platform and were hanging there like a bunch of grapes. Grishin hesitated for a moment.

"Do you know this neighborhood well?"

"I've lived here all my life."

"Is there anywhere I can freshen up and get something to eat?" He hadn't shaved since crossing the frontier.

The blue eyes studied him appraisingly. "You mean you can't pay?"

"Not right away."

"You really are new to Moscow, aren't you?"

She set off without another word, seeming to take it for granted that he would fall into step beside her. The girl followed a few paces behind.

The air reeked of soot from innumerable factory smokestacks, and the dim street lamps continued to burn, almost as if the light of day never penetrated this grim industrial suburb. Work had already started, so the streets were deserted except for a few lone pedestrians. Grishin noticed again how pallid, emaciated, and poorly dressed they were. His last vestiges of tension and apprehension melted away. He couldn't have chosen a better district in which to lie low.

"Where are you from?"

"A long way away. Baku."

"You work there?"

"I did till the Germans came. Outside Sabunchi, in the oil fields." This detail, which contained a germ of truth, formed part of Yevgeny Grigory's fictional curriculum vitae.

They passed a factory building with the torn and tattered remnants of a banner hanging from the brickwork. The slogan was illegible. The windows' iron frames were rusty and their panes thickly coated with grime, but wheels could be seen revolving in the gloomy interior. A monotonous, mechanical hum filled the air.

The woman, who had paused for a moment, peered at the shadowy figures moving around inside.

"I used to work there in the old days."

"What do they make there?"

"Linen and lace. They've stopped producing lace. We used to supply the antimacassars for all the first-class railroad cars in Russia. You can imagine how I feel when I see them in my own cars these days."

"You mean they still exist—'soft-class' seats with lace on the cushions?"

For a second she looked surprised, almost hurt. Then she said, as proudly as before, "In *my* cars they do."

They walked on.

"You can't afford to leave a train unattended for two minutes— they'd smash the windows and steal everything. The leather to sole their shoes with, the cloth from the seats, even the tumblers from the lavatories. We never leave our cars unattended. After all, they belong to the people now." The woman gave Grishin a sidelong glance. "Are you a Party member?"

"A Bolshevik, you mean?"

"The others don't count."

"No, are you?"

"Would I be wearing this uniform if I wasn't? Would I be studying at the Workers' and Peasants' College? I started at the weaving mill when I was twelve. Now I earn more in a week than my parents ever earned in a month. There were six of us in the family, and we never had more than one room between us. Now I've got two rooms all to myself, even though I never went to school. If it wasn't for the Revolution, how could I invite you to stay?"

"I didn't know you had."

"You're in luck. I've just started night shift and I spend all my spare time at the college. You really do look as if you could use some sleep. I'll feel happier with someone looking after things in my absence. Besides, no one in Moscow would take you in without asking for some rent in advance. It's a hard-nosed city."

They had now reached a residential district consisting of narrow-fronted, flat-roofed houses with grimy brick walls. People were standing in line outside a handful of grocery stores, though the windows were completely bare.

The woman paused in front of a squat building with a wooden notice board bearing the letters MPO. No one was waiting in line outside. "I'll only be a couple of minutes," she said. "I have to collect something." She emerged with a paper bag in each hand, one large and one small.

"That's another advantage of belonging to the Party," she explained. "You don't have to stand in line. You're entitled to buy food and clothing at the Moscow Cooperative."

Grishin smiled faintly. "So it pays to join."

"By the way," she said, "do you have a resident's permit?"

"Do I need one?" Nobody in London had known exactly what papers and permits were required. "Even for a short stay?" he added.

"Official forms are very important here. The comrades who produce them fulfill their quotas twice over and to spare." She handed the smaller of the two bags to the girl. *"You* get by without papers, don't you, Vera?"

"Is she your sister?"

"Vera? No, I only had three brothers. Two of them were killed in the war—fighting for the Czar, God forgive them—and I lost the other in November. Him and my father. They were buried beside the Kremlin wall, along with eight hundred others, in one huge grave. If you stay awhile, I'll take you there."

"She can't be your daughter, surely?"

The woman shook her head. "I don't know who she is. She comes and goes, waits for me at the place where I live or at the station, like this morning. I've no idea where she comes from—I don't even know where she sleeps. I'd give her a home, but she won't stay." She turned to the girl. "You keep yourself to yourself, don't you?"

The girl's expression was wary. She hugged the paper bag possessively to her scrawny chest. It was impossible to guess her age.

"Doesn't she ever speak?" Grishin asked.

"She may with Kolya, for all I know—that's the boy with the scarred face. She hero-worships him. The youngsters haven't accepted her into their gang, but she trails around after them like a dog. I call her Vera because that's my own name. Vera Ivanova—pretty easy to remember."

"I'm Yevgeny Grigory," said Grishin.

The street brought them out in a cobbled square traversed by some disused streetcar tracks that had been filled in with tar. On the far side was an open space dotted with sheds and warehouses. The windowpanes were smashed and the roofs had fallen in. Visible beyond a wrought-iron gate hanging askew on its hinges was a yard in which dandelions, thistles, and other weeds had run riot over mounds of rubble. The sign above the gate, which was still intact, read: "Vodka Distillery. M. A. Popov, Proprietor."

"Citizen Popov's house was requisitioned for us railroad employees. That's where we live these days."

"Are you all Party members?"

"Of course. Mikhail Anatolivich Popov must be turning in his grave."

The once elegant town house stood on the left of the ruined distillery, set well back from the square and separated from the factory buildings by a wall. They crossed the neglected garden and headed for the front door, to which someone had nailed a square of gray cardboard listing the new occupants. Grishin counted at least a dozen handwritten names so rain-washed and faded as to be almost illegible. And that was when he saw it.

Vera Ivanova had gone on ahead and was just about to open the door when she realized that he'd paused to look. "I don't even notice it anymore," she called over her shoulder.

Sunk in the wall beside the door was a small, glass-fronted niche, and reposing inside it was the mummified carcass of a cat. Grishin stared at the shriveled corpse with its mangy black fur and hollow eye sockets. The sharp little teeth were bared in a permanent snarl.

Vera Ivanova said, "Popov walled it up, the swine, because he thought it would protect the house against evil spirits. You aren't superstitious, are you?" She opened the door.

He glanced back before following her inside. The girl she called Vera had disappeared.

4

Vassily Ostrov emerged from the movie theater hat in hand, his gray double-breasted overcoat so neat and uncrumpled that he might never have spent the last two hours in one of the Electra Theater's cramped seats. He was among the first to leave, as if anxious to avoid contact with the other moviegoers.

Grishin watched him from the other side of the street. Ostrov paused briefly beneath the marquee to smooth his hair back, don his pearl-gray homburg, and pull on his gloves, all with a care and precision that stamped him as a man who set store by his personal appearance. Then he headed for home with brisk little mincing steps.

Grishin glanced at his watch. It was ten-fifteen. He crossed the street and set off in pursuit, but not, as on previous occasions, at a discreet distance.

Ostrov didn't take long to realize that someone was following him. He walked faster; Grishin did likewise. He came to a halt; so did Grishin. He crossed to the other sidewalk; Grishin followed suit. Genuinely uneasy now, Ostrov kept glancing over his shoulder.

Prechistenskaya was a residential district in the southeast of Moscow, so there were no stores, restaurants, theaters, or public buildings in which Ostrov could take refuge. His only remaining hope was to hail a passing droshky, but Grishin already knew where he would tell the cabby to take him. Ostrov was a man of cast-iron habits.

Grishin had slept through most of his first day in Moscow. When Vera Ivanova returned from her class at the Workers' and Peasants' College they sat together in the little kitchen–living room until it was time for her to go on night shift.

He whiled away the time between her departure and nightfall by rolling himself a stock of cigarettes. Vera's two ground-floor rooms were at the rear of the Villa Popov. As soon as it was dark he had made a tour of inspection and discovered a door that had provided the late owner with direct access to the distillery. He himself had used this side door that night and every night thereafter.

His very first expedition had disclosed what he more or less expected to see: uniformed sentries outside the British consulate and a couple of Cheka plainclothesmen lurking near the British Club in the center of the city, where Jim Hall lived.

Although various fallback procedures had been arranged with Colvin and Hall, he resolved to begin by acting on his own initiative. His prime requirements were information and a fresh set of papers, and Vassily Ostrov could supply him with both.

Grishin didn't rush things. Four days and nights of surveillance had imprinted Ostrov's routine on his mind: his working hours at Cheka headquarters, his lunch breaks, his nocturnal diversions . . .

It was Ostrov who made the first move. Unable to endure being tailed any longer by a silent, shadowy figure, he swung around and retraced his steps.

"Why are you following me? What do you want?"

"A talk."

Ostrov thrust both hands deep into his overcoat pockets. "Who are you?"

"Wouldn't it be better to talk at your apartment?"

"My apartment?" Now that he had steeled himself to confront this stranger, Ostrov had regained his composure. "What makes you think I'd want to talk with you anywhere?"

"Your natural curiosity, Vassily Ostrov."

"So you know my name—so what?" Ostrov's mirthless laugh conveyed that he now felt entirely in command of the situation. "Be reasonable, man. Stop pestering me and clear off."

"I wouldn't want to discuss your little amusements, your visits to illegal gambling clubs, and so on."

"I couldn't care less if you did."

He obviously felt invulnerable in that respect, Grishin reflected, and he was probably right. A Cheka commissar in a post as important as his might well be forgiven a secret passion for roulette.

"Penmanship," Grishin said softly. "Doesn't that arouse your curiosity?"

Ostrov's little eyes narrowed and his thin lips became thinner still. Looking at him, Grishin could tell that he must have betrayed his comrades to the Okhrana, the Czar's secret police, without a qualm.

"Penmanship," Grishin repeated. "A highly developed skill— almost an art form in its own right."

"Who are you?" Ostrov's voice was flat and expressionless.

"The pen is the forger's principal tool. He needs much more than that, of course. A steady hand, a good eye, a fertile imagination . . ."

Ostrov thrust his hands still deeper into his pockets as if anxious to conceal them at all costs.

"The Imperial Bank of Russia," Grishin went on, "employed an extremely talented man to design and engrave its banknotes. He happened to be a secret member of the Bolshevik Party, for which he forged various documents, banknotes included, and got them printed in Finland. Being constantly in need of money, he couldn't resist the temptation to betray his Bolshevik comrades to the Okhrana."

Ostrov said nothing. He turned and walked on with the same little mincing steps. Grishin kept pace with him.

"I'm talking about Vassily Ostrov, a man with strong nerves—a man who contrived to serve two masters and be two things at once: an important cog in the revolutionary machine and a highly paid informer for the Czar's secret police."

"That's absurd! No one would believe such a ludicrous story."

"Why, because Vassily Ostrov was too careful? Because he always submitted his reports to the chief of the St. Petersburg Okhrana direct and never met with him in person? Because he concealed his identity behind an apt pseudonym: 'The Pen'?"

"The Okhrana destroyed all its files."

"General Shatov took a few into exile with him."

They had reached Prechistenskaya Avenue, which bordered the Moskva River. The river had been swollen by the heavy rainfall of the last few days, and its dark, swirling waters reflected the glow of the gas lamps on the opposite bank.

Ostrov paused outside a corner house on the right-hand side of the street. It was a substantial house with a white, pseudo-Gothic façade. The glass canopy over the front door was supported by a pair of sphinxes.

"Is that worth a talk?" said Grishin. "I know it would be worth good money to a blackmailer, but our conversation may not come to that. It could take quite a different turn—different and far more beneficial to both parties."

"We can't talk in there." Ostrov indicated the house. "My wife—"

"Your wife left you seven months ago," Grishin said curtly. "She's living in Paris with Shatov. They're running a restaurant together: the A l'Ours, aptly named after the finest restaurant in St. Petersburg."

Ostrov peeled off his skintight gloves with some difficulty. The hands that came to light were slender but strong. Their combination of strength and dexterity would have graced a watchmaker or a surgeon.

"All right, let's talk."

He produced a bunch of keys from his pocket and led the way across a small but well-kept garden in which lilac trees were just coming into bloom.

Ostrov's apartment was on the third floor. He showed his visitor into a spacious corner room whose decor betrayed a taste for the exotic. Grishin walked over to one of the four big windows. The Moskva flowed past the south wall of the Kremlin only a few hundred yards away. Beyond that came a long bend. The canal ran parallel with the river, and the night was clear enough for him to trace its course as far as the point where the two dark ribbons of water converged.

"I presume you didn't come to admire the view."

Grishin continued to look out of the window.

"Who used to own this place?"

"An Armenian real estate agent. The Revolution ruined him. Now it's an apartment house for senior government officials."

Ostrov had removed his coat. The cloth and cut of his pearl-gray suit did credit to the first-class tailor who had made it. The commissar appreciated luxury, Grishin thought. Silence meant a lot to him, but money meant everything.

"Do you have any news of my wife?" Ostrov sat down on a richly upholstered divan. "Have you seen her? Spoken with her?"

"The Paris restaurant is booming. It's almost like St. Petersburg in the good old days. The same Russian aristos, the same politicians and generals, the same demimondaines. There's even a tango orchestra that rounds off the evening with 'God Save the Czar' while your wife counts her takings in the back room."

It was Colvin who had supplied Grishin with these tidbits of information.

"That's all she ever cared about, money."

"She's careful with it, too."

"You can say that again."

"Even Shatov finds her tightfisted. He was lucky enough to quit St. Petersburg in time and shrewd enough to take certain files with him, but your wife keeps him short of cash. Not unnaturally, he looked around for an independent source of income. All he had to sell was information."

"Shatov is a careless man," said Ostrov.

"I know. Nothing could be easier to arrange than a fatal accident in a Paris street, in broad daylight."

"Precisely. The Cheka's arm is long."

"Be that as it may, the general made a deal with us. The 'Pen' reports are in our possession. What we do with them is up to you."

"You still haven't told me who you are or what you want."

"My identity is unimportant. What I want is your silence and assistance in return for the originals of the reports and a substantial sum of money. Enough to enable you to settle in Paris yourself."

"Is my wife actually living with Shatov?"

"Let's get down to business."

Grishin, who had seated himself opposite Ostrov, produced the medicine bottle which the Red Guard had almost confiscated at the frontier and deposited it on the brass tabletop. Ostrov leaned forward, hugging a silk cushion, and peered at it expectantly.

"This bottle contains three photographic negatives, all of myself and all subtly different. In the case of two of them you can select the names for the papers at random—commonplace names and unremarkable occupations: bricklayer, joiner, factory worker. Age around thirty-five. I want full sets of papers complete with residents' permits, ration cards—anything and everything I'll need to justify my presence in Moscow."

"You mentioned three photos."

"The third set of papers will be worthier of your talents. They must identify me as a Cheka commissar."

Vassily Ostrov, head of the Cheka's forgery section, wasn't a gullible man. He would be bound to ponder the motive behind any such request. Grishin, who had taken this into account, thought it would do no harm to steer his thoughts in the wrong direction.

"Tell me something. Where are the Czar and his family being held?"

"That's a state secret."

"I'd still like to know."

"At Tobolsk, but they're about to be moved. What's your interest in the Czar?"

"Moved where?"

"Nearer Moscow. To Ekaterinburg in the Urals."

Grishin nodded. "That's it, then. Fix me up with some papers for a Cheka commissar from Ekaterinburg."

"You're wasting your time," Ostrov sneered. "Nobody cares a damn about the Romanovs anymore. A tango orchestra may still be playing 'God Save the Czar' in Paris, but here in Moscow the bells of St. Savior's have switched to the 'Internationale.' "

"Are you telling me that no one in the whole of Russia would lift a finger to help the Czar?"

"A lot of people doubt if he's still alive."

"So there are no plans for rescuing him?"

"He may have a few friends left, not that it'll do him any good. It's the other way around with our new Czar: plenty of enemies, but none he need fear."

"Not even the old bourgeoisie?"

"Meaning whom—'the yet-to-be-slaughtered,' as we call them these days? If you're hoping for support from them, forget it."

"So there's no one?"

"Only the other socialist parties. They hate the Czar and the Bolsheviks in equal measure, but they're split and disorganized." Ostrov paused. "What's more, they're riddled with Cheka informers. The Czar is past helping and the Bolsheviks have no one left to fear, that's the position in a nutshell. There may be a handful of men, misfits like Muranov . . . But we're wasting time, aren't we?"

In spite of what he'd just said, Ostrov made no move to rise. He continued to sit there hugging his cushion.

"Muranov?" said Grishin.

"Once a hero of the Revolution, now engaged in cleaning out stables. Pavel Maximovich Muranov, who masterminded the mutiny of the Baltic Fleet and saved the Revolution by leading Red sailors and workers to victory over the counterrevolutionary forces of Kerensky and Kornilov, plus their Cossack allies, at Tsarskoe Selo, only a few miles from Petrograd. That night will go down in the annals of the Revolution, when they're written, but you won't find any mention of Muranov. Immediately after the battle his name was writ large in Lenin's order of the day, but now most people would sooner bite off their tongues than utter it aloud."

"What did he do?"

"He voted against Lenin when it came to ratifying the peace treaty with Germany."

"Was that a crime?"

"The supreme crime. He also organized demonstrations against the treaty and published a pamphlet denouncing Lenin as a German spy."

"And now he's cleaning out stables, you said. What did you mean?"

"Just that. He's hoping to get a public trial. Meantime he keeps body and soul together by working as a stableboy at Skachki racetrack. Incidentally, his wife left him as soon as he fell into disfavor." Ostrov spoke with bitter relish. "She divorced him on the spot. Our Russian womenfolk are making the very most of the Revolution."

Grishin thought for a moment. "Do you know Lenin personally?"

"I wouldn't go so far as to say that, no. Why?"

"Because all you ever hear in this place is Lenin, Lenin, Lenin."

"He's our new idol."

"You said he had no enemies worth mentioning, but wasn't there an attempt on his life?"

Ostrov laughed as if some private joke had tickled his sense of humor. "Yes, a botched attempt at Petrograd on New Year's Day, but superstition has it that he'll die in Moscow. Everything in Russia is preordained."

"In Moscow?" Grishin's face had given nothing away, he felt sure. He reached inside his shirt and fished out his tobacco pouch, but Ostrov shook his head.

"I'd rather you didn't smoke in here."

Grishin, accepting this as a challenge to his self-control, stowed the pouch away without a word.

"All right," said Ostrov, "if you're interested in superstitions, listen to this. When Lenin arrived here on March 12 he drove from the station to the Hotel National. A big demonstration had been organized in his honor—even the schoolchildren were given the day off. The weather happened to be fine, so the car had its top down. When it got to the Tverskaya intersection, an old woman darted out of the crowd and tossed an icon into the car. It landed in Lenin's lap! The more superstitious of my fellow countrymen have taken that as an indication of where he'll meet his end." Ostrov snickered. "According to the official version, of course, the dear old thing was paying homage to our beloved leader."

Silence fell. Ostrov laid aside the cushion and rose. "May I see those negatives?" he asked. Without waiting for an answer he picked up the medicine bottle, took it over to his desk, and switched on the lamp.

Grishin had noticed a peculiar smell as soon as he entered the room. It was only now, as he followed Ostrov to the desk, that he realized what it was. Reposing on the desktop were a cork board for the preparation of butterfly specimens, various flasks and jars, some tweezers, a tin of black pins, and other items of equipment. Ostrov had recently set a moth, hence the lingering smell of ether from the killing bottle. The insect's body was pinned to a groove in the cork with its outspread wings held in place by strips of paper.

"You're a man of many parts," Grishin said. His heart was pounding against his ribs in a curious way.

"That's why I asked you not to smoke," Ostrov replied absently. "I like to preserve my specimens in mint condition." He peeled the negatives off the interior of the medicine bottle with a pair of tweezers and held them up to the light. "Good work. The same man, but every one slightly different."

"Use the one with the shorter hair for the Cheka commissar. I want you to give him the name of a real individual, unlike the others—choose someone as close to my own age as possible. How long will you take to produce these papers?"

Ostrov tossed the negatives onto the desk. "It's hackwork. My talents would be wasted on them."

"Consider how little I'm asking and how much I'm offering in return. You must be good at weighing the odds or you'd have died a traitor's death years ago."

"Damn you!" said Ostrov. "I'm not used to being insulted."

"And I'm not used to being double-crossed, so take care."

"Stop threatening me!"

Ostrov had paled slightly, almost imperceptibly, like the wings of the moth on the setting board. Grishin indicated some cabinets flanking the desk.

"Quite a collection," he said.

"I've been a collector all my life."

Grishin surveyed the cabinets. Their shallow drawers must have contained many hundreds of mounted butterflies and moths. A hot tide of anger flowed over him, but his voice remained even.

"Is there any specimen you're particularly proud of?"

Ostrov pulled out one of the glass-topped drawers and put it down on the desk. He adjusted the lamp a little, then pointed to a large, dark blue butterfly forming the centerpiece of the display.

"That's an *Apatura iris,* a Purple Emperor—the finest specimen I've ever seen. My parents owned a house in the Crimea. I'll never forget the summer I—"

He broke off. His eyes widened, first in surprise, then in horror. He was too shocked to intervene. Grishin, who had thrust him aside, smashed the glass with his bare fist and tugged the pin out of the cork lining.

Ostrov, staring at the delicate, fragile thing in Grishin's hand, uttered a strangled cry as Grishin removed the pin and clenched his fist. When he opened his fingers and extended his hand, palm uppermost, all that remained of the butterfly was a smear of fine blue dust and one or two darker, more substantial fragments.

"Why?" Ostrov asked dully. His face had gone livid.

Grishin was asking himself the same question. His pulses were racing, his temples throbbing. Sudden, overpowering rage had momentarily destroyed his capacity for rational thought and blunted his powers of recall. By the time memory reasserted itself —by the time he could picture the big white house at Baku and recall the room with the same smell of ether and the same display cabinets—he was back in full command of himself. He dusted the debris off his palm.

"When do I get those papers?"

Ostrov, still white to the lips, was staring blankly at the drawer with the shattered glass top and the missing centerpiece.

"I'll need three or four days," he replied mechanically.

"I'll let you know when and where to meet. No, don't bother, comrade commissar, I'll see myself out."

Grishin returned to Vera Ivanova's apartment by his usual route, through the ruined vodka distillery. She had recounted the story of its destruction at supper that evening.

"It happened in November, during the fighting here. The counterrevolutionaries made a last, desperate attempt to undermine our Red Guards' discipline by handing out free wine and vodka. They even distributed lists with the names and addresses of liquor stores, distilleries, warehouses, and so on.

"It was bitterly cold, Yevgeny, and everyone was starving. Before long the streets were swarming with drunken men. Disciplined units actually had to open fire on their rampaging comrades. The authorities acted fast—they ordered the destruction of every drop of liquor in the city. Our people spent a whole week setting fire to warehouses and blowing up distilleries. And that was the end of Citizen Popov's vodka factory."

Vera kept her kitchen–living room in pristine condition. She had even draped a piece of machine-made lace over the lower half of the window and arranged some potted plants on the sill. For a loyal revolutionary, her tastes were curiously lower-middle-class.

Grishin had watched her getting their meal ready the first evening. She set out the supper things with care and summoned him to table as if inviting him to a banquet. All she had to offer were some beans, stale bread toasted to make it more palatable, and an apple. She laughed when she saw the look on his face.

"No one in Moscow expects better fare than this, and then only once a day."

Their meal tonight had been just as meager. He finished off the few remaining scraps and cleared away. It was only while sluicing his face at the crude stone sink that he noticed the cut on his hand. The broken glass had inflicted a superficial wound. He dabbed it dry and retired to the inner room. Smaller than the kitchen, it contained a single bed made up with coarse blankets. There was a kerosene lamp on the rickety table, together with some textbooks and a sheaf of paper. Vera was a conscientious student. Grishin got undressed and rolled himself a cigarette. Then he extinguished the lamp and stretched out in the darkness, smoking.

He was still under the spell of his outburst at Ostrov's apartment. Again his heart began to pound, and again the pictures took shape in his mind's eye: *Colma Khan . . . the oil fields at Sabunchi . . . the Cossack captain . . . a man whose hobby was collecting butterflies . . .*

He had never dreamed when accepting Colvin's assignment that the past might catch up with him.

•5•

The main entrance at Skachki ran beneath the big stand immediately overlooking the oval racetrack. The wooden gates were painted pale green, like the spectators' seats. Grishin walked through the gateway, then slowed and came to a halt beneath the overhanging roof.

It was as if some internal alarm system had warned him of impending danger, not that he could detect anything that might have justified the sensation. Women cleaners were sweeping the aisles between the tiers of seats, and in front of him, on the long home straight, men were busy leveling the tanbark with rakes. The central expanse of turf was still drab and colorless, with only a sprinkling of new grass showing through. Farther away on a subsidiary track, some riders were doing practice gallops. To the north lay Khodynka Field, once the summer quarters of Moscow's military garrison. Facing Khodynka Field across Petersburg Avenue loomed the red and white brick walls of the Czars' coronation palace. All as it should be.

A cloudless blue sky looked down on this peaceful, unremarkable scene: a racetrack the morning before a major meeting. No one took any notice of Grishin, but he still couldn't shake off his premonition of danger.

A minute ago he'd felt too hot in his dark jacket; now he was shivering. For a moment he seriously debated whether to drop the idea of contacting Muranov and go back home. Then he recalled his conversation with Vera before setting out.

"Tell me," he'd said at breakfast, "do you ever have time for anything apart from work, lectures, and Party meetings?"

"Why do you ask?"

"I thought I'd go to Skachki. Why not skip college and come

too? It's such a lovely day—the first really fine day since I got here."

"Skachki racetrack?" Her face darkened. "No, thanks all the same."

"What's the matter, are racetracks too bourgeois for you?"

"It's too near Khodynka Field, that's why."

He realized that he'd touched some chord in her as painful as the memories revived in himself by Ostrov and his butterflies.

"Two thousand people died there," she said. "They trampled each other to death like a herd of cattle, and thousands more were hurt. That was at the Czar's coronation, may he rot in hell!" Her hands shook.

"Let me clear the table. You'll break the last of your plates."

But Vera was into her stride. "He invited everyone to celebrate the occasion. People flocked here from all over Russia. Many of them were on the road for weeks or even months—they sold everything they possessed, just to be there. Hundreds of thousands of them, half a million, maybe a million. Nobody could say for sure, afterward."

"It was a long time ago, Vera. I don't see—"

"My mother was determined to go to Khodynka Field," she went on. "I was only five, but I can still remember the row she had with my father. As he saw it, helping to celebrate the coronation of a tyrant was an act of betrayal. And do you know why my mother was so set on going? All because of a silk shawl! Every woman present was to receive a purple silk shawl with the royal couple's initials and 'Moscow, May 18, 1896' embroidered on it in gold thread."

"It's still a long time ago, Vera."

"A shawl," she said bitterly, ignoring the interruption, "—a genuine silk shawl, and all the children were to be given gingerbread and ice cream! There were gypsy orchestras, too, and dancing bears, and the Durov Brothers' circus, the most famous circus in the whole of Russia, all free of charge. I fell asleep, I remember, while my parents were still going at it hammer and tongs. However, my mother always got her way in the end. It was four in the morning when the two of us set off for Khodynka Field . . ."

Grishin frowned. "I didn't know. I'm sorry I raised the subject."

"You needn't be. I never go there anymore, that's all. Vaganskoye Cemetery lies south of the racetrack, and the railroad line to

Warsaw runs right past it. I never look out of the window when I'm
on that stretch. I never visit my mother's grave, either. Two thousand people lie buried there in mass graves. The bodies were
unidentifiable, you see—all mangled and bloody. It was the shawls
that did it. The women heard a rumor that there weren't enough to
go around, so they stormed the distribution points. If some soldiers
hadn't picked me up and passed me over the heads of the crowd,
I'd be in Vaganskoye too.

"But the festivities weren't suspended, not even for a day. The
Czar wanted his coronation program to continue regardless, so it
did: gala balls, grand banquets at the Kremlin, concerts, fireworks.
It lasted a week and ended precisely where it had begun—where
two thousand people had died—with a big military parade at
Khodynka Field, in front of the Czar and Czarina. That's why I'd
sooner you went alone . . ."

Remembering this, Grishin thought he'd identified the source of
his uneasiness, and it subsided at once. He emerged from the
shadow cast by the roof of the stand and walked over to the three
men who were raking the track. They didn't look up from their
work at his approach.

"Muranov, Pavel Maximovich—where can I find him?"

Two of the men went on working, bent over their rakes. The
third paused just long enough to shrug.

"Don't any of you know him?"

The response was the same, only more aggressive.

"Is he at the stables?"

"We're busy, can't you see? Get lost."

Grishin walked on around the oval. Riders were still exercising
on the inner track, eight of them in two groups of four. The horses
were glossy, well-fed beasts, whereas the jockeys looked thin and
undernourished in spite of the wind that inflated their blouses as
they galloped along.

Grishin was beginning to sweat in his winter clothes, which he
hadn't changed since crossing the border. Vera Ivanova had offered him a jacket and trousers belonging to one of her dead
brothers, and he now regretted having declined them.

The jockeys reined in and dismounted without quitting the track.
They stood there in a bunch, heads together, while their horses

fretted and pawed the ground. Then they all turned to stare in the same direction.

In the south, where Skachki adjoined the railroad track and a siding occupied by two or three cattle cars, some men were heading for the stables. Grishin counted around a dozen of them. The ones in the middle were carrying something. He couldn't make out what it was. They were not only too far away but partly obscured by the men flanking them.

He set off for the stables himself, walking fast, but the others got there first. Their numbers had grown. There must have been twenty or thirty of them now, all standing in a circle. No one spoke. Then, from the direction of the main entrance, came the distant, fluctuating wail of an ambulance siren.

Grishin reached the silent group beside the stables. The men were standing shoulder to shoulder, staring at something on the ground. He gently nudged one of them in the back.

"What happened?"

A weather-beaten face turned to look at him. "Were you a friend of his? I haven't seen you around before."

"A friend of whose?"

The man ran his fingers through his close-cropped, curly hair. "He was asking for trouble. Horses should be treated with respect."

Grishin recalled his unaccountable premonition of danger. "Muranov, you mean? What happened, exactly?"

"I wasn't there at the time."

"Who was, then?"

"Nobody—nobody saw what happened. Is that good enough for you?"

The man presented his back again. Other faces had turned to look at Grishin, all with the same sullen, withdrawn expression. A few of the bystanders drifted off, giving him his first sight of what lay on the ground. Someone had draped a horse blanket over the body, so all that could be seen of it was a pair of riding boots. The blanket was stenciled with a five-pointed star.

The ambulance pulled up a few yards away and the onlookers, Grishin among them, stepped aside. Most were jockeys, trainers, or stableboys with tanned, weather-beaten faces like that of the man he'd accosted. The only two exceptions, who were sallow-cheeked and wore dark suits, claimed his special attention. Grishin had encountered their type too often not to recognize them at once for what they were. They stood over the inert form on the ground, one at the head, the other at the foot, with an air of cold contempt that branded them as men whose profession was violence.

Two ambulance attendants got out. After conferring with the dark-suited pair, they stooped and picked up the body. A fold of blanket fell aside as they did so, disclosing the dead man's face. It was horribly mutilated: a pulpy red mass with two wide-open, almost animate eyes in the midst of it.

A young stableboy beside Grishin turned pale and clapped a hand over his mouth.

"Come away." Grishin took him by the arm. The sun was hurting his eyes, boring into his head, and the stables, with their promise of shade, were only a few yards away. Still gripping the youngster's arm, he pushed the half-door open and went in. The shadowy interior was agreeably cool, the air redolent of dung and leather. He heard the doors of the ambulance slam shut. Then the boy came to life with a jerk.

"I must get back to work," he said. He was a skinny youth, and so bowlegged that he looked almost deformed.

"You work here all the time?"

The boy glanced down at the halter he was holding. "I must get back to the horses."

"Did you know Pavel Maximovich?"

The boy raised his eyes to Grishin's face. They looked startlingly blue in such a tanned face. "We worked together."

"What were you doing this morning?"

"Unloading a new batch of horses."

Grishin waited.

"The new horses arrive at this time of year. Yearlings and ones that have been wintering at stud farms."

"Because of the climate?"

"That's right. Most of them winter in the south, in the Caucasus, but those we've lost because of the fighting. This season's horses are coming from the north, from the Land of the Five Rivers. It's always been good horse country." Conversation about familiar subjects, things he'd grown up with, was calming the boy's nerves.

Grishin pointed to a horse blanket draped over a beam. Stitched into it was another five-pointed star. "Is that the brand mark of the stud?"

"Yes, but the Puyachev stud doesn't exist anymore."

"The racetrack has its own siding," Grishin said, remembering the cattle cars he'd seen. "Is that where the horses were being unloaded?"

The bright blue eyes stared at him.

"What kind of horses were they? Flat racers, sprinters?"

"Trotters."

"Pavel Maximovich was a sailor, wasn't he? Could he handle horses?"

"We were all surprised how well he got on with them."

"And the accident happened during the unloading?"

"I didn't see it myself. I'd already led my horses out. So had all the other grooms and stableboys. Pavel Maximovich was the last to leave the car."

"So you knew everyone there?"

"All except the stableboys who'd accompanied the horses on the train. Them and the other two—the ones standing over the body. They must have seen what happened."

"What were they doing here? They didn't look as if they'd ever had anything to do with horses."

"Some owners don't."

"You'd never seen them at the track before?"

"Not that I recall."

"Did your horses give you any trouble?"

"No, why?"

"They didn't act up?"

"They were glad to get off the train, that's all."

"Who first called it an accident? 'Poor old Pavel Maximovich, what a way to go—imagine him getting his head kicked in.' Surely someone must have said something like that?"

"Dedya!"

Grishin's companion started at the name, which was evidently his own. The curly-haired man's head and shoulders appeared over the top of the half-door. He opened it and glared at the stableboy, who scuttled out as fast as his bow legs would carry him.

"You too," said the man. "Out!"

Grishin did as he was told. Screwing up his eyes in the sunlight, he instinctively glanced at the place where Muranov's body had lain. All he saw was a jumble of footprints in the sandy gray soil and the tire tracks of the ambulance. The eight jockeys were circling the oval again, hugging the rails in a practice gallop. The siding was empty: The cattle cars had already gone.

"And now clear off," the man said. "We don't want any snoopers here."

Further questioning would be pointless, Grishin told himself. Muranov was dead. Dead men couldn't talk, and that was why he'd come, to have a talk with him. He shrugged and walked off, then turned once more.

"Did they shoot the horse?"

"What horse?"

"The one that killed him—it must have gone crazy. Don't you usually shoot a horse when it kicks someone to death?"

The man didn't reply at once. He seemed to be pondering the question. "Accidents happen—leave it at that. Horses tuck their heads in when a storm blows up, they're smart. Muranov should have taken a leaf out of their book. He was a fool, he stuck his neck out too far."

"Where did they take the body?"

"That's enough questions. Anyway, I've no idea."

"Did he live on the premises?"

"Yes, over there with the other stableboys."

Grishin followed the ambulance's tire tracks back to the stand. Nothing much had changed. The three attendants were still raking the track, the cleaning women had swapped their brooms for mops and buckets of water and were swabbing the seats.

The stableboys' lodgings, a range of old stables converted into living quarters, were on the left of the stand. Lolling on a chair outside was the janitor, a bearded ex-soldier in a threadbare uniform with one empty sleeve. As soon as Grishin mentioned Muranov's name, he could tell from the janitor's face that he was too late again. Muranov's belongings had been removed by two men. "It was just paper, mostly. Reams of it, all covered in writing."

Had they told the janitor who'd sent them? No—they weren't the talkative kind. Did Muranov have many visitors? Only his wife —or rather, his ex-wife. Did the janitor know her name? Yes, Lena Valentinova. Whenever she turned up, the pair of them would sit poring over papers. Any idea where she could be found? Quite nearby, at a former convent. Would the janitor mind if Grishin took a look at Muranov's room just the same?

It was as the man had said. The room was cell-like, with a stone floor, whitewashed walls, and a single window set in the wall above the onetime stable door. The only furniture consisted of an iron bedstead, a table, a chair, and a clothes locker. Grishin could see at a glance that the place had been cleaned out. Only ingrained habit prompted the agent in him to examine the straw-filled mattress and look inside the locker.

They had either forgotten something or thought it too unimportant to remove. On the floor of the locker, lying in the far corner, was Muranov's sailor hat with the name *Sevastopol* picked out in silver on the band.

⬤

She had a round, rosy face and hair so short that it stood up all over her head like a shaving brush. Grishin guessed that she must be one of the convent's dispossessed nuns. She stole a glance at the sailor hat in his hand, hesitated, and came to a decision.

"Lena Valentinova is busy at present. You'd better come with me."

She led the way to some double doors on one side of the entrance hall and conducted him down a long passage with a tiled floor and a row of tall, narrow windows overlooking a cloister. At the far end were some more double doors of carved oak. She paused in front of them and turned.

"Wait outside, please. I'll tell Lena Valentinova you're here. What name shall I say?"

"Just say I'm a friend of Muranov's."

She opened the door and slipped inside. Grishin had already caught the hum of voices while coming down the passage. Looking through the half-open door, he saw a big room with a vaulted ceiling, obviously the former refectory. Scores of children were seated at long wooden tables with bowls and spoons in front of them. All wore gray smocks, and their hair was so close-cropped that the girls were barely distinguishable from the boys.

A man at the end of the room was setting up a movie camera, a rectangular black box on a wooden tripod. His clothes alone— lace-up boots, breeches and puttees, khaki shirt and polka-dot bow tie—proclaimed that he wasn't a Russian.

The woman beside him wore a simple, three-quarter-length dress of some pale material. When the girl spoke to her and pointed to the doorway where Grishin was standing, she turned. Even at that distance he was struck by the intensity of her big, dark eyes, which dominated a heart-shaped face with high cheekbones. He wondered if it had been such a good idea to come here straight from the racetrack.

The girl returned, her youthful face radiant with enthusiasm. "Mr. Crabbin is making a film about the hardships suffered by Russian children. He plans to show it all over America, to raise money for—"

Grishin cut her short. "Can Lena Valentinova spare me a few minutes?"

"Yes, if you don't mind waiting awhile."

"Were you one of the nuns here?"

She ran a hand through her tousled hair. "I'm afraid it still shows, doesn't it? Yes, I used to be Sister Anya. Now I'm Eva Dashkova again."

"How many of you have stayed on?"

"Only four out of two hundred or more. Lena Valentinova got us exempted. She said we could do more good here than at the municipal garbage dump. Have you known her long?"

"We've never met."

"Well, you'll see—she's a person who takes things in her stride." The girl smiled. "If you'd care to wait in her office . . ."

The office was bare except for a desk, two chairs, and a table with a samovar on it. Once adorned with religious motifs, the ceiling had been whitewashed so inadequately that the colors still showed through. The only window looked out on a garden enclosed by a high brick wall. Three elderly, bearded men, all wearing aprons over their Russian smocks, were busy planting seedlings.

Grishin stood at the window, watching the gardeners at work. He was prepared for the gaze of those big, dark eyes when the door behind him opened and he turned around. There was nothing small and dainty about the woman's features, neither the mouth, nor the nose, nor the planes of her forehead and cheeks. She wasn't electrifyingly beautiful, but only, he sensed, because she herself chose not to appear so. Her face had a remote, withdrawn look, as if she preferred to conceal her emotions from the eye of the beholder.

He had left the sailor hat on the desk. It was almost self-explanatory. Although she glanced at it briefly, she showed no sign of surprise or shock. On the other hand, she made no pretense of not having seen it.

"May I offer you some tea?" she said.

"If you're not too busy."

"It's made."

"In that case . . ."

She produced some cups from a desk drawer and filled them from the samovar. All her movements—the way she walked, used her hands, turned her head—had a deliberate quality. Her cotton dress, either a size too small or shrunk by repeated laundering, made her look younger than her age and lent her a girlish, almost provocative appearance. Muranov must really have been a fool, Grishin thought, not to hang on to a woman like her.

Lena Valentinova handed him his tea and looked him straight in the eye. "How did it happen?"

"You mean you've already been notified?"

She sat down behind the desk and sipped her tea.

"No," she said at length, "but it was bound to happen sooner or later."

Although Grishin had never set eyes on the living, breathing man called Muranov, he suddenly felt angry on his behalf. How could this woman, who had been his wife, react so calmly, so coldly?

"He was beaten to death, probably by several men. They'll call it an accident, of course. Officially, a horse went crazy and kicked his head in."

She finished her tea and walked over to the samovar. "How about you—another cup?" He shook his head. "Did it happen at the track itself?"

"Yes. He was dead when I got there."

"Skachki seems to be a place of ill omen."

"Does that make his death easier for you to accept?"

"Our relationship was finished—past mending. I stood by him because I'd have felt guilty if I'd abandoned him. Now that you've told me he's dead, I know it's over at last. All I can feel at this moment is relief." She paused. "But you still haven't introduced yourself. I gather you were a friend of his."

"I'd never seen him before today."

She stiffened, the anger in her eyes making them look darker and bigger than ever. "And you encouraged me to talk that way? How could you!"

Not for the first time, Grishin was tempted to get up and walk out. He wanted the woman so badly that instinct counseled him to do just that. He had never before experienced desire of such painful, animal intensity.

"When did you see him last?" At least he had his voice under control. To his surprise, she answered quite calmly.

"Only a few days ago. He was preparing his defense with my help. He refused to accept that the trial would never take place."

"The trial?"

"Pavel Maximovich was searching for the source of all the world's ills, nothing more nor less. He was a disappointed idealist. Instead of admitting that his ideals had been betrayed by his own comrades, he looked around for someone else to blame and settled on the Germans. *They* financed Lenin's party and brought him back to Russia, so *they* control and manipulate him; that's what he hoped to prove at his trial. Personally, I never thought he'd live to see the inside of a courtroom."

"What about your last visit? Did he give any hint that he felt himself to be in danger?"

"Better in danger than written off, that was his attitude—that's what he couldn't endure, being forgotten, seeing his star on the wane. If they didn't put him on trial, he said, he intended to burn himself to death in public at a race meeting, preferably on the day of the Moscow Derby—douse himself with gasoline and burn himself to death in front of the main stand, with thirty thousand people looking on . . ." She indicated the sailor hat. "Where did you find it?"

"In his room."

"And his uniform?"

"The hat was all they left."

She picked it up, traced the lettering on the band with her forefinger, and put it down again.

"He kept his uniform because he planned to wear it at his trial. Ordinary Seaman Pavel Maximovich Muranov of the battle cruiser *Sevastopol,* a son of the people transformed by the Revolution into a hero and the commander of the entire Baltic Fleet. 'Look what the Revolution has made of a simple sailor like me!' That was his message."

Grishin found her tone puzzling. It sounded almost sardonic.

"That was his message," she repeated, "and that was the root of all his problems: He posed as what he wasn't. The truth is, he came from a thoroughly middle-class family. His father was a doctor—a well-known scientist with a Nobel Prize to his credit. Pavel joined the navy under an assumed name, as an ordinary seaman. He went to great lengths to conceal his origins and concoct himself a poor, proletarian background. He was eternally haunted by the fear that his comrades would learn the truth. When his father, being a contemptible bourgeois, was forbidden to practice and turned out on the street to starve, Pavel didn't dare lift a finger to help him."

Grishin shook his head. "I must have made a mistake about you. I took it for granted you were a Bolshevik yourself."

"I certainly shed no tears for the owners of confiscated banks or palaces, but I don't believe the people necessarily own things just because they've been taken from the rich." She smiled faintly. "Do you know why Muranov was working at Skachki? Because it was the only job he could get, and he got it through my father. I use my mother's maiden name, but my father's name is Samsonov—Kyril Samsonov. Does it mean anything to you?"

"Should it?"

"Name something that comes out of the ground."

"Oil," Grishin replied without thinking.

"Oil, yes. And gold, and copper, and water, and timber. That's what interests my father—anything you can extract from the soil. Most of the horses at Skachki are his, and so is the betting concession. Wherever there's money to be made, there's Kyril Samsonov."

"He's a survivor, you mean?"

"That's one way of putting it. Unlike Muranov, I'm immune to disappointment. I don't accept the idea that you've only to change a system and everyone will be happy. If you know there's no such thing as perfect happiness you can never be disappointed, right?"

They had both failed to hear a gentle knock at the door. It opened to reveal the outlandishly attired cameraman. He had the blue eyes and pink complexion of a baby.

"Sorry to intrude, Lena," he said in English. "I only wanted to tell you I'm through here. We're taking the kids to Red Garden now."

"I won't be long."

"That's okay, Eva can manage fine without you. Take your time."

"I'll only be a couple of minutes, Mr. Crabbin."

"No need to hurry. I won't be doing any more shooting in any case—I've used up all my film. I want to check the layout of the circus, that's all. You can rely on Eva . . ."

He backed out and shut the door behind him, leaving a whiff of lavender soap behind him.

Lena Valentinova got up from her desk and went over to the table. She put the cups on it and extinguished the burner under the samovar. When she turned and Grishin looked up at her, only a yard away, her dark eyes seemed to have lost all their luster.

"Why did you want to see him?" she asked.

"Will you be going to the funeral?"

"I'm not his widow. Why did you come here?"

Again he evaded her question. He rose and spread his hands in a gesture that encompassed the whole of the bare, bleak room. "What was this place, the Mother Superior's sanctum?"

Her smile did little to disguise the weariness in her face. "How did you guess?"

He pointed to an implement lying on the desk. It looked like a pair of hair clippers, only bigger.

She laughed. It was a low, husky laugh. "Sheep shears. That's what she used for cutting off the novices' hair. She made a point of doing the job herself. They had to sit at the window while she worked on them. My first few days in this room, I couldn't look at the floor without picturing it ankle-deep in hair."

Grishin recalled the crop-headed children in the refectory. "And now you've taken up where she left off."

"Have you any idea of the state they're in when they arrive here, some of those boys and girls?"

He had a vision of the station forecourt, the ragged youngsters taking to their heels, the policemen fanning out and opening fire. He'd seen the girl Vera only once since then, and that was one night while sneaking back through the derelict distillery. He'd called her name, but she'd run off and hidden somewhere in the ruins.

"I may bring you another stray sometime," he said. "I'd appreciate it if you found room for her."

"Before you do, you should come and tour the dormitories one night—spend an hour or two listening to the children's nightmares." The color had left her face, accentuating the dark smudges under her eyes. "But don't go too near the boys' beds. One of them might wake up with a start and pull a knife on you. When they arrive we cut off their hair, strip them, wash and clothe them. We also relieve them of their knives, but we never manage to find them all. And now please excuse me, I must go."

"What's this Red Garden?"

"The children's favorite place."

"Do you mind if I come too?"

Lena Valentinova stared at him in surprise. She seemed about to say something but thought better of it and walked to the door.

Grishin followed her out. It occurred to him that she hadn't even asked his name.

●

Red Garden was only a few minutes' walk from Yelizaveta Maria. After the peace and quiet of the convent, it seemed a riot of activity, loud music and voices. Lena Valentinova was wearing a shabby knitted jacket over her cotton dress in spite of the warm spring sunshine, and Grishin wondered if she dressed badly on purpose, so no one would take it into his head to find her beautiful. Even her clumsy flat-heeled shoes seemed designed to rob her walk of natural grace.

Lena Valentinova steered Grishin toward the main entrance of the garden. Just inside, a crowd had gathered to watch a gopak dancer accompanied by a woman playing a balalaika. The swarthy man was performing a gopak with a difference—not only squatting with his arms akimbo and shooting out his legs, but simultaneously spinning around with three knives balanced point downward on his upturned face, one on each cheek and the third on his forehead.

"That's Tsorim," Lena said as she set off down an alleyway between two rows of booths, making for the circus tent that dominated the fairground. They had difficulty threading their way through the crowd. Several stallholders nodded to her, and she nodded back or exchanged a few words with them.

"Seems you're a regular visitor."

"I often come here when things get me down. I live in one of those houses across the square. Red Garden is my home away from home."

"What's the origin of the name?"

"Blood. A man's blood, shed by a woman."

"And that's why you like the place?"

She smiled. "A prince was shot dead on the roller coaster here —that's its claim to fame. The Muscovites are crazy about roller coasters, but this one's history gives them an extra thrill. They can always pretend they're riding in the car where it happened."

Grishin looked up. The cars had just reached the summit of the track. They tilted as he watched and sped downhill. Screams of delight rent the air.

"No," she said, "that car isn't here anymore. "They've put it in a revolutionary museum. You can still see it there, complete with bloodstains, though I wouldn't guarantee they're really Prince Lavyonov's."

"He was assassinated?"

"Yes, twelve years ago. The prince was a much-hated man. He owned nearly every square foot of this neighborhood—they used to call him the prince of the Moscow slums. Anyone who got behind in his rent was publicly flogged, here in this very square."

"And the assassin was a woman?"

"A girl of nineteen. She pumped several bullets into him at point-blank range, though the doctors certified that any one of them would have been fatal on its own. I was fifteen at the time and tremendously impressed. In school we talked of nothing but 'the crime.' We knew everything about the assassin—for instance, that she was five feet tall and weighed less than a hundred pounds."

"It doesn't take much strength to pull a trigger."

She gave a full-throated, uninhibited laugh. "Say what you like about Russia—it's the only country where men and women enjoy equality of opportunity, certainly as far as political assassinations go. And an equal chance of dying, naturally." Her face grew somber. "Lavyonov's Cossacks didn't kill her on the spot. They tortured and raped her for twenty-four hours . . ."

Grishin watched her as they fought their way along the crowded alleyway. She seemed to be engrossed in her own thoughts.

"Why are you called Lena? What does it stand for—Yelena?"

"No. It isn't my real name."

"Lena like the river, you mean?" Once again, as he had at the sight of Ostrov's butterflies, he felt a stirring of memory.

She stopped short, stared at him, and nodded. "I fell into the Lena when I was little. Somebody fished me out. It wasn't too difficult—the Lena can be quite placid when the level drops in summer—but my mother insisted it was a miracle, a good omen. From then on I was known as Lena." She stared at him even more intently. "And you? What's your name?"

"Yevgeny Grigory."

"Well? I've told you the story of my name. What's the origin of yours?"

He held her gaze, but he couldn't halt the flood of recollections. The Lena had been wild and turbulent that night, not calm and sluggish. The current had swept him along, sucked him under, squeezed the air from his lungs. Had Dunga Khan already found his note and the ounce of gold?—that was his last conscious thought.

"I'm sorry I asked," he heard her say.

They had reached the tent and Lena held the flap open for him. Inside was a perfectly ordinary circus ring strewn with sawdust. The warm air trapped beneath the big top smelled like a zoo, as in any circus, and the clowns in the ring wore the traditional baggy trousers, outsize shoes, and red wigs.

He followed her up a steep flight of wooden steps. The tiers of benches were crowded with crop-headed children in gray smocks.

"Move up! Make room!"

It took them a while to get settled. Whatever was happening down in the arena, it obviously appealed to the children's sense of humor, because they roared with laughter.

They squeezed onto the end of one of the narrow wooden benches, side by side. Grishin could feel the warmth of Lena's body, her thighs, through the thin cotton dress. She said something, but it was drowned by another explosion of laughter.

He wasn't listening now, he was watching, observing. He made out the shorn head and round, flushed face of Eva Dashkova, the former nun, farther along the row. Crabbin had set up his tripod in a ringside box across the arena and was trying out camera angles.

To these impressions and perceptions Grishin added others: heights, distances, the position of the exits. He noted the noise level, gauged lines of sight, lines of fire.

Instinct had warned him to steer clear of the woman beside him, but something even stronger had overridden it and brought him here. The realization jolted him like an electric shock: He had found an ideal place for an assassination.

6

Grishin made his way slowly and warily along the Solodovnikov arcades toward Theater Square.

The Bolshoi ballet school, Fridays from 3 P.M. on . . . Colvin had specified the rendezvous, but the choice must have been Jim Hall's. Grishin wondered what had made him settle on it.

It was odd: However hard he tried, he found himself temporarily unable to visualize Hall's face. The only picture that came to mind was of the big man's bulky frame wedged into a cane chair with his legs splayed and his hands clasping his paunch. He'd tied four knots in his handkerchief and converted it into a sun hat. That was in Constantinople, on the terrace of a café overlooking the Bosporus, eighteen months ago . . .

The broad expanse of Theater Square stretched away in front of him. On the north side stood the Bolshoi Theater itself, a vast building capable of seating four thousand. Workmen were busy affixing slogan-adorned banners to the portico in front of the main entrance. Other men had set up tables around a fountain in the grounds and were selling condoms and sunflower seeds.

Grishin had already seen the headlines. Few details of the "tragic accident" at Skachki racetrack could be gleaned from either *Pravda* or *Izvestia,* but both carried lengthy tributes to the "hero of the Revolution" and articles recalling Muranov's prowess. A state funeral had been decreed, and a Moscow street was to be named after him.

On the east side of the square, where the small theater stood, Grishin joined a stream of people, mostly young, who were making for the ballet school, a baroque palace with an off-white façade.

The lobby was crowded, and Grishin allowed the tide of humanity to bear him off down a corridor. He had ceased to feel uneasy about the location of his first rendezvous. It had obviously been well chosen.

The dimensions of the auditorium were vast. The walls were draped in red cloth and the lofty ceiling, with its crystal chandeliers, was picked out in white and gold. A pianist was playing in the orchestra pit in front of the stage, which sloped upward at a gentle angle.

The set, a fairy-tale palace as unreal in appearance as the palace that housed it, meant nothing to Grishin. Five dainty, fragile-looking ballerinas in white tulle, their hair pinned up and adorned with flowers, were going through their paces on the stage. Grishin stood awkwardly, feeling ill at ease in such surroundings. He tensed as a hand touched his arm.

"Easy, John, it's only me."

He turned, eager to see the speaker's face. He recognized it, of course, but he noticed a change. Jim Hall was looking older, or not so much older as more pensive.

"Yevgeny," Grishin said. "How much time do we have?"

Hall glanced at the stage. He was a good head taller than most of the spectators. "Till six. The choreographers and dancers hate these public training sessions, but that's the new era for you."

"What are they rehearsing?"

"*Sleeping Beauty.*" Hall smiled. "Man, am I glad to see you! It's been ages—a year and a half at least. Remember Constantinople? High old times, eh? Blowing up trains was child's play compared to this job."

"You sound tired."

"As my faithful Miss Cale would say, revolutions make me sick."

"Sorry I couldn't get here before."

"How long have you been in Moscow? London was beginning to wonder if we'd heard the last of you."

"How soon did they find the Latvian? He was a Cheka informer, wasn't he?"

"You mean you didn't know for sure?"

"I couldn't take the risk, Jim. When did you hear he'd been killed?"

"They brought the body here after a week and showed it to a

man named Lloyd Fleming. It was Fleming who gave me the news. Know who I mean?"

"Colvin mentioned him."

Hall covertly scanned the faces around them and Grishin did likewise. They exchanged a nod, satisfied that neither of them had noticed anything suspicious.

Grishin said, "What exactly happened?"

"Spogis really pulled the wool over my eyes. When I didn't hear from him, I waited twenty-four hours and then abandoned our Finnish safe house. Just in time, as it turned out." Hall's voice hardened. "The Cheka sent twenty men across the border. There was a skirmish with the Finnish frontier guards. In other words, the Bolshies were prepared to risk a frontier incident and a protest note, just to discover more about Hugh Thomas. It's worrying."

"You say the Cheka were there?"

"Yes, led by a commissar named Peters."

"What's so worrying about that?"

"Yury Peters is the boss of Section Nine."

Grishin waited.

"He's responsible for the personal safety of the Bolshevik leaders. Why? Why should *he* be handling the case?"

"Can you tell me anything more about him?"

"He wears embroidered silk shirts."

Again Grishin waited patiently.

"One gets to know most of these Cheka butchers in time. They sign their names in blood, and they don't care who knows it. It's one way of asserting their authority. Yury Peters is different, though. He's almost invisible."

"A Russian?"

"Yes, in spite of his name. One of the few genuine Russians in the Cheka. The usual revolutionary qualifications: tried and sentenced for sedition, several years in Siberia, many years in exile . . . Maybe that's why he's on the case. Most of his time abroad was spent in England."

"Can you find out where he lives?"

"I already know. Any other official of his seniority would have a town house and a dacha in the country, but Peters lives right next door to Cheka headquarters. He's got a suite at the Hotel Billo."

"Married?"

"He used to be, to an Englishwoman, but she stayed behind in

England. He lives here with their child, a twelve-year-old girl by the fine old Russian name of Mary. He sent her to the International School, a top-notch establishment attended by the sons and daughters of the diplomatic corps."

Grishin smiled. "I thought you didn't know much about him."

"My Miss Cale happens to be on the board of governors. They've closed it down, by the way. Under present circumstances, various foreign governments thought it wiser to evacuate their embassy children from Moscow."

"How much do you know about Section Nine, Jim?"

"Peskov, who commands the Kremlin garrison, is one of Peters' men. Cheka personnel are responsible for guarding the gates and the various buildings, manning and maintaining the telephone exchange, patrolling the vehicle park. They even supervise the preparation of our man's meals, and there's always a Cheka officer standing by when *his* Rolls-Royce is refueled."

"What about outside?"

"External security is handled by the so-called Lettish Rifles. Three full-strength companies of elite troops—a kind of praetorian guard. They're commanded by a colonel, a Latvian named Berzin. He and Peskov both take their orders from Peters."

"And our man—where's he?"

"Colvin's plan never appealed to you, I know, but there was a lot to be said for it. Our man has gone to ground in a house that used to be occupied by the Czar's gentlemen-in-waiting. The only access to the Kremlin is the Trotsky Gate. His few selected visitors need special passes, and they have to show them a dozen times before they even set foot in his outer office. He's buttoned up tight, twenty-four hours a day."

"So he spends all his time there?"

"Yes, in two rooms, so they say. Works there, sleeps there, eats there. What's more, he eats off the Czar's plates. There's a story making the rounds here. The Bolshies took over the old palace servants, one of them being a kind of majordomo named Stupishin. When our man sat down to his first dinner in the Kremlin, it was dished up on the Czar's crested china. He objected, apparently, but Stupishin put his foot down. Either eat off the Romanovs' china, he said, or go hungry. He got his way, so every time the Bolshie bigwigs look down at their plates they're confronted by the imperial eagle."

"How's his health?"

"He won't let a doctor near him, if that's what you mean, least of all a Russian doctor. He's supposed to have imported a dentist from Berlin by air—the Czar's personal dentist. I don't know if it's true. You've no idea how hard it is to tell fact from fiction in this place."

"Don't worry, Jim, I'll get to him one way or another."

"With a bit of help from me, I hope."

Grishin thought for a moment. "What does he do for relaxation?"

"Watches films. He's a regular film fan."

"Doesn't that take him outside the walls?"

"No, they've fixed up a projection room next door to his office, and he's said to spend most of his leisure time there. Documentaries are his favorites: the Ford assembly line in operation, hydroelectric power being generated at Niagara Falls, steel production at Pittsburgh, that sort of thing. It's pure chance I happen to know so much about it, but the man who gets him these films from the States is an acquaintance of mine, an American eccentric called Arnold J. Crabbin. Remarkable people, the Americans. They still preserve a few illusions."

Grishin's eyes narrowed at the mention of Crabbin's name, but he made no comment. "Anything else?" he said, as they moved to another part of the hall. "According to C, our man is fond of hunting."

"I know, I've always found that odd—he doesn't look the type. I can't picture him wielding a gun, but he regularly goes after duck and other small game on an estate near Gorky. It's a big place, all woods and hills, with a country villa in the Italian style. It was presented to the nation by Kyril Samsonov, one of the richest men in Russia. Officially it's a workers' rest home, but our man has the exclusive run of it. Security's just as tight there as it is at the Kremlin."

"How does he get there?"

"He always leaves the Kremlin by the same route, with four bodyguards in attendance. His Rolls takes him to Kazan Station via a tunnel beneath St. Savior's. Then he switches to his private train."

"Trains can be vulnerable."

Hall shook his head. "Not this one. It's the Czar's, and they've beefed up the armor plating." He smiled apologetically. "Sorry to be such a wet blanket."

"You've certainly done your homework."

"Yes, while waiting for you to surface. What else could I do?"

"He enjoys making speeches, according to Colvin."

"Not anymore, with one possible exception. They say he's got a soft spot for children. If there's anyone he'll still say yes to, however much his security men object, it's a teacher who invites him to address her class. Maybe it's because his own father was a schoolmaster, or because it's traditional for a dictator to be seen patting kids on the head."

Grishin was feeling more optimistic. He'd expected Hall to be thorough. What he hadn't reckoned with were two coincidences: Arnold Crabbin's personal relationship with Lenin, which sounded quite close, and Lena Valentinova's connection with children. Grishin had faith in coincidences. It always boded well when things took shape of their own accord.

"How much time do I have, Jim? What's the word from London?"

"The word is, don't rush things. The Allies are seeking agreement on a concerted plan for armed intervention."

"Colvin spoke of landings."

"Yes, by us in the north, at Murmansk and Archangel; by the French in the south, on the Black Sea coast; by the Yanks and Nips in the east, at Vladivostok. Talks are now in progress in the various capitals. The politicos are trying to hammer out a common policy."

"How long are they likely to take?"

"I sometimes suspect they're trying to postpone a decision indefinitely. Our prime minister's a gambler, as Colvin says. Today he's putting his chips on Red. Tomorrow he may try his luck with White."

"Fleming's Red, you mean, and I'm White?"

"You know what politicians are. They all try to manipulate each other and wind up being manipulated themselves. All I know for sure is this: The longer they shilly-shally, the more they reduce our chances of putting a stop to the Bolshies. Their present position is desperately weak. The Council of People's Commissars is said to be making arrangements to leave Moscow and withdraw to the Urals. It's also rumored that the *Polar Star,* the old imperial yacht, is standing by at Kronstadt with a full head of steam up, ready to whisk our man abroad at a moment's notice. The Reds' only chance of clinging to power is to gain time and play one off against the other. Lenin has often proved how good he is at that little game . . ." For the first time, Hall sounded uncertain.

Grishin reached into his breast pocket and produced the three envelopes he'd been given by Ostrov. He held them out.

"Here, you're an expert. What do you make of these? I took delivery of them yesterday."

Jim Hall studied the contents of the three envelopes closely and handed them back.

"If they're forgeries, they'd certainly fool me." A thought struck him. "Some people would pay a fortune for those. Who did you get them from?"

"Vassily Ostrov. Did Colvin send you his file? I told Ostrov you'd pay him. Pay him well, Jim. You don't have any money worries, do you?"

"Name a figure. Five thousand, fifteen? Pounds, not rubles." Hall chuckled. "It won't even come out of Colvin's budget. Ever since the Foreign Office discovered how heavily the Germans have been subsidizing the Reds over the years, our diplomats have suffered from the delusion that all we have to do is outbid Berlin and the problem will solve itself. I'm sitting on a stack of cash."

"Good." Grishin looked down at his clothes. "I need a few things."

Hall took an envelope from his pocket. "Rubles and German marks," he said. "You'll find they go farthest on the black market these days. Have you settled in somewhere?"

"Not permanently."

"What if I need to contact you?"

"Before our next rendezvous?" Grishin hesitated. "You can always leave a message for Yevgeny Grigory at the central post office on Myaznitskaya Boulevard. I'll drop in there every other day."

"Any information you'd like me to transmit to London?"

Grishin shook his head.

"I'll have to let Colvin know we've met."

"That's up to you."

Hall stared at Grishin, alerted by something in his expression. "Do you already have a plan?"

"Only the vaguest outline."

For the first time that afternoon, Hall showed concern. "Look," he said uneasily, "I know you're a lone operator, but everything must be cleared with London first."

"Developments sometimes acquire a momentum of their own, Jim, I don't have to tell you that."

"But the whole idea is to coordinate your assignment with the landings—in your own interests as well as everyone else's. Military intervention will create a panic, and that'll be your moment."

Grishin studied his fingernails. "International agreements can turn sour; it's one of the first laws of diplomacy."

"Don't jump the gun, that's all I ask." Hall sounded almost despairing.

The pianist in the orchestra pit had stopped playing some time ago, and the set had been changed. Four pairs of dancers emerged from the wings and the pianist struck up again. Grishin watched in silence for a while.

"What made you choose this place, Jim? I'm intrigued."

Hall didn't reply at once. "What do you think makes a good dancer?"

"Aside from talent? Training, I suppose."

"That's only a part of it. The rest is belief in an illusion—the illusion that there's no ugliness in the world, only beauty."

"I never knew you were a philosopher."

There was a trace of sadness in Hall's smile. "Anything else I can do for you?"

"Not for the moment."

"We'd better split up here. Take care."

Grishin turned away from the stage, from the world of illusion and the figures that were gliding, floating, soaring across it. He felt relieved when he regained the open air and saw the streets and sky in all their drab reality.

7

The house on Tverskaya, a street once inhabited by wealthy Muscovite businessmen and their families, had belonged to a sugar merchant named Rozanov. He still lived there now, together with his wife and two sons, in a pair of servants' attic bedrooms. The rest of the house had been officially taken over by Arnold Crabbin's relief organization.

The Rozanovs played their role as tolerated tenants to perfection. They never showed their faces, received no visitors, came and went by the back door. To survive as well as this at a time of revolutionary upheaval, however, one had to be as shrewd as Georgy Rozanov and lucky enough to find a savior like Arnold J. Crabbin.

Rozanov's next-door neighbor, a rolling stock manufacturer, had enjoyed neither of these advantages. Evicted from his house with nothing but the clothes he stood up in, he had kept starvation at bay by working as a roadsweeper. Then, one January night, he was run over by a drunken cabby. Passersby found him lying in the gutter, badly injured and suffering from exposure. They took him to a hospital in the southwest of the city, where he died without regaining consciousness.

When his wife discovered his whereabouts, hours after the event, and went to request that his body be released for burial, she was spotted and recognized by the medical superintendent. He was astonished to see her there. Her husband on the premises? Impossible! He would have been notified at once—unless, of course, the patient had been incapable of giving his name.

"An immediate operation might have saved him, but you know how things are these days. Chloroform, dressings, electricity— they're all in such short supply that we can't afford to operate in every case. We have to be selective. If only your husband had been conscious enough to identify himself, I'd have done my best to save his life."

As the anonymous victim of a road accident, Vadim Fokin hadn't belonged to the elect, yet his name appeared in big letters over the hospital's main entrance. Why? Because it was his money that had built and maintained the place . . .

Lloyd Fleming was reminded of this anecdote every time he passed Fokin's house on Tverskaya—now the headquarters of a government agency responsible for confiscating valuable furs—en route to the Rozanov mansion, with its lofty gateway, fountain-adorned courtyard, marble staircase, and neoclassical statues.

His five-room apartment on the second floor was just as the Rozanovs had left it: overfurnished and pretentious. The paintings were either copies or fakes. The library's pseudo–High Renaissance "oak" paneling was humble sprucewood from the Urals, like the white-lacquered Louis XV furniture in the drawing room.

Fleming couldn't at first understand why Lena Valentinova never lingered at the apartment and was always eager to get away. As time went by, however, he came to see the rooms with her eyes and appreciate their lack of intimacy. This morning, in fact, he had reached the welcome and reassuring conclusion that it was the apartment's frigid atmosphere that bedeviled their relationship.

Lena had turned up early. He had asked her to come, even though it was the day of her ex-husband's funeral. Muranov's parents were arriving on the overnight train from Petrograd, and she planned to meet them at the station beforehand.

Lena prepared breakfast in the kitchen and set it out on a table at one of the windows overlooking the square and St. George's Church. She poured them both a cup of tea but shook her head when Fleming pulled back a chair for her.

"I can't stay," she said, standing there cup in hand.

"I've made up my mind," he told her. "I'm going to ask Jim Hall to get me a room at the British Club."

"And desert Mr. Crabbin?"

"He'll be leaving Moscow soon in any case."

"Is he really coming to the funeral?"

"He insists on filming it. Do sit down, Lena—the train doesn't get in till nine-thirty, you said so yourself."

"I've just got time to tidy the kitchen." She put her cup down. "It's rather a mess."

"Please don't bother."

"Mr. Crabbin always says that's what he admires so much about Russian women. They learn to cook and iron before they can read."

She laughed, and her casual manner seemed as inappropriate to Fleming as her ordinary working attire. He himself had donned a dark suit and a black tie for the occasion.

"He has a Chinese couple to look after him at home," she went on, "but no one can beat Eva Dashkova when it comes to ironing shirts, so he says."

"If we must talk about housework, can't we at least be comfortable?"

Lena had left her coat draped across the arm of a red plush sofa. She went over and sat down with her elbow resting on it. Fleming tried to read her expression with his usual lack of success.

"I've something to tell you," he said, "that's why I asked you to come."

He retired to the library next door and took a sealed, addressed envelope from the desk. Before returning, he glanced out of the window at the big building on the left of the square. Once the city's largest public ballroom and a scene of aristocratic revelry, it had since been renamed the House of Soviets. Pavel Maximovich Muranov's body was lying in state in the colonnaded hall, the mangled head suitably obscured by a mass of flowers, but Fleming could see only a trickle of people filing past the honor guard stationed outside. From there the coffin would be taken to its final resting place beside the Kremlin wall in Red Square.

He returned to the drawing room and ostentatiously deposited the envelope on a table in front of the sofa. Lena was still sitting there with one arm resting on her coat as if to remind him that this was no time for lengthy conversations.

"I'm sending a letter to London," he said, "to my wife." He sat down facing her and waited. She didn't react. "I know it isn't something we should discuss in a hurry."

"As far as I'm concerned, there's nothing to discuss."

"Please, Lena. Why can't we ever have a serious talk about our relationship. Whenever I try, you evade the issue."

"Maybe it's because I don't want to discuss it, not 'seriously.' Anyway, what's wrong with our relationship, as you call it?"

"The way you say it: 'relationship!' "

Her laugh was quite unabashed. "What do you expect, Lloyd? Good relationships between men and women are few and far between. From my point of view, ours is fine the way it is."

"Talking with you is as bad as negotiating with your Bolshevik bureaucrats. They're experts at not committing themselves."

She laughed again. "I'll never forget that day at the station in Petrograd. Three hours late, and another half hour to thaw out the doors—that should have been an object lesson to you. A man like you must expect obstructionism from officialdom. One step forward, two steps back. You'll never get what you want, and it's time you realized it."

"At the moment I couldn't care less."

"You know that's not true."

"Lena! I've been meaning to have it out with you for weeks, but everything conspired. There was Muranov, for a start . . ."

She shook her head.

"You felt a continuing obligation to him—you couldn't bring yourself to desert a man in his predicament."

She shook her head again. "You see me in a completely false light."

"I should have spoken sooner, but I wouldn't be the first man to shirk an awkward decision."

She glanced at the clock on the mantelpiece, and urgency made Fleming uncharacteristically blunt.

"I've realized, Lena, that I . . . that I want you, but I also realize I can't expect you to commit yourself while I'm a married man." He indicated the envelope on the table. "That's what I've written to my wife about."

There was a momentary pause. Then she said, "I hope you were more diplomatic on paper than you're being now."

"I've given her a choice."

"Don't do anything irrevocable, Lloyd."

"If she wants a divorce—"

"Has she asked you for one?"

"Of course not, it isn't her way, but if she agrees to one I've told her she can name her own terms. That would speed things up, even under our legal system."

"Why are you doing this, Lloyd?"

He stared at her, surprised and hurt. "Why? For us, of course."

"We've slept together, well and good. That much she'll have guessed and can swallow. From what you've told me about her, she'll forgive you an affair in Moscow, but never a letter like that."

"Whether or not she forgives me is immaterial, to me at least." He couldn't remain seated any longer. "How can you be so matter-of-fact, so unemotional—so damned English?"

"Englishness rubs off on one."

Footsteps could be heard outside the door of the apartment. Lena seized the opportunity to get up. "That'll be Crabbin," she said, retrieving her coat from the arm of the sofa. "I'd better go now, Lloyd, and you'd better get something straight: She'll never agree to a divorce—she'll merely redouble her efforts to get you recalled to London."

He took the coat and held it for her. She slipped into it, then turned and looked him squarely in the eye.

"I really must go."

"Shall I see you after the funeral?"

"I don't know how long his parents are staying. I'll call you."

Before he could put his arms around her she leaned forward and kissed him lightly on both cheeks. He scarcely felt her lips.

"What about the letter?" he asked.

Lena walked to the door. "That's simple," she said. "Tear it up."

When Grishin awoke, the noises from the kitchen told him that Vera Ivanova was back from her night shift. He peered through the half-open door. She had pinned up her fair hair and was washing at the stone sink. He could see the protuberant curve of her backbone as she bent over it. The hair in her armpits was darker than the rest, like the hairline at the nape of her neck.

He watched her straighten up and turn around, unable to see him because the bedroom was in darkness. She walked to the door, opened it wide, and stood there with one hand on the doorpost. Her body was slim, with small round breasts and almost invisible nipples.

"Good morning. Did I wake you?"

"No. What sort of night did you have?"

"The usual. Nothing special."

She came in and perched on the edge of the bed. Her naked body was still damp.

"Did you find the soap?" he asked.

His bag was on the floor beside the bed. She glanced at it. "So that's what it was," she said, "a going-away present."

Grishin sat there in bed with his arms folded, regretting that he hadn't left the house before she came back.

"I'm cold," she said. "Hey, didn't you hear? I'm cold—move over." She slipped between the blankets, slid her arm behind his neck, leaned over, kissed him. Her lips were soft, and much warmer than the rest of her.

He was struck yet again by how seriously she approached the act of love. As though anxious to demonstrate that it meant more to her than mere pleasure, she rode him with vigor and determination.

She was asleep when he got up. Framed by fair hair, her face wore the same look of concentration as it did when she bent over her textbooks.

He picked up his clothes and his bag and went into the kitchen. Her dark uniform, with its red piping and shoulder boards, was neatly draped over the kitchen chair, her boots had already been polished. The package lay unopened on the table.

He lit the gas ring and put the kettle on. After a moment's hesitation he poured two cups of tea, rolled two cigarettes, and put one beside each cup.

She emerged from the bedroom with the lace coverlet around her in lieu of a robe. Looking sleepy and a little self-conscious, she ran some water into a saucepan and shared it out among the plants on the windowsill.

"Will they ever grow big enough, do you think?"

"What are they?"

"They're supposed to be tobacco plants. The seedlings came from the Crimea. A conductress on the Kiev run smuggled them here."

"It's a south-facing window," he said. "Maybe that'll help."

"You really think so?" She joined him at the table. He gave her a light and lit up himself.

"You meant to go without telling me," she said, "didn't you?"

"Have you seen Vera?"

"Yes, she was at the station this morning. Are you leaving Moscow?"

"Not just yet." He pushed the package toward her. "Why don't you open it?"

She undid the string and wound it into a ball. She also folded the paper neatly for future use and laid it aside. Then, having gingerly lifted the lid of the box, she sniffed the contents. The two bars of perfumed French soap were still in their original wrapping.

"You shouldn't buy things on the black market. It only helps the capitalists to undermine our socialist economy." She shut the box again.

"I hope you'll use them just the same."

"Yes. Thank you." Her blue eyes looked mistier than usual. "You're welcome to come back anytime," she said.

"Thanks. Take good care of those first-class cars of yours, comrade. I'll drop in again sometime, never fear."

Although Grishin had conceived his promise as a lie, he was surprised to find, when the words left his lips, that he really meant them.

●

Red Square, an elongated rectangle, skirted the Kremlin wall for eight or nine hundred yards but was less than two hundred yards wide. The square and the Kremlin itself occupied one of Moscow's seven hills, so the surrounding streets sloped away in all directions.

The sun still hung low in the sky, which was veiled in the glassy gray haze that heralds a scorchingly hot day.

Some workmen were shoveling the last of the soil from Muranov's grave in the strip of turf between the wall and the cobbled square, idly watched by five uniformed sailors armed with rifles and fixed bayonets. Another two workmen were visible atop the sixty-foot brick wall immediately above the grave. They had just unfurled a broad red banner inscribed MURANOV, MARTYR OF SOCIALIST WORLD REVOLUTION!

Fleming and Crabbin had turned up far too early, but the American had been most insistent and badgered Fleming into accompanying him to Red Square well in advance of the many thousands of mourners who were expected to flock there for Muranov's funeral.

Crabbin had set up his camera on the steps of the monument to Minin and Posharsky, just across from the grave. He was wearing his usual outfit: brown lace-up boots, puttees and breeches, freshly laundered khaki shirt, polka-dot bow tie.

"They had a harder job last November," he said, indicating the gravediggers. "The ground was frozen solid when they dug that mass grave—they had to break it up with pickaxes." He glanced at the withered wreaths beside the Kremlin wall. "They really might have replaced those for the occasion."

His normally rubicund face looked sickly, almost yellow, in the morning light, and his forehead was beaded with sweat.

"Feeling all right, Crabbin?"

"A touch of fever, that's all. Probably some infection I picked up on my last trip. Not surprising, the hundreds of hands I've shaken and the hundreds of times I've been hugged and kissed, but what can you do? People like to show their gratitude." He mopped his brow with a spotted handkerchief. "Weren't you here in November?"

Fleming surveyed the huge square. It seemed surprisingly quiet and deserted.

"No, I was ensconced in my London office, working out how much our bank had lost. It was quite a shock."

Crabbin pointed to the mouth of Nikolskaya, one of the streets leading into the square.

"I spent most of one day pinned down on that corner during the fighting. The Whites had us stymied with a machine gun. There were scores of youngsters with me, out-of-work paperboys. They made bets who could make it across the street through the machine-gun fire . . ." He mopped his brow again. "A variation on Russian roulette. Most of them were mown down, but you needn't think it put the others off their game, no sir! They carried on regardless, sprinting back and forth across the street through a hail of bullets and yelling and laughing as they did so."

Fleming stared at him. There was something weird and faintly disturbing about the American's tone. It was almost rhapsodic.

"You wouldn't understand unless you'd been there. It was bitterly cold—well below zero—and the ground was rock-hard. The gravediggers went at it with their picks and shovels all night long. Six hundred bodies, seven hundred, nine hundred, maybe a thousand. The trench beside the wall grew longer and longer . . . Ever since then, every distinguished member of the Party and the socialist movement has been buried here by order of the Bolshevik authorities." Crabbin paused. "What a day that was! And to think I'd used up all my film—there wasn't a foot to be had in the whole of Moscow. Well, I won't miss anything today. I aim to cover the funeral and the circus before I leave."

"You're off again?"

"Sure, we're having problems on the Trans-Siberian route." Crabbin twisted his white cap around so the peak shaded his face. "Did you read Lenin's tribute to Muranov in today's *Pravda?*"

Fleming didn't reply at once. The men beside the wall had completed their work. They tossed their shovels out of the grave and climbed out after them. The five sailors continued to stand there like statues. Fleming turned back to the American.

"Yes, I read it. A bit overdone, considering their differences in the past."

"I don't agree," Crabbin said firmly. "It only goes to show how badly most people misjudge Lenin. His obituary has completely rehabilitated Muranov. Is that the act of a heartless despot with ice water in his veins?"

Crabbin turned to look. The unwonted silence of the square had been invaded by the sound of horses' hoofs.

Two troops each of thirty cavalrymen came trotting up Nikolskaya and Ilinka and stationed themselves at the point where the two streets joined Red Square. A lone officer detached himself from his troops and rode across the deserted expanse of cobblestones, heading for the monument. He reined in just short of the two men and the camera, then leaned down and sullenly inquired what they were doing there.

Crabbin, looking half amused, produced the special permit that authorized him to film anywhere in Moscow, anytime. The officer examined it and wheeled his horse with a shrug.

"Hand me one of those cans of film," Crabbin said. "They won't be long now."

Fleming's uneasiness mounted. He was puzzled by the strangely unnatural appearance of the square. Where were the usual sightseers? Why weren't the buildings overlooking the square thronged with spectators? Sunlight glinted on the windows of the stores, offices, and restaurants opposite: All were firmly shut. There was no one in sight but the two troops of cavalry, the horses almost motionless, the riders erect in their saddles with carbines resting across the pommels.

"Do you know what's going on here, Crabbin?" Fleming glanced at his watch. "I'm damned if I do."

"Don't stay unless you want to, I won't be offended. Just dig out the rest of those cans for me, will you?" Crabbin broke off.

Once again their attention had been attracted by a sound. It came from the Iberian Gate at the far end of the square, through which the funeral procession could be expected to pass. There was no one in sight yet, but the two big white arches, like a pair of enormous mouths, were channeling the echoes of countless voices, some chanting, others raised in song.

Arnold J. Crabbin's face lost its momentary look of perplexity and relaxed. He climbed the two granite steps at the base of the monument and settled himself behind his camera.

Grishin had reached Sukharov Square. "Daughter of the War" was the Muscovites' nickname for this neighborhood, because it had shot up with the wild abandon of a rampant weed after the great fire of 1812. A man like Ivan Fyodorov, porter, would pass unnoticed in such a poor and densely populated part of the city. Fyodorov was one of the three pseudonyms selected by Vassily Ostrov for use on Grishin's sets of false papers.

Once in the narrow streets surrounding the marketplace, Grishin was swallowed up by crowds of people jostling and elbowing their way toward the focus of black market activity. Not all of them were prospective customers or dealers. The very poorest Muscovites derived special pleasure, masochistic as well as malicious, from visiting Sukharov market to see how prices had soared in the previous week and watch members of the outlawed bourgeoisie selling off the last of their prized possessions.

It was here that Grishin had bought the soap for Vera Ivanova. Today he wasted no time in acquiring a modest suit, a second jacket and pair of trousers, a couple of shirts, some underwear, socks, and hand towels. He also invested in two packets of coarse makhorka tobacco, some black China tea, a handful of damp, grubby cubes of sugar, and a bar of soap for himself.

After stopping briefly to eat a bowl of potato soup, Grishin left the market with his bag in one hand and his purchases tied up in paper in the other. He had already conducted a preliminary reconnaissance of Sukharov and the dilapidated rooming houses in the

vicinity. Now, after inspecting a few of the less squalid establishments, he settled on a six-storied tenement house built around an
inner courtyard. The heat hit him as soon as he passed through the
gateway. So did a stench compounded of boiled cabbage, rotting
rubbish, and urine. The janitor, a small but sturdy man in his fifties,
was built like a wrestler and had a flame-red birthmark on the side
of his neck.

"Can you rent me a room?" Grishin fumbled in his pocket for
Ivan Fyodorov's identity card.

The man gave it a cursory glance. "Can you pay?"

"Do you have a vacancy?"

"We always have a vacancy—people come and go all the time.
Pay up and you can move in right away."

"Show me what you've got."

"Those stairs are steep. It's too hot to go traipsing up them, only
to find you don't have the money."

Grishin had distributed his ready cash between various pockets
so no one would see how much he had on him. He pulled out
some greasy ruble bills and looked at them like a man confronted
by a difficult decision.

After prolonged haggling they agreed on forty rubles for thirty
days. From what the janitor said, even that modest sum was exor-
bitant.

"For forty rubles you can take your pick. Either a ground-floor
room where you get the stench from the courtyard and the din the
drunks make coming home nights, but you don't risk breaking your
neck on the stairs. Or a room on the sixth floor, where the air's
better but the water doesn't run half the time."

Grishin looked up at the square patch of blue sky overhead. "I'll
take the one at the top," he said.

The janitor showed him to the foot of some stairs leading to the
open galleries that skirted each floor. "The number of your pigsty
is 5F. You'll find a communal shithouse at the end of the passage."

"Don't I get a key?"

The man shook his head. "You only have to lift the latch. No one
who lives here owns anything worth stealing."

"Who gets rich on the rents?"

"Search me. A lawyer collects the takings. Don't ask me where
the money goes then, comrade. Certainly not to the likes of you or
me."

Grishin's room was long and narrow, with a window facing the door. It contained a plank bed plus straw mattress, a small round stove, and some clothes-hooks screwed to a plank. A naked bulb, thick with dust and fly dirt, dangled from the ceiling. When Grishin spun the faucet, all it produced was a thin, brownish trickle.

He opened the window. Moscow's twin water towers loomed above a stony waste of tenement houses. The buildings were contiguous, and their flat roofs stretched away in all directions. In an emergency, they would provide an excellent escape route. Grishin felt satisfied with his choice of abode.

He stripped completely, washed under the trickle of water, and put on the suit he had bought at the market. The spare jacket and trousers, containing some money and Ivan Fyodorov's papers, he hung on a hook. The second set of papers, made out in the name of Vada Nikulin, bargeman, he put in his pocket. His Whitechapel Road outfit and the papers for Commissar Relinsky of the Cheka he stowed away in his bag.

Before leaving the room, Grishin returned to the open window and lit one of his hand-rolled cigarettes. He was feeling good. Things were beginning to take shape. As Vada Nikulin, bargeman, he would go in search of work among the men who lived on the banks of the Moskva, earning their keep in winter by sawing up and selling blocks of ice, in summer by working on the ferries and river craft.

But first, he told himself, he must see about a gun. He'd had a precise idea of what he needed and who could supply it ever since his visit to the Durov Brothers' Circus.

Suddenly impatient, he stubbed out his half-smoked cigarette and shut the window after a final look at the bustling urban rabbit warren spread out below him. When the lights came on at night, he reflected, it might even acquire a certain charm.

The Petrograd express was already half an hour late. Nobody could give Lena Valentinova any information, and the delay, despite its predictability, was getting on her nerves. Besides, she knew in advance what course this latest encounter would take. Alexandra Mechikova's eyes would blaze with habitual, fanatical dislike of the woman who had dared to marry her son. Muranov had tried to laugh it off—"It's only because we didn't get married in church"—but he'd always hoped that things would work out between them. Muranov's mother had never shared that hope, and his death would not have diminished her animosity.

A train pulled out of the station. Smoke lingered beneath the glass roof, robbing the sunlight of its brilliance. The platform began to fill. Lena sighted an approaching train.

The blue first-class cars, three sleepers, glided past. Lena found the right number. The door swung open. A porter took the bags as they were handed out. There were ten or a dozen leather suitcases, all brand-new. After them came a man so fat he could barely squeeze through the doorway. A cigarette in a long ivory holder jutted from his lips.

Lena waited, but no one else emerged. The conductor was walking along the platform, slamming doors and locking them.

"Was this the night express from Petrograd?"

"What else?" The conductor's lack of sleep showed in his face.

"I was expecting some people. They were traveling in this car—Compartment 11B. A married couple."

"A married couple?"

"Mechikov. I made the reservation myself."

"There must be some mistake—no, wait a minute. Mechikov . . . Yes, I remember now, an elderly lady." The conductor gave Lena a look of commiseration. "The compartment was reserved for her, right enough, but she refused to travel first-class."

"She did take this train, though?"

"Possibly, but I'm only responsible for the first-class cars." He walked on, closing the doors and locking them with a brass key hanging from a chain attached to his belt.

Lena peered along the platform, which was gradually emptying. At the far end she glimpsed a tall, slim woman dressed in black and wearing a small black hat. She was standing with a suitcase beside her and a longish package in her arms.

She continued to stand there when Lena set off up the platform toward her. There was no mistaking Alexandra Mechikova, even though she'd aged in the year since Lena had seen her last. The strands of hair escaping from under her hat were completely gray. Her eyes were gray, too, but undimmed by an overnight journey of eleven hours. Their expression was as hard and implacable as ever.

"You shouldn't have troubled," was her only greeting.

"I booked you a sleeper."

"I know, a first-class compartment. Ridiculous! I travel in the class I now belong to."

The package in her arms was a bunch of flowers, their green stems protruding from the wrapping paper.

"Where's your husband?"

Alexandra Mechikova drew herself up even more stiffly. "Look, we're late already, so let's not waste time on meaningless courtesies." Her gray eyes glinted with derision. "At least you didn't have the hypocrisy to wear black. I appreciate that."

Lena stooped to pick up the suitcase.

"Don't bother."

"Let me carry the flowers, then."

"If you must carry something, I'd sooner you took the case."

They walked down the platform together. Alexandra Mechikova's coat looked too big for her, as if her shoulders had shrunk. The black dress beneath it had a narrow lace collar that lent her a forbiddingly schoolmarmish appearance.

"Precisely when and where is the funeral?" It was the first question she'd asked. "Your telegram wasn't very informative."

"We still have time. I've got a droshky waiting outside."

Not a word about her son, Lena thought. Not a sign of curiosity about the circumstances of his death. She couldn't have read the Moscow papers yet, and Lenin's tribute to Muranov had appeared only that morning.

The empty train had pulled out and the platform was filling up again. Whole families had pitched camp with baggage all around them, and a party of women were squabbling over something, their voices shrill with anger. A middle-aged couple and two children sat perched on their suitcases, striving to preserve an air of faded elegance.

"A filthy business, this revolution!" Alexandra Mechikova uttered the words with all the loathing she could muster.

Suddenly a bell rang, and a train at one of the more distant platforms started to pull out. Even the roofs of the cars were laden with passengers.

It was then that Lena caught sight of the three men at the barrier. Yury Peters, in his black leather jacket, stood in the foreground. His two companions, who topped him by a head, wore long, gray greatcoats and were armed with heavy Mauser pistols. The guns looked awesomely lethal even in their holsters.

Peters himself was unarmed. His face had an unhealthy pallor, and his cheeks were dark with stubble.

"You're a dutiful daughter-in-law, Comrade Valentinova." There was no sarcasm in his tone; he was simply stating a fact. He subjected the older woman to an appraising stare. "Where's your husband?"

"She came on her own," Lena said quickly. Anything Alexandra Mechikova might say would only make matters worse.

"Let her speak for herself, comrade." Peters was holding his mutilated hand behind his back.

Alexandra Mechikova turned to Lena, her gray eyes flashing. "Comrade daughter-in-law," she said scathingly, "if these men are friends of yours, tell them I can dispense with their company."

Lena looked at Peters. "She's just spent the whole night sitting up, eleven hours . . ." She glanced at the station clock above the heads of the other two Cheka men. "We'll be late."

Peters sighed loudly. "The next train to Petrograd leaves in two hours' time. We've made the reservations."

"I don't understand."

"I'm sorry, believe me. You've done your duty. Leave the rest to us."

"But she's here for her son's funeral!"

Peters shrugged. "There isn't going to be any funeral. The ceremony in Red Square has been canceled. Pavel Maximovich Muranov was a hero for twenty-four hours only. By the time tomorrow's *Pravda* appears, he'll doubtless be what he was before: an agent provocateur and a counterrevolutionary stooge."

Before Lena could say anything—before she could look at Alexandra Mechikova to see if *she* had grasped what was going on—the flowers slipped through the older woman's fingers and fell to the ground. They landed just in front of Yury Peters's highly polished black boots. The paper burst open to reveal a dozen white lilies, already wilting. Peters stooped, retrieved them, and wrapped them up again. Alexandra Mechikova shook her head when he held them out to her. She was suddenly showing the effects of her long, sleepless night.

Lena took the flowers herself, even though she detested lilies—their scent nauseated her. "So she's to go home without even a last glimpse of her son?'' The words were out of her mouth before she remembered Yevgeny Grigory's description of the dead man's injuries. ''On whose orders?''

''Please, comrade!''

''If he's not to be buried beside the Kremlin, where do you propose to put him?''

''That's not my responsibility. As soon as it's decided, we'll let you know. And now let's drop the subject. We'll look after this woman. You can rely on us to treat her with all due courtesy.''

Lena forgot everything she'd felt before the train came in. ''I insist on staying with her.''

Peters nodded as if he'd expected as much. ''As you wish, comrade. I'm truly sorry . . .'' He turned to the two men behind him, and his voice became cold and businesslike. ''They can wait in the station restaurant, but make sure she's on that train.''

●

''God Almighty!''

Fleming couldn't at first make out what was happening at the Iberian Gate. A yelling mob of demonstrators had erupted from the twin gateways beside the Mercy Chapel. On they came, hundreds and hundreds of them, in a never-ending stream. As though compressed by the two gate arches, they spilled out across Red Square like pent-up floodwater.

''God Almighty!''

Fleming could find no other words to express his surprise and alarm. He had seen at a glance that this was no peaceful tribute to the dead. The marchers' voices and gestures conveyed a fierce belligerence that perturbed him. Many of them were singing the ''Marseillaise'' with defiant, menacing fervor.

''Move over a bit, there's a good fellow. You're blocking my view.''

''Honestly, Crabbin, I don't think we should hang around. This is a budding riot, not a funeral procession. There's bound to be trouble. Let's get out of here while we can.''

The workmen and sailors had abandoned the open grave beside the Kremlin wall and beaten a hasty retreat. The demonstrators surged forward and crowded around it. Most of them were in their working clothes; others were wounded veterans in the coarse, striped pajamas issued to patients at military hospitals. There must have been a thousand of them or more.

Fleming watched with growing apprehension. The first banners —strips of red or black bunting—were unfurled and waved above the heads of the crowd with a vigor that rendered the slogans on them impossible to read. The strains of the "Marseillaise" died away, to be replaced by a momentary silence. Then cries rang out. Isolated at first, they combined to form a rhythmical, imperious, deafening chorus. "Muranov . . . Muranov, yes! Lenin . . . Lenin, no!" A thousand voices took up the refrain. "Muranov, yes! Lenin, no! Muranov, yes! Lenin, no! Muranov, *yes!* Lenin, *no!*"

The banners kept time with the words, fluttering to and fro, until a new babble of cries rent the air: "Hang the baron . . . Hang the German baron . . . Hang the German spy . . . Out with the Germans . . . Germans, out!" After the same initial hesitation, the demonstrators found their rhythm again. "Germans, out! Lenin, out! Germans, out! Lenin, out! Germans, *out!* Lenin, *out!*"

The cries reverberated around the square, multiplied by the echoes that rebounded from the Kremlin wall and the buildings opposite. Panic-stricken, Fleming glanced helplessly at Crabbin, who was cranking away at his camera with total concentration. The whirr of the mechanism was just audible.

"Germans, out! Lenin, out! Germans, *out!* Lenin, *out!*"

Chanting voices were suddenly mingled with the clatter of hoofs on cobblestones. The two troops of cavalry had left their intersections and were advancing across the square. Just as the demonstrators had taken time to find their rhythm, so the cavalrymen took time to develop a tight formation. One or two horses shied at the din, but they ended by maintaining an orderly trot.

"That's enough, Crabbin. For God's sake, let's get out of here!"

"Quick," yelled Crabbin, "another can! Pass me another can, and hurry!" Fleming was momentarily swayed by the American's sangfroid. He took a fresh can of film from its leather pouch and handed it to him.

They were in a kind of backwater, partly protected by the big bronze monument behind them. The troops of cavalry spread out in line abreast, heading for the Kremlin wall to left and right of them. Startled by their sudden appearance, the demonstrators fell silent, but not for long; awareness of their own numerical superiority quickly asserted itself. What could two pathetic little troops of cavalry—sixty men in all—hope to achieve against a mob a thousand strong?

The neat line of cavalrymen wavered as the demonstrators charged toward them. Horses shied and reared, riders wheeled and turned tail. The mob pursued them, snatching at their bridles and dragging some of them to the ground.

That was when the first shots rang out, crisp as whiplashes: The cavalry had been reinforced by a machine gun mounted on a converted taxicab. For a moment or two, nothing could be heard but its vicious, sustained chatter.

Bodies went flying, and the huge, compact mass broke up into knots of terrified individuals. The demonstrators ran for their lives, each intent on self-preservation, leaving the ground strewn with caps and banners, dead and wounded. As though encouraged by its success, the machine gun opened up again, firing wildly and indiscriminately.

Fleeing figures dashed past the monument, panting, ducking low. A few yards from Fleming a young woman stumbled and fell, and the red flag she had been carrying draped itself over her motionless form like a shroud.

"The camera, Fleming—the camera!" Crabbin's face was chalky white and bathed in sweat. "The camera—save the camera!"

As Crabbin fell, so did his precious contraption. His knees buckled and the white linen cap slipped off his head.

Fleming recalled later that his first impulse really had been to save the toppling camera, but it was Crabbin he caught in his arms.

He didn't see the bullet's point of entry, but just above the waistline, the freshly laundered, immaculately pressed khaki shirt began to turn red. The faint smile on Arnold J. Crabbin's waxen face seemed to convey an apology for being such a nuisance.

Something was up, Grishin could sense it. The streetcars weren't running—they stood empty and abandoned at various points along the line—so he took a droshky to the other side of the Moskva River and told the driver to drop him in the square in front of Prokovsky Church. Bazmannaya was an industrial area. The place should have been humming with activity, but all that reigned there now was a leaden, unnatural silence.

Grishin left the square and made his way along one of the grimy side streets. Factories loomed up everywhere, their tall smokestacks staining the sky black. Nothing seemed to have changed here: The place was as ugly as ever. Bazmannaya was one of those Moscow districts renowned for the fact that on sunless days the streetlights continued to burn at noon.

No outward changes were observable in Grishin's destination, either, when he finally reached it. The gray stone arch above the factory's wrought-iron gates still bore the inscription "Stefan Michelson, Manufacturer of Arms and Ammunition," and even the twin-headed imperial eagle carved in stone between the name and the description had escaped defacement during the revolution.

There was a small side gate. The janitor had dozed off in his shack with a flimsy morning edition of *Pravda* draped across his knees. Grishin tapped on the open window.

"Where do I find Josef Krnka, comrade? Does he still work here?"

The janitor came to with a start. The newspaper slid off his lap. "Krnka . . ." he muttered. "Did you say Krnka?"

"Yes, the gunsmith."

The janitor shook his head. "Never heard of him."

"What about Michelson?"

"Comrade Stefan—the comrade director, you mean? Yes, wait, I'll take you to him."

"Don't trouble, comrade, I know my way."

Grishin entered the factory yard. Ahead of him was another gate, and beyond it the central thoroughfare between the workshops. Sallow-faced workers in dirty aprons were scurrying to and fro like ants. Grishin crossed the yard to the administration building, a massive, fortresslike edifice of red granite. It was cool inside. He didn't take the elevator, but climbed the stone stairs to the top floor.

Two women were seated at their typewriters in the outer office. The elder of the two looked up first. "I don't believe it!" she exclaimed, brushing some wisps of gray hair out of her eyes. "Gregor Constantine—*you* back in Moscow!"

"Anna Andreevna, isn't it? Still at that machine of yours, I see."

She gave up trying to tidy her hair. "You haven't forgotten my name?" She turned to the girl beside her, who had also stopped typing. "Four years, and he still remembers my name! Wait till I tell the boss who's here!"

"Is he around? Would you ask if he can spare me a few minutes?"

A door at the other end of the room opened. The man who emerged was a tall, fair, Viking type in his mid-fifties. His face lit up. "If it isn't the Greek! Good to see you, Gregor. Come in, come in." He stepped aside to let Grishin pass.

"A drink?" he said, as soon as they were alone.

"A bit too early in the day for me."

Undeterred, Michelson produced a bottle and two glasses from his desk. The windows in the outer wall of the office afforded a panoramic view of the factory grounds. Every square inch of the opposite wall was covered with diagrammatic illustrations of guns, technical drawings, and production charts.

Michelson filled both glasses. It was obvious from the look of his hands that he had worked with them, so the diamond ring on his little finger seemed an eccentricity. Either that, or it was a mute announcement that Stefan Michelson, onetime mechanic and son of a Swedish blacksmith, had grown rich on the proceeds of arms manufacture. He raised his glass.

"What shall we drink to?"

"Anything you like, comrade director—isn't that what they call you these days?"

"It's a dream come true, my friend. No possessions, a life without care, no more sleepless nights spent worrying about profit margins." Michelson leaned forward. "Above all, Gregor Constantine, no more commissions payable to greedy middlemen like you! We're all brothers in the service of the same cause, the same dream. Someday the Moskva will flow with milk and honey."

"Meantime, the comrade director still drinks vodka."

"I pretend it's water, just as the workers drink water and pretend it's vodka. That's the Revolution for you." The Swede shook his head as if the new era defied his comprehension. "Nothing here belongs to me anymore, but I want for nothing. Everything here belongs to the workers, but they've got even less than before. Here in the city wages have risen five hundred percent, inflation a thousand percent, our profits two thousand percent. That's the situation in a nutshell."

"And what you say still goes?"

"Bazmannaya always was redder than red, and the workers know I'm a Red at heart. What they really hate are bureaucrats who prattle on about class consciousness when the food stores are empty. The workers elected me because I supplement their rations by black-marketeering on the side. The bureaucrats leave me in peace as long as I meet my production targets." Michelson refilled his glass. "And you, Gregor? Still in the arms trade?"

"In a manner of speaking," said Grishin, lighting a cigarette.

"I could put you in touch with the right people. The Bolsheviks are having to build up a new army from scratch. Who do you represent these days? Still working for Vickers?"

"I was thinking of buying, not selling."

"Buying? Not a hope. The arsenal at Tula is out—overrun by the Germans. Production at Sestroretsk is highly erratic because of the fighting on the Russo-Finnish border. That only leaves Yersk and the Michelson Works, alias the Nationalized Arms and Ammunition Factory of Moscow."

"Buying experience, I meant—experience and craftsmanship, comrade director." Grishin pointed to one of the illustrations on the wall. It showed a target pistol of unusual design. The lettering at the head read "Margoline TOZ-35."

"Ah, that," said Michelson. "That gun won the Russian team a gold at the Stockholm Olympics in 1912. And he only had a year to design and produce it in . . ." His big fist closed around his glass, completely engulfing it. "What idiocy! I had to dismiss twenty of my finest gunsmiths, just because they were Czechs."

"So Josef Krnka doesn't work for you anymore?"

"The Bolsheviks are having problems with the Czech prisoners of war bequeathed them by the czarist army. Some fifty thousand Czechs are living in camps strung out along the Trans-Siberian Railroad. They want to leave Russia by way of Vladivostok and join forces with the Allies in France against their former oppressors."

"But Krnka has lived in Russia for years—he's even got a Russian wife."

"The Bolsheviks are opposing the Czechs' evacuation under German pressure. The Czechs have hit back by disrupting traffic on the Trans-Siberian route, blowing up bridges, hauling Red Guards off trains, disarming them, chasing them into the steppe, and so on. Since they started doing that, Czechs have led even more of a dog's life in Russia under the Reds than Jews did under the Czars."

Grishin sipped his vodka for the first time. "There aren't many gunsmiths of his caliber in the world. Would he leave the country if a foreign firm made him a suitable offer?"

Michelson refilled his glass again. "I can put you in touch with him, but only if you guarantee to let him finish a job for me first."

"I thought you said he wasn't working for you any longer."

"He isn't, officially." Michelson grinned over the rim of his glass. "The Party's Central Committee has been racking its collective brains over what to give Comrade Vladimir Ilyich on the first anniversary of the Revolution. Someone hit on the idea of presenting him with a pair of sporting rifles—very special ones, naturally. When I was consulted, only one person came to mind . . . Give me your glass."

"I've hardly touched it."

"Never mind." Michelson hooked Grishin's glass toward him and topped it up, together with his own. "He's at Yasino. Ask for Count Sheremetyev's old place. His estate used to supply the whole of Moscow with fresh flowers—you can see the ruined greenhouses a mile away. Krnka and his wife are living there in one of the gardeners' cottages."

"If he's working for you, you must have fixed him up with a workshop . . ."

Michelson wagged his finger. "We wouldn't know anything about that, would we, Gregor Constantine? I've always valued your discretion, so let's drink a toast: to the secrets that keep us alive!"

Grishin raised his glass, and this time he downed the contents at a gulp.

The streetcars were running again by the time he reached the square in front of Prokovsky Church. One of them pulled up just as he got there. The men and women who half staggered, half fell from the crowded platforms were spattered with blood, their clothes torn and disheveled. With pale, set faces they streamed past Grishin down the street that led to the Michelson Works, some unaided, others supported or carried by their uninjured companions.

A poster on the door of the Bazmannaya Workers' Social Club, as Prokovsky Church was now called, announced that there would be dancing tonight. The strip of paper freshly pasted over it read: "Canceled."

●

The waiting room at Moscow's Petrograd Station was as big and bleak as a gymnasium. Every bench was packed, and the steamy air reeked of sweat and unwashed bodies.

Alexandra Mechikova was still wearing her coat. Her sole concession to the heat had been to remove the pins from her hat and put it on the table in front of her. Lena Valentinova, seated opposite, would have preferred to see some of the old hostility in her eyes, but they were dull with fatigue and resignation. She had taken back the bunch of lilies and laid it across her lap.

"Can I get you some tea?"

"No, don't bother . . . Tell me, that article in *Pravda* you mentioned—what did it say?"

"You were on that train for over eleven hours. Haven't you eaten anything at all?"

"There's plenty of food in my case. I haven't touched it. Well, what about that article?"

"It was a tribute to your son."

"A tribute? I thought his Bolshevik friends had written him off." When Lena said nothing, she went on, "Did you continue to see him from time to time?"

"Not very often." Lena thought of the sailor hat and was glad she hadn't brought it with her.

"Did he still hope to stand trial?"

"He had a hard time ahead of him—a hard summer."

Alexandra Mechikova straightened up. She seemed to have recovered some of her poise. "Losing your illusions is one thing, dying is another. Was it really an accident?"

Lena had rehearsed her answer to that question. "Yes," she said. "I'm terribly sorry."

"Why? Why should you be sorry? What could you have done? I couldn't do anything for him, even today, even in death. I had nothing to offer him—nothing to compare with the insane hopes his friends held out." Alexandra Mechikova's eyes roamed restlessly around the room. "If something great and good had come out of it, I don't think his death would have affected me so deeply.

All that bloodshed, just to replace one form of tyranny with another . . ."

"Take care, someone may hear."

"What did he call you?"

"I don't understand."

"Did he really call you 'comrade'—Comrade Valentinova,
Comrade Lena? And you? Comrade Muranov? Comrade Pavel
Maximovich? How can two people fall in love on those terms?"

"It was different at first."

A ghost of a smile crossed the older woman's face. "I'm happy
to hear it."

Lena glanced at the clock above the tea counter. Their time
together would soon be up. "I hope you won't find the return trip
too tiring."

"Don't worry about me. Aren't you wondering why my husband didn't come too?"

"I trust he's well, all things considered."

"Oh yes, remarkably well."

"I hardly know him, of course."

"Neither did I, believe me. Outside his professional sphere, his
clinic and laboratories, Maxim used to be a total incompetent. I
had to do everything for him—he even sent me to Stockholm to
collect his Nobel Prize. I had a terrible time of it when the Bolsheviks hounded him out of his profession. All he did was sit
around moping, day after day. More in desperation than anything
else, I suggested he do what so many others in his position had
done: go out into the countryside and try to barter some food from
the peasants. I felt sure he wouldn't even bring back a pound of
rotting potatoes."

Alexandra Mechikova looked at the clock, picked up her hat,
and pinned it back into place.

"But I was wrong. A miracle occurred: His expeditions were a
huge success, and soon he was bringing back far more food than
we needed. He started selling the surplus at certain local markets
—at a big markup. 'Markup . . .' To think that I should ever hear
him use such a term!"

She lowered her voice, less for fear of eavesdroppers than to
underline her words.

"He couldn't attend our son's funeral because he was expecting
a big consignment of contraband coffee. Maxim Mechikov, win-

ner of the Nobel Prize for medicine and physiology in 1909, has become one of the leading lights of the St. Petersburg black market . . . So don't worry on my account. One fine day I'll send you a postcard from Paris—from the Ritz Hotel . . ."

She laughed, but there were tears in her eyes. Opening her suitcase, she took out a small velvet purse and fumbled in it. Then she slid her clenched fist across the table.

"Take it."

Lena thought she wanted her to take her hand. After a moment's hesitation, she grasped it. It was so small that it easily fitted into her own. The fingers opened and were withdrawn, leaving a small, circular object behind.

"I want you to have it."

Lena shook her head. "I never wear rings."

"It's only a small ruby, but you could trade it for something."

"I'd never do that."

"Take it anyway. Please."

There was no time for more. One of the Cheka men strode over to their table. "Get your things together," he said sharply. "On your feet—you've been yakking long enough, damn you!"

His holstered pistol was level with Lena's eyes. She stared at it, dizzy with rage. She couldn't stand up. It was as if an immense weight had clamped her to the seat of her chair. Then she felt a soothing hand on hers. Alexandra Mechikova rose, slowly and calmly. She had forgotten about the flowers on her lap, and they fell to the floor.

"No," she said quickly, "leave them. They wouldn't survive another eleven hours on the train." Her gray eyes were ice cold and implacable once more.

Not until she was on the platform and had raised her hand to wave good-bye to Alexandra Mechikova, who was standing at an open window, did Lena become aware that the ruby ring was still nestling in her palm.

●

Grishin followed the woman along an overgrown path between the derelict greenhouses. They had never met before. Josef Krnka was a man of sixty, and Grishin hadn't expected his wife to be so young and pretty. She had given him a frosty reception, making it clear that she disapproved of his visit and expected no good to come of it.

The heat was more tolerable outside the city, tempered a little by the gentlest of breezes. Beyond the greenhouses Grishin glimpsed the gutted ruins of a country mansion surrounded by ancient trees and weed-infested ornamental gardens. Olga Krnka headed for an old coach house.

"One moment," she said, quietly but firmly. She knocked on the door. "Josef, someone to see you. He says he's a friend of Michelson's."

The door was opened by a lean, gray-haired man in an apron far too long for him. Olga pointed to Grishin, then silently retraced her steps to the gardener's cottage where he had first encountered her.

Josef Krnka took off his steel-rimmed glasses as if their removal would improve his eyesight. "Gregor Constantine! It's been a long time." Seen at close quarters, his eyes looked big and owlish.

He shook hands in a strangely evasive way that exposed one side of his face only. It was an ingrained habit. Thirty years earlier a propellant charge had exploded prematurely while he was experimenting with it. The right-hand side of his face, which had never regained its mobility, was peppered with countless little scars and black specks.

Grishin glanced back at the gardener's cottage. "Your wife doesn't seem too fond of visitors."

"Olga? You can't blame her for being unsociable. She lost her job the way I did, but it's even harder for her."

"I thought she was a Russian."

"If you marry a Czech, you're a Czech. She was a hospital nurse for twelve years. Now she grows vegetables, keeps a hen or two, sells stuff at the local market. She hates the work, but it helps to keep the wolf from the door."

"Michelson tells me you're working yourself."

"I try to keep busy, so my hands don't lose their touch." Krnka had the husky voice of a heavy smoker. He put his glasses on again. "Michelson sent you, did he?"

"Not exactly. I just asked him where I could find you. May I come in?"

Running along one wall of the former coach house was a big workbench equipped with various machine tools and a generator. Michelson had evidently provided his former employee with the basic necessities of his craft. The rest of the interior was occupied by a table, a couple of chairs, and an old couch.

"I work pretty late sometimes," Krnka explained. "Friends turn up too, occasionally, looking for a night's lodging. That's the advantage of being a Czech. We're used to being uprooted and shoved around—we've had generations of practice."

"I gather you're working on something special."

"Is that how Michelson put it? He's exaggerating. It's more cosmetic than anything else."

"May I see?"

Grishin went over to the workbench. The dismantled components of a sporting rifle lay strewn across it. The stock was clamped between the jaws of a vise.

"Know the make?"

Grishin shook his head.

"It's Belgian. A Lebeau-Couvally, perfect for small game. See the serial number? Any expert could tell at a glance that the gun was made for Nicholas II." Krnka pointed to a wall closet. "Michelson's given me another to work on, for bigger game. That one belonged to the Czar too. They're first-class weapons, both of them—real beauties. I even know the gunsmith who made them, a man in Liège. We're a small fraternity."

"And they're to be presented to Lenin?"

"On the anniversary of the Revolution. A bit premature, wouldn't you say?"

"Where do you come in?"

"You mightn't think it, but Lenin and the Czar are around the same height, and they're both right-handed. All I've got to change are the lenses in the telescopic sights. Lenin's eyes are weaker, especially the right one." Krnka stubbed out one cigarette, opened a battered tin box, and took out another. "The rest of the work is purely cosmetic, as I say. The guns have silver inlays engraved with St. George and the imperial eagle. I'm replacing those with new emblems."

"Doesn't sound as if it'll keep you busy long."

"It's shameful, what I'm doing," Krnka said mournfully, "—like painting out the Mona Lisa's smile."

"You could always quit Russia, a craftsman of your caliber."

Krnka shrugged. His pockmarked face looked old and dispirited.

"I'm sure I could find you a worthwhile job abroad."

"Leave the country, at my age? I've lived here since I was a boy. Besides, there's Olgla . . ." Krnka lit his cigarette and was promptly racked with a violent fit of coughing.

"As a matter of fact," Grishin said, watching him closely, "I've got some work for you here and now." He was banking on the Czech's professional pride. Krnka was the man for the job, but he hesitated even so. "Tell me," he said, "how many people know what you're doing for Michelson?"

"Just the three of us, counting you. Not even Olga knows—that was one of his conditions. It isn't a prestige job." Krnka looked at Grishin. "What are you after?"

"A gun, but a gun of a type that probably doesn't exist. Even if you solve my problem, Krnka, it won't win you any medals."

The Czech coughed again. He removed his glasses and polished them on his apron before going over to the table. "Let's start with the range," he said.

Grishin sat down opposite him. "Forty or fifty yards."

"Moving target?"

"Stationary. Any changes of position would be minor."

Krnka drew a circle on a sheet of paper. It was the size of a human head. "That big?"

"Thereabouts."

"How many shots?"

"One."

"Day or night?"

Grishin thought for a moment. "Artificial light."

"You'll need a rifle's accuracy, but I don't suppose you'd want to use anything as bulky and conspicuous." Krnka didn't wait for an answer to his implied question. "Is that a fair definition of your problem?"

"Yes. Can you solve it?"

The longer they talked, the more Grishin's doubts subsided. Josef Krnka looked rejuvenated and alert, consumed with the true artist's eagerness to tackle his next work.

• 8 •

The smell of the waiting room turned Fleming's stomach. He couldn't think straight, almost as if the hospital odor was having an anesthetic effect on his brain. His one overriding urge was to sneak out of the building and not come back. The walls were tiled to waist level, the floors covered with checkerboard linoleum. Lloyd Fleming had given up counting the squares. He couldn't get past ten.

A door behind him opened, and he heard Lena Valentinova thanking someone for showing her the way. She was there; for the moment, nothing else mattered.

Neither of them spoke at first. Then he said, "How did you find out where Crabbin was?"

"I telephoned all the hospitals when I heard."

"I never thought I'd get him here alive. It was a ghastly wound. You've no idea how long it took to get an ambulance. Who showed you in just now, a doctor?"

"A nurse. They're still operating, that's all she could tell me. What really happened? I've heard rumors, nothing more."

"They started shooting before I could collect my wits. A machine gun opened fire on the crowd without warning, quite indiscriminately. I don't know how many casualties there were. They simply left the dead and wounded lying there. Crabbin must have lost a lot of blood. If it hadn't been for his American passport, I doubt if he'd be here now. All that interested them was his film of the demonstration."

"Was it a bullet wound?"

"Yes, but a ricochet, which made it worse. I think the bullet must have hit him sideways, because the wound was so big. A moment or two before, when the crowd broke up and ran for their lives, I was on the point of following suit. Crabbin was so calm, though. He'd never have abandoned that confounded camera of his."

Fleming was beginning to feel better. Even the smell of the room seemed more tolerable, as if Lena's very presence had dispelled it.

"I'm so glad you're here," he said. "How did you get on at the station? Did Muranov's parents turn up?"

"Only his mother. Look, she gave me this." Lena displayed the ruby ring on her finger. "They sent her straight back—Yury Peters and two of his gunmen. They kept us under guard till her train left."

Fleming had never seen such a look on her face before. It was hard, almost fanatical. They sat down side by side on a bench against the wall.

"That *Pravda* article," he said, "was a bad joke."

"But a good idea."

The cynicism in her voice was equally new to him.

"Muranov was a symbol," she went on, "and symbols can be dangerous. They tend to live on, especially in Russia. Men like Lenin not only bank on that, they exploit it. If a symbol threatens them, they make it their own. They name a street after it, give it a state funeral. The idea was sound enough."

"But there wasn't any funeral!"

"The city's buzzing with rumors. The likeliest theory claims that the Germans put their foot down. They objected to the funeral on the grounds that it might spark off anti-German riots. No funeral, no demonstration: That's what their ambassador told Lenin, so the story goes."

"This country defeats me," Fleming said. "Maybe I should give up trying to understand it." Another wave of nausea assailed him, coupled with a renewed urge to flee. He went to the door and looked out into the dismal, deserted corridor. Then he came back and stood over her.

"Have you given any thought to what we talked about this morning?"

She shrugged. "All I can think of right now is Crabbin lying on the operating table and a woman in a train heading for St. Petersburg, as she still calls it."

"You're being evasive again."

"Do you know what Muranov's mother said to me at the station? 'If only something great and good had come of it . . .' She meant the Revolution. How about you, comrade banker? Do you still hope everything will turn out for the best?''

"I've never heard you talk this way before.''

"What else do you expect me to talk about? The waifs and strays at Yelizaveta Maria? My contribution to the fulfillment of paradise on earth as an associate judge on the Twelfth Extraordinary Tribunal? The cases we try and the sentences we pass: raping a nun, acquittal; stealing a loaf of bread, three years' imprisonment? Shall I talk about the doctor who issued mothers false pregnancy certificates entitling them to an extra milk ration for their starving children and got five years in a labor camp? Shall I tell you how these people haunt my dreams and point their fingers at me? Why, Lena Valentinova—why did you vote against us with the rest of the tribunal?''

Fleming eyed her thoughtfully. "You really have changed,'' he said at length.

"I'm tired.'' She tapped her chest. "Tired in here, most of all— empty, burned out. And you? Are you still the same person, the same London banker who came here as a special envoy to the court of King Lenin? Do you still cherish the illusions you had when I met you at the station in Petrograd?'' She paused. "Sooner or later you'll go home.''

"Of course I will, sooner or later.''

"Maybe you shouldn't wait too long.''

"Why do you say that?''

"Do you still believe in the success of your mission? Why not cut your losses, comrade banker? It doesn't appall you that much, does it, the prospect of returning to London?''

He said nothing.

"Go back to your bank and make some more money. Making money comes naturally to you—you enjoy it. You'll see old friends again. You'll talk together, perhaps about money, perhaps about other things, but you'll understand them and they'll understand you. Is that the life you want me to share?''

"Why not?''

"Can you see me leaving Russia forever?''

"But you just said—''

"I said I was tired, yes, but it doesn't mean I want to turn my back on this country. Russians outside Russia are like fish out of water.''

"You've lived abroad for years, in Paris, in Geneva . . ."

"I came back, though."

"There's always a way, if two people really love each other."

She remained silent, he didn't know for how long. His sense of time had deserted him again. A thought struck him: What if there was someone else? He stared at the ring on her finger with sudden suspicion.

His thoughts were interrupted by voices in the corridor. A surgeon entered, his face flushed and tense.

"He'd like to see you."

"How is he?"

"We've done all we can for him."

"Really?" Fleming said scathingly. "You tried to save his life? You didn't decline to operate? You wasted your precious chloroform on him? Why didn't you simply let him die? Because he was an American, not some poor devil of a Russian?" He bellowed the last words, and his voice rebounded from the walls of the bare room. He felt a hand on his arm.

"Please, Lloyd."

Looking at the hand, he saw the ring at close quarters for the first time. It was a modest little ruby in an old-fashioned setting. His suspicions subsided. Suddenly anything seemed possible, even that Arnold J. Crabbin would survive.

The recovery ward beside the operating room was even bleaker than the waiting room.

Crabbin was lying on a wheeled stretcher, his face as white as the iron frame, while shadowy figures moved silently behind the frosted glass door.

"I'm so sorry, Crabbin."

Had he understood? His eyelids twitched feebly and opened. The irises looked bluer and larger than usual. His lips moved, trying to shape a single word. Fleming bent down and listened until he identified it. He nodded soothingly.

"He's still worrying about that damned camera," he whispered to Lena, then turned back to Crabbin. "It's all right, old chap, don't give it another thought."

Laboriously, the American raised one hand and made a circular movement.

"The films are safe too," Fleming lied. "Stop worrying."

Again Crabbin strove to speak, but all that emerged was a series of inarticulate, unintelligible sounds. Fleming found the sight of his exertions painful. "You'll be back on your feet in no time, Crabbin," he extemporized brightly. "Another couple of weeks and you'll be sailing home across the Atlantic in a nice, comfortable stateroom. I'll come with you if you like. How about it? Utica, New York State—sounds good, eh? You'll soon be back with your wife, your family, your business interests . . ."

He broke off. With a supreme effort, Crabbin turned his head. Had he recognized Lena? "I think he wants you," Fleming said. He stepped aside, ashamed of his own relief. This time, surprisingly enough, Crabbin made sense.

"I . . . I never found it . . . The village, I mean . . ."

"I know, Mr. Crabbin."

"I really did hope . . . to find it . . ."

The door opened and a nurse came in. She felt Crabbin's pulse, then turned to them.

"He must rest now."

Crabbin's head sank back. He closed his eyes as if he had understood and was in full agreement. They opened once more, but only momentarily, when Lena bent down and kissed him on the forehead.

And then they were standing outside in the long, deserted corridor. It seemed an eternity to Fleming since he and Crabbin had left the house on Tverskaya—an eternity of waiting: for the demonstrators to enter Red Square, for the ambulance to turn up, for the surgeon to complete his work.

"I couldn't tell him the truth about his camera and the films. They confiscated the lot."

"He'll never know."

Her cool tone not only surprised him but restored a little of his own composure.

"What happens now?"

"Go home if you like. I'll wait."

Crabbin had said much the same in Red Square, Fleming recalled. He hesitated. "What did he mean when he said he never found the village? What village?"

"He didn't tell you?"

"We never talked much."

"He owns a munitions factory at Utica, near New York."

"That much I did know."

"His firm sold rifles to the czarist army for years, a million a year, twenty dollars apiece. He signed a new contract with the Kerensky government. The rifles were already on their way by sea when the Revolution broke out. Lenin would gladly have endorsed the contract, but Crabbin didn't think much of Bolshevik rubles. He canceled it."

"But he handed Lenin a check for a million dollars."

Lena smiled. "He set up a relief fund, but he hung onto the purse strings. Crabbin may be a philanthropist, but he's a shrewd businessman as well. He's one-quarter Russian, did you know?"

"Crabbin? He's so typically American."

" 'That's the great thing about America,' he used to say. 'After a couple of generations you're as American as pumpkin pie, even if you do have a Russian granny.' "

"Was it her he hoped to find?"

"No, she died in America, but she grew up here in terrible times. Her family were Jews living in Vyatka Province during the reign of Nicholas I. That made her a victim of one of the worst pogroms in our history. Jewish children were taken from their parents and driven like cattle across the icy steppe for days without food before being buried in a mass grave somewhere. Crabbin's grandmother survived, made her way to America, and married his grandfather. Crabbin heard her story when he was a boy, that's why he always meant to visit her birthplace someday. She described it in detail, apparently: the village, the church, the synagogue, the Jewish school, her family home."

"Hence all his expeditions?"

"Yes, but he never found it."

They had reached the big glass door at the end of the corridor. Lena said, "You can go, honestly. I don't mind staying."

"I'd better see the American consul, I suppose. His family will have to be notified."

They emerged into the lobby, leaving the hospital smell behind.

"And Lloyd, remember what I said about going home. Don't leave it too long. Crabbin did."

Looking at her as they stood in the entrance, he saw that she had recovered her composure.

"Know something?" he said. "I sometimes think you've got English blood in your veins."

She laid a hand on his arm, then kissed him as lightly and fleetingly as she had that morning. His suspicions flared up again.

"You may have a perfectly simple reason for avoiding me."

"What, for instance?"

"Another man."

"Sometimes," she said calmly, "I think you've got Russian blood in your veins." She turned and walked slowly back to the glass door.

She wouldn't lie, he told himself. Not at such a moment—not with Crabbin on the verge of death.

He drew several breaths of fresh, unmedicated air as he walked across the hospital forecourt. Once through the gates and out on the street, he heard a car approaching. A closed convertible coupe drew level with him and stopped.

The driver wound his window down and put his head out. Fleming felt sure he'd never seen the man before.

"Is he dead yet?"

"Who are you?"

"He hadn't a hope, not with a wound like that."

The man spoke English with a faint accent. His face was so smooth, so bland, that it was almost ageless. His fair hair looked almost white in the sunshine, like his eyebrows, which were barely visible, but their colorlessness only made his brown eyes more vivid and expressive.

"My name is Berzin, Alexander Berzin."

Fleming started to walk on.

"One moment, Mr. Fleming. I think we should talk."

The voice was calm and self-assured but quite devoid of any menacing overtones. A rarity in Russian officials these days. Perhaps that was what prompted Fleming to change his mind.

•9•

The road wound uphill, leveled out, and forked. Berzin bore left and pulled up in front of some wrought-iron gates. The avenue beyond them was flanked by trees so luxuriant that their upper branches had grown together to form a tunnel of greenery. Visible at the far end was the façade of an imposing mansion.

A uniformed guard opened the gates and Berzin parked just inside. He glanced over his shoulder at the back seat. Lying on it was a pistol in a leather holster: a Mauser, the Cheka's favorite handgun.

Fleming had been turning Berzin's name over in his mind. It meant nothing to him. His uniform, which had no collar patches, shoulder boards, or insignia, was just as uninformative. The cut and cloth were of an excellence rare in contemporary Moscow. Although that was the extent of Fleming's observations, he had sensed at once that Berzin was a Chekist. It wasn't just that his cocksure manner stamped him as one; it was the fact that few men drove around Bolshevik Moscow in a Pierce Arrow.

Fleming indicated the gun. "Aren't you going to take your toy with you?" he said. "Don't mind me."

Berzin's laugh was quite unforced. "In my opinion, Neskuchny Park is the loveliest in Moscow. It would seem tasteless, somehow, strolling around the grounds wearing a Mauser."

He got out and handed the car keys to the guard without a word. Fleming was surprised to see how much smaller he was than the impression he'd given behind the wheel. He proved to be unexpectedly short and slight, though he did his best to seem taller by holding himself stiffly erect.

Berzin set off along a narrow gravel path. The grounds were well

tended. They passed flower beds in bloom, expanses of neatly
trimmed lawn, ornamental pools.

"You pride yourself on your taste, don't you? A tailor-made
uniform, a Pierce Arrow, these grounds . . ."

Berzin paused for a moment. "You know," he said, almost
rapturously, "I really adore this view of the river."

The Moskva meandered along the foot of the wooded slopes
below them like a greenish ribbon. Immediately opposite, on the
far bank, rose the five gilded domes of St. Savior's, the most
striking and decorative of all Moscow's churches.

"Listen, why not tell me what you want and have done with it?"

"It's not as simple as that."

"No need to be evasive. I presume you're a Chekist. I know your
boss. He's a past master at conducting interviews that leave you
wondering what he actually said, what he actually offered. It's all a
verbal smokescreen."

"I belong to the Cheka," Berzin said calmly, "and I wear a
Mauser on duty, but that's as far as it goes. Primarily, I'm a soldier.
I command the Lettish Rifles. Whatever people impute to the
Cheka, rightly or wrongly, it doesn't apply to me and my men."

"Rightly is the word," said Fleming.

Berzin subjected him to a long, searching stare. "Be that as it
may, all the Lettish Rifles contributed to this morning's operation
was a brass band. The Red Guards did the rest."

"Spare me Dzerzhinsky's brand of humor. You call it a military
operation, mowing down unarmed civilians with a machine gun?
Have the dead been counted?"

"I doubt if the figures will be officially published."

"They won't be able to hush up Crabbin's death."

Berzin had walked on. "You intend to submit a report to London?"

"Of course I damn well do!"

"Your people won't know what to make of it unless someone
fills in the background."

Fleming stared contemptuously at his companion. "You pick me
up in a car that was probably purloined from the American embassy, you bring me here to admire the view, you drop vague
hints. If you think that puts you a kopek in credit with me, you're
wrong."

"You witnessed that demonstration this morning," Berzin said crisply. "Most of the protesters were workers from nationalized factories in the Bazmannaya district. Emotionally charged meetings are being held there at this very moment. They're voting on proposals for a twenty-four-hour general strike."

"Lenin's beloved workers? He must be tearing his hair out."

"To keep them in line, the government will tonight proclaim a state of martial law. That, of course, will automatically rule out any form of strike." Berzin paused. "Aren't you wondering why the funeral was canceled?"

Fleming's indifferent shrug belied his eagerness for Berzin to continue.

"We have a German ambassador here, Baron von Mirbach."

Hang the baron . . . Hang the German baron . . . Fleming recalled the chanting voices in Red Square.

"He doesn't know a word of Russian," Berzin went on. "He employs an interpreter to read him the most important items in *Pravda* and *Izvestia*. Lenin's piece on Muranov really spoiled his breakfast this morning."

"Really?" said Fleming. "Were you sitting across the table from him?"

Berzin coolly ignored the sarcasm. "The baron's an early riser, but he knows there's an equally early riser in the Kremlin. He possesses one of the few direct lines to Lenin's office, so he picked up the phone and told him—in German, naturally—what he thought of his obituary. Not only was it detrimental to the relations between their two countries, but a state funeral for Muranov would have grave international repercussions—extremely grave."

Fleming looked skeptical. "You mean a phone call was all it took? One phone call from a humble German baron was enough to intimidate the leader of the masses?"

"I expect he phrased it diplomatically. Noblesse oblige!"

Berzin's tone was no longer businesslike; it conveyed undisguised hatred and contempt. Smoldering inside this dapper little man, Fleming told himself, was a spark of fanaticism.

"He made a second phone call," Berzin said, "after the demonstration, to transmit the text of a formal note from Berlin. It stated that the slogans chanted in Red Square were directed against the German Empire and represented a slur on the Kaiser himself. Berlin therefore expected a formal apology from the Soviet government."

"May I pass that on to London, attributed to a reliable source?"

"You can tell them this too, if you like. You know how seldom Lenin sets foot outside the Kremlin. This morning he made an exception. An hour ago, he drove to the German embassy in person to apologize to Baron von Mirbach for the anti-German nature of the demonstration."

Fleming raised his eyebrows.

"He went on bended knees," Berzin said darkly. "The Germans have only to whisper and we obey. They slap us in the face and we turn the other cheek. They plunder our country and we thank them for it . . ."

They had reached the highest point in the grounds. The vast mansion, with its innumerable windows, came into view beyond a series of clipped hedges.

"Was this another of the Czar's palaces?" Fleming asked.

"It was built by Alexander II."

"Does anyone live here?"

Berzin's face broke into a gleeful smile. "I do."

He headed for a summerhouse and sat down on a stone bench outside.

"Come, let's sit for a moment." Berzin paused. "You're a banker, so tell me: What does a person need to be creditworthy?"

Fleming looked at him. "Trust. Crabbin was trusted by your new regime. He had the utmost sympathy for the Revolution, for Lenin, for Russia in general. All it earned him was a Red bullet."

"I meant the question seriously."

"I've forgotten to think like a banker, Berzin. All I see here are columns of red figures. One can absorb losses for a while, but there comes a time when they cease to be acceptable."

"You've lost all hope of balancing your books?"

"I was sent here to dissuade your government from signing a peace treaty with Germany. Result: negative. To persuade them to reenter the war against Germany, acknowledge all outstanding debts, pay compensation for damage incurred, and restore confiscated or nationalized assets to British ownership: negative. To negotiate a trade treaty granting concessions in petroleum and raw materials: negative again. For a banker, that's a pretty disastrous performance."

Fleming was surprised at himself. He wouldn't have confided

such thoughts even to Jim Hall, but he'd never been in such a mood before.

"Perhaps you've been negotiating with the wrong people," Berzin said quietly.

"Who better to negotiate with than the people in power?"

"The people to whom the reins of power will pass in the near future."

Berzin remained silent until Fleming could bear the suspense no longer.

"Are there such people? Can you give me their names?"

"Names? Shouldn't you first ascertain whether you have interests in common—whether you're mutually creditworthy?" Berzin turned and looked Fleming in the eye. "You already know one name, at least."

"Yours, you mean?"

"Colonel Alexander Berzin, commanding three companies of the Lettish Rifles stationed in Moscow, official strength three hundred, actually a thousand. You won't find a better-trained unit anywhere in Russia, if I say so myself. Every man a crack shot, superbly equipped, admirably disciplined. There are those that call us a bunch of mercenaries, I know, but they can't deny that the security of the regime is largely dependent on us. Shall I continue?"

"Why not?"

"There exists a group of men—men whose motives are as varied as their spheres of activity—who have banded together in a common cause . . ."

"In Russia? That really would be a miracle!"

"You complain of your failures, but what of the Bolsheviks'? Have they attained the Revolution's main objective? Do red flags fly over Vienna, Prague, and Budapest, Paris and London, as well as Petrograd and Moscow? Are machine guns in position on the Unter den Linden? And here? Everyone still pays lip service to the Revolution's ideals, but our socialist utopia is really in its death throes—indeed, some say it's already dead. All that matters now is power, and whether Lenin can retain his hold on it."

"Many people thought he wouldn't last three months, let alone eight."

"Nobody underestimates the man. He'll remain in power for as long as his opponents fail to organize—for as long as they're divided among themselves."

"And that's where your mysterious friends come in?"

"Back them and you could recoup your losses."

"By throwing good money after bad?" Fleming shook his head.

Berzin was undeterred. "I'm no banker," he said, "but it might be a profitable investment. There's a lot of talk these days about military intervention and the possibility of Allied landings on Russian soil. Any such landings would stand a far better chance of success if they coincided with a general uprising inside the country. Of course, the two things would have to be coordinated . . ."

"It sounds too good to be true."

"So you don't buy the idea?"

"Are you talking about money?"

"I'm talking about moral, military, and financial backing. We need the wherewithal to pay for arms and men—mercenaries, if you like. You're a banker, that's why I'm talking about money. Among other things."

Fleming was not nearly as surprised as he pretended. The fact that Berzin was alluding so openly to money—talking *his* language, in a sense—seemed more indicative of his sincerity than any other argument. Could it be that, just when he'd abandoned a confused and hopeless situation, Berzin was unexpectedly offering him a way out?

"Credit," he said, "entails some form of security."

"Britain and her allies have lodged substantial claims in respect of public and private loans made to Russia in the past."

"The British alone are demanding two and a half million pounds."

"Quite so," said Berzin, "and Lenin merely laughs at them."

"Would your friends give serious consideration to those claims?"

Berzin smoothed some imaginary creases from his uniform jacket. "I'm empowered to offer the following terms. First, active support of military intervention, including the arrest and removal of the present government, in return for financial aid. Second, a guarantee that hostilities against Germany will be resumed. Third, serious negotiations aimed at the settlement of outstanding debts, the conclusion of a trade treaty, and the granting of concessions in the raw materials sector. In return for points two and three, the Allies would bestow immediate diplomatic recognition on a new government formed by members of the group and acknowledge its sole legitimate authority."

"No names?"

"At a later stage, certainly. For now, you can refer to my friends as 'the Credit Group.' "

Fleming could feel the sun's searing heat, even in the shade of the trees beside the summerhouse. He was reminded of the abnormal silence in Red Square, the beads of sweat on Crabbin's face. The atmosphere was stifling.

"I need time," he said at length. "I shall have to take soundings at the London end."

Berzin made no comment.

"It's no use my pretending," Fleming insisted. "I can't proceed without special authorization."

"There's one proviso."

"I knew there'd be a catch in it somewhere," said Fleming.

"We want to negotiate with one person only."

"Meaning what, exactly?"

"If the response from London is favorable, I shall supply you with information about the members of the group and their aims. I shall also arrange a preliminary meeting with our representatives. The proviso is that only one person shall represent your side." Berzin paused for effect. "A banker would suit us admirably, but not an expert on icons . . ."

Fleming could find nothing to say, he was so taken aback. They rose and strolled on through the grounds.

"Speaking of credit," Berzin said after a few yards, "my friends are prepared to make a down payment on account."

"As a token of good faith?"

"The German ambassador is a thorn in your flesh as well as ours, is he not? We think it would benefit our common cause if Baron von Mirbach quit the Moscow scene, preferably for good. What would you say if His Excellency found himself unable to finish his breakfast one morning because a bullet or two had lodged in his gullet?"

Fleming stared at the spruce little man strutting along beside him. A chill ran down his spine, a faint tremor of uncertainty. Could he trust Berzin? Then he swallowed his misgivings. He *wanted* to trust him, because therein lay his only hope of leaving Moscow with his books better balanced.

•10•

Grishin was awakened by the harsh cries of ravens leaving the city for their roosts. He opened his eyes and felt for the gun at his side. Then he glanced at the window. Dusk was descending on Moscow. His time of waiting would soon be over.

He lay there motionless, bathed in sweat. The heat of the preceding weeks had transformed his rooming-house garret into a furnace. The coarse straw in the mattress beneath his bare back pricked him unmercifully, but he endured the discomfort without moving or even wincing, as if it were a form of physical training to which his body had to be subjected daily.

A man started singing in the room next door. Grishin knew what would follow. Moments later he heard the woman swearing, as she always did, and shouting at him to stop. Their quarrels, which could go on for hours, invariably ended the same way. They drank together, sang together, and either sealed their reconciliation by making energetic love or embarked on another tempestuous row.

He continued to lie there without moving. It was still too early, so he exercised the patience that was his cardinal virtue. This ability to wait had earned him his most terrifying experience, but it had also ensured his continued freedom, so he stayed prone, controlling his impatience and forcing himself not to speculate on the message Jim Hall had left for him. Like Crabbin's death, which had wrecked his plans, it was bound to augur bad news.

The room was almost dark when he rose. He was so familiar with every square inch of it that he had no need to turn the light on. He let the faucet run, went back to the bed, and picked up the gun. Krnka's idea was brilliant in its simplicity. He had modified the barrel of a Canadian deer rifle and the grip and mechanism of a Mauser in such a way that they fitted together. This hybrid weapon possessed the accuracy of a sporting rifle up to eighty yards, and the two components could be easily dismantled and concealed.

Grishin pulled the bed aside to expose the hiding place he had prepared beneath a floorboard. He had only to pry up two nails with his knife. Wrapping the components of the weapon in pieces of rag, he slid them into the cavity beneath the planks. Then he tapped the nails into place and pushed the bed back. The little bag containing the special ammunition, which was heavily greased, lay hidden in the bend of the waste pipe beneath the iron washbowl.

The trickle from the faucet had now filled the bowl. After washing, he put on a clean shirt and the better of his two suits. In addition to some money and the papers identifying him as Vada Nikulin, bargeman, he pocketed the card that had come with Hall's message.

Grishin had found it on one of his routine visits to the *poste restante* counter at the central post office. The urgency of the wording had surprised him: *Leaving Moscow tonight. Imperative meet.* Enclosed was a British Club membership card.

Grishin was ready now. He went to the window and looked out. Although a pale glow still lingered in the west, the streetlights were already fighting a losing battle with the gathering gloom. The couple next door were still squabbling, but he wouldn't know tonight how their altercation ended.

The wooden gallery was in darkness; someone had stolen the light bulbs again. Grishin kept hold of the handrail as he descended the stairs, because there was always a risk of slipping on the contents of a garbage pail or the vomit of some drunken fellow tenant. He crossed the inner courtyard, with its mounds of stinking refuse, and walked through the archway to the street. The air outside felt cool, almost cold.

He decided to walk rather than take a droshky, partly because the fresh breeze would drive the rooming-house stench from his clothes, partly to satisfy himself that no one was tailing him. For a moment he thought of Lena Valentinova, but not in any sentimental way. His plan had depended on her connection with Crabbin. Now that the American was dead, would he still be able to carry it out?

The National Hotel at the Tverskaya-Mokhonaya intersection was brilliantly illuminated. Droshkies were continually dropping guests outside the main entrance on Red Square. Lenin had stayed there in the interval between leaving Petrograd and moving to the Kremlin, and even now the luxury hotel was occupied almost exclusively by Party and government officials.

Having expected to see armed guards outside the National, Grishin noted with surprise that the entrance was still manned by two huge *schweizars* traditionally attired in long greatcoats, broad green sashes, and pillbox hats adorned with peacock feathers. All that had changed since the Revolution was that these gigantic doormen no longer handed people in and out of their cabs and cars.

Light was streaming through the hotel's lofty ground-floor windows. Guests, mostly men, could be seen conversing in the spacious lobby, with its gilded white columns and elaborate flower arrangements. Grishin watched the entrance for some time without detecting anything suspicious, then retraced his steps along Tverskaya, skirting the side of the hotel, and turned down an alley leading to the rear entrance.

The British Club was separated from the alley by a gateway and a small cobbled yard. The two tiers of curtained windows emitted a discreet glow. Only one *schweizar*—a man of average build— was on duty at the door, which had a bilingual plaque above it. He took Grishin's card. His outsize gloves had presumably been made for his giant colleagues at the main entrance.

"I suppose you aren't allowed to accept a tip these days," Grishin said.

A wary smile appeared on the *schweizar's* face as he handed back the card. "Not officially," he replied in strongly accented English.

Grishin slipped him a ten-ruble bill.

The lobby had a high ceiling and paneled walls of dark, gleaming wood. Leading off it on the right was a library with an open fireplace surmounted by a portrait of King George V. The tables were strewn with newspapers.

The smaller room on the left was a cardroom. Lights hung low over the green baize tables, three of which were occupied by foursomes silently intent on their bridge. A woman in a black evening gown was watching one of the games in progress. Catching sight of Grishin at the reception desk, she came out into the lobby.

"Good evening," she said tartly. "Tonight's a dinner night, I'm afraid. Formal dress only." She barely glanced at Grishin's card when he proffered it.

"This is the only suit I've got."

The receptionist frowned. "Very well, if you'll come with me I'll see what the vice-consul says."

She led the way down a long corridor lined with engravings of English and Scottish castles to an overfurnished anteroom. One of the double doors was ajar, and through it drifted the sound of music and the hum of voices.

"Wait here, please." Spitefully, the woman added, "You're too late for the *sakuska* in any case."

"You can keep your *sakuska* for all I care." Grishin was seldom rude to women, but his nerves were on edge; he'd hoped to see Hall in private.

The receptionist opened the door and went in. The walls of the dining room beyond were hung with red damask. Lights and voices and the strains of a well-known gypsy melody filled the spacious interior. Someone with a high-pitched voice, either a woman or a reedy tenor, was singing to an accompaniment of fiddles and a cimbalom.

The woman returned with Jim Hall at her heels. The vice-consul was wearing a dinner suit complete with boiled shirt and black bow tie. His face was flushed, and a fat Havana protruded from his fist.

"Hello there," he said jovially. "You should have been here sooner, old boy, we've already polished off the *sakuska.*"

"So I pointed out," said the receptionist, "but your friend appears to dislike hors d'oeuvres."

"I'm sorry, Miss Davidson, he suffers from poor digestion."

"In that case," she said crisply, "he'll be lucky to survive in Moscow." She withdrew, shaking her head.

"You really missed something." Jim Hall's cigar deposited its ash on the carpet. "The food here comes from the kitchens of the National, and they're the best in the city. All the biggest profiteers stuff their guts at the National, the Bolshies too, plus every kind of local bigwig." He emitted a tipsy chuckle. "Come on in, old boy."

Grishin caught him by the elbow. "One minute, Jim. Why this sudden meeting? Your message sounded urgent."

Hall stared at the cigar in his hand as if he didn't know what to do with it. Then he gave another chuckle. "Don't be a spoilsport, old bean. The boys and girls of the International School are celebrating their departure. Anyone leaving Moscow deserves to celebrate, wouldn't you say?" He wrapped an arm around Grishin and hugged him. "Keep me company, there's a good chap. They're a starchy bunch, not that there's anything surprising about that—most of their daddies are ambassadors."

Some forty boys and girls were seated at the horseshoe table in the center of the dining room, though the wall mirrors seemed to double their number. The youngest were around twelve years old, the eldest sixteen at most. All of them, boys and girls alike, resembled adults in miniature. The girls, who had put their hair up for the occasion, wore long evening gowns and antique jewelry. They moved their heads stiffly, as if frightened of dislodging a single ringlet. The dinner-suited boys were doing their best to be nonchalant, but the atmosphere was artificial and formal.

Suddenly the gypsy orchestra broke off in the middle of a waltz and played a flourish. Some doors in the background swung open, and in trooped more costumed waiters bearing huge silver platters piled high with food. The youthful diners applauded rather languidly.

"You'll have to excuse me, Jim," Grishin said. "I'm not in the mood." He was puzzled by his own lack of calm.

"At least have a drink." Hall was still slurring his words. "Just a *do zvidaniya* drink. *Do zvidaniya,* International School! *Do zvidaniya,* Moscow! *Do zvidaniya,* Russia! The youngsters insisted on having this farewell party. We suggested all kinds of treats—a historical sightseeing tour, the Borodino panorama, that kind of thing—but they voted unanimously for a slap-up farewell dinner with all the trimmings, a gypsy orchestra, waiters in Tatar costume, et cetera—a regular five-hour Russian banquet." He headed rather unsteadily for the table. "Well, I'm going to have another drink if it's all right with you."

"Have as many as you like, but let's talk first."

Hall dropped his cigar butt into an empty wineglass.

"You'll regret not having had a bracer when you hear what I've got to tell you." Once outside in the anteroom he made straight for a sofa and flopped onto it.

Grishin sat down beside him. "Well?"

Hall extracted another Havana from his breast pocket. "Here," he said, "you smoke this thing."

"What's so urgent, Jim?"

"You really do need a strong stomach in this job." Hall's tipsy smile was slowly fading. He absentmindedly stuck the cigar between his teeth. "A leather one, preferably, and a leather heart to match. I detest it when they tie an agent's hands."

Grishin leaned over. "May I?" He removed the cigar from Hall's mouth.

Hall glared irritably at the door to the dining room, where the fiddles had struck up again. "I'm leaving here tonight with a party of children—escorting the British and American kids to Vologda. Needless to say, those incompetent Bolsheviks only woke up to the fact at the last moment. They can't even run a railroad properly."

Grishin pulled up his right trouser leg. Taking the Finnish hunting knife from his boot, he used it to cut the cigar.

"Good God, are you still carrying that thing around?"

Grishin replaced the knife, lit up, and pulled an ashtray toward him.

"Miss Davidson would be delighted with you—she hates seeing ash on the carpets. She rules us all with a rod of iron. Remember we talked about that banker, Lloyd Fleming? He thought he'd landed in paradise when he moved here, but he didn't know Miss Davidson. He used to live a few doors down, with that poor devil Arnold Crabbin . . . Do you *have* to carry that confounded knife around everywhere?"

He seemed to be losing his thread, but Grishin wondered if it wasn't all an act.

"Poor old Crabbin! They actually proposed to bury him beside the Kremlin wall—after all, they had a grave already dug. His widow objected, so now he's heading for home in a zinc-lined coffin."

"You got me here to tell me that?"

Hall sighed. "I don't know when I'll be back from Vologda, and Colvin wanted the position clarified beforehand."

"The sooner you tell me what this is all about, Jim, the sooner you can get back to your party."

"Fleming was in Red Square with Crabbin when the old boy was hit. It seems to have given him the shock of his life."

"Get on with it, for God's sake!"

"This is background, John. Background's important, as well you know." Hall gave a wry smile. "I'll try to be brief. Fleming had a— a tête-à-tête with someone. I'll spare you a description of the agitated state in which he turned up at my office afterward. Anyway, he spent most of the next two weeks in our cipher room, sending coded signals to London and receiving coded replies. Back and forth, back and forth it went. They really burned up the ether."

"The Foreign Office?"

Hall nodded. "Fleming came to me with a fantastic story. Alexander Berzin, who commands the Lettish Rifles, was proposing to overthrow the Bolshevik regime—or words to that effect. What it boiled down to was that a clique of dissidents calling themselves the Credit Group had banded together and were offering London their cooperation. London insisted on a further meeting at which Berzin became a little more specific. He hinted at the existence of a sort of shadow cabinet. He wouldn't name names, but he did give some idea of the kind of people involved: a general with forty thousand Czech legionnaires at his disposal; representatives of the three White Russian commanders, Denikin, Kolchak, and Yudenich; a financial expert from the former Cadet Party—"

"What was that you said at the outset—about tying an agent's hands, I mean?"

Hall ignored the question. "The story stank to high heaven, didn't it? Personally I'd have held my nose and run, but our banker friend wouldn't be pried away from the cipher room at any price. Mark you, I can understand why. He saw a chance of reasserting himself. He never liked your trespassing on his territory, so to speak—"

"One moment, Jim. How much does Fleming know about me?"

"He took your arrival like a gentleman. He was very tactful, very quick to accept that your presence here wasn't a legitimate topic of conversation between us. He wondered about you, of course, but that's all. He's had a hard time of it, our banker. A steady diet of empty promises doesn't do much for a person's morale. Him I can understand, but the Foreign Office?"

Grishin relit his cigar and waited.

"They actually bought his story. In the normal way, they'd have gone on raising queries and objections until the affair petered out

of its own accord, but this time they acted with incredible speed—
by their lights. Their instructions were brief and to the point: Fleming was to be the choreographer and dance the solo part as well."

"Go on."

"Do you know what finally clinched it? This Berzin fellow offered them a bonus in the person of the German ambassador to
Moscow. He's undertaken to have him bumped off."

"I'll watch the papers."

"It's no joking matter."

"Who's laughing?"

"Well, there you have it: London wants the new scheme to go
ahead without any interference from you."

Grishin seemed engrossed in his cigar ash.

"How does all this affect me, Jim? Whatever the FO says, Colvin
is his own master. He makes the rules."

"Your assignment has been shelved. Colvin's orders."

Grishin felt anger well up inside him. He knew it didn't show,
just as he knew that Hall would be stung by his outward indifference. This was one of the occasions when Hall expected him to
display emotion.

"For how long?" was all he said.

"Don't make me feel worse by taking it so damned calmly."
Hall's tone was earnest. "I fought the idea, John. I spent just as long
in the cipher room as Fleming. I tore the scheme to shreds—I told
Colvin he was wasting precious time."

"And what did he say?"

"The same as the FO. Suspend preparations, take no action that
might tread on Fleming's corns, await developments. Your assignment has been put on ice."

Slowly and steadily, Grishin slid the hand holding the cigar
across the table. The ash broke off and landed in the ashtray.

"Well," said Hall, "will you cooperate?"

Grishin nodded.

"Colvin wants your confirmation."

"Of course. Signal him yes."

Hall, who had clearly expected tougher resistance, heaved a
sigh of relief and sat back. "Why not come to Vologda with me? I
could put you up in style there—a nice house with a view of the
river . . ."

"Thanks, but no."

"Summer in Moscow is hell, John. No one stays here in July and August unless they absolutely have to."

"How long will you be gone?"

"A week or so. It depends when they can get us a train for the onward journey to Archangel—the kids are being evacuated by sea. What do you plan to do?"

Grishin didn't answer at once. He smiled genuinely this time, but behind the friendly demeanor his mind was working overtime.

"Colvin cast me in this play," he said eventually. "Now he's bringing down the curtain halfway through the first act. No actor likes that."

Hall gave him a long look. "I know, it was the first thing that crossed my mind when his signal came in. I wondered why he should be taking such a risk."

"Did you come to any conclusion?"

"The only answer I came up with was that Colvin doesn't see it as a risk—he's sufficiently sure of himself to believe you'll hold off till he gives you the word." Hall rose. "Let me know where I can reach you." He seemed to have sobered up completely.

"I'll be in touch," said Grishin.

"What about money? Need any?"

"Not at present. Did you settle up with Vassily Ostrov?"

"Did I! You should have seen him take the envelope from me. He didn't know how much it contained, and it was all he could do not to tear it open on the spot. From the way he fingered it, I'd guess that there's nothing he wouldn't do for money."

"Which reminds me," said Grishin. "The man who sold us the lowdown on Ostrov, General Shatov—we don't need him any-more, do we? I was going to suggest to Colvin that Shatov might have an accident. The traffic in Paris is a lot heavier than it is here . . ."

Hall nodded. "What now? Feel like a drink?"

Grishin stubbed out the remains of his cigar and got to his feet. "No, don't let me keep you from your party."

"It isn't *my* party, for God's sake, it was all the kids' idea! Look, John, I told you how much I deplore this business. It goes against the grain to—"

Hall broke off as the dining-room door opened and a corpulent youth appeared. The black dinner suit emphasized the boy's un-healthy pallor. He might have been Hall's son, Grishin thought.

"Could you come, Mr. Hall?" the boy said. "The waiters are being awfully slow with the dessert."

Hall waved him away. Then he shrugged and gave in. At the door he turned. "You'll keep in touch?"

Grishin nodded. He'd meant to ask if he could safely use the telephone, but calls from the British Club would almost certainly be tapped by the Cheka. He wondered, as he emerged into the street, whether Lena Valentinova would still be at the convent at this hour. His eagerness to see her again surprised him.

The audience sat spellbound as the Moloch's head filled the entire screen, smoke gushing from its cavernous mouth. A group of terrified children cowered on the monstrous idol's lolling tongue, about to be devoured at any moment.

The Electra Theater's resident pianist belabored the keys unmercifully, striving to heighten the dramatic impact of this tragic scene from the Italian spectacular *Cabiria.*

The narrow, tunnel-like auditorium, which had only five seats in each row, was steeply inclined. Most of the moviegoers were men, and every face looked waxen in the reflected glow from the screen. Grishin scrutinized each one in turn as he made his way up the side aisle.

Vassily Ostrov, with his homburg on his lap, was seated at the end of a row near the back. Grishin bided his time. Looking for Ostrov here was a long shot, but it had paid off.

Ostrov began to fidget, glanced casually at the figure in the aisle, concentrated on the screen again. Then he turned once more, but not casually this time. He jerked his head around and stared hard.

Grishin didn't react. He merely waited, leaning against the wall. After a moment's hesitation, Ostrov tried to ignore him and focus his attention on the screen. Then the suspense became too much for him. He got up.

"What do you want?" he hissed. "I've done all I can for you."

Grishin took him by the arm and steered him down a narrow passage to the rear exit. Ostrov squirmed in his grasp.

"We made a bargain. I kept my side of it."

"I've got a couple of questions for you. All you have to do is answer them."

"Questions?" They were standing beside a small door with a dim green light above it.

"Do you know Alexander Berzin?"

"Who?"

"Berzin—he commands the Lettish Rifles. Has your section done any work for him lately?"

"My section, for Berzin? No."

"Does the term 'Credit Group' mean anything to you?"

"Never heard of it. Why?"

"Have you recently produced any documents—forgeries, I mean—relating to the following: a Czech general, a financial expert late of the Cadet Party, Admiral Kolchak, Generals Denikin and Yudenich?"

"Yudenich? Yes."

"What did you have to do?"

"Fabricate some correspondence between the general and a young German lieutenant."

"To what end?"

"Yudenich and his White Russian troops are giving us trouble on the northern front. The object was to compromise him. The letters were—well, of an erotic nature."

"You're sure that's all?"

"I forged them myself." Ostrov snickered. "Not that I've had any personal experience in that line."

"What about London?"

"The usual thing."

"Meaning what?"

"False papers for our agents operating in England. Material designed to incriminate people working against us there. We feed it to the press or the police. More often than not, it's easier than hunting them down ourselves."

"Nothing connected with Berzin, though? Nothing about a resistance group here in Russia?"

"No, I swear it."

Satisfied that he was telling the truth, Grishin released him.

"Keep your eyes and ears open. Something of the kind may come your way. I'll be in touch." He paused. "How did you like the envelope? Were the contents adequate?"

Ostrov nodded silently.

"Do you get any Paris newspapers at Cheka headquarters?"

"A couple. Why?"

"Watch them during the next few days. Look out for the name Shatov. You'll find it in the 'Deaths' column. *Au revoir.*"

Grishin reached for the door handle.

"Wait!"

Ostrov looked as if he'd seen a ghost.

"Listen," he said urgently. "Stay away from the vodka distillery, *Yevgeny Grigory . . .*"

"What did you say?"

"I only saw the name this evening, in a routine report from a Cheka informer living in a house formerly owned by someone called Popov. The description matched the personal particulars of a man on our 'Most Wanted' list. That's why it gave me such a shock when you turned up here."

"Don't let me keep you," said Grishin. "You'll catch the end of the picture if you hurry."

He opened the door to the rear exit, closed it quietly behind him, and drew a deep breath. He now had one more urgent errand to run.

●

It had turned cooler. The sky was almost cloudless, the waxing moon three-quarters full. Grishin went as he had come, on foot. He needed time to marshal his thoughts.

The streets were deserted. A strange stillness brooded over the city, and whenever he was overtaken by an occasional droshky the noise seemed startlingly loud.

The farther he went the emptier the streets became. When he turned into the cobbled square in front of the vodka distillery, he found he had it entirely to himself.

Grishin knew he shouldn't have come. Even if he was in time to warn Vera Ivanova, how would that help her? He scanned the house beside the distillery, trying to recall the sequence of her day and night shifts. Few of the windows were lit, and then only dimly. Being conscientious Party members, one and all, the tenants faithfully obeyed their government's injunctions to save electricity.

He slowly crossed the square and walked up to the rusting wrought-iron gate that led to the rear of the house, entering the derelict distillery by way of the warehouse. A sound came to his ears—a soft, rhythmical, shuffling sound.

Grishin froze. Then he made out a figure in the gloom. It was the girl Vera had named after herself. The sound he could hear was the slap of her bare feet on the flagstones. She was alone, dancing on the spot in a sort of trance, the upper part of her body almost motionless. Grishin tiptoed nearer and whispered so as not to startle her.

"Vera?"

She continued to dance, intent on her strange little jig.

"Vera?" he repeated, edging closer. "What are you up to?"

Still she danced on with her head bowed and strands of hair flopping over her face, watching her feet as if they had taken on a life of their own. Grishin followed the direction of her gaze. At first sight her feet looked merely grimy in the faint moonlight. Then he saw that they were smeared with some dark, sticky substance.

"Stop it!" he said. His voice sounded preternaturally loud in the empty warehouse.

She stopped dancing at last and looked up with an air of bewilderment, swaying slightly. Grishin guessed that she might have found a stray bottle of vodka somewhere.

"What's the matter with you?"

She opened her mouth, but all that emerged was a muffled, inarticulate groan.

"Have you cut yourself?" It was a logical conjecture. The warehouse floor was littered with broken glass.

She shook her head, staring at him wide-eyed. He waited. There had to be some explanation for her odd behavior.

"How's Vera—Vera Ivanova? Have you seen her tonight? Is she at home?"

He was halfway to the door at the back of the warehouse when the girl came to life. She ran past him and barred his path with her arms outstretched, shaking her head violently.

He thrust her aside. His internal alarm system sounded, but his present mood was so fatalistic that he ignored it.

The back door of the Villa Popov was shut, as it should have been, but unlocked. Leaving it open, Grishin slowly and silently made his way along the passage. He could hear nothing unusual, just faint voices, distant footsteps, gurgling pipes.

He opened the door to Vera Ivanova's kitchen inch by inch, half expecting to be jumped at any moment, then pushed it wide with his foot. Nothing happened. Enough moonlight was coming through the kitchen window to show him that all seemed unchanged: the table, the sofa, the gas stove, the sink, the potted plants on the windowsill. Looking at the moonlit window, he was able for the first time to discern the pattern woven into Vera's homemade lace curtain: a two-headed eagle and the Cyrillic characters "KA," the initials of the old imperial railroad.

"Vera?" His voice reminded him of the girl's muffled groan. There was no sound, no movement anywhere.

He tiptoed to the middle of the kitchen. Her uniform was neatly draped over a chair with her boots side by side beneath it.

The bedroom door was open, the bedroom itself in darkness.

"Vera?" He stood motionless, listening intently for the rhythmical sound of breathing, waiting for her to stir in her sleep, and while he stood there pictures flitted through his mind unbidden: a little girl clinging tightly to her mother's hand, losing hold of it, clutching it again, being towed through the crowd toward the booth on Khodynka Field where silk shawls were being distributed; the same girl as a pale and skinny twelve-year-old, timidly tending the looms and their racing, whirling bobbins; Vera in her uniform with the red piping; Vera standing naked in the doorway, one hand resting on the jamb, exactly where he was standing now . . .

He walked to the foot of the bed, saw the outlines of a naked body stretched out on it. Then he caught a sour whiff of vomit and almost vomited himself. Recoiling, he slumped against the wall. All that dispelled his numb foreboding was a sharp, localized stab of pain where the electric light switch was digging into his back.

There was no point in his having come. There was even less point in his staying a moment longer or turning on the light to confirm what his other senses were already telling him loud and clear, but he did. Although the naked bulb shed a wretched, feeble light, to him it seemed harsh and glaring.

Vera Ivanova was lying face down in a welter of blood. Her slim white body seemed uninjured, but there was blood everywhere: on her splayed legs, on one of her outflung arms, on the blankets— even on the floor where Grishin was standing. He wished himself back in darkness, knowing that he had still to see the worst.

As though magnetized, he moved to the head of the bed. She must have washed her hair that evening, because it looked more than usually fair and fluffy. He bent over, put out his hand, and gently turned her head. The sight of her battered face was like a recurrent nightmare, but not of Muranov lying on the ground at Skachki racetrack, surrounded by onlookers. This nightmare was one that had haunted him since his boyhood.

Hearing a sound behind him, Grishin braced himself for the confrontation he'd been expecting. He turned with the feeling that overcomes one on emerging from a nightmare, a mixture of bewilderment and relief.

But it was only the girl Vera. Seemingly unaware of him and the body on the bed, she was gazing down at her feet through the strands of hair falling over her face. Her toes were dabbling in the blood on the floor, flexing, expanding, contracting. Grishin realized that she must have been in the room before.

"Stop it! Stop it, for God's sake!"

She raised her big, burning eyes to his, but without comprehension. Her toes continued to toy with the blood.

He drew back his hand and slapped her face so hard that he himself felt the pain of the blow. Her eyes grew bigger and bluer still. Then she started to cry, tearlessly, with her mouth alone.

She didn't speak in the droshky, just sat there beside him, stiff and silent, outwardly uninterested in where they were going. The knotted handkerchief on her lap contained her few belongings.

She had shown him her hiding place among the ruins, one of the distillery's brick-built, wood-fired furnaces. She could crawl through the stokehole and close the circular iron door behind her. The interior was lined with old blankets and stacked with cardboard boxes full of oddments pilfered from all over the city: corks, reels of cotton, tubes of paint, toothpicks, electric plugs.

Grishin wasn't sure that he was doing the girl a favor by taking her away from her lair, but he couldn't bring himself to leave her behind. Someone must know of his existence, so there was no point in trying to cover his tracks. On the other hand, if the person in question had counted on his returning to Vera's apartment, why hadn't he been ambushed there?

The central post office, where Jim Hall's message had been awaiting him that afternoon, was open day and night. Telling the cabby to wait, he went inside to look up Lena Valentinova's address and telephone number.

As soon as he heard her voice, he said, "I must see you." He was about to hang up when she said, "Well, here I am."

"No, not at your place."

"Where are you calling from?"

Again he felt tempted to hang up. Then he realized that her motive in asking the question was simply to fix a convenient rendezvous.

"I don't mind where we meet," he said. "You suggest a place."

"Red Garden, the main entrance," she replied. "Will that suit you?" She spoke with as little hesitation, as little sign of surprise, as she had shown at the unexpected sound of his voice so late at night.

"I'll need a little time."

"I'll be there anyway."

Grishin told the cabby to pull up at the south end of Red Garden. The fairground was deserted. The booths were dark and silent, and the trestles of the roller coaster, whose undulating track stood outlined against the sky, looked frailer and more skeletal than ever. The cars were parked in a row, chained together to deter vandals. The only light to be seen was a dim yellow glow from the circus tent.

The girl Vera padded along at Grishin's heels, a pace or two to the rear. There had been no shoes among her bits and pieces, so her feet were still bare.

Lena was waiting just inside the main entrance, where the gopak dancer had been performing. She was wearing another of her ill-fitting dresses with a knitted jacket over it.

Grishin breathed a sigh of relief. "Thank you for coming," he said.

"It wasn't far." She kept her hands deep in the pockets of the woolen jacket.

"And thanks for making things so easy on the phone."

"It sounded important."

He looked at her, experiencing another fierce upsurge of the physical desire she'd aroused in him at their first meeting.

"I'd like you to look after someone for me." He turned. "Vera? Vera, come here."

The girl was standing beside the roller coaster's cars, which were painted to resemble birds and beasts: swans, horses, pigs. In the act of climbing into one, she had straddled the side with her legs apart. Grishin, reminded of Vera Ivanova's splayed thighs, felt sick again.

Lena went over to the girl. He heard her say, "Have you ever had a ride in one? Know what it feels like? Like a bellyful of butterflies!"

Grishin reached Lena in a few swift strides. He gripped her roughly, aggressively, by the shoulder.

"Don't be so naïve!" he said. "This girl is from the streets—she's as sly as an alley cat, so don't waste your time. Take her with you, dump her in a bath, give her something to eat, and find her a pair of shoes—but don't expect her to love you in return. She'll steal from you and run away again." He broke off awkwardly. "Maybe she'd be better off on her own," he said. "I don't know—I honestly don't know if I was right to bring her here."

"Why not tell me what's happened?"

It was pointless to talk about it. He'd said all there was to say, but he hesitated nonetheless. The glow of the tent caught his eye.

"The Durovs work late."

"Yes, shall we go and watch?"

He nodded and set off along the alleyway between the booths. The dusty ground was strewn with lottery tickets discarded by unsuccessful gamblers. Lena fell into step beside him. When she glanced back over her shoulder, he said, "Don't worry about the girl, she'll follow us. Even if she doesn't, you won't be able to keep her against her will."

"Her name's Vera?"

"Who knows? She's dumb—at least, she acts like it. I've never heard her speak."

"You told me the last time we met you might bring me a stray someday."

"It was only a vague idea at that stage." He paused. "The stuff on her feet is blood."

Lena took one hand from her jacket pocket and rested it briefly on his shoulder. Grishin appeared not to notice.

"A woman was murdered tonight," he said.

"That was how you sounded on the phone."

"Her name was Vera Ivanova. She put me up for a while when I arrived in Moscow. I . . . I needed a place to stay, so she shared her home with me."

"A total stranger? Women are odd creatures."

"I think it was partly pride. She wanted to show off what she'd achieved. *Two* rooms all to herself! The Revolution was far and away the best thing that had ever happened to her. She was a student at the Workers' and Peasants' College and a senior conductor in charge of three first-class cars. You should have heard her talk about them. How people broke into railroad cars if you turned your back for an instant—how they ripped out the seats and hacked off the leather window straps, but that was never going to happen to *her* cars because she'd defend them to the death . . ."

Grishin turned his head and looked at the woman beside him.

"I found her the way I found Muranov, with her face battered beyond recognition."

"Yevgeny—"

"Except that it didn't make sense. She knew nothing—she couldn't have told them a thing about me."

"Them?"

"The people who murdered your ex-husband."

"The Cheka? Are you sure? Isn't it possible that Vera Ivanova made a habit of inviting unknown men back to her apartment?"

He stared at her, nonplused by her calm tone of voice, but also by the idea itself. "They may have wanted to make it look like a straightforward murder. The fact is, they killed her for no good reason. She knew next to nothing about me, and the little she did know she'd gladly have told them. She was a devout Communist —she owed the Party everything. If they'd said, 'Assist us with our inquiries, comrade,' she'd have told them every last little detail."

"Not if she was in love with you."

"There was nothing like that between us."

"Women are protective by nature."

"But I gave her no reason . . ."

"Didn't you make love to her?"

Grishin fished the old tobacco pouch out of his shirt. His fingers felt so numb he had difficulty rolling a cigarette. His silence told Lena that he had.

"May I have one too?" she asked.

"You smoke?"

"Now and then. Did you leave the—the body where it was?"

Suddenly aware of how much he'd already revealed, he didn't reply. The agent in him revived.

"You don't trust me, do you?" When he still said nothing, she asked point-blank, "Did you really kill that man at the frontier? With a knife?"

He recoiled as if she'd pulled a gun on him.

"Just before you turned up at the convent, I heard a description of someone who'd killed a Latvian on the Finnish border. His face, his clothes, his boots . . ." She pointed at his feet. "Tatar boots with flat soles. I wondered, but it seemed impossible. The man sitting in my office was Russian, even if Yevgeny Grigory wasn't his real name, whereas the description related to an Englishman called Thomas. I had my doubts, but now?"

A curious sound impinged on the silence around them, a sort of smothered laugh. Looking around, Grishin saw that they had reached the circus tent, and that the girl Vera was standing at the entrance. She had lifted the flap and was watching something inside. Whatever had occasioned the strange sound, she was its source.

"Shall we go in?"

He didn't reply.

"May I have a light, please?"

Grishin had lit his own cigarette and entirely forgotten about hers. He struck a match. When he held it out, she leaned forward and grasped his hand to steady it. Then she looked up, and he saw her face by the light of the match. Her big, dark eyes were ringed with fatigue and filled with tension.

"You have beautiful eyes," he said.

The match had gone out. "What color are they?"

"Black," he said.

"You remembered?"

"I remembered."

"Does it bother you?"

He pulled at his cigarette, but he couldn't feel it between his lips. He took a step toward the girl. "Take care of her, won't you?"

"What shall we do, Yevgeny?" Lena tossed her cigarette away. "Shall we stop now and remain the two strangers we still are, or run away together?"

"This isn't the time."

"People fall in love at the worst of times. They fall in love in squalid, unromantic surroundings. They fall in love under the most impossible circumstances."

"You know nothing about me."

"I know you killed someone. I know you're a wanted man."

"You don't know why I'm here." Again the words slipped out.

"I know it must be important to you. I know you wouldn't abandon your—your plans even if I asked you to, so I won't." She smiled with an effort. "I know you find my eyes beautiful. Maybe that's as much as I want to know."

He gripped her shoulders with both hands. He said nothing, just gripped them hard. Then he drew her fiercely to him and kissed her. Far from resisting, she put her arms around him and kissed him with the same fierce urgency. It was fear and passion combined that flowed in their veins, flowed from one body to the other, fused them together—indeed, it seemed momentarily impossible that their two bodies could ever be parted again.

Lena released him with a sharp little intake of breath like the muffled sob that greets a sudden stab of pain.

"Yevgeny," she said, "Yevgeny . . ." She embraced him once more and almost simultaneously pushed him away from her. "You remember the girl who assassinated Prince Lavyonov? She was only nineteen and five feet tall. I'm twenty-six and five-feet-three without my shoes, but I'm afraid."

This time it was she who drew him fiercely to her. She kissed him, then hurriedly broke away and walked over to the circus tent. "I'll take you to the circus," she told the girl in a normal tone of voice. "That's a promise."

The girl didn't take her outstretched hand, but she followed her obediently.

It was less dark than it had been. A wind had sprung up and dispersed the remaining clouds, so the stars were more clearly visible. Strange noises—sounds that hadn't been audible before—drifted across the fairground. One of them sounded like a train getting under way.

"Warsaw Station," Lena said. "It's quite close."

They made their way back to the main gate. The street, the houses opposite, the flickering gas lamps—everything had taken on a strangely theatrical, two-dimensional appearance.

Lena indicated one of the houses across the street. "That's where I live," she said diffidently. "You can come up if you like."

Again he heard distant sounds from the station. They conjured up visions of a train's illuminated windows gliding through the

night, of the morning he'd arrived in Moscow and the band of
ragged children in the forecourt of Vindau Station, of Vera Ivanova
in her uniform. But as all these mental images began to fade, the
speeding train acquired a different significance: He pictured himself on board, leaving the city far behind.

"I'll be gone for a while," he said.

Lena nodded. "You know where to find me."

She held his gaze for a moment, then turned and put out her
hand. The girl ignored it as before, but set off after her.

Grishin had a sudden thought. "Don't cut all her hair off," he
called, uncertain if Lena could still hear him.

⁂ PART TWO

June–August 1918

11

The train was toiling across the steppe. It was hours since Grishin had seen a station, a village, a farmstead, a tree—anything other than this dusty, featureless plain. Even the few clouds floating in the burnished blue sky might have been composed of dust.

The blazing sun created a wall of heat which the train seemed to penetrate with difficulty. From time to time the whistle emitted a warning blast. There was no need—the train was traversing an endless, trackless plain—so the plaintive shriek resembled the cry of a frightened beast endeavoring to keep up its spirits in desolate, forbidding terrain. Sporadic rifle shots rang out from the head of the train whenever the Red Guards thought they glimpsed a target in the shimmering heat haze.

Thirty or forty of them sat huddled together on a flatcar behind the locomotive. The front of the boiler had a red star painted on it, and two crossed red flags fluttered behind the smokestack. Machine guns had been mounted on either side of the flatcar, and the Red Guards themselves were as heavily armed as if they were bound for the White Russian front.

Their operational objective was, in fact, quite different. They had been sent out into the plains to requisition wheat, potatoes, and cattle for the starving inhabitants of Moscow. Grishin had ascertained that as many as ten such expeditions left Moscow daily, bound for all points of the compass. The commissars in charge of these trains, which always enjoyed right of way, were not only empowered to seize foodstuffs but adept at discovering where the peasants had ingeniously hidden them. The first five cattle cars of Grishin's train bore the following ominous inscription in big white capitals visible at half a mile:

DEATH / TO ALL / GRAIN / SPECU / LATORS!

The train was now crawling, at a laborious twenty miles an hour, toward the so-called Land of the Five Rivers, a fertile breadbasket south of the Uvaly highlands. Grishin had boarded it at Kostroma, a city on the Volga some two hundred miles northeast of Moscow. For eight hours, the underpowered locomotive had been hauling its fourteen cattle cars eastward along a track leading into the Urals by way of Vyatka and Perm. The rearmost car was set aside for passengers. There had been around a hundred of them at the outset, but their numbers had gradually diminished—seeping away, as it were, into the surrounding plain. The dozen or so that remained were ragged vagrants with grimy faces. The sliding door was open. Grishin sat in the doorway while his companions lay sprawled in the straw, uninterested in anything as long as the train kept moving—probably indifferent even to its destination.

●

Grishin himself had once belonged to the rootless fraternity that roamed the country by rail, allowing chance to determine the course of their lives. No one had ever disputed his right to a privileged place beside the door, even when he was only thirteen, and although no one knew that this lean and lanky youth had already killed his first man, the toughest of his fellow travelers treated him with a certain wary respect.

He had waited four long years for a chance to kill Vadim Nekrasov, exhibiting a patience and perseverance inherited from his mother. She possessed those qualities to the full. He recalled her standing outside the villas in Baku's most exclusive neighborhood—luxurious white villas overlooking the Caspian. Whatever their design, they had to be white—white above all else. He scarcely recognized his mother when she stood gazing at them. She became another woman altogether, oblivious even of the boy at her side. He heard her sigh, saw her expression: infinitely covetous while her eyes rested on the white villas, infinitely resentful when she finally tore herself away.

At night in his room back home on the edge of the Sabunchi oil fields, after returning from one of these excursions, he would hear her furiously haranguing his father. The poor man's silence, which only enraged her still more, would eventually be succeeded by lame assurances in which she had long since ceased to believe.

A thousand boreholes in ten thousand square meters of ground —such were the "naphtha wells" of Sabunchi on Cape Apsheron. They were owned by Sweden and by Alfred Nobel, the inventor of dynamite. Young Mikhail Grishin's father, Yegor, a Georgian, was the oil company's senior engineer.

The house, which went with the job, was situated between the outer row of pumps and the refinery. Most of the petroleum was obtained from open wells. An unattractive green in color, the viscous stuff got everywhere. They tracked it into the house on their shoes, their clothes reeked of it—even their food tasted of it, so Mikhail's mother said. Then there was the sound of the machines: the thousand eternally squeaking pumps that extracted the oil from the sandstone fifteen hundred feet down. At nights, when Mikhail lay awake in his attic room, which was lit by the refinery's dancing flames, the mournful sound of the pumps seemed to echo his mother's complaints.

●

Another rifle shot rang out from the front of the train. Grishin saw a spurt of dust in the distance, but that was all. The ragged, grimy scarecrows on the floor of the cattle car came to life. One of them crawled over to the doorway on all fours. He swore obscenely.

"What the devil are they shooting at?"

A second hobo brushed the straw from his hair and gave vent to a string of even riper oaths. The other men slowly sat up in response to the sixth sense that told them when some new development was afoot.

The scenery had changed. Instead of beating down on a barren, dusty wilderness, the sun was gilding the stubble of harvested grain fields. The blue bank of cloud that seemed to hover on the horizon, just above this shimmering golden expanse, was really a tree-clad mountain range. For Grishin, who hoped to find Dunga Khan there, the sight of it held special significance.

A narrow farm track had converged with the railroad line and was running parallel to it. In the distance, barely visible through the heat haze, a village came into view, its pale blue onion dome and cluster of roofs reflecting the sunlight.

The train began to slow. The first of the hobos tossed their bundles out of the car and jumped after them, heads tucked in, backs rounded. Only two stayed behind, a boy of around fourteen and a sturdy man with blind, milky eyes.

They pulled into the station five minutes later. The wheels stopped clanking, and the vacuum they left was filled by a great silence. All that still hung in the air was the locomotive's asthmatic wheezing. It had an exhausted, almost human quality. Grishin jumped down, grabbed his bag, and settled it on his shoulder. Now that the train was at a standstill, the heat felt even more oppressive. He was hungry and thirsty, having eaten and drunk nothing since the last stop at five that morning.

The station's waiting room, ticket office, and buffet were all one room. Grishin was agreeably surprised to find some charcoal already glowing under a samovar filled with water. His bag contained a mug, cubes of compressed tea, sugar, a loaf of bread, half a roast chicken, and a can of sardines. He had also bought himself an old Nagant revolver from a black marketeer at Kostroma—not a particularly accurate weapon but effective enough at close range.

Looking through the window, he could see the engineer and the stoker replenishing the tender from a woodpile. The horses he'd seen tethered some yards away had disappeared, together with the commissar in charge and most of his men. Two of the remaining Red Guards had taken up their positions on the roof of an adjoining shed, one leaning on his rifle, the other scanning the plain through binoculars.

Grishin finished his meal and went outside. As he was making his way over to the fountain he saw the main body of the expedition galloping toward the village in a cloud of dust.

The stationmaster was chatting with the engineer and the stoker. Beside the woodpile was a siding waist deep in grass, and on it stood a rusty handcar.

The stationmaster joined Grishin at the fountain. He shuffled rather than walked, as if his boots were too heavy for him. Removing his cap, he dunked his handkerchief in a bucket of water and mopped his perspiring face. Then he wrung out the handkerchief and inserted it between his neck and the collar of his black smock.

"Hot enough for you?" His eyelids were swollen and inflamed. "We don't get many travelers here, not these days."

One of the sentries on the shed roof gave a yell. An oath and

several rifle shots followed. Two Red Guards who had been dozing in the shade jumped up and vanished behind the building.

Grishin glanced inquiringly at the stationmaster, who shrugged.
The Red Guards returned dragging the carcass of a dog, an emaciated beast with mangy fur and protruding ribs. The rooftop sentries
and the machine gunners from the flatcar had all left their posts
and clustered around the animal. They bent over it, arguing heat-
edly. At length one of them fetched a bale of straw from the shed,
scattered it over the carcass, and set fire to it. The flames were
almost invisible in the sunlight.

"Why?" asked Grishin, recalling the isolated shots fired en
route.

The stationmaster dunked his handkerchief in the bucket again.
"Maybe they thought it was sick—maybe they were simply passing the time. Are you from Moscow? I'm told the Muscovites won't
even have dogmeat to eat before the summer's out."

"No, I'm from Kostroma."

"Let's go inside, it's like a furnace out here."

The stationmaster's office doubled as switch tower and living
quarters, complete with a cot and a table on which lay an unfin-
ished game of chess. The calendar on the wall was pre-Revolution-
ary. The stationmaster, who had brought the bucket with him,
deposited it beside a chair in the middle of the room. Kicking his
boots off, he dipped one of his bare feet in the water and smiled
slyly.

"No reason why one shouldn't make the best of things. My
name's Bibikov, by the way—Anatoly Bibikov."

Grishin sat down facing him with his bag on his lap. "Are you
expecting another train today?"

"Another train?"

"The samovar . . ."

"Ah, that was for the commissar's benefit, but he told me tea
was a waste of time." Bibikov shook his head. "Time-wasting . . .
I reckon that's a term they invented in Moscow."

Grishin pointed to a telegraph in the corner. "Does that thing
work?"

"Sure it works, but it hasn't been in use for weeks. In the old
days we had five trains a day through here from Kostroma and

another five from Vyatka, not to mention the wealthy landowners who used to come and go in their private cars."

Grishin rolled a cigarette and offered it to Bibikov, but the stationmaster pointed to his inflamed eyelids and said, "Hay fever." One of the three windows overlooked the locomotive, the tender, and the machine gunners, who had returned to the flatcar. Grishin nodded in their direction.

"What are they scared of?"

"Who knows?" Bibikov moistened his handkerchief again. "Do you play chess, by any chance?"

"When does the train go back?"

Bibikov spread his hands as if the question presented too many complications. "The peasants should have delivered their quotas of grain and cattle to the station, ready for loading, but they've become even more pigheaded since they were granted their freedom—to use the official term."

"In Kostroma there are rumors of disturbances. Foraging parties sometimes meet resistance, so they say."

"Countryfolk are slow on the uptake. They don't understand the new era. The land around here is rich and fertile. It all belonged to landowners with big estates. The peasants were slaves, beasts of burden. Then everything changed. Agitators came along and told them the land was theirs. Land, buildings, livestock—all they had to do was take it, and if the owner tried to stop them they were legally entitled to liquidate him."

"What's so hard to understand about that?"

Bibikov smiled so broadly that his watering eyes became slits. "The peasants seized the land and started working it themselves. Then along came the commissars. Bravo, they said—the land belongs to you now, i.e., to the people. But to make sure the people really benefit, comrade peasants, what's needed is a touch of discipline and organization. Someone has to manage the confiscated estates, distribute seed corn, decide what crops to grow, install farm machinery. Don't get us wrong, said the commissars— everything belongs to everyone, to the people as a whole, but every collective farm needs organizing. If everything is collectively owned, comrade peasants, your comrades the factory workers can't be allowed to go hungry . . ."

Grishin continued to smoke in silence. With a job as solitary as his, Anatoly Bibikov clearly enjoyed holding forth to a captive audience.

"Confusing, eh? But it gets even worse when village priests tell the peasants, 'Beware the collective! Cross yourselves three times at the very word! Collective farms are the work of the Devil, and God will destroy their crops. Not an ear of grain will ripen on the stalk.' And to give God a helping hand, the priests go the rounds at night and poison the seed corn with chemicals. And when spring comes and the collectives' fields remain barren, what better proof of God's omnipotence?"

Bibikov removed one foot from the bucket and substituted the other.

"The commissars have a few tricks of their own, of course. They round up a priest or two, erect gallows on the barren land, and hang them as an argument in favor of collectivization. What are the peasants to do now, hand over their grain or hide it? And what are the Red Guards to do, obey their commissars' orders and fire on their brother peasants, or turn a blind eye?" Bibikov sneezed. "Ah yes, my friend, these are confusing times indeed."

"Has anything like that happened here?"

"At Unshaskoye? No, the commissars have never paid us a visit till now. The local peasants have an alternative: they ferry their grain across the river—drive their cattle across the Unsha into the Khan's territory." Bibikov removed the handkerchief from his neck and fanned himself with it. "What heat! There's bound to be a storm before long . . ." He cocked an eye in Grishin's direction. "I'd steer clear of the village if I were you."

"I wasn't intending to go there."

"Where, then? The Kostroma-Vyatka line stops here now, didn't you know? This is a kind of frontier post."

"Because of bandits, you mean? I hear they ambush trains and rob the passengers."

Bibikov leaned forward confidentially. "Mail cars carrying money for the big banks, that's more their mark, not wedding rings and small change."

"Have they blown up the bridges?"

"No point. How can they ambush trains that aren't running any longer? No, traffic was suspended because of the risk."

"Forty Red Guards and a couple of machine guns should be enough to defend a train."

"Against a band of robbers, maybe, but not against a well-armed, well-disciplined body of men. What can one describe them as—irregulars, partisans? Nobody even knows how many of them there are." Bibikov glanced at the circular clock on the wall above the obsolete calendar. "Those Red Guards must have reached the village by now. They'll find it empty—no grain, no cattle, no men—and the Khan will have gained another fifty recruits."

"If they're fighting the Bolsheviks, are they Whites?"

"Neither Whites nor Reds. There's a song they sing on the march." Bibikov sang the words in a low voice. "No plunderer I, nor slayer of the defenseless. Neither White nor Red, I am the bird that plucks the ripe grain . . ."

"And their territory starts on the other side of the Unsha?"

"They control the whole area between the Unsha in the west, the Vyatka in the east, the Vetluga in the south, and the Vigal and Yug in the north—the Land of the Five Rivers, in other words. They also have the Severniye Uvaly highlands at their backs, a perfect hideout in an emergency."

"What do you know of Dunga Khan?"

Bibikov's sweeping gesture seemed descriptive more of infinity than a human being. "He's a Siberian, a Tatar, a Mongol. He's lost an arm or a leg. He's a eunuch with seven wives. Your guess is as good as mine."

Grishin walked over to the window farthest from the track. Looking out across the shimmering yellow plain, he could now see the mountain range far more clearly than he had from the train. It brooded on the skyline like a purple rampart, almost indistinguishable from the bank of low cloud that lent it an impression of even greater height.

Bibikov removed his foot from the bucket, hooked it over his knee, and mopped it with his handkerchief. "They don't like people taking too close an interest in them, as the Red Guards learned to their cost." The handkerchief was sodden. He gave up and pulled his boots on anyway.

"The Red Guards," Grishin said, "—what happened to them?"

"There was a famous stud farm not far from here, the Puyachev. Superb horses, Moscow Derby winners among them. The brand was a five-pointed star—you know, from the Land of the Five Rivers." Bibikov stared reminiscently at the ceiling. "The Red

Guards sent out a ten-man patrol. I saw the only one that returned. The Khan's men sent him back alive, but not before they'd branded him on the forehead . . ." He frowned. "Why on earth do you want to cross the river?"

"Let's say it's because I'm neither White nor Red, just a bird that plucks the grain." Grishin hummed a snatch of the tune.

Bibikov moved a chessman indecisively to and fro. "I can't get you a horse. The ones you saw are the only horseflesh left this side of the Unsha."

"What about that handcar out there?"

"What about it?"

"Does it work?"

"It'd probably need oiling." Bibikov pointed to the chessboard. "A shame you don't play."

Grishin nodded in the direction of the telegraph. "If a message comes for Vada Nikulin, will you take it down and keep it for me?"

"How would I get in touch with you?"

"I may drop in for an occasional game of chess. Will you lend me the handcar?"

"It belongs to the people, and the people includes you. I don't see why not." Bibikov fetched a grease gun from the top of a locker. "I hope you've got some really good friends across the river, comrade."

"How far is it?"

"To the Unsha? Five miles. And don't forget: Once you're over the bridge you're on their territory."

The handcar had been rusting on its overgrown siding for months. Even when it was thoroughly greased, Grishin had to exert all his strength to operate the rocker arm that drove the rear wheels.

The heat was overpowering now that the sun had reached its zenith, and he was streaming with sweat after only a few yards. It trickled into his eyes, almost blinding him. The blue hills on the horizon, with their promise of shade and refreshment, became a vague blur. All he could see with any clarity were the two rails stretching ahead of him. To his smarting eyes, they seemed to be melting in the white-hot glare of the sun.

Dunga Khan and Colma Khan were brothers, Colma being the younger of the two. They belonged to a dwindling Circassian tribe resident on the northern flanks of the Caucasus Mountains and devoted to the breeding and stealing of horses. Dunga had once told Grishin that the title "khan" was common in his tribe because Circassians judged a man by three things: his horsemanship, his skill at arms, and his singing voice—in that order. In their estimation, anyone in full possession of those attributes was a khan, a prince among men.

Colma was a khan on Sundays only. That was when he donned the Circassian male's traditional costume: a long, close-fitting *cherkeska* bristling with cartridge cases sewn to the chest like organ pipes, the belt adorned with pistol and dagger. At Sabunchi he was plain Colma, the man in charge of the oil company's numerous teams of horses.

Horses were important in the oil fields. They hauled heavy equipment across rough ground to the drilling sites, barrels of crude oil to the refinery, and kerosene or gasoline to the harbor. The two hundred beasts under Colma's care were better fed and tended than the workers.

That was yet another reason why Mikhail Grishin's mother hated the company house on the edge of the oil fields so much: the hardship and misery of the workers, which clung to her engineer husband like an aura still more noisome than the stench of petroleum.

Their plight preyed on Yegor Grishin's mind. He couldn't restrain himself from harping on the terrible accidents that occurred, the burning and maiming of overworked laborers because exhaustion bred carelessness, and the company claimed that it was already spending too much on safety measures. Being responsible for maintaining output and replacing disabled workers, Yegor Grishin felt a compulsion to get such things off his chest, but his wife had no wish to hear about them. Enough was enough, she said. The least he could do was to keep off the subject in their son's presence and refrain from inviting men like Colma to the house.

But Colma had long been young Mikhail's idol. Colma used to take him on trips, let him hold the reins, teach him how to handle horses. Colma always had time for nine-year-old Misha, as the boy was universally known. He took him to places of which other Baku youngsters only dreamed—to the fire worshipers' temple at Surakhani and the Tatars' Forbidden City, where the most mysterious things were offered for sale, among them a variety of yellow scorpion whose sting was fatal only in August of every year. The boy was doubly impressed because all of them—Dunga Khan, Colma Khan, and he himself—had been born in that month. The coincidence seemed strangely significant.

One Sunday in November, Colma was too busy to devote himself to Mikhail. He could only suggest that the boy might like to help him distribute some handbills. Freshly printed on a small hand press the night before, they called on the company's labor force to attend a mass meeting that same afternoon.

It had been raining for days on end, and soon there were sodden, discarded handbills strewn everywhere. It seldom snowed in Baku, and Mikhail, who was Baku-born, had never seen snow lie. But that Sunday, thousands of handbills blanketed the muddy ground like a snowfall.

Late in the afternoon the sun came out and the onshore wind dropped, as it usually did an hour before dusk. That might have been why so many workers turned up after all. The procession filed past the derricks to the administration building with Colma and Yegor Grishin in the lead and Mikhail trotting along between them.

The petition they intended to deliver was couched in the mildest terms. It pointed out that most of Sabunchi's fatal accidents occurred in the vicinity of open, unprotected oil and gas wells. The company's own engineers had recommended the introduction of various safety measures. All the workers asked was that these be put into effect.

The meeting had been purposely called on a Sunday to avoid any loss of output. No strike was threatened, and the peaceful nature of the occasion was underlined by the presence of Yegor Grishin, the company's chief engineer. Furthermore, Colma had expressly urged the demonstrators to refrain from singing or chanting provocative slogans.

The management, which had no intention of making any concessions, put a more sinister construction on Colma's initiative, especially as he was rumored to have links with revolutionary elements. They duly sent for a detachment of the Cossack cavalrymen who were, in their view, enjoying an altogether too leisurely existence at garrison headquarters, a palace formerly owned by one of the khans of Baku.

To Captain Vadim Nekrasov, the Cossack commander, the situation seemed crystal clear: He was faced with a budding insurrection. More importantly, it presented him with an opportunity to shine in the eyes of his superiors at Tiflis. No command could have been less calculated to enhance an officer's promotion prospects than that of a tranquil backwater like Baku.

That was how the workers found themselves confronted by a squadron of mounted Cossacks. After the tedium of a day spent distributing handbills, Mikhail Grishin was surprised and delighted by the spectacle of a hundred horses, each finer than the next, a hundred Caucasian saddles with silver pommels and cantles, a hundred Circassian coats. He mistook the cavalrymen for fellow tribesmen of Colma's, unaware that the Cossacks had adopted the *cherkeska* as their uniform. The cartridge cases protruding from the little pockets on their long tunics glinted in the waning daylight.

Later he would recall the short-barreled cavalry carbines, the knouts, and the officer's face: thin lips, cold eyes, waxed mustache with upturned ends. It was suddenly quite close, that face, because the officer rode over to them. He halted in front of Colma Khan, reins in one hand, saber in the other.

"Stick your petition on the end of that. Then about-face, all of you!" His voice was firm but not unfriendly.

"Since when have you belonged to the management, Captain? Kindly let us pass."

From that moment on, everything became telescoped in Mikhail Grishin's memory: Cossacks charging, knouts whistling through the air, demonstrators backing away, Colma being seized and dragged twenty or thirty yards to a timber tripod—being lashed to it with leather belts and hoisted into the air above an open borehole.

There he dangled, bound hand and foot, his massive, muscular body writhing impotently as half a dozen Cossacks took it in turns to flog him with their knouts. Some of their comrades held off the crowd, carbines at the ready, while others lit torches. The light was fading fast by now.

Mikhail remained at his father's side. The officer promised that no harm would come to either of them. Yegor Grishin was an engineer, a man of his own class, said the officer, but it was time he learned the folly of associating with malcontents like Colma.

The boy recalled the steadily increasing pressure of his father's hand and his plea to the officer: "In heaven's name, captain, let the boy go home!" The little mouth beneath the waxed mustache twitched contemptuously. "It was your idea to bring him along." Later, his father said, "Don't look, Misha! Shut your eyes!"

How had the tripod come to be there? Was the whole thing prearranged? At an order from Nekrasov, the Cossacks who had been flogging Colma withdrew. One of them leaned far out of his saddle and tossed a blazing torch into the open borehole.

"Colma! Colma!"

Mikhail's cry was drowned by a muffled explosion as the mixture of gas and petroleum ignited.

"Don't look, Misha! Shut your eyes!"

He clamped his eyelids together. A wave of heat smote him. He screwed up his eyes even tighter. Everything went red. The heat penetrated his eyelids, seared his face, bored into his brain, his breast. This much he could recall perfectly: Even before he opened his eyes, before he heard the roar of the flames and Colma's agonized screams, before that frightful stench filled the air—even then, something had caught fire within himself.

The urge to look became too great. He opened his eyes.

Was that Colma? Impossible! How could that blazing torch be a man strong enough to lift a barrel of petroleum unaided, a man who wore the thinnest of shirts, even in winter, and rode like a god? How could anyone hope to destroy a body as indestructible as his?

In that moment Mikhail Grishin learned everything about the world he needed to know. No subsequent experience would ever change that, and all that happened to him in later life was relative to that one, terrible moment of truth.

The demise of Chief Engineer Yegor Grishin a few seconds later was attributed to mischance. Even Captain Nekrasov pronounced himself deeply affected by the accident. It was occasioned not only by the fact that a horse had shied at the fire but also, to be fair, by an injudicious and easily misinterpreted move on the victim's part. He had lunged at one of the Cossacks and tried to wrest the carbine from his grasp. Had he seriously intended to use it? That was an open question and must remain so. Suffice it to say that the gun had gone off without hitting anyone—the autopsy established that beyond doubt. The deceased had sustained multiple injuries consistent with their having been inflicted by the hoofs of a panic-stricken horse, but no gunshot wound was found.

It was Captain Nekrasov himself who rescued young Mikhail from the ensuing turmoil and took the petrified, speechless little boy home. He told his mother what had happened, expressed sympathy, and offered to assist her in any way possible. He not only returned the next day and reiterated his offer of help but attended her late husband's funeral.

From his widow's point of view, Yegor Grishin's death heralded a change for the better. For one thing, she was able to leave the house she hated and move elsewhere—if not into one of the coveted white villas, at least into something halfway there. The directors of the oil company, being as deeply affected as Nekrasov by the sad and unpleasant nature of her husband's death, generously assigned her a rent-free apartment and volunteered to pay her his salary for another year.

The Cossack captain—his hopes of promotion were not immediately fulfilled, though it was hinted that they might be "once the dust has settled"—continued to visit the widow Grishin at regular intervals.

Nekrasov's promotion came through twelve months later. He moved Mikhail and his mother into a white villa overlooking the Caspian and formally proposed marriage.

"What do you think, Misha?" the widow asked her son. "I wouldn't want to do anything you disapproved of."

The boy nodded.

"Of course," she went on with a girlish little laugh, "it would mean changing our name."

"I know." The words were muffled and almost unintelligible.

"You see? Even your voice is coming back."

Mikhail had been unable to speak for some time after "the sad occurrence," as his mother always called it. The local physicians were mystified, but Dr. Krimholtz, a specialist summoned from Tiflis by Nekrasov, diagnosed the trouble as a straightforward case of membranous diphtheria. He cauterized the boy's tonsils, which were coated with a white film, and made him gargle with milk of sulfur. His voice gradually returned, but with a curious aftereffect: It was deep and husky, and remained so for the rest of his life.

His mother blossomed. She mixed with people whose society she had always craved and dressed as she had always yearned to, in floating pastel gowns. She became a different and more beautiful woman, and the transformation was not lost on her son.

Mikhail, who now bore his stepfather's surname, gave the Nekrasovs no cause for complaint. Although he remained taciturn, he treated his stepfather with unremitting courtesy and respect. He remained aloof from other children of his age, scored good marks in school, kept his room tidy and made himself agreeable to visitors. His mother, who received numerous compliments on Mikhail's behavior, never failed to pass them on to her husband. The credit, she said, belonged to him and his paternal affection for her fatherless son.

In reality, it was Mikhail who made the running. Nekrasov was a fine horseman, so he asked for riding lessons. Nekrasov was an outstanding shot, so he asked to be allowed to accompany him on hunting expeditions. Nekrasov's only civilian hobby was collecting butterflies, so Mikhail assisted him with net and killing bottle and learned how to set and mount the specimens they caught.

In spite of the boy's docility and good manners, however, Vadim Nekrasov always felt faintly uncomfortable in his company. That was why he suggested enrolling him in the cadet academy at Tiflis. Wasn't he a born soldier? Didn't he have all the makings of one, with his amazing physical stamina and proven intellectual ability?

"What do you think, Mother?"

His mother was taken with the idea. "Don't you mind the thought of leaving home?"

"No, Mother."

"Well, if it's really what you want . . ."

"Yes, Mother."

"In that case, Misha, I couldn't be more delighted for you. It's an honor, being awarded a place at the cadet academy."

The day of Mikhail's departure fell just before his thirteenth birthday. His cadet uniform and riding boots had been purchased, his trunk packed, his seat on the Tiflis express booked. Nekrasov had given him a letter of recommendation to the commander of the 1st Army Corps, who also commanded the Imperial Cadet Academy, and a letter of credit on the Tiflis branch of the Imperial

Bank. He had additionally presented him with a farewell-cum-
birthday gift: a Cossack carbine made to order by the finest gunsmith in the Caucasus, Fritz Haegele of 19 Golovinsky Prospekt,
Tiflis.

Early on the morning of his departure, three hours before the
Tiflis express was due to leave, Mikhail knocked on the door of the
bedroom his mother shared with his stepfather. The Nekrasovs,
who had returned home late from a reception at the Grand Hotel,
were fast asleep. It was his mother who eventually woke.

"Who is it?" she called drowsily.

Mikhail came in. The double bed was immediately facing the
door. He walked to the foot. His mother whispered so as not to
wake her husband. Mikhail had never entered the room before.

"What are you doing here at this hour?"

"It's all right, Matushka. Don't turn the light on."

Nothing in his manner aroused her suspicions, she later testified
to the police. He had spoken quite normally, in his deep, husky
voice. Besides, she was touched: It was the first time he had ever
addressed her by the affectionate diminutive *matushka*.

She waited for him to come closer. Instead, he moved to the
other side of the bed. She vaguely noticed that he was fully dressed
and wearing his Tatar boots.

But hadn't she noticed the gun in his hand? It was a bulky
weapon, a cavalry carbine weighing nearly six pounds and firing
16.5-millimeter ammunition. The barrel was only twelve inches
long, or little longer than that of a revolver. It was the gun
Nekrasov had presented to his stepson.

All Mikhail's mother discerned in the half-light of dawn was his
outstretched arm leveled at her sleeping husband's face. She recalled thinking that it looked oddly elongated, like an oversize
artificial limb.

"What are you doing, Misha?" his mother had whispered. The
boy had turned his head and gazed at her a second or two. When
he spoke his tone was grave and serene.

"Please don't look. Shut your eyes."

The artificial limb exploded. The whole room exploded, drown-
ing her horrified scream. In the silence that followed she heard a
dull thud as Mikhail dropped the gun on the floor, heard him walk
quietly to the door, heard his parting words.

"Don't try to find me, not ever."

She tugged at the pull switch of the bedside light but fainted before she actually saw that nothing remained of Vadim Nekrasov's face.

●

Grishin sighted the river and the horsemen almost simultaneously. He counted twelve men, six on either side of the railroad track, plus a few spare horses laden with water and provisions.

Once across the bridge he finally let the handcar coast to a halt; his five-mile journey had seemed interminable. The horsemen continued to sit motionless, watching him. All save one wore bandoliers and were armed with brand-new semiautomatic Mosin Nagant carbines. Their horses were fresh and well fed. Their boots were dusty, but their clothing was clean and in good order. The Red Guards at Unshaskoye station had resembled a ragged band of brigands by comparison.

Grishin secured the brake and dismounted. He held his arms a few inches clear of his body as he scrambled down the embankment. One of the horsemen detached himself from the rest and rode over.

Everything about him surprised Grishin when he recalled the type of men Dunga Khan had surrounded himself with in the old days. He was unarmed, and all that adorned the front of his well-tailored hunting jacket was a pair of binoculars suspended from a thong around his neck. Elegant was the only word Grishin could find to describe the way he guided the horse with his thighs, the harmony of movement between rider and mount. Though young, possibly in his mid-twenties, he was clearly the leader of the party. His fair-skinned face and brown eyes conveyed an air of melancholy. It was a face that had taken generations of breeding to evolve.

The horseman brought his horse to a stop by knee pressure alone, holding the reins an inch or two clear of its mane.

"Few people venture across the Unsha these days, didn't anyone tell you?"

"Yes, the stationmaster."

"Bibikov? How is he?"

"Feeling sorry for himself."

"Ah, so it's hay-fever time again." There was a brief pause. "What brings you here?"

"I'm looking for the Khan."

The young man raised his hand in an unspoken command. One of his companions galloped past them up the embankment and made for the handcar.

"You arrived on the train this morning?"

"Yes, from Kostroma."

"How many Red Guards remained behind at the station?"

"Half a dozen. Two lookouts on the roof of the shed, two manning the machine guns, two off duty." The young man hadn't inquired about the rest, so Grishin assumed that their movements must be known to him.

"Machine guns, you say. What kind?"

"Russian Maxims, the latest model. Belt capacity two hundred and fifty rounds, rate of fire five hundred a minute."

"An expert, eh?" The young man patted his horse on the withers as though congratulating it. "What was that firing we heard?"

"They shot a stray dog."

The other horseman came trotting back and tossed Grishin's bag at his feet. "One revolver," he said, "one box of ammunition. Nothing else of interest." His face was sharp, with a beaky nose. He rejoined the others.

The first horseman looked down at Grishin. "Take your things and go back where you came from."

"That handcar's hell to keep moving—it hasn't been used for months—and five miles is quite a stretch."

"I'm advising you for your own good, Expert."

"So did Bibikov."

"You say you're looking for Dunga Khan . . ." The horseman made a sweeping gesture. "You might as well look for a needle in a haystack."

The others had stationed themselves so that the sun was in Grishin's eyes. Their horses stirred uneasily, shook their manes, brushed flies away with their long tails, pawed the ground. Grishin waited. Patience was his only asset.

"Does he know you?" the young man asked at length.

"He'll remember. We go back a long way."

"Do you have a name?"

"May I move my hands?" Grishin squinted up at him, dazzled by the sun.

"If you're careful, Expert. You don't mind my calling you that?"

Grishin's shirt was open at the neck. He reached inside and eased the string of the tobacco pouch over his head. The brown eyes followed every move he made. Not venturing to throw the pouch, he held it out by the string. The leather was black and stiff with age. The man took it and hung it on his pommel.

"We'll see," he said with a sad, weary smile.

"It'll mean more to him than any name."

"If you say so, Expert. We don't go by our own names here, any of us." He indicated his companions. "We have certain rules on this side of the river. Two of us will ride with you. You'd better do as they say."

He tossed the pouch to one of his men, then wheeled his horse. Once again, rider and mount moved as one, with fluid elegance, but it was something else that caught Grishin's eye. Slung from the cantle of the young man's saddle was an iron rod the length of a man's arm, and welded to the end was a brand in the shape of a five-pointed star.

Grishin had only a rough idea of which way they were heading and how far they had ridden through the forest. He was dependent on his sense of smell alone. At the last change of horses and escorts, in a clearing waist-deep in bracken and surrounded by spruce trees, he had been blindfolded. His wrists were already tied behind his back.

The tang of resin gave way to a cloying fragrance so intense that it swamped the reek of sweat from his exhausted horse and his own drenched body. From time to time he felt something prickly brush his cheeks.

He rode without difficulty. His horse was equipped with a Caucasian saddle of the type that had curved, silver-sheathed horns fore and aft, and to anyone familiar with such a saddle nothing could be safer or more comfortable. His captors' manner toward him had grown perceptibly less abrupt when they saw how well he sat a horse.

He estimated that six or seven hours must have elapsed since the mounted patrol had intercepted him. His escorts had changed every hour, and fresh horses were always ready and waiting. The long ride across the plain to the hills had demonstrated, again and again, how far the Khan's authority extended and how firmly under his control this territory was.

The area had looked deserted at first, yet every field had been harvested or tilled. The farmsteads and villages they passed seemed to have been abandoned by their inhabitants: no sound of voices, no dogs barking, just heat, dust, and silence. And then, within seconds, a dozen of the Khan's men would appear from nowhere and the scene would be transformed: boisterous salutations, laughter, mountains of snow-white bread, roast chickens, butter, cheese, hot tea for Grishin and his companions, water and oats for their horses.

The character of the countryside had changed. It became greener, more fertile, threaded with streams. The physical appearance of his escorts changed too. The softer and lovelier the landscape, the fiercer, darker, and more oriental their cast of feature. They were armed with knives and daggers as well as rifles or revolvers. Grishin could tell that he was nearing his destination. Dunga Khan's original band had been recruited in the Caucasus from just such men as these.

For the last half hour they had been winding their way up a steep track. The air was still laden with the same sickly scent. The rider ahead of Grishin came to a halt. His own mount followed suit. For several seconds he heard nothing but the three horses' heavy breathing. Then came a shrill birdcall, very close at hand, followed by an answering cry in the distance. Someone took his horse's bridle and led it along for a few yards. The ground underfoot was soft, presumably carpeted with pine needles. Nimble fingers untied the rope around his wrists.

"Dismount," said a voice.

He slid to the ground and waited, massaging the stiffness from his wrists.

"You can remove that blindfold, Expert." The name had stuck.

He couldn't undo the knot at once, so he pulled the scarf down and left it around his neck. Dusk was falling, but he could see that the trunks of the spruce and beech trees around them were overgrown with prickly bindweed. The cloying scent that filled the air came from the clusters of greenish flowers visible among its jagged, leathery leaves.

"He's all yours now, Cherry." The speaker was the man who had untied his wrists.

It was only then that he noticed the girl standing at the mouth of the narrow forest track with a hunting rifle slung from her shoulder.

She wore a tightly belted red dress that overlapped her boots and a colorful Tatar cap on her sleek, dark head. Her skin looked the color of bronze in the twilight. Grishin grasped the origin of her nickname when he saw her mouth, which was as full and round as the ripest of cherries.

"Bring your horse and come with me."

He led the beast by the bridle. It was slightly lame in the right foreleg. The girl walked a few yards ahead, one hand on the sling of her gun. The path ran steeply downhill. Twice she paused to imitate a birdcall, and twice it was echoed from somewhere deep in the forest. Sentries materialized, exchanged a few whispered words with her, and vanished into the gloom again.

The path leveled off, the trees thinned. At the end of the path Grishin saw a clearing and a small lake with two campfires reflected in its glassy surface.

A number of men were seated around the campfires, eating. Nearer the lake, horses were grazing in a corral.

The glow of the fires and the light of the rising moon revealed that the clearing was surrounded by tall ash trees, and beneath them stood several log cabins constructed of freshly felled timber.

"This is your hut, and that's Soso. He'll look after you when the Khan's away."

A thickset, middle-aged man had been leaning against the doorpost. He stepped forward hesitantly, with a look of disbelief that accentuated his most salient feature, a prognathous jaw.

"Varya?" he said. "You here? Nobody told me . . ."

"Soso! My God, Soso, what are you doing so far from Georgia?"

Soso bared his strong yellow teeth in a wry smile, looking more bulldog-like than ever.

"My wife, Varya—she finally ran off with a younger man. When I heard that Dunga Khan—"

"Is he here?" Grishin asked quickly.

The girl began to fidget. "Come on, you can talk later."

Soso unslung Grishin's bag from the cantle of his saddle. "She was crazy about you, Varya."

"About me? You're dreaming, Soso. I was only a boy."

"She always did fall for much younger men, but who cares? I'm back with the Khan again, even if I am a long way from Georgia." Soso carried the bag to the door of the hut, then turned and pointed at the sky. "Wait till the moon rises, Varya. You'll see—the moon here is almost as good as a Georgian moon . . ."

The girl had walked on along the edge of the clearing. Another log cabin loomed up before them, much larger than the first. It had a stone chimney with a plume of smoke rising from it. The girl paused outside.

"Give me your horse."

"It's lame," Grishin said. "Riding blindfold isn't easy. I couldn't give the beast much help."

"Just a thorn, probably." She took the bridle, looking at him as she did so. The next moment she started to laugh. It was a strange laugh, carefree as a child's and sensual as a woman's. "A thorn in a man's flesh," she said, "—that's far worse. Don't worry, the horse will be attended to."

She led it away, still laughing. The door of the log cabin opened and steam billowed into the night air. A young woman appeared, a Mongol with slanting eyes and a round face.

"Your bath is ready."

He said nothing and she stood there patiently, looking up at him.

"You are a friend of the Khan's. Friends get a bath—only friends. It will make you feel better, so come."

The outer room was hung with rugs and lit by oil lamps with shades of colored glass. Peering through the steam, Grishin made out two bodyguards seated cross-legged at the entrance to another room screened by a bead curtain. They were Koreans or Chinese, small but wiry men whose faces were a mass of fine wrinkles. Arms folded, they inclined their heads in Grishin's direction.

The hot, humid atmosphere made him more than ever conscious of his fatigue. The slant-eyed girl started to unbutton his jacket.

"What are you doing?"

"I only want to help you."

"Help me how?"

" 'Cloud,' the Khan told me, 'do everything to make Misha comfortable.' " She tittered suggestively.

"Thank you, but no."

"Surely you will not refuse a gift from the Khan. He will be very angry with me. Is that what you want? He can become very angry, the Khan—very, very angry. You have seen him when he is angry, no? Then let me do as he says." She lowered her voice. "I shall

undress you . . . I shall bathe you . . . You will feel good . . .
Cloud knows her business, ask the Khan."

"Where is he?"

A second girl appeared, also an Asiatic, and the two of them
proceeded to undress him. They giggled meanwhile, whispering
together in their own tongue. The first girl handed him a towel and
surveyed his naked body.

"It is just as the Khan said. White skin—white all over. He was
right, the Khan."

They started giggling again, only to be reduced to silence by a
powerful bellow of laughter from the inner room.

"Come in, Misha!"

Grishin parted the bead curtain and made his way inside. Another colored glass lamp was suspended from the ceiling, and
beneath it stood a round wooden tub from which clouds of fra-
grant steam were rising.

A few inches above this pall of vapor Grishin could see the head
of Dunga Khan. The close-cropped hair and beard were grizzled
and the cheeks crisscrossed with a multitude of little furrows, but
the eyes beneath the drooping lids radiated a love of life that some
might have found almost indecent in a man on the threshold of
sixty.

He took one arm from the water and draped it over the edge of
the tub. The arm was robust and sinewy, the shoulder above it far
more muscular and well developed than its counterpart on the
other side, which terminated in a stump.

Grishin, overwhelmed by a flood of memories, was recalled to
the present only for brief moments by Dunga Khan's boisterous
words of welcome.

"Still shy with women, eh, Misha?" The big man squinted at him
over the rim of the tub. "So you didn't drown yourself in the Lena
after all. I always had my doubts—I always knew you were a born
survivor . . ."

●

The last-known photograph of him—more properly, of a boy
named Mikhail Nekrasov—had been taken on the day of his mother's second marriage. Though long out of date, it was reproduced
on posters offering a substantial reward for information leading to
his arrest.

Six months had elapsed before he plucked up the courage to examine one himself. Mikhail listened to the bystanders talking among themselves and overheard their surprised, incredulous remarks. They found it hard to reconcile a child's photograph with the printed text below it, which gave a detailed account of the cold-blooded murder at Baku. Mikhail himself didn't recognize the boy in the photograph, who bore no resemblance to the person he was now. The faded photograph seemed as unreal as the details of the crime itself, which he had expunged from his memory. His sole concession to the past was that he allowed a few people, but only a few, to call him Misha.

He hadn't boarded the Tiflis express, of course, nor had he enrolled at the cadet academy. He never received any further formal education. City streets, cattle cars, railroad stations, municipal parks, rooming houses—those were his school from now on.

Being a sturdy youngster, he was seldom out of a job. He survived by working as a shipboy aboard the barges that plied the Caspian, on tobacco plantations, in vineyards, cement factories, silk mills, grain stores. When he couldn't find work he kept himself afloat by stealing or smuggling. The Caucasus, with its wild and inaccessible mountains, remote upland valleys, and warlike tribes, had long been renowned as a haunt of bandits, smugglers, and rebels.

Dunga Khan led one such band whose exploits were the talk of every village in the area. Mikhail had first met the Khan when Dunga visited his brother Colma at Baku. Then only nine years old, he had felt insignificant and de trop, so he left it to chance whether or not their paths crossed again. He had an iron physique, after all, and the digestion of a young ox: he could fend for himself and survive unaided.

It was hot that August even at Gori, a small town situated beside the Kura in a rugged mountain valley forty miles northwest of Tiflis. Nearly all the inhabitants were Georgians like Mikhail's employer, a blacksmith and hostler responsible for looking after the horses that hauled the imperial mail coaches. His name was Soso—or rather, that was what everyone called him because it was his favorite way of prefacing or concluding a remark.

On the day in question, almost a year after Vadim Nekrasov's murder, the usually phlegmatic Soso was in a state of high excitement. When he set off for Gori station at noon, leading a team of four fresh horses, he forbade Mikhail to accompany him. All he would reveal was that an urgent consignment of cash from the Imperial Bank at Batum was to be transferred from the mail train to a mail coach. The Gori-Tiflis line had been cut that morning, reportedly because a violent summer storm had destroyed one of the bridges over the Kura.

Soso duly set off with his four stout horses, but not before he had currycombed them with more than usual care, given them a double ration of oats, and patted them repeatedly on the neck. His young wife couldn't wait to get him out of the house. "Come into the kitchen with me, Varya, you must be starving . . ." She fanned her flushed cheeks and unbuttoned her blouse. "Come on, Varya, he won't be back for ages . . ."

But Mikhail, alias Varya Kolzov, had sneaked off to the station regardless of Soso's instructions and his young wife's blandishments. When he got there he found it guarded by Gori's entire police force and a detachment of Cossacks. Intrigued by these abnormal security measures, he waited to see what would happen.

The mail train pulled in with a sealed freight car bringing up the rear. The Cossacks promptly threw a cordon around this car while it was uncoupled and shunted onto a siding. They formed an even tighter cordon while sacks and boxes stenciled with the imperial eagle were being transferred to the waiting mail coach. It was a slow and laborious procedure, checking each item, exchanging signatures and receipts, sealing the doors of the coach.

And then everything happened at once. Hand grenades hurtled through the air and exploded among the policemen and Cossacks. The mail coach rocked and skidded perilously as its startled team took off at a gallop, but another grenade stopped the horses in their tracks. Ferocious-looking figures converged from all sides. They unhitched two of the injured beasts and put them out of their misery. Other bandits vaulted onto the box and drove off at top speed while a rear guard held the forces of law and order at bay with rifle fire.

High in the rugged mountains five or six miles east of Gori, a series of interconnected sandstone caves combined to form a subterranean redoubt. One cave served as a makeshift hospital for the casualties of the raid. The proceeds—money destined for the

Imperial Bank at Tiflis, including freshly minted seven-and-a-half-
and fifteen-ruble gold coins—were counted in another. The total
haul amounted to fifty thousand rubles.

On returning to the smithy, where Mikhail was awaiting him,
Soso grudgingly admitted that he was one of Dunga Khan's men.
With equal reluctance, he was persuaded to take Mikhail along to
the caves. At long last, after the wounded had been tended and the
spoils distributed, Soso presented him to the Khan.

"The boy has worked for me for some weeks, Dunga. He—he
saw the raid in progress. He's hell-bent on joining us."

They were standing at the entrance to one of the caves. Dunga
Khan called for a lantern and held it up so that the light fell on
Mikhail's face. Soso, hovering in the background, said hurriedly, "I
told him the decision would be yours . . ."

"Leave me alone with him."

Mikhail heard the others make their way outside, heard them
excitedly discussing the raid with the men guarding the horses. He
himself was quite calm.

"Soso insists on calling me 'the boy,' " he said. "I may be a boy,
but I can do a man's work."

"How old are you?"

The lantern light lingered on his face. "As Varya Kolzov?" he
replied coolly. "Eleven months and ten days old." It was the time
that had passed since the murder.

Dunga Khan lowered the lantern and whistled through his teeth.
"I thought your face was familiar," he said. "Misha Grishin, isn't
it?"

"Grishin, Nekrasov, Kolzov . . . I sometimes wonder *who* I
am."

"And you want to join us?"

Mikhail hesitated. "I'm not sure. I've been managing all right on
my own. I wanted to see Colma's brother again, that's all."

"Go back to Gori with Soso. I'll think it over and you do likewise. Then we'll see."

Three weeks after the raid a horseman turned up at Soso's
smithy leading a spare saddle horse. Five minutes later Mikhail was
on his way into the mountains. Soso felt doubly relieved. Not only
had the Khan forgiven him his indiscretion, but the boy would now
be out of range of his wife's alluring glances. Only a few days later,
Mikhail rode with the Khan's men at Kedabek in the Armenian

highlands when they attacked a wages convoy bound for the Siemens Brothers' copper mines and smelting works.

Mikhail Grishin, alias Varya Kolzov, was a diligent pupil, just as Dunga Khan was a willing and skillful teacher. He knew how men should be led, and the meticulous planning of a raid appealed to him as much as its actual execution. Last but not least, his choice of victims endeared him to ordinary folk. The Khan never robbed private citizens; he preyed only on targets of popular loathing such as banks, foreign-owned corporations, and imperial institutions. To the lower orders and his own men he seemed the embodiment of an age-old dream: the individual's triumph over authority.

Dunga Khan liked his raids to involve the use of grenades and explosives—anything that made a bang. The louder the bang the more it unnerved the enemy, and the lighter their resistance the fewer the casualties. He was always on the lookout for experts in this field, but it too often happened that the bombs and mines they devised failed to go off or exploded prematurely. It was his insistence on being present at one such experiment that had cost him his right arm.

The end, when it came three years later, took everyone by surprise, and it was preceded by one of the Khan's most resounding successes.

Again it was a hot August day, and again the scenario presented classic features: A consignment of paper money was on its way from the imperial mint at St. Petersburg to the Imperial Bank at Tiflis, which overlooked Loris Melikovskiya Square in the center of the Georgian capital. Dunga Khan had stationed his men at various strategic points, and Mikhail had volunteered to drive the haul to a hideout on the city's northern outskirts, following a prearranged route.

Punctually at 10:30 A.M. the imperial mail coach came into view escorted by two troops of cavalry, one in front and one behind. As soon as the coach entered the square, the cavalrymen were scattered by grenades and gunfire. The terrified horses pulling the mail coach broke into a gallop but were brought up short by more grenades. The coachman surrendered, the policeman on the box beside him was shot dead, the soldiers and the rest of the police were held in check by rifle fire while the Khan's men emptied the coach and transferred its contents to Mikhail's waiting wagon.

Several of the escorting troops were killed and fifteen wounded. The attackers sustained no casualties at all.

The size of the haul surpassed all expectations. The hideout in the north of the city was piled high with paper money: three quarters of a million rubles, largely in brand-new five-hundred-ruble bills. It was Dunga Khan's biggest bank robbery ever, and, at that time, the biggest on record.

The members of the gang split up, as they always did after a large-scale raid. On this occasion Dunga Khan had decreed a two-month standstill. In mid-September, however, he was alarmed to hear that one or two of his men had been picked up and detained.

He himself, together with Mikhail and several other associates, had retired across the frontier into Persia and were safely installed at Bandar Anzeli. This Caspian seaport was a major transshipment center for the illegal arms trade, and the Khan intended to return to Russia with a new arsenal of weapons.

Disturbing reports continued to reach Bandar Anzeli, however. More arrests had been made, apparently because the police were being tipped off by an insider, but at the end of September Dunga Khan and his companions decided to return regardless.

Their intended landfall was Lenkoran, the nearest port on Russian soil. They sailed by night in two identical fishing boats, one laden with arms, the other with fish. The boat with the innocent cargo went on ahead. Before long, the prearranged signal came back: nothing suspicious sighted. Lenkoran was, in fact, swarming with police and troops, and the crew of the first boat had been overpowered. An hour later Dunga Khan's party fell into the trap. Before the day was out they were on their way to Tiflis in a heavily guarded train, chained hand and foot.

Although Dunga Khan's men had always lived well, none of them had managed to accumulate much money. It was the Khan himself who purchased arms, ammunition, and horses, bribed informers, and paid doctors to tend the wounded. Discounting the women he kept in his various hideouts, he lived like any other member of the gang—from hand to mouth—so he could hardly have failed to salt away a fortune from the proceeds of his robberies in recent years. His associates sometimes speculated on its size, but none would have dared to quiz him about it.

Anticipating public interest in the case, the authorities at Tiflis had fitted out one of the city's theaters for the occasion. It remained unused. The trial was held in an ordinary courtroom. The sentences, too, did not come up to general expectations. Although they were severe—lifelong banishment to Siberia for Dunga Khan, terms of fifteen to twenty-five years for his confederates—everyone had taken it for granted that the Khan would hang. It was promptly rumored that he had made a deal with the Imperial Bank, but this was never to be proved.

Seventeen-year-old Varya Kolzov—such was the name on his papers, and it never occurred to anyone to connect him with a certain Mikhail Nekrasov, born Grishin—was sentenced on grounds of youth to fifteen years' hard labor in Siberia.

The labor camp known as Bakhanai III was situated at the confluence of the Unjulyung and the Lena, little more than thirty miles from the Arctic Circle. Almost ten miles wide at that point, the Lena was already icebound when the party arrived late that November.

The camp itself, a cluster of crude log cabins beside a bend in the river, was a so-called mixed camp for convicted criminals, exiled revolutionaries of both sexes, and hundreds of Chinese forced laborers. In summer the prisoners, men and women alike, panned for gold on the banks of the fast-flowing Lena. In winter the women chopped firewood while the men dug for gold in the frozen ground.

Mikhail soon realized that a life sentence was tantamount to a death sentence. What with the poor food, a working day that lasted from first light to nightfall, and winter temperatures that could plummet to minus sixty degrees Fahrenheit, Bakhanai III had the highest mortality rate of any camp in the region. Any inmate not carried off by tuberculosis or typhus could expect to die a lingering death from fatigue and malnutrition.

From the first day on, Mikhail's one obsession was to escape while he still had the strength. In May the ice on the Lena began to break up. For two weeks the air was filled with the deafening sound of ice floes grinding together and piling up on top of each other. As the ice melted, so the river overflowed its banks and became wider still.

Early in July, even though Dunga Khan dismissed his scheme as reckless and suicidal, Mikhail broke out of camp. He was recap-

tured a month later and brought back under guard. The Cyrillic
characters branded on his back—the C and the K that now identified him as a Siberian escapee—oozed pus for weeks to come.

The short Siberian summer was drawing to a close. They had
been panning for gold all day long, lashed by an icy wind from the
tundra. Mikhail was standing outside the hut when a female work
party returned from chopping wood escorted by guards as robust
and well fed as the dogs trotting beside them. With their close-
cropped hair, clumsy boots, and baggy, tattered clothes, the fifty-
odd women were as alike as peas in a pod. And then he saw *her*.

She was striding along, head erect, at the front of the column.
She looked slimmer than the rest, and she walked differently, with
a kind of jaunty defiance. The hair escaping from under her fur cap
was long and curly.

He stared at the apparition: her face, her walk, her long auburn
hair—long hair banned by the camp authorities because it ham-
pered women at work and reduced their output by causing accidents; long hair in a place teeming with lice and destitute of soap.
Suddenly, when she was a mere ten yards away, she glanced at
him, whipped off her cap, shook out her hair, and smiled. Then she
was gone.

Mikhail stood rooted to the spot, trembling all over. He had
always been shy with women. Even in the case of Dunga Khan's
camp followers, who slept with one man one day and another the
next, he had always held back and endured his comrades' derision.

And now, here of all places, his diffidence and reserve had fled
and been replaced by an overpowering desire to possess this one,
unknown woman. Only minutes earlier he had been exhausted to
the point of collapse, numb with cold and hunger. His hutmates
had fought like wild beasts over the thin cabbage soup and hunks
of moldy bread awaiting them on their return from work, and the
thought of escape had been uppermost in his mind. All that was
forgotten now. Now, the camp had become transfigured.

He turned to Dunga Khan, who was standing beside him.

"Who is she?" He could hardly speak.

"Our Misha has caught fire at last." The Khan sounded less
jocular than uneasy. "Stamp the flames out quick, Misha, you'll get
burned."

"Do you know who she is?"

"It wouldn't help if I told you."

"So you do know?"

"She's a common whore, that's all."

Mikhail laughed. "Since when have you had anything against whores? What's her name?"

"Anna Rodovna. She worked at a brothel in Yakutsk, a garrison town crawling with army officers, all of them bored to death. Anna was the main attraction. She used to pump officers for information and pass it on to her revolutionary friends. They sentenced her to fifteen years."

"And you call that whoring?"

"She still does it here in camp, but only for profit. One-Ounce Anna, they call her, because that's her price. I tell you, one ounce of gold would see us both halfway to freedom!"

The Khan had already begun to hoard gold. Particle by particle he smuggled it from the river and the mines, past the checkpoints, and into camp, where he concealed it in various hiding places. Month after month he added to his hoard with one idea in mind: Someday he would use it to bribe guards, buy horses and guns.

When winter came, gold had to be blasted out of the icebound soil with explosives. The camp acquired a new commandant, supposedly because his predecessor had been too lax. He inaugurated his reign by stringing up three Chinese coolies whose pockets had been found to contain a pinch of dust with a few grains of gold in it. Their frozen corpses were left dangling on the camp parade ground as a deterrent.

Worried by this development, Dunga Khan continually moved his cache from place to place. Mikhail was neither dissuaded by his warnings nor repelled by what he had told him about Anna Rodovna's background. A man possessed many advantages in the fight for survival; a woman like Anna had nothing but her beauty and sex appeal. He had duly begun to collect his ounce of gold: dust so fine that it had to be swept up with a hen's feather, grains the size of barleycorns, more dust, more grains, sometimes a tiny nugget.

One ounce of gold . . . It assumed the proportions of a mountain in his mind's eye—an icy waste to be traversed, as much of the River Lena to be panned as would fill an ocean. The winter seemed interminable . . .

One morning, water began to drip from the coolies' stiff, ice-encrusted corpses. The floes on the Lena melted. Spring was followed by a short summer notable for its brilliant blue skies, then August, the first biting winds from the tundra, and his birthday. He was nineteen now, with nearly two years in the camp behind him. On the first Sunday in September, the only day of the week when no work was done in the afternoon, he extracted his gold from various nooks and crannies and poured it into his leather tobacco pouch.

He left the hut with the pouch around his neck, tucked away beneath his shirt and jacket. The September sun was shining, devoid of warmth, in a deep azure sky. His mood was half exuberant, half apprehensive. Rumor had it that typhus was raging in the women's sector of the camp.

To reach their huts he had to cross the parade ground, the place where the gallows stood and floggings were administered, but he gave no thought to that now. His thoughts were of a face: fair skin, brown eyes with long lashes, full lips, a mane of auburn hair.

On the far side of the parade ground stood the commandant's quarters, a large log cabin with a tin roof. Smoke was rising into the air, straight as an arrow, from the tall iron chimney. Sentries with dogs stood guard at each of the building's four corners. Muffled singing and laughter could be heard. The sun was already so low in the sky that its orange rays had set the windows aflame.

He had to pass quite close to the hut. When he was only ten yards away the door burst open and the commandant himself emerged, stretching luxuriously. Not a tall man, but so thickset that he almost filled the doorway, he was wearing boots, a pair of black breeches held up by suspenders, and a gray undershirt with long sleeves. Even if he hadn't been holding a bottle by the neck, anyone could have seen he was drunk.

Why should Mikhail have noted all these details? Did he already sense what was going to happen?

The commandant took a step forward, swaying a little. In the act of raising the bottle to his lips, he paused and looked back into the hut.

"Come on out," he called. "Come on, the air's nice and fresh out here."

She appeared in the doorway behind him. Her long hair fell to her shoulders, more luminously auburn than ever in the rays of the setting sun.

The commandant took a pull at the bottle, then offered it to her. She gave a full-throated laugh and shook her head. He laughed back and flung the bottle away. The sun was just above the horizon now, red as a blood orange. He pointed to it. Then he lurched toward her, groped for her.

"Come on, Anna," he said thickly, "let's do it out here. Haven't you ever done it in the open at sunset? You've no feeling for nature, you bitch!"

She gave another full-throated laugh. It was impossible to tell from her voice if she was drunk too.

"Who says so?" she retorted. "I'm a child of nature!"

Did she realize that he was standing there watching? What of the guards, too, and the other onlookers who had been attracted by the commotion?

Anna Rodovna leaned against the wall beside the door of the hut. The bull of a man stationed himself in front of her, gripped her shoulder with one hand, pulled up her skirt with the other. She continued to stand there with her back to the wall. Releasing her shoulder, he slipped off his suspenders. His breeches slid down over his buttocks, and that was how he took her.

He was shorter than she was at the best of times, and his crouching, thrusting stance reduced his height still more. She topped him by a head in consequence, and Mikhail, looking into her eyes, could see that they were alight with triumph.

Back in his own hut he tore a strip off one of the sheets of oil paper that had been stuck to the windowpanes to protect them from the coming frosts of winter. Then he took a pencil stub and wrote:

Don't bother to look for me. I'll be under the ice till spring comes.

Before leaving the hut, he concealed the note and his gold, carefully folded into another fragment of oil paper, in a place where he knew Dunga Khan would find them.

It was dark by the time he reached the river after wading through the marshes that bordered it. The Lena stretched ahead of him in the gloom, an infinity of turbulent, fast-flowing water.

Almost before the cold hit him, before the current swept him

away and sucked him under, before he gagged on the first wave to
break over his head, he had begun to fight for his life . . .

●

After the steam and heat of his bath the air outside was pleasantly cool and pellucidly clear. The moon, occasionally obscured
by clouds, seemed to be promenading at its leisure through the
trees overhead. Soso had been right: It was very like a Georgian
moon, buttercup yellow with an aureole of gold.

"Come, let's eat." Dunga Khan led the way to one of the
campfires.

His two Chinese bodyguards sat down a few feet away with
cavalry carbines across their knees. Even the Khan carried one of
these short-barreled weapons.

"You don't seem very hungry."

"Your men fed me well on the way."

"We live like cows in clover here." Dunga Khan chuckled.
"Every army marches on its stomach, so they say." He looked
Grishin in the eye. "Did you really mean to drown yourself that
time?"

"I don't remember."

"No one in camp gave you a chance."

"I was lucky. Some nomads happened to be out fishing. I was in
their tent when I came to, smeared from head to foot with some
vile-smelling ointment. They swore it had even brought the dead
back to life."

"They move north at that season of the year."

"Yes, I stayed with them all winter and most of the spring. They
hunted seal in the Lena delta and along the coast. At Tiksi I found a
schooner filling its water tanks in the harbor—another sealer, in
fact. The captain was English, most of the crew were Koreans.
They'd lost a man, a Britisher who'd been killed in a tavern brawl
on the waterfront. I inherited his job and his seal knife."

"The sea is seldom ice-free before June."

"Three months, that's all. You spend the whole day on your feet,
skinning seals in a welter of blood, and the salt eats your hands
away. In September, just before the channel froze up, we slipped
through the Bering Straits. I left the ship at Yokohama, exactly a
year after I escaped. The first thing I treated myself to out of my
pay was a Turkish bath."

He omitted to say that the Englishman who had lost his life at Tiksi and been buried at sea was called John Blade. In addition to his knife, Grishin had appropriated his papers, which he found in the dead man's sea bag. John Blade had been four years his senior, but Grishin looked at least four years older than his age. At Yokohama he'd employed a forger to replace Blade's photograph with his own.

Dunga Khan produced the leather tobacco pouch from his pocket. "You've carried this ever since?"

Grishin took it from him. "Was it an ounce?"

"I thought you were crazy when I found that gold."

"I was never able to weigh it, so I couldn't be sure."

"Yes, my son, it was a good ounce."

They fell silent for a while. The moon climbed higher. It was almost full, only three or four days from plenitude.

"The cold, that was what I really hated," said Dunga Khan. "Even now I sometimes feel as if I'm frozen to the marrow. All that cures the sensation is a dip in that tub of mine." He smiled. "The girls distill an essence from the flowers of the bindweed. That's what does the trick, according to them."

"How long were you at Bakhanai III?"

"Four thousand eight hundred and ninety-eight days—thirteen winters. When I think how much gold we must have mined in that time . . ."

Grishin rolled himself a cigarette and waited.

"News travels slowly in Siberia," the Khan went on. "One day we marched back from the mines to find the camp deserted except for a man waving a red flag and shouting something about a storm. A *burya,* a hurricane, had swept the Czar away. There'd been a revolution. He told us it had happened at St. Petersburg six weeks before."

"This was in February of last year?"

"Yes. The commandant and his guards had fled. And listen to this: The last consignment of gold—the whole of the winter's output—had been dispatched from the mines precisely four days earlier. All that was left in camp was what had been mined in the past four days. It was hardly worth stealing." He indicated his Chinese bodyguards. "While the others were getting drunk, the three of us headed for Yakutsk. Anna Rodovna came with us."

Grishin took a smoldering twig from the fire and lit his cigarette.

"I hoped to catch up with the gold there." Dunga Khan gave a rueful laugh. "But all we found at Yakutsk were revolutionaries and red flags. Everyone was making long speeches—they'd all become veteran revolutionaries overnight. Anna Rodovna was the only one who didn't change. She remained what she always had been, a whore."

"The Bolsheviks don't tolerate nuns or whores."

"True. They've probably sent her back to Bakhanai by now. Anyway, we didn't find any gold train—we couldn't even get places on an ordinary train out of Yakutsk. Travel permits were reserved for delegates, Party members, political exiles—privileged individuals of that kind, not common criminals like us—so Chin and Chan and I bought ourselves some horses and guns and decided to found a brotherhood of our own." He began to sing in a surprisingly high-pitched, melodious voice:

> Brothers, my wounds are hurting.
> Brothers, for what did we fight?
> The comrades are making merry.
> Is that why we shed our blood?

Dunga Khan got up, and his diminutive Chinese bodyguards promptly rose to follow him like bisected halves of their giant master's shadow.

The moonlight made all the corraled horses look the same color. The girl Cherry was kneeling beside Grishin's last mount. She got to her feet and came to meet them.

"It was a thorn," she said, addressing the Khan. "Nothing of consequence."

"I hate to see a horse suffer."

She shook her head. "It isn't in pain. Some spider's web ointment and a bandage soaked in gutta-percha should work wonders."

"Shoot the beast if you have to."

"Of course, Khan, but it won't come to that. Your friend will be able to ride it again two days from now."

Dunga Khan had already turned away from the lake and the firelit clearing. Grishin walked beside him with the two bodyguards still following on behind.

The big man shook his head. "I find it more distressing to see a horse in pain or dying than a man."

"You didn't seem too distressed at Gori and Tiflis."

"Not outwardly, perhaps, but that was the aspect of our transactions I liked least."

"Transactions, eh? I don't remember your calling them that in the old days."

"I try to move with the times." Dunga Khan chuckled. "The redistribution of wealth—that was Colma's term for our banditry. You were too young to understand."

"He was my hero. That was good enough for me."

"Colma thought the world was on the brink of a golden age in which all men's dreams would come true. He may have been ten years my junior, but he was a thousand years ahead in his ideals."

"He never managed to convert you, did he?"

"He stopped trying. All he ever discussed with me in the end was money."

"Money? Colma interested in money?"

"Not for himself, for the cause."

"Did you ever contribute to it?"

Dunga Khan hesitated. "I did after his death. The head of his revolutionary cell at Baku came to see me. The movement was a tender little plant, he said, so couldn't I water it a bit?"

"You mean you gave them a share of our loot?"

"Yes, damn it! The men didn't go short, did they? I didn't go short. Anything we didn't spend on ourselves or our equipment went to them, in memory of Colma. I never did enough for him while he was alive."

"How much did you give them?"

"Too much. It went to their heads."

"Is that why we were caught after Tiflis, because you suddenly cut them off without a kopek?"

Dunga Khan laughed. "On the contrary, they got all the big-denomination bills we took—over two hundred thousand rubles. The money was too hot for my liking in any case. However, instead of feeding the bills into circulation gradually, the idiots sent couriers to Stockholm, Berlin, Paris, and London with instructions to change the whole lot on the same day."

"And the banks had the serial numbers?"

"Of course. Those wretched revolutionaries were in deep enough trouble already. They didn't want to swing for a gang of thieves and cut-throats from the Caucasus so they made a deal, the way people do when their backs are to the wall: They sold us out."

The Khan had set off along a well-trodden path leading into the forest. Two sentries appeared as they rounded a bend. One of them was Soso.

"Are there any others left from the old days?" Grishin asked.

"Only a handful."

"How many are you in all?"

"Too many. A hard core of a hundred and twenty men divided into ten detachments."

Neither White nor Red . . . Grishin hummed the tune he'd heard Bibikov sing.

"Neither White nor Red, but gold. The Golden Horde, Misha, that's us." Dunga Khan turned to his two shadows. "Chin, Chan, come here. Show him how much you give for the Revolution."

The pair approached, lithe and slender as boys. One of them held his hand up, and Grishin saw that the little finger was missing. The other pointed to the stump and said, "That much, Khan."

Dunga and his bodyguards burst out laughing. It was a curious mixture of sounds: one deep-chested bellow of laughter echoed by two high-pitched giggles.

"And how much would you give for gold?"

"For gold? All nineteen fingers—*and* our arms and legs." They giggled again and broke into a gleeful little dance. "One day, Khan, we shall be worth our weight in gold."

"I won't be needing you any more tonight," Dunga Khan said. Seeing them hesitate, he added, "This man is my friend. Get some sleep, we leave early tomorrow."

They obeyed reluctantly, with many a backward glance. Dunga Khan watched them go.

"They know the inside of every mine in Siberia," he said. "They came to Russia during the Kolyma gold rush. Some of the best prospectors are Chinese, and Chan is the finest explosives expert I've ever come across." He produced a stick of something from his pocket and bit a piece off. "That's another souvenir of the camp, my bad teeth. The girls doctor this chewing tobacco for me. It's the only thing that kills the pain." He paused. "How much gold did Bakhanai produce, do you reckon?"

Grishin smiled in the darkness. "You've got a one-track mind."

"Thirteen years and five months . . . We must have mined a mountain of it in that time."

The trees had thinned, and the path petered out in a clearing punctuated by rocky outcrops. Visible beyond them was a row of wooden cages. Dunga Khan paused in front of the first. Two dogs were stretched out inside with their heads resting on their paws.

"Soso's been overfeeding you again, eh?" Still chewing his plug of tobacco, the Khan spoke indistinctly. "You're getting lazy." The dogs, big, lean animals of indeterminate breed, scrambled to their feet, excited at seeing their master.

"Idle beasts, lazy Russian mongrels—it's time you earned your keep." Dunga Khan walked on down the line of cages.

"Why don't they bark?" Grishin asked, but the Khan was pursuing his favorite theme.

"Grains, flakes, nuggets—that's how we dug it out of the ground. Now it's all melted down into nice, shiny bars. Four thousand eight hundred and ninety-eight days' worth—I see it all the time, our gold: Chin's gold, Chan's gold, my gold, and an ounce of yours, my friend . . ."

"The dogs—look, they're opening their jaws—why don't they bark?"

"Chan cut their vocal chords." The Khan seemed irritated by this digression.

Grishin was momentarily taken aback. "A useful man, Chan," he murmured.

"I want that gold, Misha—all of it! I want the whole goddamned mountain." Dunga Khan tapped Grishin on the chest. "Did you know that Russia's gold reserves are still intact? The mob stormed the Winter Palace—they burned and looted and destroyed—but they never got at that gold. And now Lenin's sitting on it. He never mined an ounce of gold in his life, our new Czar, but he's sitting on a king's ransom. What's more, he's scared stiff of losing it. He didn't trust the banks at Petrograd, so he took it to Moscow. But it wouldn't have been safe enough for him in the vaults of a Moscow bank either, so he moved it into the Kremlin with him."

"Who says so?"

"Everyone knows I pay well for inside information and never divulge its source." Dunga Khan chuckled. "So tell me, Misha: Where would *you* keep gold if no one place seemed safe enough?

You'd stick it in a vault that was permanently on the move, wouldn't you?''

Grishin stared from the Khan to the caged dogs and back again, thinking hard. Suddenly the events of the past few days fell into place.

"A train?"

"Correct. An armored train, heavily guarded and forever changing direction.''

"How does that help you?''

"The Bolsheviks' territory has shrunk. They've got German armies in the south, White generals and Czechs in the east, Finns and more Germans in the west. What does that leave them? The north —the Severniye Uvaly and the Severniye Urals. That, Misha, is why the moon above us isn't a Georgian moon.''

"I still don't see what you have in mind.''

"Wait. Maybe I'll get a chance to show you before long." Dunga Khan bent down and addressed the occupants of the nearest cage. "Brave bastards, brave Russian mongrels! You won't let me down, will you?''

They walked back in silence. The campfires in the clearing had been extinguished. Horses were grazing quietly, sentries patrolling the edge of the clearing in pairs. Two women appeared, one of them carrying a lantern, and hurried on ahead of the Khan.

"Why did you come, Misha?''

"Moscow was depressing. I needed a change.''

"What have you been doing all these years?''

"Surviving. I learned that from you, among other people.'' Grishin hesitated for a moment. "You're leaving early, you say?''

The big man laughed. "I have my kingdom to attend to.''

"May I ride with you?''

"Chan will wake you.''

The two women had paused outside the door of a log cabin. They were the Asiatic girls from the bathhouse.

"They're nice, gentle creatures, my friend,'' said Dunga Khan. "They know every way there is of soothing a man in mind and body. I cater to my men's needs. A bandit should sleep soundly while he can.''

The girls smiled. Seen by the lantern's dim light, their flowerlike faces and dark eyes exemplified all the beauty of their race. Although Grishin knew he wouldn't sleep, he said, "Make sure Chan wakes me, won't you?"

Inside the hut he found his bag beside a couch heaped with thick, soft furs. He was still awake when the first light of dawn tinged the clearing with gray.

12

The horses were alarmed by the dogs' proximity. They whinnied and twitched their flanks. Grishin had only once before seen horses so nervous, and that was one night in the Caucasian highlands, when they had scented wolves. These dogs were wretched beasts imprisoned in portable cages, but they had not been fed for days and were almost demented with hunger, which might have been what alarmed the horses so much.

The riders kept their mounts on a tight rein and clamped their thighs together to quieten them. They were forty men of all races, all ages, every social background: runaway peasants with broad cheekbones and hands like mattocks; lean, gaunt townsmen, and genuine bandits who had seen the inside of many a prison and committed every conceivable crime. All wore bandoliers and carried guns.

They dismounted, patted the dust from their clothes, and watered their horses. Dunga Khan was wearing a long *cherkeska* in spite of the heat, and his grizzled head was adorned with a faded Chinese skullcap. He was mounted on a gray mare, Chin and Chan rode a pair of shaggy Siberian ponies, and Grishin had been assigned his original horse, now completely recovered from its injury.

It was noon, and the plain near Unshaskoye was shimmering in the white glare of the sun. Riders and horses had taken refuge in an open-sided barn that not only provided shade but was invisible from the railroad track some two miles away, which skirted the Puyachev estate. A lookout sat perched in one of the three trees overlooking the well between the barn and the main house.

The stud farm had been looted and gutted by fire; now only one wing of the house still stood. Grishin had seen dozens of these relics of the Revolution in recent weeks. They dotted the country-side like a plague of boils: derelict mansions with soot-stained window embrasures, scarred walls, painted ceilings riddled with bullet holes, smashed furniture, torn books and photographs, slashed canvases.

The farms and villages in the Land of the Five Rivers, where the Khan held sway, presented a striking contrast with their well-tended fields and orchards, brimming barns and granaries. Grishin had soon realized, however, that Dunga Khan's thoughts—his days-long absences, his mysterious trips by calash to Vyatka, his clandestine meetings with informants—were entirely centered on the gold train.

As the weeks went by, Grishin himself fell prey to the same obsession. Jim Hall had sent him only one message in all this time: Baron von Mirbach, the German ambassador, had been murdered at his Moscow residence. A postscript in cipher informed Vada Nikulin that London was ecstatic, likewise "the banker."

That had been at the beginning of July. Since then silence had prevailed, and since then Moscow had seemed ever more remote.

"The train! The train!"

The words were uttered in a hoarse croak. The lookout at the top of the maple tree had been sweltering in the sun for nearly an hour. He cleared his parched throat and repeated the cry.

Horses pawed the ground nervously and started circling on the spot. Their riders soothed them with clucking noises.

A cloud of dust appeared in the distance. As it drew nearer, Grishin recognized the lone horseman ahead of it as the youthful commander of the patrol that had intercepted him at the Unsha. He brought his sweating horse to a halt in front of Dunga Khan.

"They're coming right enough—your information was correct. They're across the river already."

"A locomotive and a flatcar?"

"An armored locomotive unlike any I've seen before, plus two flatcars and forty or fifty Red Guards. Each car has a machine gun mounted on it. Your friend the Expert can tell you what type."

"We won't get close enough for their machine guns to do them any good."

The young man hesitated. Then he said dryly, "We both have our spheres of command, Dunga Khan. Shouldn't I lead this attack?"

"I don't wish us to lose horses and men for no good reason. This train ride is a foolish demonstration. They know they can't achieve anything by coming here. Their only motive is wounded pride, and wounded pride breeds stupidity."

"Shall I get the men into position?"

"Let me handle this my way," Dunga Khan said impatiently. "What happens afterward is your affair, right? Water your horse and relax in the shade—and tell the lookout to warn us when the train gets within a couple of miles."

Grishin caught a second glimpse of the branding iron hanging from the young man's saddle as he wheeled his horse and rode over to the well. He shouted an order to the lookout overhead, then dismounted and lowered the bucket into the well. Nothing could be heard for a while but the creak of the windlass.

A curious expression appeared on the Khan's face, a mixture of distaste and malicious amusement.

"Had you noticed, Misha? None of my men drank from the well, and some of them crossed themselves before watering their horses at it."

Grishin glanced at the well, the slim young man in his hunting jacket, the branding iron suspended from his cantle.

"Who is he?"

"Hardly an attractive idea, drinking from a well that once contained your father's corpse." The Khan's tone matched his expression. He sounded half repelled, half amused. "I don't know how deep it is, but it can't have been easy, fishing him out. I refer to Puyachev Senior, 'the Old Prince,' as he was known."

Dunga Khan chewed on his tobacco plug, pursed his lips, and spat it out.

"This is rich and fertile country, Misha. Sow a kopek, they say, and you'll harvest a ruble. The Puyachevs owned everything in sight: the grain fields, the horses, the cattle, the peasants—absolutely everything. They employed agents to squeeze the land and the peasants for all they were worth. They themselves visited here once a year at most. The rest of the time they spent at St. Petersburg, in the Crimea, in Paris, Baden-Baden, Monte Carlo. Nikolai was the first Puyachev to run the estate himself. He introduced a lot of improvements. When the Revolution broke out and the family was dispossessed overnight, he was the only landowner in the district to cooperate with the newly elected peasants' committee. He helped them to allocate the land, machinery, buildings, livestock. Everyone was satisfied . . .''

Dunga Khan's horse shied, whinnied nervously, threw back its head, and abruptly froze. They heard a faint hiss, saw a snake gliding through the dust toward it.

Chin and Chan darted forward, but Dunga Khan was too quick for them. He slid from the saddle in one swift, graceful movement. His hand shot out and gripped the reptile just behind the head. Three or four feet long, it was gray with yellow markings. The body writhed briefly. Then it went limp and dangled there, quivering a little as the life drained out of it. Dunga Khan climbed back into the saddle, draped the carcass around his neck, and went on with his story as if nothing had happened. He pointed to a gutted chapel near the ruins of the main house. The tombstones in the little graveyard beside it had been uprooted.

"The Puyachevs didn't live here, but they all insisted on being buried on the estate. The peasants detested the old prince—with good reason, I suspect—and the idea of burying him here was needlessly provocative: It rekindled their hatred. The Party authorities at Vyatka were unhappy enough already about his son's arrangement with the peasants, which conflicted with what they termed 'revolutionary consolidation,' so they sent an agitator to stir things up. He didn't find it difficult. 'They propose to bury this exploiter of the masses in the soil that used to be his, do they? What impudence, comrades! Bury him on *his* land? I thought the land belonged to you now . . .'

"Young Nikolai underestimated what was going on. He tried to reason with the peasants, but they were too infuriated, too carried away, too drunk on the Party's free vodka. They broke open the coffin and dragged his father's rotting corpse from the chapel. After dumping it down the well they ran amok and set fire to everything—destroyed their own property, in other words."

"What about the son?"

"He escaped the old man's fate by the skin of his teeth. When I turned up here, he joined us." The Khan peered around. "Some of those drunken vandals are now under his command."

"What became of the body?"

"I've never asked him."

The lookout's hoarse voice broke in. "The train! Two miles now!"

"Very well, down you come!" Dunga Khan urged his mare out of the barn's shady interior and rode to a knoll some distance away.

Grishin rode after him. Far to his right he could make out the blackened ruins of Unshaskoye, which the Red Guards had burned to the ground after finding it deserted and its granaries empty. Looking leftward along the railroad track, which glinted in the sunlight like two parallel threads of gold, he could just discern some tiny puffs of smoke. The sound of the locomotive came faintly to his ears, carried by the breeze.

"Misha, I'm getting an erection." Dunga Khan laughed, wild with excitement. The snake's carcass slithered from around his neck and fell to the ground. He ignored it.

Nikolai Puyachev, who had followed them, was gazing out across the plain with the immobility of an equestrian statue. His face was dry and smooth as parchment, Grishin noticed, but there was a feverish glint in his brown eyes.

"Shall we go?" he asked in an expressionless voice.

"Divide the men into two groups and station them on either side of the track—and Nikolai, stay out of range of those machine guns. The Red Guards aim to put on a show of strength, but so do I. Until my experiment turns out one way or the other, hold your horses."

The young man's nod was almost imperceptible. "You're the Khan," he said.

"Don't charge those machine guns whatever you do. Cut off their line of retreat and blow up the track if necessary."

The men were already moving out when they got back to the barn. The horses seemed as relieved as their riders to be off at last.

Sudden silence replaced the commotion of the general exodus, the shouts and hoofbeats. Two tall, gaunt Georgians had been looking after the caged dogs throughout the expedition. Apart from them, Grishin himself, and Dunga Khan, only Chin and Chan had remained behind.

At a nod from their master, the Chinese got off their ponies and picked up a long black box with metal handles. Grishin noticed how carefully they lifted it out of the straw and carried it over to the cages. The four dogs panted and whimpered as the Georgians released them one by one.

Kneeling down, Chin and Chan spoke soothingly in their own singsong tongue. The animals licked their faces and lay down obediently with their forepaws extended. What Grishin had mistaken at a distance for yellow fur turned out to be jackets specially designed with pockets in the sides, each big enough to accommodate a sizable explosive charge.

"Good dogs, plucky little bastards . . ." Dunga Khan might have been translating the Chinese words for Grishin's benefit. "Easy, easy, you'll soon fill your bellies . . . There's a regular feast waiting for you. All you have to do is go and get it."

Chin removed the round gray sticks of dynamite from the box; Chan inserted them in the pockets, three bundles a side, and secured the flaps.

"Ready, Khan." Chan looked up, his slanting eyes alight with anticipation.

"What about the detonators?"

Chan shook his head. "Not here, Khan, not yet. Trust Chan."

Once more they emerged from the shade of the barn and rode out into the blinding sunlight. Chin and Chan entrusted their ponies to the Georgians and set off on foot. They kept well ahead of the others, each holding a pair of dogs on long leashes.

The train, a big black locomotive hauling a tender and two flatcars crowded with Red Guards, had drawn nearer. Suddenly the puffs of vapor from the smokestack dwindled and became a stationary haze: The train had come to a stop.

The sun continued to beat down. Grishin had a fanciful notion that, if only they waited long enough, the metallic monster—like some oversized beast—would shrivel up and die. He reached for the canteen slung from his pommel.

The two Chinese had halted fifty yards ahead. Dunga Khan dismounted.

"No, Khan, no closer! Stay where you are."

Chin and Chan repeated their performance of a few minutes earlier. They squatted down beside the dogs, talking softly and persuasively as they connected the detonators. The firing mechanisms, which had taxed Chan's ingenuity to the full, were activated by thin metal rods designed to set off the charges when bent at a critical angle by coming into contact with an obstruction overhead.

Dunga Khan turned to Grishin with glowing eyes. "You see how hungry they are? They haven't had a square meal for days, but they know they need only crawl beneath a locomotive to find food—

that's what we've trained them to do." He looked at the dogs. "Don't let me down, you poor bastards."

Grishin saw Chin and Chan remove the leashes and straighten up. The four animals hesitated for a moment, then darted off.

They remained bunched together for the first few yards, neck and neck, steel rods whipping to and fro. Then they diverged. Running at full stretch, they raced along the furrows of the field that lay between them and the railroad track, four yellow dots trailing four plumes of dust.

They had covered nearly two hundred yards, a third of the distance, when the Red Guards spotted them. Rifle shots rang out, crisp and staccato, and little fountains of dust sprang up at the points of impact. The men on the flatcars had the sun in their eyes, and the speeding dogs were no easy target.

The first explosion came like a bolt from the blue. One of the yellow dots vanished in a cloud of dust and smoke.

Chin covered his face in his hands and groaned, but the Khan's excited bellow silenced him.

"That still leaves three!"

Then came another flash, another detonation, another mushroom of dust and smoke—so close to the train this time that it was momentarily obscured from view.

The last two explosions followed an instant later. The bulky black monster straddling the rails was lifted bodily into the air and engulfed by a dazzling fireball.

When the dust settled they saw the shattered locomotive lying on its back, wheels uppermost, and beside it, where the track had been, a crater with scorched sides. Dark, inert forms littered the embankment, but a score of uninjured Red Guards were running away.

"Plucky little bastards!"

Although the Khan's eyes were still shining exultantly, Grishin detected a preoccupied look on his face, as if his thoughts were already elsewhere.

Chin and Chan clapped their hands and uttered jubilant cries in a mixture of Chinese and Russian. Grishin caught the odd word.

"The gold train, Khan—now for the gold train!"

A tall column of smoke continued to hang over the site of the explosion. Some of the surviving Red Guards were making for the river; others, overcome with panic, had stopped short and discarded their rifles in readiness for surrender.

The two detachments of horsemen were already on the move. Like the dogs, they kept together for a while before fanning out and cutting off the fugitives' line of escape. As the net drew tighter, so the first shots rang out. The bandits were adept at firing from the saddle.

Abruptly, the Khan turned away. "Everyone claims to be fighting for some kind of cause," he said, "but all it amounts to is looting and killing. That's Russia for you."

"Why so moody?" Grishin said. "You should be feeling good."

The furrows in the big man's face were awash with sweat. He screwed up his heavy-lidded eyes against the sunlight.

"Sooner or later, Misha, they'll beat us. Sooner or later they'll scatter us like chaff. Our numbers will dwindle. We'll recruit some men and lose others, but our losses will outnumber our gains. Our territory will shrink, little by little."

"Russia's a big country, Khan."

"I spit on Russia!" Dunga Khan's eyes widened, and something of their usual sparkle returned. "You're right, though: a bandit can always make himself scarce—it's no disgrace, is it? Other mountains, another moon, another encampment . . ." He gazed across the sun-baked plain to where the wooded highlands brooded on the distant skyline. "The wide blue yonder, that's the only country for the likes of us."

He wheeled his horse and spurred it into a brisk gallop. It was all the Georgians and his bodyguards could do to keep pace with him.

Grishin brought up the rear, his eyes on the purple hills.

❖ PART THREE

August 1918

13

"**Y**our vote, Comrade Valentinova—may we have your vote now?"

The room where the Twelfth Tribunal sat in judgment was cool and spacious, but Lena felt unbearably hot. Her throat burned whenever she swallowed. I'm getting a fever, she thought. Let's hope it isn't typhus.

"A simple 'guilty,' comrade, or is that too much to ask of you?"

Martov was his usual unruffled self. A man of fifty with a bland, clean-shaven face and an engagingly gentle voice, he never bullied or hectored.

She cleared her throat, still incapable of replying. The two other members of the tribunal had already joined Martov in voting for a conviction, so nothing could save the woman prisoner now. The expression she turned on Lena was less reproachful than inquiring. Explain the charge, it said. Do I really stand accused of suspected espionage?

The prisoner's husband, a regular army officer in the Czar's service, had been dragooned into the Red Army by law and sent to the Kazan front. He had deserted to the Whites at the first opportunity. His wife had neither known of his intention nor been in touch with him, having parted from him months ago "for personal reasons."

Lena looked up and said, "I abstain."

She saw Martov stiffen. He removed his glasses, polished them on the sleeve of his jacket, and nodded to the court stenographer, a thin youth with a sallow complexion.

"Comrade Valentinova abstains."

Martov then delivered the verdict and passed sentence—twelve months in a penitentiary plus three years' deprivation of the right to reside in Moscow—in his quiet, dispassionate voice. Once the guards had led the woman away, he sat back and sighed.

"You've been sitting with us for five months now, comrade, and all our verdicts to date have been unanimous." He studied Lena closely. "There's nothing wrong, I trust?"

Should she ask him to adjourn the session? She surveyed the courtroom, formerly the ballroom of a mansion in the Sushchev-skaya district, but said nothing.

The judges sat at a long table. On the wall behind them, framed by folds of drab gray cloth, hung a portrait photograph of Comrade Lenin. The accused stood behind a wooden rail screwed to the parquet floor. There were no chairs or benches for defending counsel or witnesses. The Extraordinary Tribunals had replaced the "old, corrupt judicial system," and their rules of procedure were simple in the extreme: The chief judge and the public prosecutor were one and the same person.

Every urban district had its own tribunal. Lena Valentinova, being a Party member, had been elected an associate judge by her local section. No one ever declined such an appointment, nor had she felt uncomfortable in her role for quite some time. Burglary, theft, robbery with violence, drug dealing, speculation, murder—all these had increased alarmingly in post-Revolutionary Moscow, and ninety percent of the tribunal's cases had fallen into that category. Of late, however, there had been a sharp increase in the number of political cases brought before it. The situation being critical, the tribunal was expected to be more critical in its approach. It had, in Martov's words, to "suppress any feelings of compassion, laudable in themselves though these may be." There were even some who charged the Sushchevskaya tribunal with excessive leniency and pointed to other tribunals whose members proceeded with "exemplary severity" against those who "jeopardized the achievements of the Revolution."

"Here, drink some of this."

Martov filled a glass from the carafe.

"Thanks. I'll be all right."

"We have one more case to try, comrade."

He looked through his papers. She knew he was doing so only to give her time. Martov scarcely needed to refresh his memory, he was always so well prepared. He headed the State salt monopoly, and malicious tongues whispered that, because the Bolsheviks had no salt mines left in the territory under their control, he had plenty of time to spare for perusing files.

"It's quite straightforward, comrade. You'll have no grounds for abstaining this time. May we proceed?"

She nodded. Perhaps she was only looking for an excuse, she thought as Martov called out the defendant's name. It wasn't Martov and the cases that had changed, but she herself, prompted by a wholly unimportant, selfish, bourgeois emotion. She had been irritable and discontented ever since Yevgeny left Moscow. Why did she continue to torment herself with that humiliating desire to hear his voice, feel his touch, have him beside her in the flesh, share her bed with him? She wrenched her mind back to the matter in hand.

The accused was a man of forty or thereabouts. He looked puny beside the two sturdy guards flanking him. What with his dark, wavy hair, floppy cravat, and frock coat, he seemed at pains to convey an "artistic" impression. Lena privately forecast that this would earn him a black mark with Martov.

The guards escorted him to the rail. He swayed for a moment when they stepped back, almost as if he missed their support. When he rested his slender hands on the rail, Lena noticed that the nails were badly bitten—something else that Martov would hold against him.

"You're already acquainted with the indictment," he began. "Fostering anti-Soviet sentiment, engaging in anti-Soviet agitation, disseminating criminal rumors about Comrade Lenin and others, making false and slanderous statements to enemies of the people for financial gain . . . State your name for the record."

The defendant stood there stiffly with his chin tucked in. Looking more closely, Lena saw that he adopted this curiously rigid stance to conceal an unsightly goiter.

"Your name," Martov repeated.

"Voroshin, Konstantin Nikolaevich."

"Age?"

"Forty-four."

"Occupation?"

Voroshin coughed. "Wigmaker."

"Louder, please."

"Wigmaker."

"I didn't know there was any demand for such persons in our socialist society. Your address?"

"At the moment—"

"Yes, I know. At the moment you're in custody at the local jail."

"Petrovskaya, Block 7, Staircase L, Apartment 271."

"The number of your house committee?"

Voroshin coughed again and tweaked his cravat.

"No house committee," Martov dictated for the stenographer's benefit. "No Moscow resident's permit, no regular occupation, no ration cards. Tell me, Voroshin, what do you live on?"

"I used to have a certain, well—income."

"Earned income?"

"There's not much call for a wigmaker's services at present, not a theatrical wigmaker."

"When your room was searched, the following sums of money came to light: four hundred French francs, twenty American dollars, and twenty-four pounds sterling. In other words, Konstantin Nikolaevich Voroshin, foreign currency to which you had no legal entitlement."

"Yes, but . . ."

"But what?"

Voroshin thought for a while, then shook his head.

"You moved to Moscow from Petrograd five months ago, at the end of March. At the same time, be it noted, as Comrade Lenin and the government."

"From Viborg, actually. I worked in Petrograd, at the Mariinsky —the Mariinsky Theater," Voroshin added proudly.

"So we're led to believe."

"As wigmaker to the Mariinsky, I worked for all the greatest actors. The wigs for all the leading roles were made by me." Voroshin had found his voice and was looking more confident now. He even stopped plucking at his cravat.

"You also owned a shop."

"A studio," Voroshin amended.

"Where you manufactured wigs?"

"Yes."

"For workers?"

"Well, not exactly . . ."

"I have here a list of your customers. Would it be true to say that they all belonged to the property-owning class?"

"What with materials and labor, a good wig—"

"Would have been beyond the means of an ordinary worker, is that what you were going to say? Or were you going to tell us that a worker would have felt too much of a fool, parading around in a wig? That brings us to your absurd lies." Martov's voice rose by several decibels. "Lies and slanderous allegations about men who live like ordinary workers, eat and dress like workers, toil day and night for the good of the country—and all for a worker's wage! It was at Petrograd that you first began to spread ridiculous rumors about Comrade Lenin, among others. You had the effrontery to claim that Lenin, Comrade Vladimir Ilyich, wore a wig!"

"Yes, of course—that's to say, I made it myself."

"You made it yourself? For Comrade Lenin?"

"Yes."

Martov sighed. "For what leading role?"

"To help him escape from Petrograd."

"Really?" The sarcasm in Martov's voice was withering.

"Yes, in July of last year. Kerensky and the provisional government intended to charge him with high treason, so he had to lie low."

Martov sat back in his chair with a pitying smile. "You met with Comrade Lenin in person, of course?"

"Yes indeed. He was hiding out at the home of a carpenter who also worked for the Mariinsky. It was the carpenter who sent for me."

"To make a wig for Comrade Lenin?"

"He needed a false passport to get him across the border into Finland, so he had to have a photograph taken."

"Kindly describe it."

"The wig?"

"No, don't bother, we already have your signed deposition on the subject. I quote: 'A gray wig that came down low over his forehead.' Why gray?"

Voroshin looked puzzled for a moment. "I suppose he wanted to look older than his age."

"You actually saw Comrade Lenin wearing this wig?"

"Of course. I had to make sure it fitted. Even if you take accurate measurements—"

Martov thumped the file in front of him.

"That's enough! I never thought you'd dare to repeat that ludicrous story here." He glared around the room. "First a wig for Lenin, then a false beard for Comrade Kamenev prior to a meeting of our Party's Central Committee—a meeting at which the very future of our country was to be decided. According to your testimony, Prisoner Voroshin, all the members of the Central Committee turned up at that meeting in wigs, false beards, false mustaches. Can anyone here imagine a more ridiculous fabrication? Can anyone conceive of a crime more heinous than the exposure of our country's leaders to scorn and derision?"

The courtroom was hushed. No one expected Voroshin to utter a word in his defense, but he did.

"That's how it is with such stories—people *enjoy* hearing them. It was the same at the Mariinsky. They never tired of listening to my little anecdotes about Chaliapin and Monachov and Madame Gorky."

Martov turned to the other members of the tribunal. "You see? He'd struck gold, our Citizen Voroshin. He was now a celebrity himself: wigmaker to Lenin! He duly proceeded to exploit his vein of gold. He gave interviews to the foreign press. He accepted payment in foreign currency. When Lenin and the government moved to Moscow, so did he, because that was where the source of his ill-gotten income now lay." Martov rounded on the accused. "James Turner . . . Does that name ring a bell?"

"I'm not sure."

"With *your* memory for detail? You're unaware that Mr. Turner is an Englishman who writes for *The Times* of London?"

"You may be right—yes, I remember now."

"Did he pay you for a story about Comrade Lenin?"

"Everyone's interested in Lenin, and so little is known about him. He proposed to write an article and needed information."

"And so, not being in possession of any facts, you told him these outrageous lies!" Martov produced a clipping from his file. "I quote: 'According to information received from a man on intimate terms with the new Russian czar—"

"On intimate terms? No, I never said that, and I certainly never called him our new czar."

"You saw the article?"

"I can't read English."

"I have here an accurate Russian translation of Mr. Turner's fairy tale, Voroshin. According to you—"

"Comrade Martov," Lena broke in.

"Comrade Valentinova?" Martov's tone was amiable. "You think we've heard enough? I agree with you. The tribunal has already devoted more than enough time to this individual and his anti-Soviet agitation."

"The basis of the indictment," she said, "is the story of the wig. The accused has testified that he was summoned to Lenin by a carpenter at the Mariinsky Theater." She leafed through her papers. "His name is Viktor Kluyev. He's a Party member of long standing, Comrade Martov—a man to be trusted."

"Well?"

"I see his name on file, but no affidavit. Hasn't he been questioned about the case? He could either corroborate the defendant's story or refute it."

Martov smiled thinly. "Why don't we consult Comrade Lenin himself?"

"Yes, why not? In view of the severity of the sentence you'll probably impose—"

Martov cut in. "I'm being very patient with you today, comrade." He turned to the prisoner. "You state that you subsequently attempted to see Comrade Lenin."

"Yes, I did."

"For what purpose?"

"I hoped he would help me. My application for a Moscow resident's permit had been turned down. 'You mustn't hesitate to ask me if you ever need help'—that's what he told me at Viborg."

"It was a promise, you mean?"

"I wouldn't let him pay for the wig."

"I repeat: Are you implying that Comrade Lenin made you a promise and failed to keep it?"

"I only know I was refused admittance."

"You tried to see him at the Kremlin?"

"Yes."

"And later at Gorky?"

"I thought I stood a better chance there. He mightn't have been so busy."

"So Lenin refused to see you on both occasions, at the Kremlin and at Gorky, in spite of his promise? You also claim to have written to him. 'Up to a dozen times,' you say in your statement."

"Or thereabouts, yes. I couldn't think of any other way—"

"To remind him of his promise?"

"Yes."

"Comrade Lenin never made any such promise! Why not? Because he never met anyone named Konstantin Nikolaevich Voroshin—because it never even occurred to him to slink out of Petrograd wearing a wig."

Voroshin stood there with his head tucked in, tortoiselike. His cravat had come undone, exposing the goiter beneath. He struggled to retie it, but his hands were trembling too much. He was clearly frightened now. His lips moved, but no sound emerged.

"Well, have you anything more to say?"

Voroshin looked up at the photograph on the wall above Martov's head; he said nothing.

"Are you deaf?"

Voroshin bowed his head as if the photograph itself had dashed his last remaining vestige of hope—as if he had vainly expected Lenin to sprout a gray wig.

When Martov next spoke, he might have been addressing a courtroom filled to capacity with avid spectators, not merely his fellow judges, two guards, and the prisoner.

"We have heard enough," Martov boomed. "The Revolution will not be thwarted by puppets and parasites like you, Konstantin Nikolaevich Voroshin. At a time when the Party and the country were beset by dangers of the greatest magnitude, you saw fit to spread lies and panic and ally yourself with that section of the international bourgeoisie which is striving to overthrow our system by force. There is no room here for men like you—for agents of foreign powers intent on undermining the state. In the case of crimes such as yours, this tribunal has not only the right but the duty to impose the supreme penalty. We shall now take a vote." Martov looked at Lena. "You first, comrade."

"I request an adjournment."

"I see no reason." His eyes were expressionless. "This time, presumably, the vote will be unanimous. Well, comrade?"

She felt bemused and exhausted when it was all over—ashamed, too, even though hers had been the only dissenting voice. She could still see Voroshin standing there, puzzled and incredulous at first, then numb with shock and deathly pale. He just managed to retie his cravat before the guards wheeled him around and marched him out.

Martov had nodded to her at the same moment, taken her by the arm, and steered her to a small door at the back of the court-room. The suite of rooms beyond it had not been converted into Party offices but used as a dumping ground for any effects and objets d'art not considered valuable enough to inventory and re-move from the premises. The room Martov chose for their inter-view might have been a junk dealer's warehouse; they could barely move for statues, mirrors, stacked furniture, crates of china and books.

Martov bent over one of the crates and pulled out a piece of old lace. Having eyed it with disdain, he dropped it on the floor and brushed the dust off his fingers.

"Your attitude, comrade, is as outmoded as that thing there, and it's time you admitted it."

"But a death sentence! You must be out of your mind!"

It surprised her to hear her voice at all, it was so faint and hoarse. The mere effort of saying "Not guilty" seemed to have used up all her energy.

Martov shook his head. "Your ideals do you credit, but they're out of date. I advise you to sleep on your verdict. Tomorrow you can ask me to amend the record."

Another shiver ran down her spine. She couldn't make up her mind if she was feverish or simply afraid.

"I'm convinced he was telling the truth."

Martov shrugged. "Would it allay your sentimental misgivings to learn that Comrade Lenin has expressed an opinion on the case?"

"There was nothing about it in the file."

"Nevertheless, I took the trouble to ask Comrade Lenin for a written statement."

"But the file—"

"His reply was, and I quote from memory: 'In all honesty, Comrade Martov, I feel disinclined to intervene in this matter. I am satisfied that you, being a veteran Party member, a guardian of the law, and a conscientious president of the Twelfth Extraordinary Tribunal, will arrive at the only right and proper verdict without any prompting from me. The Kremlin, August 12.' Does that clear your head, comrade? From now on, I trust you'll vote with the majority."

"I shall resign."

"Think it over first."

"I shall submit my resignation in writing, Comrade Martov."

His eyes were cold and speculative now, like those of a doctor weighing a patient's chances of survival. He kicked a cardboard box. "Trash, rubbish, abandoned property. Why should we bother about such things—why should we jeopardize our authority for the sake of a few obsolete ideas? Don't lag behind the others, comrade. Stay with the herd."

"Or the wolves will pick me off?"

"Don't look at me like that. I'm not the butcher you seem to think. These are critical times. The enemy is at the gate—the whole situation is poised on a knife edge." He chuckled. "Tomorrow, we ourselves could be swinging from a lamppost. Human life has never counted for much in Russia, comrade. It didn't under the Czar, so why under us?"

Impelled by a craving for fresh air, Lena hurried to the door and out of the building, only to be enveloped in the heat of a sultry August day. Her legs felt like lead, her body oozed sweat from every pore.

Some workmen were busy stacking sandbags in front of the windows, presumably in preparation for street fighting. They paused for a moment, startled by the sound of a motor vehicle backfiring as it turned out of the lofty gateway into the street. It was one of the black vans with barred windows used for transporting convicted prisoners to their places of detention. The Muscovites called them "Black Ravens." Blue smoke gushed from its tailpipe, contaminating the air with a stench of low-grade gasoline.

Lena passed few pedestrians, saw no lines outside the food stores. She didn't seem to be walking along the street so much as floating down a long, empty tunnel of pure heat. The only sound she registered was the tramp of marching feet. A company of Red Guards was proceeding in the direction of the railroad station, bound for the Kazan front.

She felt better when she got to Red Garden. She sipped a glass of tea substitute, her tension gradually subsiding. At the entrance to the double row of booths and stalls, Zorim the gopak dancer was juggling with knives to the strains of a balalaika. She joined the little knot of spectators.

The music speeded up. The dancer's movements accelerated too. He brought the performance to a whirlwind close, tossed his knives into the air, and caught them in quick succession. Lena felt herself stiffen suddenly. Whether or not her imagination was playing tricks, she had the distinct impression that someone was coming up behind her. Her heart beat faster from fear or excitement, she couldn't tell which. She found it physically impossible to turn around.

The balalaika had struck up again. Someone just behind her began to hum the melody. The voice was deep and almost inaudible, but her senses were attuned to it. No one else could have heard that voice; it was meant for her ears, her body, alone. At last she turned.

The tanned, lean face was fringed with a week-old beard. Recognition dawned slowly.

"Is it really you?"

"I happened to be passing." The words were little more than a whisper. He ran a hand over his beard. "I need a shave. Know where I can get one?"

She took a step toward him and rested her head against his chest. "I've missed you like hell."

He said nothing, just put his arm around her shoulders. He left it there as they crossed the street, walked along it to her apartment house, and climbed the stairs to the top floor.

There was a slip of gray paper pinned to her door, an official notice rubber-stamped by the Sushchevskaya district council. It was nothing alarming or unusual, merely an announcement to the effect that, in compliance with some new regulation, the electricity would be cut off from 9 P.M. on.

•14•

Grishin had been back in Moscow since that morning. He had already kept an appointment with Jim Hall, who had telegraphed Unshaskoye stating the time and place: twelve noon at Vaganskoye Cemetery, a huge burial ground in the northwest of the city.

Groups of mourners were standing in line outside the main gate, a monumental edifice which itself resembled an ostentatious memorial to the dead. Once inside the octagonal cemetery, they slowly dispersed in all directions. The long, straight central thoroughfare was flanked by rows of ugly tree stumps—all that remained of an avenue felled for firewood the previous winter.

Grishin tagged on to a large funeral procession. The coffin, a child's casket of unvarnished deal, was being trundled along on a simple handcart. He followed the mourners when they turned off down one of the narrow paths that converged on the avenue and halted in front of a freshly dug grave with a mound of peat-dark soil beside it. Grishin noticed many such graves, all of them only a few days old and all marked with plain wooden crosses.

For a moment he'd felt tempted to seek out the mass grave in which the victims of the Czar's coronation largesse at Khodynka Field lay buried, but twelve o'clock was fast approaching. He set off in search of the grave Hall had specified.

He found it in an older part of the cemetery. The plots were family plots and the tombstones more imposing—indeed, many were miniature mausoleums. At Vaganskoye the class system had yet to be abolished.

Grave 37 in Row M was a recent addition. The plinth at the head supported a white marble figure in the shape of a female angel with a pair of tiny wings sprouting from her shoulders. The date of death was given as November of the previous year. Grishin calculated that the woman in question, Dagmara Fyodorova, must have been only twenty-eight when she died. Unlike most of the neighboring graves, this one was adorned with fresh flowers. Someone had laid a bunch of chrysanthemums at the angel's feet.

Grishin heard footsteps approaching and turned. It was Jim Hall, elephantine body bursting out of a white linen suit, moonface crimson with sunburn. He looked exhausted.

"This heat!" He displayed the backs of his hands, which were covered with little white blisters. "I'm like that all over." He gave Grishin a clumsy pat on the arm. "So you made it. It's good to see you again."

"I only got in this morning."

"Summers in Moscow are as extreme as everything else in this godforsaken country. The Russians don't know the meaning of moderation. Imagine kicking the bucket at this time of year! They don't even possess a crematorium."

"Why pick this place if you find it so depressing?"

"I thought it might cheer me up to see how many of our Russian comrades are biting the dust."

"I didn't know you were a cynic."

"I'm not, that's the trouble. Come on, maybe we can find a spot of shade somewhere."

He led the way, plodding along on short, sturdy legs. His white linen suit was crumpled, the back of the jacket bisected by a streak of sweat.

Funeral processions were still filing through the main gate, streaming down the avenue, fanning out along its tributaries. Hall paused beneath a young maple tree and eyed Grishin's tanned face resentfully.

"You never peel, do you?"

"Not since I was a boy."

Hall gestured at their surroundings. "They promised conditions would improve in the summer, when harvest time came, but they've gone from bad to worse. Typhus is raging, people are dying like flies. Disease and malnutrition are carrying them off faster than the Reds can shoot them—and they're shooting plenty just to stay in power."

"You really did pick the wrong spot."

"No, it's perfect—it makes me even madder at them. The goddamned Bolshies could have done this country a good turn. Instead, they've gone and ruined everything." Hall gave a wry smile. "But I'm neglecting my duties—I'd better fill you in. First, they finally put paid to the Romanovs, did you know? The Cheka slaughtered them—Czar, Czarina, kids, and all."

"I haven't noticed any peasants weeping, Jim."

"It isn't generally known yet. Point number two: The Czechs have captured Kazan. If they succeed in crossing the Volga there'll be nothing between them and Moscow but open country. Third, there are the landings. The Americans and Japanese have occupied Vladivostok and the French have put troops ashore on the Black Sea coast. Our own chaps have landed at Murmansk and Archangel, but that still leaves a lot of questions unanswered. How far have they advanced? How many men do we have up there, ten thousand—or a hundred thousand, as some people say? I'm completely in the dark. I can only try to guess what's happening from the Reds' reactions."

"Aren't you in touch with London?"

"Not directly. The Cheka turned up within hours of the news reaching Moscow. I'd been tipped off, so I managed to burn my codes and secret papers. They arrested over two hundred French and British nationals and closed the consulates down. We were released twenty-four hours later, but my code books were destroyed." Hall drew the back of his hand over his perspiring brow. "I presume they lost their nerve. First reports spoke of a hundred thousand British troops. The sky was blue, like today, but it turned black with smoke. The Bolshies were burning their records in a panic."

Grishin shrugged. "I don't know why you're looking so down in the mouth. The news could be a lot worse."

"News? Rumors, you mean. One person has it on good authority that the Reds intend to abandon Moscow and withdraw to the Urals. Never, says someone else. They're going to defend Little Mother Moscow to the last man—the imperialist invaders will find less here to gloat over than Napoleon did."

"So why have I been recalled?"

"It's to do with your assignment."

"What assignment?"

"Your man, John. I've seen it again and again since I've been here: Somehow, he always manages to turn a hopeless situation to his advantage."

"I see." Grishin smiled. "You mean you're untying my hands at last?"

"Untying them? Possibly. London hasn't formally declared war, but our troops are on Russian soil. That's an act of war. First they arrest us all. Twenty-four hours later we're back on the street again. Why? Lenin must have some kind of card up his sleeve, but what?"

"What am I expected to do with my hands tied?"

"I could tell you they're untied, but it isn't as easy as that."

"Oh?" Grishin was feeling uneasier by the minute.

"Everything's set for a coup d'état."

"Really? Tell me more."

"All the Bolshevik leaders are to be arrested at one fell swoop." Hall eyed Grishin steadily, trying to gauge his reaction. "Hell, it wasn't my idea. I detest it when amateurs butt in, but fair's fair: Fleming's mysterious friends delivered the goods. They murdered the German ambassador right enough."

"I know, I got your message."

"Our banker has had the bit between his teeth ever since—it's been one secret meeting after another. There's only one thing missing."

"And that's where I come in?"

"Not exactly. They can't launch a coup without an alternative government. A new premier, foreign minister, minister of the interior, et cetera."

"How closely are you involved?"

"I'm just their paymaster."

"You still haven't told me why I'm here, Jim."

"Everything depends on whether they can put Lenin out of action."

"And can they?"

"All the Reds' troops are on the Kazan front, down to the last cripple. The barracks are empty—except for Berzin's Lettish Rifles. You remember Alexander Berzin? The plan is to arrest Lenin and his cronies on a Thursday, when the Central Committee meets. Instead of shooting them, it's proposed to put them on trial—stage a nice, big show trial and wash their dirty linen in public. Shooting them would only make martyrs of them." Hall grinned. "There's even a suggestion that Lenin and the rest should be marched across Red Square in their shirttails for the delectation of a jeering mob."

Grishin frowned. "What about London? Are they in on this?"

"It's the usual form. If the scheme works, they'll take the credit. If not, they'll feign total ignorance."

"And Colvin?"

"Colvin's waiting to see which way the cat jumps."

"That leaves you, Jim." Grishin was worried by the fat man's obvious misgivings. "I've never known you to run an agent blindfolded before. Why not come clean with me?"

"It's Fleming. He makes me nervous."

"Why?"

"Because he's an outsider, a banker playing the part of an agent. His plan seems watertight enough. It's always worth keeping a weather eye open, though, and four eyes are better than two."

"You think the group's been infiltrated?"

"Not necessarily, but it might be worth checking to see if there's a weed or two growing in Fleming's rose garden."

Hall groped in the pocket of his baggy suit and pulled out a pack of cigarettes.

"In here you'll find a list of Berzin's leading associates—what London refers to as the shadow cabinet—though they prefer to call themselves the Credit Group." Hall spoke with renewed assurance. Even his suit seemed suddenly to fit him better. "The final meeting is scheduled for a week from today. That's when they hope to settle a few outstanding points and sign an agreement."

"A written agreement?" Grishin raised his eyebrows.

"Yes, dealing with economic matters—reparations, concessions, that sort of thing. There's a banker at work here, don't forget. The meeting is on August 29. 'Foreclosure Day' will be a week after that." Hall grinned. "Sorry about the financial terminology, but that's their code name for the great day."

Grishin nodded and put the cigarettes in his pocket. "Where's this meeting to be held?"

"At a dacha outside the city. I've given you a note of that too."

"One thing, Jim: Has Fleming mentioned this business to Lena Valentinova?"

"I doubt it. If the coup succeeds he'll be the hero of the hour. He wouldn't want to risk an anticlimax by telling her prematurely."

"All right, I'll take a look around." Grishin's somber face broke into a smile of genuine amusement. "You got your way in the end, didn't you?"

"Meaning what?"

"Meaning we're back in harness together."

"No harm in that, is there?"

Hall set off down the path between the graves without another word. They came out into the central avenue just beside the funerary chapel.

The west door was open. As they passed it Grishin saw that the nave was crowded, possibly because a funeral service was in progress, or because the chapel housed a celebrated icon, the Sacred Virgin of Voha. Even the forecourt teemed with mourners or worshippers. Two priests were stationed on either side of the portal, each holding an icon for the benefit of those unable to get in. The men, women, and children filing past them paused for a moment, knelt down, kissed the icons, kissed the priests' hands, and moved on.

Hall looked away sharply. "Incredible, isn't it, with all the typhus going around." He came to a halt. "Let's keep in daily touch from now on. Call me at the club—tomorrow night at eight to begin with, fifteen minutes earlier each time after that." He gave Grishin's arm another clumsy pat. "We'd better say good-bye now."

"Why did we meet here, Jim?"

"Sorry, old chap, I don't get you."

Grishin noticed the change in Hall's expression only because he'd known him for so long. His face was still puce and perspiring, but the brown eyes were veiled and the mouth had become a stubborn line.

"The grave, Jim."

"What grave?" Hall's tone was as uncommunicative as the look on his face.

"Our rendezvous: Row M, No. 37, Dagmara Fyodorova." For a split second, but no longer, Grishin thought he'd succeeded in penetrating Hall's defenses.

"I picked a number at random, that's all." He nodded to Grishin and waddled off in the wake of some mourners who were just leaving the cemetery. His linen suit looked startlingly white against their rusty black.

Jim Hall was hiding something, Grishin felt certain, and the thought made him feel better. Somehow, it reassured him that all was as it should be.

•15•

It was getting dark outside. Although the windows were wide open, the top-floor apartment was stiflingly hot. Lena's naked body seemed to burn like fire in his arms. Her hair, when he touched it, was as wet as if she'd just emerged from a shower.

"Are you all right?"

Her only response was to nestle even closer. "May I ask you a question?"

His arms tightened around her. "Try me."

"A silly question?" She turned her head and kissed him. "Do you mind it that I'm not very experienced?"

Looking at the face above him—the parted lips, the big, dark eyes—he detected something he'd never seen before except in men: an almost animal hunger. It lent her face a reckless, provocative quality and rekindled his desire for her.

He took her by the shoulders and turned her over on her back. He had been very gentle, very restrained the first time, but her change of expression had transformed her into a different woman, so he made love to her differently, swiftly, almost roughly.

"Yes," she said afterward, "it was a silly question."

Her eyelids flickered, her breathing became slow and regular, her body relaxed. Very slowly, he withdrew his arm from beneath her. "You're not going?" she murmured, but without really waking. By the time he was on his feet beside the bed, she had drifted off again.

He tiptoed to the window. The fairground booths were shut, the roller-coaster cars chained up for the night, and the big top was in darkness. He closed the window and drew the heavy velvet curtains. The brass rings rattled softly as they slid along the rail.

The place was not so much an apartment as one big room

running the full width of the house. The few pieces of furniture must have belonged to a previous occupant. Grishin could not imagine that Lena had chosen the decor herself. There were some cheap rugs, two plush armchairs, a battered table, the divan on which she lay asleep, and a rosewood piano. The dominant feature of the room was the wallpaper: cockatoos with silver wings and bright red pomegranates in their beaks, fluttering through a luxuriant green jungle.

The little kitchen, with its china cupboard, spirit cooker, and sink, was partitioned off by a screen. A french window opened onto a small balcony overlooking the inner courtyard. Grishin closed this too and drew the curtains.

His bag was on the kitchen table, where he'd left it after shaving in the washroom next door. He hesitated for a moment. Then he got dressed, picked up the bag, and went back to the main room. Lena was stirring restlessly and talking in her sleep. The words were unintelligible.

It was so dark by now that he could see her body only as a dim shape. Her convulsive movements had thrown the bedclothes off. He put his bag down and drew them over her. Her bare shoulders felt hot and moist.

She woke and sat up, shivering. He retrieved her blouse, which was lying on the floor.

"Here, put this on. I'll make some tea."

"I don't know what's the matter with me. I'm freezing—I can't think why, in this heat. Will you be able to find everything?"

He lit the kerosene lamp beside the bed and went back to the kitchen. When the tea was made, he carried it in on a tray. Lena said nothing throughout. He pulled the little table up to the divan and deposited the tray on it. Having arranged the pillows behind her back, he poured a cup of tea and handed it to her.

"Drink it while it's hot."

There was no gratitude or tenderness in her expression. It was watchful and wary, as if his solicitude was a danger signal. Her eyes traveled from his face to the bag on the floor.

"You were going."

He poured himself a cup of tea and perched on the edge of the divan. "It won't do you any good unless you drink it while it's hot. I really should have taken your temperature first."

She laughed aloud. "You seriously think I'm the kind of person who keeps a thermometer in the house?" She drank her tea and handed the cup back.

"Is there a doctor in the neighborhood?"

"Thanks, you make a good cup of tea. It's no use calling a doctor. Whatever he prescribed would be unobtainable." She leaned back against the pillows and sighed. "Tea and talk, that's how Muscovites keep themselves alive these days."

"Have you had any cases of typhus at the convent?"

"Let's change the subject, shall we? Have you noticed the wallpaper? Parrots in here, butterflies and daffodils on the staircase. Oleg Voyeikov, wholesale dealer in wallpaper and furnishing fabrics, Moscow-Paris-London. He used his home as a showcase. There's a different hand-blocked paper in every room in the house."

"So you have had some cases at Yelizaveta Maria?"

"Careful, comrade!" She smiled sardonically. "Children take priority in our socialist society, didn't you know? Our schools have been allocated the finest premises—their pupils eat better than our leaders in the Kremlin. Within a few months, our educational establishments have attained standards of hygiene never before enjoyed in Russia. You're spreading anti-Soviet rumors, Comrade Yevgeny Grigory."

"Many cases?"

"Twenty or so, seven of them fatal. Sometimes we have camphor and strychnine but no syringes to inject them with, sometimes it's the other way around. Everything gets stolen from the hospitals and sold on the black market."

"Is Vera all right?"

"She only stayed ten days. One morning she was gone."

They fell silent for a while. Lena hugged the bedclothes to her, still shivering.

"You really ought to see a doctor."

"Maybe you're right, but what I really need . . ."

He turned the lamp down and waited.

"You remember I told you about the girl who admired the girl who shot Prince Lavyonov?"

Grishin nodded.

"Picture the same girl two years later. She was eighteen and studying in Paris because Russian universities didn't admit women. One day in winter—it was almost like Russia, the weather was so icy—a double funeral took place. The two coffins were draped in red flags. The couple had committed suicide because they were old, because the revolution they longed for seemed more remote than ever—this was in 1911—and because they'd lost all hope that it would ever come to pass. Their memories were as sacred to revolutionaries everywhere as icons are to an Orthodox priest. The dead woman's father was Karl Marx and the cemetery was Père-Lachaise, where members of the Paris Commune were executed—hallowed soil, in other words. That was why our Russian girl turned up there.

"Every revolutionary of note had hurried to Paris for the occasion. There was a lot of speechifying, but nobody spoke for long because of the cold. The last speaker was a man who'd used scores of names in his time and still hadn't made up his mind which one to adopt for good. That day he stuck to the middle-class name he was born with: Vladimir Ilyich Ulyanov . . ."

Lena paused. Then, sensing Grishin's interest, she went on.

"He announced his intention of speaking in Russian. Could anyone there interpret for him? The Russian girl stepped forward—a dark girl in a thin, threadbare coat, no hat or gloves. A strange girl who had run away from home and refused to accept a kopek from her immensely wealthy bourgeois father . . .

"She translated Vladimir Ilyich's funeral address into French. He delivered it standing on a platform with someone holding an umbrella over him to keep the rain off. She stood close beside him, anxious not to miss a word of what he said. Nobody held an umbrella over her, and nobody spared her a thought once the proceedings were over. Her only reward was a week in bed with a high temperature, but as soon as she was back on her feet she made her way to No. 4 Rue Marie Rose in the 14th Arrondissement. Believe it or not, Vladimir Ilyich not only deigned to see her but invited her to do some chores for him. First a translation, then some reference work at the Bibliothèque Nationale. Oh yes, and could she make a trip to England with instructions for the comrades there? His passport wasn't in order . . ."

Her voice trailed off. She smiled wryly. "One shouldn't talk about dreams when they're over."

"When did it really end, your dream?"

The question seemed to alarm her. She looked at something over his shoulder.

"Would you mind trying the telephone?"

It was on the wall beside the door. He got up and went over to it.

"Is it still connected?"

He lifted the receiver and listened. "Yes. You want me to call someone for you?"

"No. Hang up and come back, please."

He sat down again.

"Was I talking in my sleep? Did you pick out any words—a name, for instance? A name like Voroshin, Konstantin Nikolaevich, wigmaker?" She pulled the bedclothes up to her chin. "They may have shot him already . . ."

He studied her in silence. She looked close to tears, on the verge of breaking down, but he knew it wouldn't come to that. She radiated strength and determination, even now. There was too much love and hatred inside her to leave room for anything else.

"What about the telephone?" It seemed the simplest question he could ask.

"You're sure it was still connected?"

"Quite sure."

"It's a great privilege, a private line—an honor reserved for comrades true to the cause. I've broken faith and abused that privilege. The first thing they'll do is cut me off. It's the usual routine."

"Shall I make some more tea?"

She didn't appear to have heard. "They've gone mad! He makes a wig for Lenin and they sentence him to death. The great man can't bring himself to admit that he once gave his enemies the slip wearing a wig." She shook her head. "Why, Yevgeny?"

"Why what?"

"Why this myth, this legend of a better world? Did it ever exist? *Will* it ever exist? Which are at fault, our recollections or our expectations?"

"I'm not qualified to answer."

"Who is, then? The man who killed to get across the frontier? The man who came to Moscow to kill again?" The bedclothes slid off her shoulders as she sat up straight and stared at him. "Are you really prepared to die for *that?*"

He met her gaze, knowing that this was his last chance to walk out and never see her again—knowing that he shouldn't utter another word.

"I'd better go now." He spoke coldly, with an unmistakable note of warning in his voice.

"But I love you, don't you understand? Damn it all, why do I have to spell it out? A total stranger sits on the edge of my bed, makes me a cup of tea, and I tell him I love him. It's funny. You might at least laugh. Go on, laugh!"

He leaned forward and took her by the shoulders. "What do you want me to say?" His voice was even lower and huskier than usual.

She smiled suddenly, with complete self-assurance, and kissed him. "Come back soon," she said.

He picked up the tray and carried it into the kitchen. When he returned he pointed to the piano. "Do you play?"

She shook her head, puzzled by the question.

"All right if I leave something with you?" He opened his bag and took out the bundle containing the old Nagant revolver. The piano strings jangled faintly as he lifted the lid and stowed the gun inside.

"I'll pick it up in due course."

"Yevgeny," she said, "I want you back alive—I need you alive. You're no good to me dead or in a prison cell."

"That won't happen."

He turned the wick of the lamp still lower, bent down, and kissed her one last time. When he reached the door he heard her say, "The telephone?" It was the drowsy voice of someone already dozing off.

He removed the earpiece from its hook and listened to the jumble of sounds coming down the line. Even when you got a number in Moscow you felt you were conversing with every other subscriber in the city at once.

"You're still connected," he said, and hung up.

A long, deep sigh of relief came from the divan. He opened the door and closed it softly behind him.

Grishin had thought it was hot in Lena's apartment, but the room on the sixth floor of the lodging house near Sukharov market felt like the inside of a blast furnace. By the time he reached the window and flung it open he was streaming with sweat and gasping for air.

Everything was as he had left it: his spare suit, Krnka's gun and special ammunition. The only difference was that even the couple next door were finding it too hot to pick a quarrel.

He was tempted for a moment. Waking up with Lena in his arms would have been infinitely preferable to waking up alone on a lumpy palliasse in this hothouse of a room, but he banished the thought by concentrating on what lay ahead. The desire to complete an assignment was, after all, a form of lust in its own right.

The light was fading when Grishin and Lena reached Kammeny Bridge, an iron structure with latticework sides, after walking along the left bank of the Moskva. People with paper bags or rolled towels under their arms streamed past them in the direction of Ivan Baths, Moscow's largest public bathhouse, which stood on the other side of the twilit river.

The heat had abated since Grishin's return to Moscow a week earlier, and it was a pleasant summer evening. The embankment was crowded with other couples strolling arm in arm. The climate-conscious Muscovites were already thinking ahead: the weather could change overnight at the beginning of September, and the first heavy rains would cast a chill over the city.

They had set out early, at about seven. Lena, who had grown up in St. Petersburg, missed the waterways of her native city.

"Over sixty canals, over six hundred bridges—more even than Amsterdam or Venice . . . Are you listening?"

"Of course," he said, but he was listening with only half an ear, intent on his forthcoming rendezvous with Ostrov at the Electra Theater and the meeting at the dacha. He was restless, tingling with expectancy at the knowledge that things were coming to a head at last. He had completed his preparations; just how adequate they were, only time would tell.

"It irritates you, doesn't it?"

"What does?"

She laughed. "Walking arm in arm with a woman."

Once again, he hadn't even noticed. They left the river and climbed the broad stone steps leading to the square in front of St. Savior's. The church was just a huge gray shape in the dusk, but its four gilded domes, lit by the afterglow of the sunset, seemed to be floating in midair.

"Is this the way to the Electra?"

"A shortcut."

They crossed a small park and turned down an ill-lit street. The illuminated sign above the movie theater's entrance could be seen at the far end.

"I haven't even asked what we're going to see."

"An American picture, *The Clansman*. Three thousand extras, eighteen thousand horses, eight months in the making. Every house has been sold out for a month now."

"Really?" she said dryly. "Well, I suppose going to the movies is one way of forgetting about an empty belly."

"How are you feeling?"

"A bit shaky. Otherwise as good as new."

She had called the doctor after all, that first night. The fever had persisted for four days, accompanied by rigors and spells of dizziness. Now, after two days' convalescence at home, she was venturing out for the first time. She had lost weight. Her eyes looked even bigger and deeper set, her high cheekbones more prominent, and her face had acquired a delicate transparency that only enhanced its beauty.

"Just look at all those people."

Grishin had been too preoccupied with her to notice the milling throng outside the Electra. He took her arm and steered her out of range of the nearest streetlight.

Standing in the shadows a couple of hundred yards from the theater, they could hear the bystanders buzzing like a swarm of bees and see them gesticulating excitedly. An open car drove up, tires squealing and exhaust backfiring, with policemen overflowing onto the running boards. A second police car and an ambulance followed moments later.

Lena said, "There must have been an accident." Then, as if divining his thoughts, she asked, "Were you meeting someone there?"

He said nothing, just watched the policemen leap from their cars and fan out.

"Shall I go?" she said. "Would you like me to find out what's happened?"

"No, stay here."

"But you need to know—I can go for you." As if it was all settled, she added, "What exactly do you want me to find out?"

Again he gripped her arm. She realized at once that he was focusing her attention on himself, not holding her back.

"If there has been an accident, find out who was involved—and find out where the ambulance goes, if you can."

"That shouldn't be too difficult."

"Don't go asking questions, just keep your eyes and ears open. Be as inconspicuous as possible."

She nodded and set off. He watched her walk up to the theater and mingle with the crowd. She was just in time. The police forged a path through the inquisitive onlookers, and two ambulance attendants disappeared inside carrying a stretcher.

Grishin had a recurrence of his waking nightmare: Muranov dead on the racetrack, Vera Ivanova dead on her bed. Why should Vassily Ostrov be the next victim—why Ostrov, of all people, with his long experience in the art of survival?

The police had a hard time holding the crowd back when the ambulance attendants returned. The stretcher was draped in a blanket, but there could be no mistaking what lay beneath it.

Lena reappeared at last, walking slowly back down the street. Twenty yards away she broke into a run. "You were right," she said breathlessly. "A man was murdered—strangled. And Yevgeny, he was a Chekist . . ."

"Easy, easy, get your breath back first." He took her arm. "Let's get out of here."

Grishin turned off before they reached St. Savior's and the river, on the lookout for a cabstand where he could find a droshky to take her home.

"So," he said eventually, "begin at the beginning again. A man was murdered. Where, in the auditorium itself?"

"Yes, he was strangled in his seat—garroted from behind with a wire noose." Her tone was calm and matter-of-fact. "Nobody heard anything. The place employs a pianist."

"I know. Did you hear anyone mention his name?"

"No, but he seems to have been well known there. I heard an usherette say, 'Oh, I know him—he must have seen the picture a dozen times at least.' Does that help?"

"Yes."

"There's something else. Just as they were carrying the body outside, someone ran up with some things he said belonged to the dead man: a hat—a gray homburg—and a silver-topped cane. Not the kind of thing anyone carries these days."

Grishin said nothing.

"Was he the man you were to meet?"

"What about the ambulance?"

"That was odd. Someone asked the driver, quite casually, 'Where are you taking him?' and was promptly hustled away by the police." Lena's face darkened. "I've left the worst part till last, Yevgeny. There was someone else there, someone from the Cheka . . ."

"In charge, you mean?"

"No, just watching in the background. I know him—his name is Peters." She looked uneasy for the first time. "I wonder what *he* was doing there."

"Yury Peters? Did he spot you?"

"No, I'm sure he didn't. I was careful, very careful. How do you know him?"

"I only know him by name."

"He's one of Dzerzhinsky's deputies."

"So? Maybe he likes going to the movies."

She hesitated, then it dawned on her. "You were going to meet that man there, but he was murdered first. Did his murderer know about your rendezvous?"

A shrewd question, Grishin thought—a question he would have to ask himself, but not now. Later, at his leisure.

They had reached Prechistenskaya Gate. Two droshkies were standing at an intersection on the broad boulevard running north of it, which bore the same name. It was so dark by now that Grishin could see the cabbies' cigarettes glow like fireflies when they took a puff. He thought of the dacha and hoped the moon would have risen by the time he got to Kuntsevo. He walked Lena to the cabstand.

"I'm sorry about our evening."

"You're sending me home?"

He opened his jacket, unbuttoned his shirt, and produced a bulky envelope. "Here, take this."

She made no move to do so. "What is it?"

"Money."

"For the man you were to meet? Why can't you tell me about him?" When he didn't reply, she said, "How much money?"

Grishin involuntarily pictured Ostrov sitting at the back of the Electra, sauntering home with his silver-topped cane, relaxing in his apartment. What would become of his butterfly collection? Why should he, Grishin, feel a kind of compassion for Ostrov dead when he'd despised him alive?

"How much?" she repeated.

"Enough for him to quit Russia and start a new life somewhere else. Enough to rent a small apartment in Paris, open a restaurant à la russe, employ a chef and a couple of waiters, and not worry even if the place failed to pay for a year or two. But I don't know if that's what he really wanted it for."

Lena strove to read his expression in the gloom.

"If you'd been sitting there beside him they might have killed you too."

"The possibility had occurred to me."

"Very reassuring, I must say! And you expect me to go home and not worry myself sick?"

Grishin shared at least some of her concern. Had he genuinely been in danger? "You knew about that Latvian I killed on the frontier. Who told you? Try to remember."

"It was . . ." She hesitated. "It was Yury Peters. What does that signify?"

He put one arm around her, still holding the envelope in his other hand.

"For the moment, nothing more than a curious coincidence. I'd tell you if I knew myself. Please take the money now."

"If it's as much as all that, why don't we keep it ourselves?" The idea sounded quite spontaneous. "I assume it's in foreign currency. If so, why don't we use some of it to bribe someone—a conductor, say, who'll find us a sleeper on the next train going west. We could be across the frontier in twenty-four hours. Why not, Yevgeny? Let's try—let's take a cab to the station and see if there's a night train out of here."

But she must have realized that the die was cast, because she took the envelope and put it in her pocket. "I'm going to find it hard, waiting for you."

"I won't be long."

"Don't be. Those parrots on the wallpaper get you down when you're alone."

"One more thing, Lena: Steer clear of Lloyd Fleming."

"I haven't seen him for weeks, but why?"

"Keep it that way. If he calls you, think of an excuse—say you're under doctor's orders. Steer clear of him till the dust settles."

He walked the last few yards to the cabstand with his arm around her waist. One of the cabbies, a Mongol with a broad face and slanting eyes, tossed his butt away and opened the door.

Seeing her hesitate, Grishin said, "Do you have some small change?"

She nodded and held him close. "Are you sure you won't take that train?"

The cabby, who had already resumed his seat on the box, glanced at them over his shoulder.

"Take your time, comrades," he said, "you're only young once."

•17•

A thin thread of smoke was rising from the dacha's chimney. The clear sky was filled with stars, but they gave little light, just swathed the heavens like big banks of luminous cloud.

The windows were shuttered and the house looked deserted. That, coupled with the smoke, lent it a faintly sinister appearance.

Grishin had an unobstructed view of the dacha from a hill overlooking the site. All he could see of the neighboring houses were some roofs jutting above a dense plantation of spruce and birch. The trees around "his" dacha had been felled—so recently that the raw stumps showed up in the gloom. Felled for firewood, or so that no one could approach the place unobserved?

Compared to its neighbors in the colony, which numbered around a dozen, the house was little more than a large hunting lodge. The outside walls consisted of stout tree trunks laid on a stone foundation, the roof was tiled with hardwood shingles. Discounting the smoke, Grishin had seen no sign of life in the two hours since his arrival.

His commanding position enabled him to look out across the gently undulating terrain west of Moscow. In the distance he could make out the winding river, the railroad tracks leading to Kuntsevo station, where he had left the train, and the road to Moscow itself, a pale ribbon intermittently severed by dark strips of woodland. The countryside looked entirely uninhabited. Though less than four miles from the heart of the capital, he might have been in another world.

Glancing back at the dacha, he noticed that smoke was no longer rising from the chimney. Puzzled, he focused his attention on the crisply defined ribbon of road. Fleming, Berzin, and the others would have to come that way.

Another half hour went by before he detected a low hum in the distance and saw headlights stabbing the darkness.

He peered at his watch: it was just after eleven, so they were on time. He made out two cars, a black limousine and an open coupe with a long hood. They disappeared briefly behind a clump of trees before turning into the drive. The entrance to the drive, a big wrought-iron gate flanked by a pair of stone sentry boxes, was more imposing than the dacha itself.

Grishin carefully stubbed out his cigarette against a tree trunk. The ground was tinder-dry after such a prolonged heat wave. Then he heard the gate swing back on its hinges. Two men held it open for the cars to pass, then closed it again and remained on guard.

The cars made their way up the winding drive to the dacha. He counted the limousine's occupants as they got out. There were seven of them. They stood there for a minute, clearly glad to stretch their legs after traveling in such cramped conditions. Then they headed for the dacha in single file and disappeared from view. Both the men who emerged from the second car remained outside, presumably on guard like the two at the gate.

Grishin had seen what he expected to see. It was a relief to move after standing on the spot for hours. He had no difficulty in finding his way in the darkness. Counting tonight, this was his third reconnaissance of the area.

He halted a few yards short of the private road leading to the dacha. Set in the wall enclosing the property was a small side door hidden by undergrowth. Having forced the rusty old lock on one of his previous visits, he satisfied himself that the damage had remained undiscovered. Then he hurried across the road, through a small pinewood, and across another road to a fenced-in site with a half-completed water tower in the middle. It was eleven-thirty when he took up his position beside the rutted track leading to the construction site.

He saw the car's headlights even before he'd finished another cigarette, and withdrew to the shelter of some trees. The two-seater coupe's lights went off, then on again, twice in quick succession. He stepped out onto the track. The driver pulled up beside him, doused his headlights, and switched off.

Grishin opened the passenger door and got in. It was a relief to see Jim Hall's Buddha-like figure ensconced behind the wheel.

"Well, did they show up? I'm not late, am I?"

"How on earth can you bear to drive with the windows up on a night like this?"

"The handle's stuck." Hall chuckled. "Glad you made it. I lost my way twice—no sense of direction, I'm afraid."

Grishin tried the handle. It was stiff, but he got the passenger window open.

Hall chuckled again. "You're a mechanical genius. I'm hopeless."

Not when it comes to blowing up bridges, Grishin thought. Aloud, he said, "Nervous, Jim?"

"As a kitten. I've got the Bank of England on board." Hall jerked a thumb over his shoulder. "There's more cash back there than either of us'll ever see again: a million sweet pounds of it. The very thought brings me out in a sweat."

"Whose car is this?"

"The Italian ambassador was kind enough to lend it to me. Next time I'll borrow something more my size."

"Can't you adjust the seat?"

"Now you're being mechanical again." Hall reached for the ignition key. "All right, let's go and get rid of our christening present."

Grishin laid a restraining hand on his arm. "One moment, Jim. I'm not sure the baby deserves a present after all."

Hall waited in silence. His capacity for silent attention was unique, and that was what Grishin needed—a good listener. He lit another cigarette.

"Your baby has turned out to be an abortion. They just killed Ostrov."

Hall shrugged. "I can't say I'm surprised. He had it coming."

"We met twice in the past week. I'd fixed a final rendezvous for this evening. Someone else got there before me."

Hall smiled his Buddha's smile. "Don't expect me to shed any tears for Ostrov."

"There's more. You asked me to check the dacha out. All the houses around here have been requisitioned for Party bigwigs and senior officials. They used to rely on wells; now they're building a water tower. There wasn't any electricity; now, every house is connected to the city grid."

"Still no telephones?" said Hall, unimpressed.

"The houses are administered by Section Six of the Cheka. That includes the dacha in question."

"Alexander Berzin is a Chekist, we already know that."

"So was Ostrov. I gave him your list of names and asked him to investigate them. He said it would be a waste of time. I scored a direct hit, Jim: he knew the names already, every last one of them."

"How come?"

"Because he invented your shadow cabinet himself."

Hall shifted in his seat, but that was all. Grishin had been pondering the information all evening. It was only now, thanks to the fat man's aura of composure, that his own ideas were falling into place.

"Vassily Ostrov was the finest forger they had—he headed the Cheka's forgery section. A week or two ago, around the time when Berzin first made contact with Fleming, Ostrov was sent for by Dzerzhinsky himself. Dzerzhinsky moved him into a special office of his own and gave him an assignment so secret that no one else was allowed to get wind of it. His task was to invent five personalities from scratch, complete with names, backgrounds, papers, letters of recommendation, et cetera. The product of his labors was your list of names: an entire shadow cabinet, the famous Credit Group. All your prominent counterrevolutionaries, ministers, generals—your Messrs Voronsky, Arbatov, Semashko, Isakovsky, and Lashin—were figments of Ostrov's fertile imagination."

"Excuse me." Jim Hall groped for the door handle and finally got it open. He walked a few yards into the trees and relieved himself copiously with his back to the car. Then he came waddling back, still wrestling with his fly buttons. The sight was so comical that Grishin momentarily relaxed.

"Well," Hall grunted, squeezing in behind the wheel again, "what can I say?"

"Ostrov invented those five men. He was going to hand me the documentary evidence this evening."

"And that's what the extra money was for?"

"Yes, but he never got it. He got a piano-string necklace instead." Grishin paused. "You realize what this means, don't you, even without any conclusive proof? Your quintet are agents provocateurs. The Credit Group is simply an elaborate Cheka trap."

"May I say something?"

"By all means. Prove I dreamed the whole thing."

"Try looking at it from the other side. The Cheka get to hear that secret meetings are taking place—that the British are flirting with a bunch of dangerous counterrevolutionaries. They fail to track the Credit Group down, but they employ Ostrov to *dis*credit them. If that's the case, you're the one who's fallen into the trap."

"I thought of that, Jim, but why should they kill him? Ostrov would have been far more useful to them alive."

"Perhaps they thought he'd outlived his usefulness."

"There's something else—a minor detail, but it's significant. Forgers are strange characters. They tend to have a perverted sense of humor."

"Well?"

"Voronsky, Arbatov, Semashko, Isakovsky, Lashin . . . Ostrov was given carte blanche to pick the names himself, so what did he do? He picked five names whose initials spelled his *own* name."

Hall muttered them to himself. "V . . . A . . . S . . . I . . . L . . ."

"It's a trap right enough, don't you see? The moment Fleming puts his signature to that agreement, they'll move in. Can't you see the headlines in *Pravda?* 'British Plot Foiled in the Nick of Time!'— 'British Secret Service Planned Lenin's Murder!' You asked me what card our friend in the Kremlin could still have up his sleeve. Well, I'm afraid that's it."

"Are you through?"

"Yes."

"Feeling better?"

"Yes and no."

"You want to call it a day?"

"We both should. Most of all, we should both avoid that dacha like the plague."

"Fleming's in there, and Fleming's one of ours."

"Oh come on! Nothing'll happen to Fleming, he's got diplomatic status. Anything they did to him, we could do to the Soviet envoy in London. It isn't a country's official representatives who foot the bill for its blunders."

"That's why I'll ask you again: Do you want to bail out?"

Grishin's instinct urged him to respond with a simple, unequivocal affirmative. To say yes would clearly convey what he felt. A "no" would fundamentally be a lie. He had never regarded espionage as anything other than what it really was: a dirty business. If he'd sometimes, though very rarely, felt he was doing a worthwhile job, he owed that feeling to Jim Hall alone. Although Hall had never tried to sell him his own sense of duty or patriotism, some of it must have rubbed off. Perhaps that was why he said, "Not if you want me along."

"Thanks. I can't just leave Fleming in the lurch."

"Apart from delivering the cash, do you have to put your name to anything?"

"No. Fleming's the daddy. My job is to stay there and hold his hand till the baby's born."

"Do you have a gun?"

"What if I do?"

"Where is it?"

Hall hesitated. "Under your seat."

Grishin leaned forward. His groping fingers came into contact with something small and hard wrapped up in a piece of rag. The bundle turned out to contain a short-barreled revolver little bigger than the palm of his hand.

"Cute little toy, isn't it?" Hall's laugh sounded rather forced. "Easy to conceal—a favorite with cardsharps, bartenders, brothel-keepers. Don't underrate it, though. It's surprisingly accurate and extremely lethal . . . I think we'd better be going."

He pressed the self-starter. The engine coughed a couple of times, but that was all. He tried again with similar results.

"Damn and blast!"

He's only calm on the outside, Grishin thought. He's worried—he likes this business as little as I do.

"Shall I get out?"

The gun, which was still lying on his palm, might have been made for him. Its perfect balance imparted a sense of security. Grishin briefly debated whether to hide it in his boot, but that seemed too inaccessible. He tucked it into his waistband.

"Want me to swing the handle for you?"

Just then the engine fired. The long hood vibrated as they got under way.

"Take it slow," Grishin said. "You have to turn off pretty soon—I'll tell you when." He could feel the gun nestling against his stomach.

Hall drove in the middle of the road, bending low over the wheel and peering through the windshield.

"Another fifty yards, then make a right."

The road became narrower and degenerated into a dusty, unpaved track.

"Not so fast, we're nearly at the turnoff."

"I can't get the damned thing to go any slower."

The car took the bend. The headlights picked out the wall enclosing the grounds of the dacha. Grishin put his hand on Hall's arm.

"Stop here."

"Why here?"

"Pull up and leave the engine running." The car almost stalled.

"Damn it, John . . ."

"You see that corner where the two walls meet? About ten yards this side of it there's a clump of bushes and a big branch of elder overhanging the wall."

"Well?"

"There's a door there. I couldn't see any footprints inside or out, so I assume it's escaped their notice. It's only a couple of hundred yards from there to the dacha."

Hall turned and stared at the hand on his arm. "I've never run a couple of hundred yards in my life. I'd have a heart attack."

"You won't have to. I suggest you drop me off and let me deliver the money for you."

"The hell I will!"

"Once you've dropped me, drive back here. Turn the car around and park it as close to that side door as possible. Keep the engine running."

"But it's me they're expecting."

"What matters is the money."

"They'll only smell a rat—I mean . . ." Hall broke off, conscious of the implication.

"If Berzin and his friends are on the level they'll have no reason to be suspicious, and if I'm imagining things it'll make no difference to them who delivers the money. If not, we'll stand a better chance this way."

Nothing could be heard but the engine ticking over.

"Why you?" Hall said eventually. "Besides, you're the better driver."

"We could always toss for it."

"Let go of my arm, damn it!"

Grishin hadn't realized that his hand was still there. He removed it.

"All right," said Hall, "you win."

Grishin sat back. As he did so the gun in his waistband gave him another reminder of its presence. It felt bigger and heavier against his stomach than it had in his hand.

By the time they drove up to the gate, he had forgotten about the gun altogether. It had become an extension of his body.

The graveled drive, which was steep and winding, proved longer than Grishin had thought. One of the men on duty at the gate escorted him a couple of paces to the rear.

Though not intimidated, Grishin felt far from sanguine. The handle of the suitcase was biting into his fingers, and the case itself seemed to get heavier with every step he took. Once he had skirted the parked cars, the dacha loomed up before him on its foundations of rough-hewn stone. The veranda running the breadth of the house was protected by an overhanging roof. The moon had risen, illuminating the reddish brown bark of the tree trunks that formed the outer walls.

A man emerged from the shadowy recesses of the veranda. He might have been the first guard's twin brother.

"Only one of them?" His thin lips barely moved when he spoke.

"His friend couldn't wait—said he was expected back in town."

The man on the veranda stepped forward and put his hand out. "I'll take that."

Grishin relinquished the suitcase and climbed the stone steps. He counted four of them; in his predicament any detail seemed worth noting. Holding the case in one hand, the second guard knocked on the door. Grishin made another mental note: His knuckles sounded as hard as the wood itself.

The door opened. Grishin screwed up his eyes, momentarily dazzled by the light. He counted six men seated at a table in front of a big open fireplace but didn't see the man who had opened the door until he spoke.

"You're very punctual. Come in." His English was good, with only a trace of an accent.

The guard deposited the case on the floor. "I haven't searched him yet."

"No need, I'm sure. We're all friends here." The man made a gesture of dismissal and turned to Grishin. "Permit me to introduce myself: Alexander Berzin."

Grishin nodded. "Don't let me interrupt you."

"Make yourself comfortable." Berzin pointed to an empty chair. "We've made good progress tonight—we won't be much longer."

Although they varied in age, the men around the table had one thing in common: Their chins were dark with stubble, almost as if they had made a simultaneous resolution to stop shaving and grow beards. It didn't escape Grishin that they all avoided his eye and feigned an intense preoccupation with the papers in front of them.

"Do you know Mr. Fleming?" asked Berzin. "Civilian or no civilian, he's the most important person here."

Lloyd Fleming was wearing a double-breasted gray suit. Perhaps because he knew him to be a banker, Grishin couldn't help likening his pallid complexion to the white of a British five-pound note.

Fleming, who had half risen, stopped short. A look of surprise and annoyance dawned in his eyes.

"Where's Jim Hall?"

"He couldn't stay. Something urgent cropped up at the consulate." Grishin held his gaze. Fleming had never seen him before, he reflected. Suspicious he might be, but he couldn't be sure of anything.

"A million pounds is a lot of money to entrust to someone else."

Grishin smiled. "I imagine you'll count it before you give me a receipt."

"Do you have a name, at least?"

"My name doesn't matter. I'm just an errand boy."

Berzin politely but firmly terminated this exchange—almost, thought Grishin, as if he were coming to his rescue.

"I suggest we adjourn for a drink and then complete our business as quickly as possible."

"We needn't detain him," said Fleming, still looking at Grishin.

Berzin laughed. "Surely you don't expect the poor man to walk home? Arbatov, do the honors."

Glasses were filled and drained, toasts proposed and drunk, though Fleming made heavy weather of his vodka. Berzin picked up a pencil and rapped the table. The others resumed their deliberations as if oblivious of Grishin's presence.

Grishin's glass was still full. He sat there on the sidelines with a curious sense of detachment, only half registering the course of the negotiations, the exchanges of documents, the minuting of agreements.

"The term of the lease should be set at ninety-nine years . . ."

"Sixty years at most, certainly in the Kamchatka region . . ."

"I find that wording too imprecise. The new government must do its utmost to ensure . . ."

Grishin was aching for a cigarette, but he didn't want to draw attention to himself by moving. With the exception of Berzin and Fleming, the others had all removed their coats. The room was stiflingly hot. Not for the first time, Grishin glanced at the open hearth, convinced that a fire must be blazing there, but the stone recess was as bare and empty as ever.

His eyes combed the walls again and again. He found nothing to confirm his suspicions, and yet, as he scrutinized the paneling inch by inch, his certainty persisted that men were lurking in another room somewhere behind it—a room where a fire had been burning not long before. He never for an instant doubted that they would make their entrance when the time came.

Till then he could only watch and wait, remain alert, trust his nose for danger—and the gun, of course. That was a comforting thought. Although he hadn't identified the make beyond doubt in the darkness, he guessed it to be American, probably a derringer. That meant it had six rounds in the cylinder. Each shell was tipped with an ounce of lead—enough to tear a huge hole in a man's gut. Another thought struck him: An ounce of metal, albeit gold rather than lead, had done him little good in the past. He was fortunate not to be superstitious.

"So we'll leave it at next Thursday, when the Central Committee's in session." Berzin was speaking. "And don't forget, my friends, burn your notes before we go."

The meeting seemed to be drawing to a close. Grishin forced himself to concentrate on what was being said and done at the table. He rested his right hand on his thigh, only inches from the gun.

"If we're all agreed, Voronsky will now read the final text over to us. Then we can sign it."

Berzin again. Grishin wondered why he was so unmistakably in charge.

"Silence, please."

The words were accompanied by more rapping on the table with his pencil. Was it a signal, and if so to whom?

Voronsky had a dry, brittle voice. Grishin studied the others one by one as he read out the text. The red-rimmed eyes and unshaven faces were eloquent of fatigue, but there was something more than exhaustion in the stiff and unnatural way they sat there. Yes, he thought, they're all on edge, even Berzin. Fleming was the sole exception. He looked weary too, but his eyes shone with triumph.

"Well, Mr. Fleming, I think that meets all your requirements. Shall we proceed with the final formality?"

To Grishin's ears it sounded theatrical and false. Berzin's uneasiness was now almost palpable.

"You sign first, Voronsky."

Nothing broke the silence but the scratch of the pen. Voronsky passed it to his neighbor and slid the document across to him. *Voronsky, Arbatov, Semashko, Isakovsky, Lashin* . . . Grishin wondered if Ostrov had rehearsed them all in person.

Lashin finished signing and straightened up. He offered the pen to Fleming, but the banker waved it aside with a shake of the head. Grishin detected a sudden flicker of alarm in Berzin's eyes. A moment later all was explained: Fleming had declined the pen only because he deemed it unworthy of such a momentous transaction. He reached into his breast pocket and produced a black fountain pen embellished with silver.

He unscrewed the cap and bent over the document with a contented smile. Having checked the other signatures, he initialed each sheet in turn until he came to the last, then paused. Berzin drummed nervously on the tabletop. Fleming signed.

Don't do it! The words were on the tip of Grishin's tongue, but they remained unspoken.

The lights went out. Simultaneously, the room came alive with noise and movement. Grishin's hand went to his gun, but the darkness rendered it a futile gesture. Before he could locate the source of the danger—a concealed door that had escaped his notice—his wrists were seized and twisted behind his back. Something fell to the floor with a clatter. The pain was excruciating, but nothing compared to the pain he felt when an arm wound itself around his neck and compressed his windpipe like an iron band. The scream he tried to utter emerged as a strangled grunt. The pain traveled from his throat to his nose, eyes, and temples until something exploded inside his head and he lost consciousness.

Someone or something was emitting weird moaning sounds. He strained his ears and tried to locate them, but they eluded him. As soon as he stopped concentrating, they started again. Grishin had no idea that he was making them himself. He opened his eyes but promptly shut them. The light and the pain in his head were unendurable.

A voice was saying something, apparently from a long way off— an unfamiliar voice. Was he still at the dacha? He forced himself to reopen his eyes.

It was the same pine-paneled room, but deserted except for himself, the men who were pinioning his arms from behind, and the man facing him.

A yard, two yards? Grishin's smarting eyes couldn't gauge the distance. He saw the man's face as a smooth, round blur. What he did make out more clearly was a Russian blouse with colored embroidery at the neck. He registered something else, too: The man was holding his right hand behind his back. The pose was vaguely reminiscent of an executioner sparing his victim a sight of the ax till the final moment.

Grishin was relieved at his ability to think straight again. The blurred face became more distinct, acquired a puzzled frown. Why should the man be looking puzzled?

"Who the devil is this?"

Berzin swam into view. "He brought the money."

The man in the Russian blouse swore angrily. "That's not what I asked you," he snapped. "I want to know who he is. Doesn't he have a name?"

Berzin shrugged. "I think he's fit enough to answer for himself."

Grishin's throat felt like one big, open wound, his eyes throbbed, the room was gyrating. He swallowed hard. Perhaps his head wasn't as clear as he'd thought.

The unknown man seemed to have recovered his equanimity. He continued to stand there with one hand behind his back. Berzin came closer, still holding his pencil. He leveled the point at Grishin's right eye.

"Leave him to me, I'll find out who he is."

Grishin's captors, who obviously approved of this proposal, tightened their grip on his arms. He was afraid, but not of Berzin, who no longer counted. The other man was clearly in command now. Then he caught sight of someone walking slowly and unsteadily into the room like a man striving to keep his balance on a tightrope. It was Fleming.

"I demand an explanation," he protested feebly. "What's the meaning of this, Peters?"

Peters . . . The name triggered another explosion in Grishin's head.

The hand—who had told him about the mutilated hand? Peters at Yelizaveta Maria. Peters outside the Electra. Yury Peters, Cheka commissar, head of Section Nine, responsible for the security of the Bolshevik leaders . . .

As the pain in his head subsided, he heard Peters say, "You're an idiot, Fleming."

"You owe me an explanation," Fleming retorted, but it sounded less like a protest than a feeble request.

"Shut up! You've dug your own grave, Fleming. It's deep enough already, so shut your mouth!"

"As an accredited representative of His Britannic Majesty's government, I—"

"What are you waiting for, Berzin? Take him away."

Berzin laughed. "It's incredible. The poor fool still hasn't taken it in."

"Did you hear me, Berzin?"

"Yes, yes, right away. Come with me, Mr. Fleming."

Fleming had already tottered off. At the door he paused abruptly, as if brought up short by some unseen obstacle, and half turned.

His eyes came to rest on Grishin, blank and uncomprehending at first. A look of hatred and resentment suddenly crossed his face. Then, as he left the room, his expression changed yet again, and all that remained was resignation.

"Well?" said Peters. "How about you? He was taken in, but you?" He answered the question himself. "No, you weren't deceived. You knew it was a trap." His voice rose to a shout. "You knew it, but you came here anyway!"

The blow was so unexpected that Grishin couldn't have dodged it even if his arms had been free. The mutilated hand slammed into his face like a set of brass knuckles.

His head exploded a third time. One cheek felt as if splinters of bone were protruding from the skin. His nose went numb and began to swell. Blood trickled into his mouth and down his chin.

But the pain this time was quite different. Every throb seemed to carry a hidden meaning: *It's all an act, an act, an act . . .*

"Take him out to the car."

The pain subsided. He remained conscious only of a pressure in his midriff, a fist boring into his stomach. He almost cried out when he realized that the gun was still in his waistband.

Hadn't he lost it in the scuffle? What had clattered to the floor? He looked down, but all he could see was some broken glass, no sign of a revolver. Was it really still in place, and did Peters know it?

The two men were propelling him toward the door when Peters said, "Kyril, the suitcase."

The man on his right hesitated, then released him. He felt as if a tourniquet had been removed. The blood seemed to shoot up his arm and into his heart—an illusion, perhaps, but the sudden, violent pounding in his chest was very real.

It was cooler outside, and much darker than before. The sky had clouded over and the wind had freshened. Grishin breathed deeply. The man named Kyril was preceding him down the steps with the suitcase. The other was still beside him, marking his every move.

The cars had backed and turned. He could see their taillights at the mouth of the drive. A third car, a compact-looking black sedan, was parked outside the dacha.

Kyril opened the trunk. He turned as he was lifting the suitcase in and laughed. "It feels like a fortune."

Peters, who was still on the veranda, said, "Hurry up, you're wasting time."

Whether or not the words were meant for him, Grishin acted on them. His right hand dived under his jacket and went for the gun. Simultaneously he pivoted on the spot, breaking the grip on his left arm. The man's hands parted like the jaws of a pair of pliers. Grishin almost fell, but he recovered his balance and sprinted off into the darkness. Although his legs felt like jelly, the strength came flooding back into them at every stride.

"You damn fools! You idiots!"

Peters bellowed the words at the top of his voice, but to Grishin they seemed to carry the same message as before: *It's all an act . . .*

Still running, he turned and fired a couple of unaimed shots. It was only then, when he felt the gun kick in his hand like a living thing, that he realized he'd escaped. The Cheka men were firing back, but only at random.

The car was there, just beyond the door in the wall. Jim Hall had backed it up to the bushes and left the engine running.

Grishin wrenched the passenger door open and jumped in. Nothing happened. He turned. Even though the headlights were off, Hall's linen suit showed up white in the gloom. He was slumped over the wheel with his arms hanging limply at his sides.

"Jim?"

The only response was a faint groan.

"Jesus Christ, Jim, what happened?"

Grishin laid his hand on Hall's broad back. He heard another groan. The cloth beneath his fingers felt wet and sticky.

He didn't stop to investigate. Jumping out again, he leaned into the car. Hall's massive body was a dead weight, but he managed to drag him onto the passenger seat, then sprinted around to the other side and got in behind the wheel.

He slammed the coupe into gear. As it bounced across the uneven ground and onto the private road, he could see out of the corner of his eye that every jolt induced a corresponding movement in the limp and unresisting form beside him. Glancing into the rearview mirror, he spotted headlights farther back along the narrow, dusty cul-de-sac. They were closing fast. He put his foot down hard and kept it down, wondering how Hall could have complained of the car's speed. It seemed to lumber along like a medieval warhorse.

The mouth of the cul-de-sac loomed up. He swung left onto the asphalt road that led through the woods, then left again at the next intersection. He was driving almost blind with the headlights off, so he saw it only in the nick of time.

"Jesus Christ, Jim!"

Grishin was conscious neither of the speed at which the car was traveling, nor that the glare of his pursuers' headlights had vanished from the rearview mirror. He didn't even realize that he'd just, for the second time, invoked a name that had seldom crossed his lips before.

•18•

The only light in the big corner room on the top floor of Cheka headquarters came from the reading lamp on Dzerzhinsky's desk. He had pushed his chair back, so his face was in shadow. The deep-set eyes beneath the high forehead resembled a pair of dark cavities.

People called it a high forehead, Peters reflected, but to him it was just a receding hairline. He and his chief were the same age. Did Dzerzhinsky resent going bald at forty-one? Not in the least, so he didn't have a complex about it.

For a moment Peters felt a mixture of annoyance and envy. Then it subsided. He himself had a complex about his mutilated hand, but that was all right with him. People were welcome to poke fun at his vanity in private as long as it kept them from discovering anything else about him. It had its uses after all, that claw of his.

The darkness outside was unrelieved by any hint of dawn. The four big windows looked like black, blank mirrors. The wind, which was even more noticeable six floors up, kept spattering the panes with raindrops. Peters and Berzin were still wearing their coats.

"Why don't you take those wet things off?" Dzerzhinsky suggested. "Dump them anywhere—the place is a pigsty anyway."

Peters had noted with surprise that Dzerzhinsky's desk still bore the debris of an early breakfast. The Cheka boss was usually a stickler for cleanliness and tidiness in his official domain.

"Once, just once," Dzerzhinsky went on, "I ask for some breakfast and a shave at five in the morning, and what am I told? A canteen breakfast I can have, but no shave. It's against the law—a law we made ourselves. Barbers are day workers, and workers mustn't be exploited." His hand appeared in the glow of the lamp.

He adjusted it so that the light shone on the two chairs in front of his desk.

"I've been meaning to ask you, Yury: Do you shave yourself these days? Sit down, both of you."

"Yes."

"You never seem to cut yourself."

Peters looked surprised at the question. "Left-handed, you mean? It's just a question of patience and practice." He was pleased with himself. He'd struck precisely the intended note.

Dzerzhinsky pointed to a folder lying on the desk.

"Really sensational, this document you brought me from the meeting at Kuntsevo, Comrade Berzin—genuinely useful, too. A British conspiracy unmasked! It's a long time since I've had more welcome news to give Comrade Lenin—better than anything our military commanders can report from the front these days. My congratulations."

Berzin sat back and stretched his legs. "Thank you."

"Just a minor detail." Dzerzhinsky paused. "I'm not sure Comrade Lenin wouldn't have preferred to be shot. This plan to parade him through the streets of Moscow without his trousers . . ."

Berzin cleared his throat. "It was a British plan, don't forget."

Dzerzhinsky laughed dryly. "Nobody seems to appreciate my little jokes anymore. Not even you, Yury."

"I think it's your reputation," Peters said coolly, "—it overawes people." He nodded at Berzin. "May I endorse your congratulations? Comrade Berzin's planning and execution were quite admirable." Praise is the best method of attack, he thought—a time-honored tactic, but still one of the best.

"Amazing people, the British. A banker with a sense of patriotism—truly amazing!"

Berzin cleared his throat again. "Have you questioned him yet? He doesn't deny it's his signature, does he?"

"At the moment he's too stunned to deny anything. I even get the impression that he's quite relieved to be locked up in his cell downstairs. Relieved that the suspense is over, I mean."

"I can't claim all the credit, of course," Berzin said. "If my five conspirators hadn't played their parts so convincingly, the scheme would never have worked."

To Peters, Berzin's modesty sounded false. Besides, he seemed to have missed the underlying problem. Dzerzhinsky's outwardly innocuous question was predictable.

"Are they celebrating their success?"

"Yes. I've kept them together, as you instructed."

Dzerzhinsky moved his chair closer. "You realize, comrade, that their task is still incomplete? If we make this conspiracy public, we can't indict an imperialist banker on his own." He opened the folder and leafed through it. "They signed this document too— here are their signatures. If there's a trial they'll be charged with the same crimes as Fleming. After all, a conspiracy by definition must involve more than one person."

Berzin's face was showing the effects of his long, sleepless night. "Of course," he said, "they all understand that."

"So they'll continue to play their parts as convincingly in court?"

"I think so—yes, I mean."

"Even when they're sentenced to death?"

Silence fell, broken only by the patter of rain on the windows. Berzin laughed, but he stopped abruptly when Dzerzhinsky glanced at Peters and shook his head. "*You* realized I wasn't joking that time, didn't you, Yury?"

Peters felt almost sorry for Berzin, who was kneading the back of his neck and looking bemused. He still seemed to have missed the point.

"Sooner or later," Dzerzhinsky went on, "our five worthy comrades would want to tell their story—the true story of their contribution to a Cheka tour de force. It's only natural, wanting their own little share of the credit." His voice rose. "But needless risks, Comrade Berzin, must be avoided at all costs. To conclude, therefore, I want the five of them isolated in some nice, secure, comfortable place—Marfino will do. They're to have privileged treatment and privileged supervision until the future course of this affair has been decided."

His words settled like a pall over the big room. It was Berzin who broke the silence. "Is that why Comrade Ostrov was—had an accident, because he knew too much about this plan?" He shut his mouth quickly, as if shocked at his own audacity, but Dzerzhinsky remained calm.

"What's your opinion of Comrade Berzin's conjecture, Yury?"

"Ostrov wasn't in my section. I'm not competent to judge."

"Perhaps you'd care to hazard a guess. Do *you* think we got rid of him because he knew too much?"

"He may have used his talents to line his own pockets."

"An interesting theory. Could the British be behind it? Might Ostrov have been in contact with this man James Hall?"

"Perhaps Comrade Berzin knows."

"I asked you."

"Then I'll have to repeat myself: The investigation wasn't my responsibility."

Dzerzhinsky ignored this. "What of the remarkable coincidence that Ostrov should have been murdered on the very night of the Kuntsevo meeting? Can you explain it?"

"Perhaps that's just what it was, a coincidence." Would Dzerzhinsky let it go at that? Peters remained on the alert, mentally preparing himself for further questions.

"Any news of Hall?"

"No trace of him so far. He didn't return to the consulate or the British Club. We're keeping both places under surveillance."

"You realize, of course, that we shall have to repatriate Fleming eventually. Hall's another matter—he's a Secret Service man, so the British will abandon him to his fate. That makes him all the more important to us. Has the car been found?"

"No trace of that either."

"Your answers are becoming a trifle monotonous."

"We've set up checkpoints on all the approach roads. We're also watching the railroad stations. It should be easy enough to spot a man of Hall's build."

"How reassuring." Dzerzhinsky leaned forward. "Correct me if I'm wrong, but wasn't Hall supposed to deliver the money in person?"

Peters studied his hands, saying nothing.

"I asked you a question, Yury."

"Shouldn't it be addressed to Comrade Berzin? He made all the arrangements."

"I'm not interested in who made the arrangements. The man who brought the money got away, and you were the one who lost him, damn it! Do you have an explanation? If so, I'd be fascinated to hear it."

"He had a gun."

Dzerzhinsky stared at Peters in disbelief. "Is that all?" He didn't raise his voice, but the menace in it was unmistakable. "Is that all you have to say? He had a gun, and it wasn't found? Didn't anyone search him?"

Peters waited, confident that his nerves were stronger than Berzin's. He had only to stick it out for another few seconds and Berzin would speak.

"Comrade Peters and his men remained behind the scenes," Berzin said hurriedly. "We agreed that he wouldn't go into action until the document had been signed." He paused for a moment. "I didn't search the man myself because I had no grounds for suspicion. He'd brought the money, after all. Besides, it might have put Fleming off. It was a mistake, I realize that now. Very well, the mistake was mine." He rounded on Peters. "If only you'd left him to me! He'd have talked, and he'd be here now, under lock and key. And another thing, Peters: You can keep your backhanded compliments to yourself!"

Dzerzhinsky had been watching the other two with an air of amusement. "Much as I enjoy a good dogfight," he said, "I must reluctantly forgo the pleasure. We don't have the time to spare." He paused. "So neither of you had seen this man before?"

They both shook their heads.

"You're absolutely positive?"

Then Berzin had a flash of inspiration. "He was an Englishman sent by Hall. Fleming claimed he didn't know him, but it may have been an act."

"He still insists the man was a complete stranger to him."

It's over, Peters thought, but his sense of relief was premature.

"The man's description, Yury—doesn't it remind you of something? Don't we already have a similar description on file?"

Peters furrowed his brow as though thinking hard.

"Perhaps I can help you. The man who cut the Latvian's throat on the Finnish border—any resemblance to him?"

Peters looked up, amazement on his face and in his voice. "Yes, now that you mention it . . ." He seemed to ponder the idea. Then he shook his head. "No, he wouldn't have run the risk, not that man. He killed the Latvian because he scented a trap. Would he really go blundering into another?" He shook his head again. "To me it doesn't make sense."

"We've never traced him—we've never even come close. Odd, Yury, isn't it? Any thoughts on the subject?"

"There are two possibilities, as I see it. Either London recalled him at once and he never reached Moscow, or he got here and they recalled him so as not to upset the banker's plan."

"Is that why you've more or less stopped looking for him?"

Peters said nothing.

"Well?"

"If you feel I haven't been thorough enough, comrade, you can always relieve me of my post."

The sky outside was beginning to pale, the light from the desk lamp losing its brilliance. Dzerzhinsky pushed the lamp aside, perhaps because it had ceased to be an effective aid to interrogation.

"I'm wasting my time on you, it seems." He replaced the document in the folder. "One last question, Yury, just to satisfy my personal curiosity. Why did you hit him?"

The question came as such a surprise that Peters was momentarily at a loss for an answer. He hoped that his voice, at least, wouldn't betray how much it had caught him off balance.

"I don't follow you, Felix Edmundovich."

Dzerzhinsky was lolling back in his chair with his eyes half closed. "It's quite simple. You punched our mysterious stranger in the face. Why?"

Peters thought fast. He couldn't have heard it from Berzin, so he must have questioned the two guards. It was uncharacteristic of Dzerzhinsky to concern himself with such a minor detail.

"I suppose I lost my temper when he wouldn't talk. I still don't see the point of your question."

"Mere curiosity." Dzerzhinsky chuckled to himself. "You wouldn't for an instant hesitate to shoot a man who defied you, but punching him in the face? That doesn't sound like the Yury Peters I know."

Peters shrugged. "With respect, I still find your question puzzling."

"Very well, let's drop the subject. Get one thing straight, though, the pair of you: I want results. I want James Hall and I want the other man, whoever he is."

The desk lamp seemed to distract him again. He switched it off, plunging the office in gloom, then switched it back on and rose to his feet. The other two followed his example.

"The detection of this conspiracy is a stroke of luck," Dzerzhinsky said. "It gives us a little breathing space, but the worst is far from over. There are foreign troops on our soil. The Czechs and the Whites are breathing down our necks. The peasants are resisting collectivization, the workers are striking for more food and higher wages. We're surviving by arresting people in droves and shooting them. I'm sick of sitting here signing death warrants—it's giving me writer's cramp."

He switched off the lamp for good and walked to one of the windows. They really looked like windows now, not mirrors.

"I want results, do you hear, so make sure I get them!"

Peters and Berzin lingered with their coats over their arms, uncertain whether or not they had been dismissed. Dzerzhinsky continued to stand there with his back to them, staring out of the window.

Peters could picture the scene outside as clearly as if he were standing there himself: a sea of buildings, and dominating them the fortresslike Kremlin with its massive walls, towers, palaces, and churches.

Dzerzhinsky seemed far away, but Peters felt sure he could tell what was passing through his mind. There was nothing above Moscow but the Kremlin and nothing above the Kremlin but heaven, so the old saying ran, but the man at the window would not have acknowledged the ultimate truth of that statement. In his estimation, the top floor of Cheka headquarters overtopped the Kremlin and heaven itself.

Dzerzhinsky opened the window. The patter of rain grew louder. Then it was drowned by another sound, distant at first but steadily growing louder and more strident: The ravens were launching their daily invasion of the city. Their harsh cries drifted into the room. Dzerzhinsky shut the window and turned.

"You heard the ravens?" Although his eyes were on the other two, it was hard to know if his words were directed at them. "I listen to those birds every morning. Nothing could convey more clearly that this is Asia, not Europe at all. Asia, comrades!"

The sentries outside Cheka headquarters saluted as Yury Peters emerged, but he was too engrossed in his thoughts to notice. He stood beneath the canopy for a moment, surveying the empty square. The rain had drawn a dismal gray veil over everything in sight—the streets, the buildings—even the blanket of low cloud from which it came.

A streetcar clanged in the distance. The sound brought Peters to life. He set off briskly for the Hotel Billo, still carrying his coat over his arm. There seemed no point in putting it on, the hotel was so near.

At least he hadn't missed Mary; he could see his official car parked immediately outside.

The glittering chandelier in the lobby created an impression of old-world, rather shabby splendor. The air was warm and stale, redolent of wet coats and coffee substitute. Laughter and conversation drifted across from the breakfast room, which was always crowded at this hour. Peters suddenly felt that life had resumed its normal course.

The porter, a man with a lined gray face and gray hair that looked as if he powdered it, slid a key and the morning papers across the desk. "Good morning. I suppose you haven't had breakfast yet. Shall I have it sent up to your suite?"

He always contrived to avoid the word "comrade," Peters noticed, as if it would have been out of keeping with his bourgeois surroundings or disgraced his porter's uniform, however threadbare and shiny.

"Has my daughter had hers?"

"Oh yes, Miss Mary breakfasted in her room. Give me your coat. The weather has changed with a vengeance—rather early this year, wouldn't you say?" The porter glanced across the lobby. "That may be her now. A remarkable young lady, your daughter, if you don't mind my saying so."

Peters picked up his key and the papers, crossed the lobby to the elevator, and stood waiting beside the gilded grille. The arrow on the dial above it showed that the cage was descending.

The first to emerge when the grille slid back was Peters's driver, carrying a child's coat and satchel.

Mary Peters had strikingly fair, flaxen hair and a wealth of not altogether natural ringlets that made her look older than her thirteen years. The face itself was still childish, but her china-blue eyes had the seductive allure of a grown woman. She turned them on her father.

"You missed breakfast again, and you did promise!"

"I'm sorry." Yury Peters, usually so self-assured and self-possessed, sounded rather at a loss. "I really did try to make it."

"All right, I believe you." She smoothed her blue velvet dress, which had a little lace collar. "I'm glad I saw you, at least. Now I must go." She gave the driver a nod.

The driver helped her into her coat, which was also of blue velvet but a trifle darker than the dress. The collar was trimmed with a narrow strip of ermine.

"You think it's right to wear that coat to school?" Peters said.

She laughed a tinkling, rather affected laugh. "It isn't my fault they've closed the International."

"It was pretty ostentatious, Mary, even for the International."

She tossed her curls. "Everyone in school knows who I am—I mean, who my father is. Nobody would dare to say a word against the way I dress, and that includes the teacher. I really must go now. Don't I get a kiss?"

Peters bent down and kissed her on the cheek. The kiss she gave him in return was just as coquettish as her laugh.

"Are we lunching together?" she asked.

"I expect so, yes."

"I hope you'll have shaved by then."

Peters watched her cross the lobby with the gray-uniformed driver at her heels. A bellhop hurried up with an umbrella. He opened the door and escorted them outside.

•19•

As long as he confined his gaze to the body under the blanket, he could persuade himself that there was still a chance. Once he looked at the face, he knew it was hopeless. Jim Hall's massive frame appeared to be fighting on, but not his face. His expression was mournful rather than agonized. A syringe and three empty ampoules lay in a bowl beside the bed.

A tremor ran through the dying man's body. His eyes opened, staring blankly at the ceiling. His neck was so heavily bandaged that he couldn't have turned his head if he'd tried.

Grishin glanced at Olga Krnka, who merely shook her head. Her face looked as weary as he felt, but it radiated the calm, cool professionalism of the trained nurse.

"He's in pain again," Grishin said.

She looked at him with disfavor.

"Can't you give him another shot?"

"That was my last," she said. "Just be thankful I still had three left."

"What's taking your husband so long?"

"Go to the kitchen and make yourself some tea. I'll stay with him. And don't pin any hopes on the doctor," she added. "He can't do any more for him than I've done."

It was a miracle that Hall had withstood the trip at all. He'd been shot three times at point-blank range. One bullet had penetrated his shoulder beside the neck and emerged beneath his arm, shattering the upper ribs. The loss of blood from that gaping wound should have proved fatal by itself. Two more slugs had lodged elsewhere in his back. It was a heaven-sent coincidence that Yasino, where the Krnkas lived, was little more than a mile from the dacha, and that Grishin had recalled this in the nick of time, when he was already on the Moscow road.

"Jim?" He avoided looking Hall in the eye and concentrated on his bloodless lips.

Olga Krnka frowned. "Leave him alone," she said.

He bent lower over the bed. Could a miracle happen? Would he be able to communicate with Hall, ask questions, elicit answers?

"Can you hear me, Jim?"

"That's right," Olga said tartly. "Encourage him to talk, perhaps he'll die quicker that way."

Grishin said no more, but he continued to bend over the dying man. He couldn't be sure, but he thought he saw a gleam of comprehension in Hall's eyes, and his pale lips seemed to shape the name "John."

"No, Jim, forget it. Just take it easy."

"The grave, John . . . the grave . . ."

Olga rose and went to the window. Grishin noticed for the first time that it was already light outside.

"I think they're coming."

He looked back at Hall. His lips, which were closed again, fluttered a little as each labored breath escaped them. Grishin hesitated, then walked around the bed and joined the woman at the window.

The rain had stopped and the sky was brightening. The car's tire tracks, deeply imprinted on the grassy track between the greenhouses, were full of rainwater. They led to the coach house Krnka used as a workshop.

Two figures were approaching the cottage, both wheeling bicycles. One was Krnka, the other a young man with a medical bag strapped to his carrier.

"It's better the doctor shouldn't see you—better for you and better for him. He's a Czech and a friend of Josef's, but one shouldn't impose too much, even on friends."

"Coming here was our only chance. I'm sorry."

"Not as sorry as I am. I knew you were trouble the first time I saw you."

"I couldn't have foreseen this."

Like the expression on her face, an austere oval outlined by the white kerchief she was wearing, her voice softened a little.

"We've all had a long night. Why not go and make that tea? I'll call you if necessary."

The cottage kitchen seemed vast compared to the little room where Hall lay dying. Grishin lit his first cigarette for hours and listened to the murmur of voices in the passage.

The cigarette tasted of nothing—he couldn't even feel it between his lips. Peters's blow hadn't broken any bones, just split the skin over his cheekbone, and Olga Krnka had stitched that superficial wound together. The swelling was already going down, though breathing through his nose presented problems. It was almost devoid of sensation and bled at frequent intervals.

Josef Krnka came padding into the kitchen carrying his muddy shoes. His jacket and trousers were also sodden and splashed with mud. He nodded to the man he still knew as Gregor Constantine.

"Sorry I took so long."

Krnka's eyes disappeared behind a film of condensation as his steel-rimmed glasses steamed up in the warmth of the kitchen. He removed the glasses and placed them carefully on the kitchen table.

"Would you mind putting some wood on?"

Grishin choked back the question he was itching to ask and went over to the kitchen stove. Some embers were still glowing in the grate, so he added a couple of billets from the box of firewood beside it. When he turned he saw that Krnka had already stripped off his wet things and was standing there in his coarse gray underclothes.

"I only have one suit," he said as he hung the sodden garments on a line near the stove. "That's all we Czechs are allowed. Tell me, how's that face of yours?"

"Your wife's a miracle worker," Grishin replied, wondering why Krnka didn't tell him whether or not he'd made the call.

"Twelve years a nurse, four of them at the front—there's nothing she hasn't seen, nothing she can't do . . . You must be hungry. I'll see if I can find us something to eat."

"She told me she's working at a hospital again."

"Yes, we got divorced. A curious solution, but it meant she got her Russian citizenship back."

Grishin wanted desperately to ask him straight out. Perhaps he'd forgotten to telephone in all the excitement.

"There are some potatoes and an egg or two," said Krnka, busying himself at the stove. "I'll make us some tea, too. You must eat something."

"Did the doctor ask a lot of questions?"

"I wouldn't have fetched him if he was the inquisitive type. He's a good doctor. If there's anything to be done for your friend, he'll do it."

Krnka carried the plates to the table, and they ate in silence. Grishin was hungry, but he tasted as little of the food as he had of his cigarette. Krnka rose, turned the clothes on the line, and came back with two big mugs of tea. Grishin, who had his ears pricked for sounds elsewhere in the house, noticed that Krnka was listening too.

The Czech polished his glasses with his vest and replaced them on his nose. "Olga doesn't show it," he said, "but she's scared they'll find you here."

"I'll be gone by the time she comes home from work, Krnka. So will my friend and the car."

"But . . ."

"Did you call the number I gave you?"

"Of course. I should have told you right away."

"Was it still connected?"

Krnka took a cigarette from his battered tin box. Grishin lit it for him.

"Thanks. Yes, the number was in order. I followed your instructions to the letter. When a woman answered, I passed on the message and hung up at once."

Krnka cleared his throat a couple of times. Then he said, "It won't be too easy, getting out of here. All the roads I saw this morning were being watched. There were roadblocks and checkpoints everywhere."

Grishin felt strangely calm. "I've paid several visits to Kuntsevo in the last few days," he said. "My papers were examined every time."

"They check to see if the peasants going to market have their permits, true, and they're always on the lookout for deserters. But this morning—well, that was different."

"Where did you fetch the doctor from?"

"Nemchinovka, that's why I took so long."

"That's on the main road, isn't it—the one that runs beside the railroad track?"

"In this weather it's the only road passable by car, and today there were five soldiers manning the roadblock beside the bridge. I used side roads on the way back, but there were checkpoints there too."

"Five sentries at the bridge, you said?"

"I'm not saying it's all on your account, but there's certainly something up."

Grishin's nose started bleeding again. He tilted back his head to stem the flow and reached for a rag.

"You move around too much," Krnka said. "Sit quietly for a while and . . ." He broke off. Voices could be heard in the passage again.

He's dead, thought Grishin.

The voices ceased. Olga Krnka opened the door and glanced at her husband. "Leave us for a moment, would you?"

"I'm in my underpants," Krnka grumbled, but he got up and went out.

Olga shut the door behind him, and Grishin knew: everything she did conveyed it. She removed her kerchief, shook out her hair, went to the stove, warmed her hands at it, poured herself a mug of tea.

"Why didn't you call me?"

She stared at him over her mug. There was no sympathy in her expression, just reproach. Grishin had turned and was on his way to the door when she broke the silence.

"He died of internal bleeding."

Grishin spun around. "As I see it, he died because somebody sneaked up on him in the dark and shot him three times in the back."

"The real damage was done by two projectiles which—"

Grishin laughed. *"Projectiles?* Did you learn that term from your husband, or does it just sound more innocuous?"

"One of them penetrated the left lung and caused massive hemorrhaging. The other damaged the spinal column and—"

"Stop it! He's dead, isn't that enough?"

"There's something you might like to know. In the doctor's

opinion, he wouldn't have survived even if you'd take him straight to a hospital."

But Grishin, who had already left the kitchen, didn't hear.

When he was alone with the body in the other room—alone with the blanket-enshrouded form that might have belonged to a big, strong, healthy man playing dead—he couldn't even bring himself to fold the blanket down and look at Hall's face.

He stepped back a pace. He had no real sensation of being alone with death. For a moment he felt something akin to anger at Jim Hall, and both of them—his anger and the man beneath the blanket—were very much alive. *I told you it was a trap—well, didn't I? We should have avoided that dacha like the plague— you knew it yourself—but no: Our man's in there—we can't leave our man in the lurch. Well, I'm your man too, but me you've walked out on for good!*

They were both in the kitchen when he returned. Olga didn't seem to have stirred from the spot. She was still standing beside the stove, cradling the mug in her hands.

"Did he say anything more?" Grishin asked.

She took a sip of tea. "It sounded like a name."

"Russian?"

"Yes. A woman's name."

He suddenly remembered the few words Hall had muttered and the white marble figure at Vaganskoye Cemetery, Row M, Grave No. 37.

"Did you catch it?"

"I'm not sure. Could it have been Dagmara?"

"Dagmara Fyodorova?"

"Yes, I think that was it." She put her mug down. "I have to go now."

Krnka made an apologetic gesture when the door had closed behind her. "You've got to see it from her point of view."

Grishin rolled himself a cigarette. To his surprise, he could taste the tobacco again.

"Did you finish off your job for Michelson?" he asked, purely for something to say.

"Yes. Just in time, too. Stefan Michelson isn't the 'comrade director' anymore."

"Why, what happened?"

"They caught him blackmarketeering—trading guns for food for his workers." Krnka paused. "Anything I can do for you?"

"Could I put my head down for an hour or two before I go?" He had to reach a decision. He knew there was probably no correct decision open to him, but he also knew that he would reach a better one if he was rested.

"You can have my room. Anything else?"

"Yes, the car—I think the radiator's sprung a leak. Would you mind topping it up for me?"

"How do you propose to get that car . . ." Krnka's voice trailed off when he saw Grishin produce the gun from his waistband.

Grishin couldn't recall how many shots he'd fired. He now saw that four of the six chambers were empty.

"Do you have any ammunition for this thing?"

Krnka peered at the revolver with furrowed brow and narrowed eyes. "May I see it?"

Grishin noted the change that took place in him as soon as the gun was in his hand. He seemed less edgy, displayed the same professional composure Grishin had observed in his wife all night long.

"Superb workmanship." Krnka's fingers closed around the butt. "Fits the hand beautifully—perfectly balanced. A little gem of a gun. I never even noticed it on you." He continued to study the revolver from all angles. "I suppose you know what it is?"

"A derringer, at a guess."

"Correct, but there are derringers and derringers." Krnka was not so much conversing as communing with himself. "Some are cheap and shoddy, but a few . . ." He cocked the revolver on an empty chamber, aimed, squeezed the trigger. "This one was made by a master craftsman. Know what we call such a weapon in the trade?"

Grishin recalled Jim Hall's description: a gun for cardsharps, bartenders, brothel-keepers.

"The Assassin," said Krnka. "Easily concealed and absolutely lethal at close range. The Americans have used it on two of their Presidents." He broke the gun and ejected the remaining shells. "Unusual caliber . . . An ounce of lead . . . No, I've nothing of the kind in stock. Still," he added quickly, "if you're going to lie down for an hour or two I can make you some. Anything else?'

"A couple of minor details, but we can discuss those later."

Krnka nodded, already halfway to the door. He looked as if he could hardly wait to get to his workshop.

Grishin felt far less like sleep once he was stretched out on Krnka's bed. The dead man seemed much closer than before. It was as though Hall had made him two bequests: a gun, and a name.

Who was Dagmara Fyodorova, and what had been her relationship with the dead man? She herself had died in November 1917, at the height of the Revolution. A ballerina? Jim Hall had answered those questions by default—by his silence.

But the gun? What kind of legacy was that?

Jim Hall had known all about the gun. He hadn't actually referred to it by the same name as Krnka, "the Assassin," but that meant nothing. Hall had always loved codes and ciphers—the intelligence agent's puzzle books—more than anything else in the world. Was the gun's sobriquet merely coincidental, or had he meant it to convey a hidden message?

Before Grishin fell asleep he pictured Jim Hall smiling inscrutably, one dimple in each fat cheek, the way he always smiled when playing some diabolical trick on the opposition.

Go on, the smile said, *figure it out for yourself.*

•20•

The boy knew precisely what was happening. Lena Valentinova couldn't recall his name for the moment, but he was an observant youngster, and he'd been in the convent's infirmary long enough to know what it meant when a bed was screened off from the rest of the ward. He must often have heard her whispering behind the screen with the doctor. Sometimes, too, he must have heard the cries of the dying.

This boy wouldn't cry out, Lena felt sure. It wasn't his way, and besides, he was probably too weak.

The boy's face—why *couldn't* she recall his name?—was beaded with perspiration and his eyes were closed. She concentrated on his face because she couldn't bear to look at the rest of him. His body was covered with lentil-sized red blotches, some of which were oozing blood, and his breathing was as labored and erratic as if all his ribs had been broken.

Half delirious, he muttered a word she failed to catch. Unable to think of anything else that would have excited such concern in his feverish brain, she wondered if he had a knife hidden under his mattress.

"Can you make out what he's saying?" The doctor, a quiet-spoken little man shorter than Lena herself, was close to exhaustion but steadfastly courteous and considerate.

"I'm afraid not." She would have regarded it as an act of betrayal to mention the possibility of a knife.

He felt the boy's pulse and shook his head.

"Can't you give him a shot of strychnine?"

He hesitated, then let go of the boy's wrist and beckoned her outside the screen.

"Look," he said, "I'm keeping it for the ones with a reasonable chance of survival. In his case it would merely prolong the agony."

"Please try. It's so seldom we have any."

"There's no point. Listen, why not get some rest?"

"Try it, please!" She didn't know herself why she was being so insistent.

He retired behind the screen again, alone this time. Lena could never bring herself to watch a needle piercing human flesh. She stood outside, waiting for the clatter of the ampoule and syringe as the doctor put them back in the enamel bowl.

Eventually, when nothing happened, she peeked around the edge of the screen. The doctor was in the act of pulling the coarse gray sheet up over the boy's face. She suddenly remembered his name.

"Too late, I'm afraid."

He took her arm and steered her away from the bed. She was glad that the long ward was in semidarkness despite its numerous windows. Rain was teeming down out of a gloomy, overcast sky. There were a dozen beds on either side of the central aisle, all of them occupied. Lena felt she was the focus of twenty-three pairs of eyes.

"Go and get some rest now, I'll attend to the others. Just for the record, what was his name?"

"Ilya."

"Is that all?"

"Yes, damn it, that's all!"

She turned on her heel, feeling tired and disconsolate. Her head ached as she made her way between the twin rows of beds. The boy had been a favorite of hers, even though he, more than most, had always brusquely rejected any friendly overtures.

Eva Dashkova, who had been hovering outside the ward, held the door for her. Her hair was now so long that she had to tie it back with a ribbon.

"How's Ilya?" she asked, but Lena's face was answer enough. "I'll tell Dimitry," she said hurriedly. She pointed along the corridor. "There's someone to see you."

"When you fetch Dimitry, tell him he'll probably find a knife under the mattress."

"He would have looked anyway."

"Tell him to bury it with the body," Lena said curtly. The knife had been Ilya's sole possession—the only thing he valued. It consoled her a little to think that he and his knife would not be parted.

He was standing at one of the windows in the entrance hall with his back to her, but she recognized the black leather jacket at once.

Although he must have heard her coming he continued to stand there, leaning forward slightly and gazing down at something in the convent's inner courtyard. Joining him at the window, she saw some men unloading sacks from an open truck—sacks of precious white flour.

"What on earth!"

Her exclamation was born of sheer surprise, but all she felt when she turned and looked into Yury Peters's bland, round face was fear—fear mingled with an uneasy recollection of the strange phone call that morning: the voice with the foreign accent, the brief and far from reassuring message. So that's why he's here, she thought. Her fatigue disappeared in a flash, and so did her blinding headache. If she couldn't banish her fear of the man, at least she was on her guard.

"A gift," he explained, "from the haves to the have-nots."

"I thought the haves had been liquidated."

"Let's say there are still some citizens of our Soviet republic who enjoy more privileges than others."

"So we'd noticed." It sounded ruder than she'd intended.

"I heard you were suffering from a temporary bottleneck in supplies, to use the current phrase." He eyed her quizzically. "Well, don't I get any thanks?"

"All that flour—where has it come from?"

"Does it matter?" He grinned. "From somewhere that has inherited your temporary bottleneck."

"I'm not in the mood for jokes, especially not today."

"More typhus?"

"Another death."

"One of the children? I'm sorry, truly sorry."

Oddly enough, Lena thought, he sounded sincere. His face had darkened.

"You didn't come here to express your sympathy, I'm sure."

He started to speak, but something distracted him. He was facing in the direction of the infirmary, so he'd caught sight of them first. The two men had rolled up the boy's body in a gray blanket and were carrying it along the passage, one at either end. They were such an ill-assorted pair—Dimitry, a giant, towered head and shoulders above his much shorter companion—that the limp gray sausage dangled between them at an extreme angle. Dimitry must have been helping to unload the truck in the courtyard, because the back of his smock was white with flour.

"Poor child . . . How sad!"

Lena was surprised yet again to hear the compassion in Peters's voice.

"How old was she?" he asked.

"Twelve." Then his exact words sank in. "It was a boy."

"A boy? I don't know why, I took it for granted . . ." Abruptly, he seemed to lose interest. "Can we talk somewhere? Your office, perhaps?"

"Do we have something to discuss?"

From the way he nodded, she felt more than ever convinced that he was there on Yevgeny's account.

"Well?" she said, as soon as Eva Dashkova had served tea and left them alone together. "I don't have much time. Would you mind coming to the point?"

"I'll try. To be honest, though, I'm taking a bit of a risk, and it goes against the grain. I'm not a gambler by nature." Peters stroked his chin. He'd shaved, but he still looked as if he'd been up all night. "How long have we known each other? My first sight of you was in Paris, at Père-Lachaise. I'd come over from England for the funeral. You, of course, had eyes for no one but Comrade Lenin— or was it still Ulyanov in those days?"

"Why rake over the past?"

"You joined the Party soon afterward, didn't you? You, the daughter of Kyril Samsonov, one of the wealthiest men in Russia. Strange but true . . ." Peters seemed engrossed in long-forgotten memories. "Those were great days, happy days. Rich or poor, what did it matter? None of us cared whether we ate or went hungry. We nourished ourselves on our beliefs, our hopes. Our heads were in the clouds. What prospects, what infinite possibilities . . ." He leaned across the desk, and his tone changed. "To return to the present. Is it true you've been having certain differences of opinion with Comrade Martov of the Twelfth Tribunal?"

"Is that what this is about?" Relief surged through her.

"Some comrades in your position might be apprehensive, but you're made of sterner stuff." He watched her intently. "That's what I'm pinning my hopes on."

"I don't understand."

"Your friend Lloyd Fleming was arrested last night."

Lena recalled Yevgeny's words of warning. "I haven't seen Mr. Fleming for weeks," she said casually.

"He's locked up in a cell at Cheka headquarters, accused of conspiring against Lenin's life—among other things."

"Is that all?"

Peters had a talent for silence. His silences could be more intimidating than any volley of threats, but Lena was unafraid. She knew she could hold out.

"You don't seem unduly concerned," he said at length. "I'm glad, because it implies that all the gossip in Moscow about your relations with Fleming was merely that and nothing more."

Lena was feeling surer of herself. "Isn't our conversation becoming a little too personal?" she said boldly.

"Mr. Fleming blundered into a Cheka trap. Another Englishman lost his life: James Hall."

"How does that concern me?"

"I regret to inform you," Peters said, "that a third man was involved." Still watching her face intently, he nodded as if to confirm the truth of what he saw there. "Ah yes, Lena Valentinova, I can see it in your eyes. My hopes have been fulfilled. I can see even more than I expected. *That* information did strike a chord somewhere!"

Lena held his gaze, but without any certainty that she would be able to endure another of his silences. She was relieved when he broke it himself.

"My problem is, how can I induce you to trust me? It would militate against all your instincts, wouldn't it?" He sighed. "May I have some more tea?"

"It'll be cold by this time."

"Never mind."

She refilled his cup, willing her hands not to tremble, but Peters made no move to drink.

"We needn't give this third man a name—a name would mean nothing in his case, so let's dispense with one. At all events, he's a man who knows how to survive, who doesn't make mistakes—or didn't until last night.'' He reached for his cup so roughly that tea slopped over the rim. "I'm sorry."

Her headache was coming back. Any excuse to move was welcome, so she fetched a cloth and mopped the desk.

"You know who I mean," Peters said when she'd sat down again. "Remember the frontier incident at Easter? Remember our conversation? That was when the subject first came up. You didn't know him then, of course, but you do now." He hadn't raised his voice or injected any note of menace into the words. He had simply made a statement without expecting her to confirm it. "Didn't it ever occur to you that, in spite of his talent for survival, the man in question needed help from some outside quarter?"

Again he played his silent card, and this time it was Lena who spoke first.

"Why are you telling me all this?"

"Do you believe me?"

"What if I did?"

"Has he ever told you why he came to Moscow? I see from your face that he hasn't. That's good. His blunder last night infuriated me, can you understand that?" He looked at her inquiringly. "Have you any means of contacting him?" Another pause. "I see, so we're back where we started."

"Would it be like him to tell me where he can be found?"

"He may get in touch with you."

Her fears came flooding back. How could she have admitted so much, even by implication? How could she have thought herself a match for a man like Yury Peters?

"I hope he does get in touch with you," Peters said. "I really do —it's his only chance . . . Any tea left? No?" He looked around for something to fiddle with. All he could find were the mother superior's sheep shears. Their function seemed to mystify him. He turned them over in his hands and put them down again.

"He may, of course, have abandoned his plan." Peters shook his head as though to convince himself that this was unthinkable. "Listen to me. It's a month since a certain man has ventured outside the Kremlin. All he ever sees is the view from his window. He lives on his private Olympus. He knows nothing of Russia anymore, and Russia knows nothing of him. I needn't mention his name, need I? No mere mortal should take the name of his god in vain!"

Lena wasn't sure she'd heard him aright, but there was no mistaking the violence of his emotions. Could he really be talking about Lenin? When he continued, the words poured forth like a pent-up flood.

"It wasn't always so. You could speak with him in the old days—anyone could. He was accessible to the humblest worker, sailor, peasant—even to a wigmaker, comrade!—but now he's a god. Not Christ crucified, but one who crucifies others, who drives the thorns and nails into their living flesh . . ."

He's crazy, she thought. She was confronted by a stranger, a demented stranger. And then, from one moment to the next, like red-hot iron plunged in water, he became the Yury Peters she knew: cold, supercilious, dispassionate.

"Listen carefully, comrade. Our god has finally recognized the need to come down from Olympus, just this once, and address his devotees. He intends to deliver speeches at two factories whose workers are threatening to go on strike: the Aleksandrovsky Railroad Works and the Moscow Arms and Ammunition Factory, formerly the Michelson Works . . ."

He eyed her coldly and appraisingly. Like a gardener waiting for parched soil to absorb one application of water before giving it another, he was allowing her time to digest his words.

"Both speeches are scheduled for this evening. Their timing is as follows: six-thirty at the Aleksandrovsky Works, eight-thirty in the newly constructed workshop at the Michelson Works. He insists on being driven to both functions in his gray Rolls-Royce. A second Rolls of the same model and color will follow on behind. Traveling in it—are you listening, comrade?—will be a decoy, a man who closely resembles him."

Again he paused to let the words sink in.

"Security precautions for the double will be nominal only. The real man will be surrounded by four bodyguards, all of them a good head taller, three of them with very fair hair . . . Well, will you pass that on?"

"You're mad!"

"I told you, I'm no gambler," he said. "This isn't a sudden brainstorm; I'm giving your man a last chance."

"I still don't know what you're talking about." Lena was afraid to say anything else.

"Tell him, that's all I ask. Leave the decision to him."

Peters nodded to her and rose. At the door he turned.

"Was it really a boy? A boy of twelve? There seemed to be so little of him."

•21•

It was raining again. Not as hard as it had last night, but the ground was still sodden and muddy. Grishin had wasted an hour trying various side roads in the hope of getting through without having to pass a checkpoint, but they either brought him out on the only main road to Moscow or proved so narrow and impassable that he almost got bogged down and had to return to the main road willy-nilly.

From his own recollections and what Krnka had told him, he was less than a mile from the roadblock on the outskirts of Nemchinovka. He pulled over and got out. The road was flanked by willows, the adjoining ditch awash with rainwater. Torn off by the gale, the first autumn leaves were drifting along on the turbid surface of the stream.

The road and the railroad track ran parallel for several hundred yards before crossing a small river. The roadblock must be just this side of the bridge. The visibility was too poor for him to see anything in detail at this range, but a long line of stationary farm wagons indicated that the roadblock and the men guarding it were still in position. Peering through the drizzle, he could just discern the jagged gray outlines of Moscow in the distance.

Grishin removed his jacket and got back into the car to complete his preparations. He barely glanced at the body wedged in behind the seats, though he could now look at it without a twinge of emotion. It was just an anonymous corpse. Jim Hall was someone else, someone wholly remote and unconnected with it: a man to whom he, Grishin, had given his word.

Spreading the jacket across his knees, Grishin took the scissors he'd begged from Krnka and unpicked the hem. Secreted inside the lining was the identity card made out in the name of Cheka

Commissar Relinsky. He sewed up the hem and propped the card on the dashboard, photograph outward, just beneath the rearview mirror. Then he combed his hair down over his forehead, like the Grishin in the photograph, and cut a straight fringe two inches above his eyebrows, trimmed his eyebrows themselves, which were on the bushy side, and snipped away the hair around his ears to accentuate their size. He retrieved the black peaked cap from under the seat, where he'd left it the previous night, and put it on so that it exposed a little of his fringe. Finally, he pocketed the identity card and slipped a red armband—a last-minute addition made from an old dress of Olga Krnka's—over the left sleeve of his jacket.

There was nothing to be done about the cut on his cheek, so he had removed the dressing altogether. The angry red wound and the black stitches protruding from it lent him a tough, ferocious appearance quite in keeping with his new persona.

Having jettisoned the scissors, needle, and thread in the ditch, he took the revolver from his waistband and weighed it in his hand. It was fully loaded now.

Krnka had woken him after six hours of deep, dreamless sleep. The Czech had barely given him time to shave and get dressed, just hovered there impatiently until Grishin followed him into the kitchen. Neatly arrayed on the kitchen table was a row of shiny cartridge cases, each tipped with a dull gray cone of lead. The gunsmith's eyes had shone no less brightly than his cylinders of burnished brass . . .

Grishin was finding it hard to distinguish the road clearly through the windshield, which continually misted up in the damp atmosphere. He switched on the headlights, not to help him see better, but to advertise his approach. The road was so thick with mud that he could scarcely detect the asphalt surface beneath.

A freight train overtook him on the single-track line to his left and slowed as it neared the bridge. Some wagons on the far side of the river waited for the train to cross and were then waved on.

He could see the sentries now. One was checking papers while his companions kept watch on the line of wagons and pedestrians. Five dark figures with ankle-length greatcoats brushing the ground and rifles slung, they stood out clearly against the rainwashed sky.

They caught sight of him when he was a hundred yards away,

waved the wagons on the bridge to a halt, and stared in his direction.

Grishin accelerated, but not too much. He wanted to give them the impression that he was in a hurry, not that he intended to bull his way through without stopping. At fifty yards he flashed his headlights, at twenty he sounded his horn, at ten he leaned out of the window and started shouting.

"Clear the road! Let me through! Get those people out of the way!"

One man stepped out into the middle of the road and raised his hand. The others unslung their rifles. Beyond them stood several wagons filled with peasants. There might have been just enough room on the bridge for the coupe to have squeezed past if Grishin had simply put his foot down, but he wouldn't have survived a hail of rifle fire.

He pulled up right beside the man in the road, who proved to be a sergeant. At a sign from him, the others surrounded the car with their rifles at the ready. Their fresh young faces were ruddy-cheeked and beaded with moisture. Grishin ignored them. Only the man beside him counted. He leaned farther out of the window, one hand on the wheel, the other on his thigh.

"You there! Get those confounded peasants out of my way!"

"All in good time, comrade, all in good time."

The sergeant was a thickset, sturdy man with a drooping gray mustache. The collar of his greatcoat was up and his cap pulled down low. He was so short that his eyes were almost level with Grishin's, but the look in them suggested that he was more used to giving orders than receiving them. He rested one hand on the roof of the car.

"Where are you bound for, comrade?"

Grishin watched him inspect the interior. His expression hardly changed when he caught sight of the big, inert form behind the seats.

"You're holding me up," Grishin snapped, far from certain that he was making any impression on the man at all. "Is there a telephone near here?"

"Where to, comrade?"

"I asked you a question. I advise you to answer it."

"You do, do you?" The sergeant laughed grimly and turned to his men. "If he makes any trouble, shoot him."

Grishin sighed. "If they do, Comrade Sergeant, at least go to the nearest phone and call Moscow 134." He paused for effect. "That's Cheka headquarters, in case you didn't know. Ask for Comrade Dzerzhinsky—maybe you've heard of him? Felix Edmundovich Dzerzhinsky . . . Tell him you've just shot one of his commissars."

The sergeant removed his hand from the car roof. "May I see your papers?"

Grishin produced the identity card from his breast pocket and held it out of the window, photograph upward. If he thought that would be enough, he was mistaken. The sergeant took it and stepped back a pace. He looked at the photograph, then at Grishin, then at the photograph again.

"Comrade Relinsky?"

"Commissar Relinsky." Grishin sounded more irritable than angry. "What is it now?"

He watched the sergeant's face, unsure whether a Cheka commissar's papers would be sufficient to overawe him. Even though his chances of survival would have been slender, he was still poised to drive straight on.

"What happened to the man in the back?"

Grishin sighed again. "What does it look like? He's dead."

"That doesn't answer my question, comrade."

"Listen! I'm not obliged to answer you at all, but let's not make life any harder than it is already. That's an Englishman's carcass back there—he was shot in a raid last night. Now may I have my papers back?" Grishin scowled. "Make up your mind, Sergeant. Either let me through or get to a phone and call that number. Tell Comrade Dzerzhinsky he needn't worry about the English spy anymore, you've seen his body with your own eyes."

The sergeant's manner remained wary. Grishin could almost see his brain churning. He had his orders, but "Cheka" and "Dzerzhinsky" were potent, intimidating names. That was his problem: orders versus fear.

The rain was dripping off his cap. He sucked in his lower lip and proceeded to chew it.

The two men eyed each other in silence, one hoping against hope, the other cogitating furiously. Without surrendering the identity card, the sergeant circled the car once and returned to the driver's window. He indicated the steam escaping from the radia-tor cap.

"You'd better top that up," he said, "or you won't get much farther." Grudgingly, he handed the identity card back.

Fear had won the day, Grishin thought—it usually did. Aloud he said, "Now perhaps you'll get those goddamned peasants out of my way!"

The sergeant barked an order. His men slung their rifles and doubled toward the bridge, baying like a pack of hounds and waving the peasants aside. Grishin let in the clutch. The wheels spun in the mud and failed to grip. The sergeant smiled sardoni-cally.

"You're overloaded, Comrade Commissar. English spies must eat better than honest revolutionaries!"

Grishin glared at him. "Tell your men to give me a push."

Two of the soldiers braced their shoulders against the back of the car. Grishin let in the clutch and stepped on the gas. The wheels started spinning again, then gripped. The men jumped aside, swearing volubly, as mud spurted into the air.

After a few yards Grishin felt the iron plates of the bridge be-neath him. The other two soldiers bellowed at the peasants to stand clear. They stared at Grishin with hatred written on their workworn faces. One of them spat as he passed. A glance at the rearview mirror told him that the sergeant was still standing in the middle of the road, gazing after him, but he scarcely registered the fact. The car was claiming his full attention: its squeaks and rattles, the steam now jetting from the radiator cap, the fuel gauge, the speedometer.

He had left the bridge behind and was driving along an asphalt road flanked by squat suburban houses. The car was making pro-testing noises. He saw he was driving too fast and took his foot off the gas pedal. It suddenly occurred to him that he'd flipped the derringer's safety catch before reaching the roadblock. He re-moved one hand from the wheel and felt for it. His fingers were trembling so much, it was all he could do to depress the little lever.

The room on the top floor of the house overlooking Red Garden felt chilly. Lena sat perched on the edge of the divan, cradling a cup of tea in her hands and staring at the telephone. The light was already fading.

Her initial hope that he would contact her at Yelizaveta Maria had dwindled with every passing hour, to be replaced by mounting uncertainty. Then, just before going home, she had received an unexpected phone call from Peters.

Jim Hall's body had been found in a side street near the Italian embassy, in the back of the ambassador's coupe. The car had suffered from the attentions of a street gang. The youngsters had removed the tires, stripped the leather off the seats, and rifled the dead man's pockets. They had taken his money but left his identification and the strange note pinned to his jacket. Some passersby had seen them at work and called the police.

Peters's account of the find was brief and businesslike, but Lena couldn't fail to detect the triumph in his concluding words: "That means he's back in town!" She had hung up before he could say any more.

She rose, still holding her cup of tea, and went to the window. A gale had sprung up and snapped some of the big top's guy ropes. She could see figures scurrying around in the gloom, struggling to recapture the billowing canvas and peg it down. The tea stalls were shut and the roller coaster had suspended operations for the night. It saddened her to think she might never see Red Garden again.

She made her way to the kitchen, put the cup down, and retired to the little washroom next door. It was so dark in there that she switched on the light. When she saw her pale, haggard face in the mirror, she wished she hadn't.

What if he comes here!

She washed her face and dabbed it dry. The only makeup she possessed was an old box of mascara, a relic of her Paris days. Very carefully, taking her time, she applied some to her lashes and traced the line of her eyebrows. In default of lipstick or rouge, she bit her lips and pinched her cheeks the way her mother used to. Feeling slightly better, she combed her hair and returned to the living room.

With the light on and the curtains drawn, she pulled a suitcase from under the divan and proceeded to pack a few things: underclothes, a couple of dresses, her only other pair of shoes. Then she opened the lid of the piano. The envelope of money Yevgeny had given her was inside, together with the cloth-wrapped object he'd hidden there weeks ago. It had neither surprised nor alarmed her to discover that the bundle contained a gun. She had always smiled at Muranov's habit of keeping a similar weapon handy at all times, even on the bedside table at nights. Putting the gun in a paper bag to keep the oil off her clothes, she stowed it and the money at the bottom of the suitcase, secured the clips, and draped her coat over it.

Just then the telephone rang. She froze, unable to move.

I won't tell him about Peters, she thought, I'll simply listen to what he has to say. He'll probably tell me where to meet him, that's all. Of course—that's why he's calling! He knows I'm ready to leave. We're going away together after all. She could already hear his deep, calm voice above the insistent ring of the telephone.

She dashed across the room, quite forgetting that the first thing she heard would be the flat, impersonal voice of the operator.

"Six-one-four? Are you there, six-one-four?"

"Yes, speaking."

"What took you so long?" Lena heard the customary babble of distant, disembodied voices, then the operator again. "Go ahead, please." A noose seemed to tighten around her throat.

"Lena?"

She found her voice at last. "Yes?"

"I hear you're leaving town and going to stay with friends in the country. Is that right?"

She drew a deep breath and forgot her fears. He was saying precisely what she wanted to hear.

"Where shall we meet?"

The disembodied voices rose to a crescendo and the line seemed to go dead before she heard his voice again.

"Don't postpone your trip, understand? Leave at once."

"Why," she said, "aren't you coming too?"

"What's wrong, Lena?" No amount of background noise could disguise the urgency in his tone. "Lena? You'd better tell me."

"I had a visitor today."

"Well, go on."

"My things are all packed. I'm ready to leave right away."

"This visitor—did he give you a message for me?"

"I haven't even told you who it was."

"You don't have to."

"Promise me you won't go . . ."

"Lena, please!"

"It sounds so crazy."

"The message, Lena!"

"What time is it?"

"Just after eight."

She breathed a sigh of relief. "Then it's too late anyway . . ." She knew he was waiting for her to go on—knew he wouldn't give up till she'd told him. Why shouldn't she trust him to make the right decision? "He's addressing the staff of the Michelson Works half an hour from now."

"You say you're packed?"

"He'll be driven there in his car, a—"

"Lena, listen to me: Leave the apartment at once."

"I didn't want to mention it, but now I'd better tell you everything."

"You've already told me all I need to know. Just *listen,* I beg you."

"All right." There was nothing she wanted more than to hear his calm, reassuring voice.

"Only take the barest essentials—nothing compromising, know what I mean? Go to Yaroslavl Station and take a train to Kostroma —the first one out. At Kostroma change to the Vyatka-Perm line and get off at Unshaskoye . . . Unshaskoye on the Unsha."

"What about you, Yevgeny? Will you—"

"The stationmaster at Unshaskoye is a man named Bibikov. Tell him Vada Nikulin said to look after you. I hope you can play chess. That's all, Lena. I'll see you at Unshaskoye . . ."

The earpiece hissed and crackled for another few seconds. Then it went dead. Lena waited awhile before hanging up. All she felt at first was relief. She could forget about Peters and his visit, Martov and the Twelfth Tribunal, even the convent infirmary—yes, even that, without a pang of conscience. One thought alone possessed her: the prospect of sitting in a train leaving Moscow.

Unshaskoye . . . She'd never heard of the place, but the very name sounded like a promise.

Opening the suitcase again, she removed the money and the paper bag containing the gun. He was right—the risk of a random search was too great. She replaced them both inside the piano and put her coat on. Then she picked up the case, went to the door, and listened. All was quiet. Ever since her altercation with Martov she'd been in the habit of checking the phone before leaving the apartment. She did so again, and this time the line was dead.

She put the suitcase down, jiggled the hook, cranked the handle to attract the operator's attention. No answer, no background noise: The phone had been disconnected. She repeated the whole procedure until she was quite sure.

She went back to the divan and sat down, feeling dazed. Why now, of all times, just after he'd called her? Coincidence? Could it really be a coincidence, or had they been waiting for that one call?

She summoned up a detailed recollection of Peters's visit, his words, his demeanor. Yury Peters on her side? How could she have believed that for a single moment? Why should a man like Peters have come to Yelizaveta Maria, wormed his way into her confidence, said those crazy things? Why had it mattered to him so much that Yevgeny should learn of those meetings? There could be only one explanation, of that she now felt quite convinced: It was a trap laid by the Cheka for the man who had eluded them for so long.

I should never have told him. He's on his way there this minute, just because I passed the message on. I should never, never have told him!

All that mitigated her sense of doom—all she clung to—was one short sentence uttered in a deep, calm voice:

I'll see you at Unshaskoye . . .

She knew nothing of Unshaskoye, but she could picture the station, a red brick building with an overhanging canopy and a garden enclosed by a white picket fence; the stationmaster,

Bibikov, a man in a baggy black uniform and clumsy boots; a chessboard with all the pieces set out except two pawns, one black and one white. She could see Bibikov conceal them behind his back and hold them out for her to choose.

But she could also picture another scene—one that was more familiar to her: a vast, crowded hall and a platform draped in red bunting. She could see the man on the speaker's rostrum—or rather, she wanted to see him. All she actually saw was his photograph on the wall of the Twelfth Tribunal's courtroom. It was that almost irrelevant image which infuriated her most of all. The picture was taken years ago, she thought, but that's the one he insists on displaying everywhere—that and no other!

She went back to the piano and took out the brown paper bag containing the gun. The suitcase she left where it was—she didn't even bother to lock the door behind her.

It was damp and raw for an August night. She hugged the bag to her chest, but no one gave her a second glance. Muscovites made a habit of carrying paper bags wherever they went, just in case they passed a store with something on the shelves worth buying.

• 23 •

The wind was gusting harder than ever. Dark clouds scudded low overhead, and hundreds of handbills were swirling around the square in front of Prokovsky Church, alias the Bazmannaya Workers' Social Club. When Grishin picked one up, the printer's ink was so fresh it came off on his fingers. Little effort had been made to hand them out, it seemed—either that, or the workers had discarded them because the paper was too poor to roll tobacco in.

He paused and surveyed the square. The street leading to the Michelson Works was feebly illuminated by a few flickering gas lamps. The bare brick walls of the factory buildings on either side lent it a cavernous appearance. The square was almost deserted, yet not far away, Grishin knew, was a huge hall crowded with workers. If the meeting had begun on time, his decision couldn't be delayed much longer.

He felt for the revolver to satisfy himself that it was securely tucked into his waistband. There had been no time to retrieve the hybrid pistol concealed beneath the floorboards of his room near Sukharov market. It simply meant that he would have to get closer to his target.

Buttoning his jacket, he walked quickly across the square to the Workers' Club. His mind was made up.

The string of colored bulbs above the former church door did little to create a festive impression. Neither did the music coming from inside.

He opened the door and went in. The nave was lit, though only dimly, by more colored bulbs strung between the stone columns, which were additionally festooned with paper chains. The church windows had been draped with the inevitable red bunting, the altar demolished and replaced with a wooden platform. Occupying a quartet of plain kitchen chairs on this platform was the band: three male accordionists and a woman with a tambourine. A dozen-odd couples were dancing a paso doble on the old mosaic floor, stumbling occasionally as they tripped over the indentations left by the knees of generations of worshipers.

Then he saw what he'd been looking for: a trestle table in one of the side aisles. Several men were standing at this makeshift bar, drinking some dark concoction which the woman behind it ladled into their glasses from a cooking pot. A notice on the wall above her head bore the following injunction:

FOR YOUR HEALTH'S SAKE, COMRADES, KEEP THIS PLACE CLEAN!

Grishin was hailed by a bearded giant with a gentle face. "Nothing much happening yet, comrade—too early."

Grishin nodded rather diffidently. "What does one drink here? I don't have much money."

The bearded giant grinned. "It's not worth paying for," he said thickly, and turned to the woman behind the counter. "Give him some of that rat poison."

The band stopped playing and the couples on the dance floor split up. The women, most of whom had been dancing barefoot, retired to a bench at one end and slipped their shoes on. A few of the men loitered near them. The others drifted over to the bar.

Grishin picked up his glass and sampled it. The contents were warm and potent but unidentifiable. He whistled softly.

"God help my stomach!"

One of his neighbors, a round-shouldered man in thick-lensed glasses, glared at him with mock outrage. "No blasphemy, comrade, not in this holy place!" He laughed uproariously and turned to the others. "I move that our comrade here be censured for blasphemy. Who'll second the motion?"

"Relax," said a rat-faced, gypsyish-looking man. "This is a social club, not a Party meeting."

The bearded giant burped loudly. "Come on, Lisa, our glasses are empty!"

They toasted each other and drank while the band launched into another apology for a paso doble. The women got up from their bench and waited to be asked to dance, swaying listlessly to the music.

"It's too early," the bearded man repeated. "Wait till later, though!"

Grishin evinced sudden interest. "After the demonstration at Michelson's, you mean?"

"I spit on all demonstrations," said the gypsy, "especially this one."

"Do any of you work there?" Grishin glanced toward the door. "I've got a brother at Michelson's—we arranged to meet here." He paused. "Maybe one of you knows him: Ivanov, Stepan. He's five years older than I am, but we're pretty much alike to look at." He smiled his newfound, diffident smile. "Except that Stepan's lost a thumb."

The bearded giant guffawed. "We must have fifty Ivanovs at least, and take it from me, comrade, half of them are short of a thumb or something else. If we could sew all the missing bits back on, we'd increase our output by twenty percent!"

"He was supposed to meet me here at eight. It's about his wife . . ." Grishin left the sentence in midair.

"He must be keen to hear Comrade Lenin speak, your brother," said the gypsy. He assumed an oratorical tone. "These are dark and difficult days, comrade workers! How can you even think of your empty bellies when the Revolution is in mortal danger?" His voice reverted to its normal pitch. "We're cattle, that's all, and all they give us to chew on are slogans."

"I move that slogans be abolished!" The shortsighted man's eyes twinkled behind his glasses. Encouraged by yells of approval from the others, he went on, "I move that every worker have his stomach surgically removed. No stomachs, no starvation!"

Hands shot up to an accompaniment of catcalls, whistles, and cries of "Hear, hear!"

"Passed unanimously!" the bespectacled man declared with a beaming smile. The gypsy looked at Grishin. "What about you? I didn't see you vote."

Grishin laughed and patted his midriff. "No point, comrade. I don't have a stomach anymore."

"Lisa, more rat poison!"

They clinked glasses, drank, quieted down. Boredom set in.

"Well," Grishin said eventually, "it really is like a morgue tonight, this place. Have any of you ever heard him speak—Comrade Lenin, I mean?"

"They all talk the same drivel," growled the gypsy.

"Still, it might be more fun than here. I'm off. Anyone feel like coming with me?"

The shortsighted man took off his glasses and polished them enthusiastically. "Why not? Let's go and put our resolution to the vote!" It was the bearded giant who clinched it. "I'm with you," he roared. "Our comrades need reinforcements. We mustn't let them down!"

Grishin was reasonably familiar with the layout of the Michelson Works. He had debated whether to try to sneak in somewhere— via the railroad siding or a deserted construction site he'd noticed on his last visit—but security was bound to be particularly tight at those points, and the risk of running into a patrol in the darkness was too great. His safest bet was to enter by the main gate, prefera- bly with a crowd.

It wasn't until they were outside in the windswept square that he realized how much drunker his companions were than they'd seemed to be in the club. There were six of them including the three he was counting on most: the bearded giant, the stoop- shouldered man in glasses, and the gaunt, swarthy gypsy.

They stood there swaying for a moment, then linked arms for mutual support and set off, singing lustily.

With Grishin in their midst, they took up almost the full width of the street. Their voices rebounded from the high brick factory walls on either side. Half startled by the echo, they broke off, began again, listened. Some of them bellowed with drunken laugh- ter, but the farther they went the less ebullient they became. Their singing, which had already dwindled in volume, died away alto- gether when they caught sight of two figures in gray greatcoats lounging beneath a streetlight. The soldiers, smoking with their rifles slung, just stared at them as they went by.

They lurched on down the street, still arm in arm but silent now. When another pair of uniformed figures appeared, three of the party wavered, turned, and retraced their steps. The trio Grishin had pinned his hopes on weren't among them.

Whether latecomers or idle spectators, a little crowd some forty or fifty strong stood clustered around the main entrance to the Michelson Works, watching something. Two dungaree-clad workmen had propped a ladder against the wrought-iron gates, and were removing a banner inscribed FEED US OR WE STRIKE!

The onlookers uttered no protest when the banner was eventually taken down. Grishin peered through the gates into the factory yard, which was dimly lit by gas lamps bracketed to the corners of the red granite administration building. Beyond the inner gate leading to the workshops the night sky looked paler, as though tinged with the reflected glow from a building ablaze with lights. Was it his imagination, or could he really hear the distant hubbub, the beehive hum, of a vast assembly?

The bearded giant shouldered his way through the crowd and accosted one of the workmen.

"Hey, Shadrin, have they voted yet? Which way did it go?"

The workman shrugged. "No idea. All I know is, a commissar ordered us to take this thing down. If a commissar says so, that's good enough for me."

He gathered the big strip of cloth into a bundle and headed for the side entrance with Grishin and the trio from the Workers' Club at his heels.

The old janitor leaned out of his window. "You're too late, comrades. The place is bursting at the seams. You wouldn't even get your noses around the door."

The bearded giant chuckled. "Don't worry about us, papashka."

"You're wasting your time, believe me."

Sentries had been posted along the walls of the administration building. More uniformed figures were cordoning off the forecourt in front of it. One of them came sauntering out of the gloom. He was a slim, erect man of thirty or thereabouts. His army greatcoat was so long that it flapped around his boots, and he wore a Mauser in a black leather holster on his belt. A cigarette with a cardboard mouthpiece dangled from his thin lips. A few yards short of the gatekeeper's shack he came to a halt and spat out his cigarette.

"Trouble, papashka?"

The gatekeeper leaned still farther out of his window. "Not really, comrade commissar. They're notorious latecomers, these fellows—I know them of old."

"Notorious, eh? Where d'you pick up a long word like that, old man?"

The gatekeeper was momentarily abashed. Then he grinned. "I

read *Pravda,* comrade, like every good Communist. All I meant was, they're great at clocking in late. They won't even get their noses around the door, and I told them so."

The bearded giant lumbered through the side gate and into the yard. The other two followed, and Grishin, rather than be the last in line, sandwiched himself between them.

The commissar barred their path.

"Are you deaf? The old man's right, you won't get your noses around the door."

The bespectacled man fidgeted with his glasses, the gypsy stared at the ground. Grishin turned his jacket collar up and crossed his arms as if he found the night air too chilly for comfort. The bearded giant, their self-appointed spokesman, drew himself up to his full height.

"We vote with our hands, comrade, not our noses."

"And which way do you propose to vote, for a strike or against?"

"We'll listen to what Comrade Lenin has to say, comrade commissar—then we'll see. That's fair, isn't it?"

The commissar nodded and waved them on. Whether or not he meant the gesture to be magnanimous, he seemed content to have asserted himself. Turning on his heel, he stalked off with the skirts of his greatcoat flapping around his boots.

"Arrogant swine!" muttered the gypsy.

Grishin held his breath and stared after the commissar's retreating figure, but he had either failed to hear the remark or chosen to ignore it. If Grishin hadn't looked in that direction, he might not have spotted the two cars parked in the forecourt of the administration building. Both were gray, and both were Rolls-Royce limousines. Their doors and windows were closed, and standing guard over them were a dozen men in civilian clothes.

Grishin couldn't afford to lag behind his companions. The gypsy was still cursing as they passed through the second gateway and set off down the central thoroughfare between the workshops. Sentries were posted on either side at intervals of twenty or thirty yards.

Towering above the other buildings was a new workshop the size of an airplane hangar, with massive brick walls and a flat roof supported by steel girders. The six-foot gap between the roof and the top of the walls was glazed, and the light that streamed through the big glass panes drew a dazzling white line across the dark sky. From inside, like the fluctuating roar of surf on a beach, came the sound of innumerable voices.

●

Lena Valentinova left the streetcar at a stop less than half a mile north of the Michelson Works. The shabby, featureless houses around the square looked uninhabited. Only the Bazmannaya District Hospital, which boasted a light above the entrance and a handful of illuminated windows, gave evidence of life within.

The four streets leading off the square were sparsely lit and equally deserted. Being a stranger to this industrial slum on the far side of Moskva, Lena had expected to be guided to her destination by crowds of demonstrators converging on it from all directions. Her only recourse was to accost the three women who had followed her off the streetcar—nurses, to judge by their starched white caps and long capes.

"Excuse me?"

One of them turned. "Yes?"

"How do I get to the Michelson Works?"

"Take that street over there—you can't miss it." The nurse peered at her more closely. "Is anything the matter?"

"No, I'm a stranger here, that's all." Lena hugged the brown paper bag to her chest. "I'm late. Lenin's speaking tonight."

"Lenin?" The nurse's youthful face stiffened. "If you see that man, tell him . . ." She broke off, turned on her heel, and hurried after the others.

Lena crossed the square. Sentries were stationed at the mouth of the street the nurse had pointed out to her. There were four of them, two on either side, all wearing standard gray greatcoats and round caps, all armed with carbines. They leered at Lena, but she didn't notice. She clutched the paper bag even tighter, half afraid that it might slip through her clammy fingers. There was something strangely reassuring about the feel of the hard, unyielding thing inside.

●

Grishin estimated that there must be three thousand people in the hall. They were jammed together so tightly, he felt, that if one of them moved the repercussions would be detectable throughout

the building like ripples on a pool. Clouds of tobacco smoke
floated above this human sea, contributing to the density of an
atmosphere already thick with the stench of stale sweat and damp
clothing. The combined hubbub of three thousand voices was
deafening.

The speaker's rostrum, draped in red and picked out by a light
immediately overhead, had been erected in the middle of the hall.
Its present incumbent was someone other than Lenin. In spite of
his stentorian voice and extravagant gestures, he was finding it
almost impossible to make himself heard. Every word he uttered
seemed to bounce off a wall of hostility and was drowned by
howls of rage and derision.

"At this supreme moment, when our comrades at the
front . . ."

This drew another barrage of yells and whistles. Individual heck-
lers could be distinguished: "Why aren't you at the front yourself?"—"Get lost!"—"We've heard enough!"

"Please, comrades! A little self-discipline!"

The sole response was a crescendo of jeers and catcalls. Pande-
monium reigned.

Grishin and his three companions had begun by trying the various entrances, only to find them blocked by a solid mass of bodies.
The gypsy eventually secured a view of the proceedings by scaling
the outside wall and joining several other agile spectators on a
narrow ledge below the line of windows. The bearded giant appropriated a ladder from somewhere and climbed up beside him, but
the bespectacled man gave up and sat down outside to await the
end of the meeting.

Although Grishin had wormed his way into the building and
progressed a few yards through the crowd, all his further efforts
proved futile. He was beginning to wonder if he could achieve
anything at all with his gun. He was still some thirty yards from the
rostrum. The derringer might just kill a man at that range, but how
was he to draw it, let alone aim it, in such cramped conditions?

The uproar, which had died away when the speaker left the
platform, defeated, broke out afresh when his place was taken by a
woman. It was several minutes before she got her message across.

"Comrades! Comrade Vladimir Ilyich requests you not to
smoke! Comrades, kindly extinguish your cigarettes and pipes!"

The only response, once again, was a chorus of whistles, cat-calls, and sarcastic laughter.

Grishin spotted movement of some kind beyond the rostrum: Four tall, broad-shouldered men were forging a path between two ranks of uniformed guards. They were so tall that the man in their midst remained invisible until they halted at the foot of the plat-form.

The uproar did not diminish when the man stepped forward and climbed the wooden steps. It became louder, angrier, and more menacing.

Grishin, who had studied photographs and newsreel shots of Lenin from Colvin's archives, was seeing him in the flesh for the first time. He was unprepared for the reality of the man—for his squat stature and the way his massive, balding head seemed to sprout from his shoulders without the intervention of a neck. The coarse, thick jacket and crumpled shirt looked none too clean, and the slit-eyed face was devoid of its famous black goatee. Lenin was growing a new beard, from the look of it, but the thin, reddish fuzz on his chin bore scant resemblance to what had been there before. He looked almost like an impostor, Grishin thought—an actor trying to impersonate a great man but proving unequal to the part.

Did the other three thousand feel the same? Their whistles and boos gave way to a low, hostile growl that gained in volume and animosity moment by moment.

Grishin could hardly draw breath. The bodies around him seemed to be swelling, expanding, demanding more space than the hall could encompass.

The thickset figure on the rostrum might have been a statue. All that moved were the narrow, slanting eyes beneath the domed forehead, looking still narrower and more oblique as they prowled the air above the heads of the crowd. Lenin waited, seemingly deaf and blind to the hostility around him. He stood there leaning forward slightly, gripping the sides of the lectern. The faint, sar-donic smile on his face became more pronounced as the low growl of anger subsided and finally ceased.

"Citizens, workers, comrades! If you give me a hearing, do not expect a political speech. You have heard too many speeches—true. Slogans fill no bellies—true. The masses are tired and hungry—true. We live in troubled, anxious times—true. More of our people will die of cold and starvation—true. More of our soldiers will die in battle—true. All these things are true, comrades, but there are reasons. Who or what, you will ask, is responsible for our trials and tribulations?"

Grishin listened to the voice rather than the words. It was hoarse and strained. He understood why the woman had asked everyone to stop smoking. Lenin spoke without the aid of rhetorical gestures. He continued to stand motionless, leaning forward a little with his hands gripping the lectern. His only weapon was that hoarse, insistent voice whose sheer monotony compelled the crowd to listen in silence.

"Why did we take up arms in the first place? That peace might be restored. That the land should belong to the peasants. That the factories should belong to the workers. That power should belong to the people. We not only fought but triumphed: Power passed to the revolutionary workers, soldiers, and peasants. Peace and the Revolution seemed secure. Our victory seemed complete. The welfare and future of our people were in good hands at last. But do not be deceived, comrades! Our common enemies are still at work, still doing their utmost to foment unrest, starve us out, spill our blood, destroy the Revolution. The truth, comrades, is as follows. Only last night, the most brazen of all counterrevolutionary conspiracies was uncovered here in this city, in Moscow, in our very midst: a plot to overthrow the Revolution and liquidate its leaders! I propose to read you extracts from the conspirators' own program, confident that you, who form the backbone of the Revolution, will give our foes the only right and fitting response . . ."

Spellbound and stupefied, the vast crowd made no sound. The speaker's monotonous, unflagging voice droned on without interruption. Grishin could sense the mood of his audience changing.

"Your answer, comrades, will decide the issue. Are we to abandon our aims? Are we to tolerate the destruction of all that has been achieved at the expense of so much blood? The choice is yours. Do you wish the world to believe that the Russian Revolution is over, or do you wish to tell the world: Make no mistake, we shall finish what we have begun?"

What a voice, Grishin thought. It was indefatigable, unquenchable, irresistible. He himself felt at one with the crowd gazing raptly at the man on the rostrum: a man like themselves, ill dressed like themselves, weary like themselves. Scattered cries of approbation and encouragement rang out. Three thousand people were willing his voice not to fail, willing him the strength to continue, hanging on his every word.

Grishin turned and inched his way through the crowd. Behind him he could hear the speaker embark on his peroration in the same unchanging, almost mechanical tone.

"I came here armed with no promises, comrades. I came here in the simple belief that the people's welfare is in strong, safe hands. Steadfast determination and iron discipline will crush the counter-revolution, by the people and for the people. The future belongs to us. Long live the Revolution!"

Grishin reached the exit. Just as he did so the hall seemed to explode. A single, overpowering wave of sound smote him in the back. The people inside were too jam-packed to applaud, but they could cheer, and they did.

When Grishin turned for a last look at the rostrum, Lenin was standing exactly as he had stood at the beginning of his speech: motionless, with both hands gripping the edge of the lectern. He accepted the homage of the crowd as dispassionately as he had earlier accepted their hostility. The ovation went on and on, and still he continued to stand there unmoved and unmoving. The only discernible change in him was an intensification of the sardonic smile that hovered around his lips.

The night air felt cold after the steamy warmth of the hall. Grishin shivered, waiting for his eyes to become accustomed to the darkness. Inside the hall, a resolution was proposed and passed by acclamation.

Cautiously, he skirted the building. Lenin and the other speakers must have entered it from the far side. Peering around the corner, he saw some uniformed figures drawn up in two ranks facing inward. An officer with a flashlight was checking their alignment. There were no cars in sight.

Grishin returned to the other side of the building, which now resounded to the strains of the "Internationale." He looked back along the central thoroughfare to the factory entrance, but no cars were visible in that direction either. Although the lighting was dim, he could just make out the yard and the wrought-iron gates. The crowd in the street beyond them seemed to have swelled to three or four times its original size.

Hugging the shadows in the lee of the nearest workshop, he crossed a stretch of open ground and made for the perimeter wall, which was topped with broken glass. There he stopped to listen. The singing from the hall came faintly to his ears, but everything around him was still. He made his way along the wall to the rear of the administration building.

The wall and the building itself were separated by a narrow alleyway leading to the forecourt. It was so dark he had to grope his way along it step by step. He was three quarters of the way to the forecourt when the sound of voices stopped him in his tracks. Two men were talking together, but not in Russian. They sounded like Estonians or Latvians. The voices died away. Grishin waited. A car started up, then another. He almost panicked for a moment, fearing that he was too late, but breathed a sigh of relief when neither car drove off.

He crept to the mouth of the alleyway. With his back glued to the wall he peered around the corner into the forecourt. Illuminated by the gas lamps on the front of the administration building, two Rolls-Royce limousines gleamed as if their paintwork had never been exposed to the elements. Both drivers were in their seats, and one of the cars already contained a passenger. Although Grishin could only see the back of his head, he looked startlingly familiar.

His gaze traveled past the cars to the factory yard. It was cordoned off from the forecourt by armed guards, and stationed in front of them was the commissar in the long greatcoat.

Grishin took a last look at the cars: the drivers, each behind his wheel; the anonymous passenger, stiff and motionless as waxwork dummy; the plumes of vapor from the exhausts. He was close enough, he decided.

He withdrew behind the wall. All he had to do now was wait. The workers would be reluctant to let Lenin go—they would stream out of the hall and follow him. However many sentries had been posted, they would never be able to control a cheering mob thousands strong.

He unbuttoned his jacket and felt the gun, forbidding himself to think of Jim Hall—forbidding himself even to reflect that the gun had been his. He regretted not having tested it for accuracy. The shots he'd fired that night at Kuntsevo had been loosed off at random.

Something impinged on his consciousness: a distant commotion, a medley of shouts and singing. It was coming from the far end of the central thoroughfare. He peered around the corner again. At a signal from the commissar, the first car crawled forward with the second one following bumper to bumper.

One hand on his gun, Grishin darted along the wall to the other side of the forecourt and secreted himself in a pool of shadow with his back to the brickwork.

The cars halted midway between the forecourt and the factory yard. The drivers stayed put. Guards opened the rear door of the leading Rolls. The second car was ignored. The doors remained closed, the back of the passenger's head could still be seen through the rear window.

The din redoubled as the crowd reached the inner gateway and poured through it into the yard. Harassed soldiers linked arms and held the excited workers in check, leaving a narrow lane clear.

It was like a repetition of the scene when Lenin had made his way to the rostrum. The four bodyguards hid him from view so effectively that his presence in their midst could only be surmised.

Grishin drew his gun, flipped the safety catch, and held it at his side with his arm fully extended. He had time, plenty of time, now that he was so near his target. His moment would come when Lenin boarded the car—when his bodyguards had to stand aside and could shield him no longer.

The four hulking men were still half a dozen paces from the car's open door when Lenin paused and waved to the cheering, tumultuous throng. They grew impatient, closed in on him, tried to hustle him along.

Grishin raised the gun. He held it at arm's length, two-handed, crouching a little as he adjusted the position of his feet. Drawing a deep breath, he aimed at a spot twelve inches below the top of the doorframe. Another few seconds, and the big, balding head would appear in his sights. Nothing could prevent the bullets from finding their mark. He could visualize his target in every detail: the high, domed forehead, the slanting, faintly Asiatic eyes, the sparse reddish beard—even the sardonic smile.

The stocky little man would have no time even for a lightning realization of what was about to happen. He would have failed to gauge a situation correctly for the first and last time in his life. All his perspicacity and prudence would avail him nothing. Death was a phenomenon even Lenin could experience only once.

Seconds ticked by, and still the doorframe remained empty. Grishin had to breathe again despite himself. He lowered the gun and looked.

Lenin and his security men might have been part of a tableau: They hadn't moved from the spot. All the movement was elsewhere. The main gates had been opened for the cars to make their exit, and through them, yelling wildly, poured the crowd that had been waiting outside in the street. Soldiers formed a line and headed them off, but a small group of women succeeded in breaking through the cordon.

Two of Lenin's bodyguards seized him by the arms and tried to tow him to the car, but he shrugged them off and took a step toward his admirers as though inviting them to approach him—as though eager to hear what they had to say. He had just confronted three thousand hungry, exhausted, rebellious workers and persuaded them to cheer him to the echo. He was a sorcerer who had demonstrated his magical powers. Perhaps his weeks of self-imposed incarceration in the Kremlin had deprived him of this sense of power for too long. Perhaps he simply wanted to try out his magic on another batch of willing subjects.

"Vladimir Ilyich!"

Grishin heard the woman's voice, saw the figure in the thin coat, heard the cry repeated. She had raised both hands, and clasped in them was something dark and metallic.

He froze, unable to believe the evidence of his senses. It couldn't be Lena Valentinova who had called Lenin's name, just as the object in her hands couldn't be a gun. His brain balked at the very idea. Like everyone else, he stared at her transfixed. "No," he said, not realizing that he had actually uttered the word.

And then it dawned on him that the scene had changed in one important respect: The bodyguards were nowhere near their charge. The short, stocky figure was standing there alone and unprotected.

Grishin's heart pounded wildly. He raised his gun, but he was still taking aim when a shot rang out. It reverberated from the surrounding walls. The forecourt sprang to life, shouts and words of command rent the air. Only two men, the would-be assassin and his intended victim, seemed unmoved by the uproar.

Grishin squeezed the trigger. Lenin flinched, threw up one arm, turned his head. Grishin knew instinctively that he had aimed too low and hit him in the shoulder. He raised the gun a fraction of an inch. Peripheral vision disclosed that the bodyguards were converging on his man, but he got off another two shots before they reached him.

Lenin staggered, performed a half pirouette, and collapsed face down. It was only then that the bodyguards threw themselves on top of him.

The crowd remained frozen with panic for several seconds. Then people started yelling, running in all directions, flinging themselves to the ground. In the heart of this turmoil, like a different kind of tableau, the four big men continued to lie motionless on top of their invisible master.

Grishin's work was done. His instinct for self-preservation took over, banishing even the thought of Lena from his mind. He withdrew to the end of the wall and made his unhurried way across the forecourt to the mouth of the alleyway. He didn't put on speed until he was out of sight behind the administration building, and it was only then that he noticed the gun in his hand. After a moment's hesitation, he tossed it over the wall.

The whole width of the central thoroughfare was choked with workers still emerging from the hall. Once he had insinuated himself into their midst, Grishin began to breathe easier. They were slowly but steadily wending their way toward the factory yard, and he was so completely hemmed in by them that he had only to relax and allow himself to be borne along on the human tide.

Something other than shuffling footsteps became audible. It was a sound he failed to identify at once: A confused murmur, almost a groan, had originated at the head of the column and was drawing nearer. He nudged the man in front of him.

"What is it?"

The man slowly turned his head. His aging, weary face was frosted with white stubble, but the fatigue imprinted on it was overlaid with a look of utter dismay. He opened his mouth and closed it again, unable to get a word out.

Another man, who had overheard the question, answered for him. "Somebody just shot Lenin."

•24•

There was a sort of bed in the cell, an iron grid covered with a thin straw mattress. She lay on it, flat on her back, without fully grasping where she was.

The cell was dark, that much she did know, and she was in pain. She wasn't afraid because the pain dominated all else. She wouldn't be able to think clearly while this frightful pain held her in thrall.

It was everywhere. Her legs hurt, her arms burned like fire, her ribs seemed to creak when she breathed. Her head hurt worst of all. It felt as if every nerve ending had been laid bare. When she touched it the pain increased a thousandfold.

She experimented once more—gingerly, with her fingertips. Her cheeks were deeply scored and encrusted with dried blood. The touch of her fingertips on her cheekbones was like an electric shock. She discovered more cuts and lacerations on her neck. One pain caused her special torment. It was in her mouth, sharp and piercing as a jagged sliver of glass: She had bitten a fragment off the tip of her tongue, and her swollen mouth tasted of blood.

Stand up, she told herself. Stand up!

She tried to turn on her side. It was an agonizing, interminable process. Pain transfixed her from the crown of her head to the tips of her toes. She tried again and again until she succeeded. Drawing up her knees, she swung her legs over the edge of the bedstead and heaved herself into a sitting position.

She sat there swaying, clinging to the iron frame with both hands. She turned her head, first one way, then another. The pain sickened her, but she persevered.

Proud of her success, she took stock of her surroundings: a cell measuring six feet by nine; a stone floor and brick walls; a steel

door with a spy-hole in it; high up in the opposite wall a barred
window; at the foot of the bed a metal washbowl with one cold
faucet; in the other corner a pail with a wooden lid. She was glad
her swollen nose had lost its sense of smell.

She noticed only now that she'd lost her coat, that her dress was
torn—that one sleeve was completely missing. At once she began
to tremble all over with cold. She was afraid now, too, as though
the veil that pain had drawn across her memory was lifting at last.

She still failed to grasp the full extent of what had happened.
Everything was clear to her up to the moment when the factory
gates swung open and she and the others rushed into the yard. She
could remember calling "Vladimir Ilyich!" How naïve of her to
have called his name! *Vladimir Ilyich, look at me, cast your mind
back. Remember me, Lena Valentinova, the girl from Père-
Lachaise?* No, at least she hadn't shouted that.

The cell felt colder than ever. She shivered, striving to recall the
rest. What else? The gun, of course. She had removed it from the
paper bag as soon as the gates opened. She had raised it in both
hands because it would have been too heavy for her otherwise—
raised it, pointed it at him, and pulled the trigger. But then? What
had happened then?

She had been entirely alone, or so it seemed—alone with the
gun and Vladimir Ilyich—but an instant later they had hurled themselves at her. *That's her! Get her, grab her! Yes, that's the one!*
Savage yells, faces contorted with hatred, clawing fingers.

Why? They were the same hungry, angry women who had
waited outside the gates with her, the ones that had come to
protest, to voice their impotent rage and support their menfolk in
calling for a strike. Why should they now vent their spleen on her?
They rushed at her, punched her, tore her clothes, pushed her to
the ground, trampled and kicked her. Their feet were everywhere.
She tried to crawl away on her hands and knees, but they dragged
her back. Fists thudded into her face . . .

At that point memory failed.

She braced her hands against the iron bedframe and struggled to
her feet, but her legs gave way. She crawled to the washbowl on all
fours, hauled herself erect, leaned against the metal rim, waited till
she could summon up the strength to turn the faucet on. Bending
over, she spat out an accumulation of blood. Then she let the
water run into her cupped hands and immersed her face in it.

Back on the edge of the bed again, she felt her aches and pains receding. She could think more clearly now.

The soldiers had saved her from a lynching. They had wrested her away from the mob and whisked her off before she lost consciousness. She could recall the interior of a moving car, a gateway, a yard enclosed by high walls, an endless succession of passages and stone steps, a door clanging shut behind her, the rattle of a key . . .

Suddenly it dawned on her: No one had questioned or searched her, asked her how she had acquired the gun or why she had used it. She stared at the opposite wall, pondering this mystery. Then, still aching in every limb, she rose and went to the window.

Looking up, she could see a patch of night sky with low clouds racing across it. She strained her ears. A faint rumbling sound was audible in the distance. It drew nearer, grew louder and more distinct, then faded and ceased altogether. There was no mistaking the sound: A train had just pulled into a station.

But what station? How far had she traveled by car? Was she still in Bazmannaya? If so, the station would be the terminus of the line to Kazan.

She tottered back to the bed and sat down again. Picking up the thin, gray blanket, she draped it around her shoulders.

Why deceive yourself? she thought. There's another station close by—Yaroslavl Station. That was where he told you to take a train to Kostroma and change for . . .

She sat there shivering with the blanket around her shoulders, trying to recall the name, but it eluded her.

●

Lloyd's Fleming's cell in the basement of Cheka headquarters was clean and spacious. It contained a table, a chair, and two bunks, one above the other.

Fleming was stretched out on the lower of the two with his arms folded behind his head. Being the sole occupant of the cell, he had appropriated both pillows and three of the four available blankets.

The light was still on. The guards had either forgotten to turn it off or left it on deliberately.

Workmen had been redecorating some nearby cells during the day, and a smell of paint still lingered in the air. Fleming didn't dislike the smell. On the contrary, it stirred some pleasant recollection, though its precise nature temporarily escaped him.

In his heart of hearts he was glad to be there—glad the whole sorry business was over. He had spent the long hours between his sessions with Dzerzhinsky doing what his career had trained him to do: drawing up a profit and loss account. He was abandoning the role that had been forced on him and becoming what he had always been: an English banker whose forebears had been City of London financiers for seven generations and paid small heed to anything that couldn't be expressed in numerical terms.

The thought of Lena Valentinova was the only really bitter pill he'd had to swallow in the last twenty-four hours. After this latest fiasco—even he could find no other word for it—how would he ever be able to face her again? For the moment this problem was solved by his confinement to a cell, but in any case, Dzerzhinsky had hinted that he wouldn't be allowed to see her again prior to deportation.

He had loved her for all that, and he still did—or liked to think he did. He would always remember her, just as he would always remember Russia. The more time went by, the less distressing his memories of her would become. Would he eventually be able to enter Lena in the assets column of his balance sheet?

He suddenly remembered what the smell of paint reminded him of: his investment in a Birmingham dye works on the verge of bankruptcy. He'd been the junior member of the board, and all the other directors had voted against a rescue operation. He had ended by investing his wife's money, purely on the strength of a young industrial chemist's assurance that a process he had developed would put the firm in profit again. Within five years, the Birmingham company's new synthetic dyes had captured forty-two percent of the world market. The annual dividend ranged from twenty-two to twenty-nine percent.

Fleming looked at his watch. It was ten to eleven—ten to nine London time. That thought conjured up a vision of the house in Grosvenor Square—far too big for a childless couple , he'd always felt, but his wife had overridden his objections. "The secret of success, Lloyd, is to keep open house." His mild protest—"And for that we need a dozen servants?"—had fallen on deaf ears.

Ten to nine in London. Dinner would be drawing to a close. Was it Friday today? Friday meant turtle soup, *saumon au court bouil-*

lon—they employed a French chef—and a cheese soufflé. In spite
of strict wartime rationing, his wife always managed to track down
the requisite ingredients.

Time to take coffee in the drawing room. His wife's taste in
furniture was on the baronial side, but the lighting was pleasantly
subdued. A fire would be blazing in the grate and the latest edition
of *The Times* awaiting him on the coffee table in front of the deep,
luxurious sofa.

One particular evening surfaced in his memory. Harrow, his old
school, had lost to Eton yet again in the annual cricket match at
Lords. His wife gave him a sympathetic little nod, totally failing to
grasp how much this mattered to him. He read on. "Had you
heard? The Liberals didn't muster enough votes in the House to
increase the standard rate of income tax. It's staying at a shilling in
the pound." That *did* interest her, being a person who considered
five percent far too high already. "However, they did hammer the
big landowners. From now on, real estate valued at a million
pounds or more will be liable to tax at fifteen percent." His wife
cast her eyes up to heaven. "Scandalous, that's what it is. Lloyd
George is little better than a Communist!"

It was Lloyd George, the prime minister, who had sent him here
as his special envoy. His wife had been all in favor at the time.
Money was at stake, after all—a lot of money. Vast amounts of
capital had been plowed into Czarist Russia. All England, from the
Treasury and the major banks to the aristocracy and the private
investor, had trembled for the safety of those investments.

That aspect of his balance sheet looked truly disastrous. *That*
had been his big mistake, a reluctance to write off losses in good
time. He would be returning to London empty-handed. One never
knew, though—times might change for the better. Russia might
change hands again, and her future masters might need foreign
capital. Perhaps his balance sheet would end by looking healthier
after all. Perhaps . . .

He wished they would turn the light out. How could they have
forgotten? He listened, but the entire cell block was wrapped in
silence.

He would try to sleep in spite of the light. He hoped to be back
in London soon. He hoped so if only because of an untoward noise
that had woken him that morning. It had come from the inner
courtyard near his cell, and it sounded like a firing squad at work.

Grishin lit a cigarette and peered at his watch before the match went out. It was almost eleven-thirty. He'd been standing there for over half an hour.

It had started to drizzle again, but it was such a fine drizzle that he could see the droplets only when he looked up at one of the streetlights on either side of him. With one notable exception, the square and the streets leading off it were strangely silent and deserted.

In a city like Moscow, news spread fast by word of mouth alone. Three thousand people had either witnessed or heard about the attempt on Lenin's life, yet the same silence reigned everywhere. The few people Grishin had encountered on the street gave him a wide berth and hurried past without so much as a glance in his direction.

The two buildings he was watching stood opposite, across the broad expanse of Lubyanka Square. The Hotel Billo was largely in darkness. Discounting a handful of rooms on the upper floors, only the entrance and a few of the big ground-floor windows were illuminated. Cheka headquarters, on the other hand, was ablaze with light. It was also the only focus of activity.

Men had been converging on it in an endless stream, singly or in groups. Cars drove up, disgorged more men, and joined the steadily lengthening rows of vehicles already parked under guard in the square. Grishin had seen no one leave the building since he began his vigil. It was as if all who entered it had gone to ground there.

He took a last pull at his cigarette and tossed the butt away. It landed on the wet cobbles and expired with a hiss. Still he didn't move, as though the mere act of standing there and staring at the lighted windows would present him with a solution. He pictured the feverish activity inside the building, saw grim-faced men hurrying along the corridors, telephoning police stations, barracks, the Kremlin, a hospital, heard them requesting information and issuing instructions. But what really preoccupied him, and what he strove with all his might to banish from his mind's eye, was another vision altogether: a darkened room, a chair in the center, and on it a woman with the dazzling beam of a spotlight aimed at her face. There were men around her, invisible in the gloom, putting questions—always the same questions—over and over again . . .

One of the parked cars, a black limousine, started up. Grishin watched it back, turn, and head for the main entrance in a wide arc. The driver pulled up and got out, walked around to the other side of the car, and opened the rear door.

Three men emerged from the building and stood talking for a few moments. Two of them got into the car. The third watched it drive off and disappear through Vladimir Gate before making his way slowly along the sidewalk to the colonnaded entrance of the Hotel Billo. There he paused and glanced in all directions.

Grishin waited, motionless, until the man had climbed the steps and gone inside. Then he turned his jacket collar up and set off across the square. He wished he still had Jim Hall's derringer but instantly suppressed the thought. Killing the man he hoped to see would be tantamount to killing off his only hope of ever seeing Lena Valentinova alive again.

The fourth-floor corridor of the hotel was decorated with a flowered wallpaper almost indistinguishable in design from the gilt-framed flower pieces that hung at intervals along it. The air was stuffy, as if it had been stagnating there ever since the place was built.

Grishin ran his eye down the odd numbers on the left-hand side. The night porter had told him 403–405. The door of 403 was slightly ajar, and he could see a thin shaft of light escaping. He wished yet again that he still had the gun.

Someone inside the room laughed.

"Don't bother to knock, come right in."

The laugh and the tone of voice told Grishin that Yury Peters's state of tension was quite as extreme as his own.

The room was so overfurnished that he almost failed to see the man at first. Heavy mahogany tables, pleated lampshades, plush armchairs, more floral wallpaper and gilt-framed pictures—the whole decor reminded him of London apartments he'd rented in the past.

Peters himself was seated at a massive Victorian desk lit by an onyx lamp with a tasseled shade. He was leaning back in a carved oak chair, his face partly in shadow. One hand rested on the desk top, the other on his thigh near a half-open drawer.

"So you're Relinsky today!" He gave another edgy laugh. "This name-changing business is becoming de rigueur. If you don't have at least a dozen pseudonyms these days, you aren't a genuine revolutionary—or a genuine agent. Vladimir Ilyich is said to have used a hundred in his time. Personally, I've always stuck to plain Peters—against everyone else's advice, of course . . ."

"Both hands on the desk," Grishin said.

Peters removed his hand from the vicinity of the drawer and put it on the desk beside its fellow. The lamplight emphasized the contrast between them: one scarred and twisted, the other shapely and well manicured.

Grishin made his way around the desk. Lying in the drawer was a Mauser automatic, black, glinting, menacing. Peters made no attempt to go for it. If his face wore any expression at all, it was curiosity.

"You plan to shoot me?" His tone was a trifle more self-assured now. "What for?"

Grishin took the pistol. Hatred surged through him at the feel of it in his hand. Was this the gun that had killed Jim Hall? He returned to the far side of the desk and stepped back a pace, unable to endure the proximity of Peters's face. He could tell from the weight of the gun that the magazine was full.

It was Peters who spoke again. "Would shooting me make you feel better?" He seemed to ponder the question seriously. "Yes, I suppose it might, but for how long? And then?" Another pause. "Shall I tell you something? I've had plenty of time to think about you since the day you crossed the border—or rather, since I saw that Latvian preserved in ice with his throat cut. It's odd how engrossed you can become in someone of whom you know nothing, or next to nothing—odd how he gradually comes to life for you. You end by believing you really know him. We've met before, but that time didn't count." He smiled. "I laughed before you came in because I was thinking: What if you're wrong—what if he's nothing like your mental picture of him? In that case, Yury Peters, you're a dead man."

Grishin scanned the room again, more than ever reminded of an overfurnished Victorian parlor. "What's next door?"

"My bedroom." Peters indicated one of two communicating doors, then, with a trace of reluctance, the other. "A second bedroom and a sitting room. May I continue?" He didn't wait for an answer. "On the other hand, I said to myself, the fact that he's here may equally mean that your assessment of him is correct. He's here because he wants to talk—he isn't the kind of man to go off half-cocked."

Grishin glanced at the telephone on the desk. "I know," said Peters, "I had plenty of time to call someone after the night porter informed me of your arrival, but I didn't. I simply sat here waiting for you. Why not make yourself comfortable? We both have problems, so why don't we talk them over? We don't have to like each other, but we need to talk. Am I right?"

"Get up."

Peters rose. He was wearing a Russian blouse very like the one he'd worn the night before, with intricate embroidery around the neck.

"Go and sit over there." Grishin pointed to one of the deep plush armchairs. Once in it, Peters would find it hard to get up in a hurry.

Peters went over and sat down. Covering the back and both arms of the chair were embroidered antimacassars held in place by pins with colored glass heads. Peters's mutilated hand lay on his lap. The fingers of the other roamed idly over the embroidery. He was looking at Grishin, but his thoughts seemed to be elsewhere, and his voice, too, took on a different note. "All my own work, can you imagine?" He laughed. "A strange form of recreation for a man like me, sitting at home in the evenings doing embroidery. I haven't done any since . . ." He didn't finish the sentence. He didn't even raise his misshapen hand, but his meaning was clear.

Grishin pulled up a chair and sat where he could keep an eye on the doors as well as Peters. Depositing the Mauser on a small table beside him, he rolled a cigarette, stuffed the tobacco pouch back inside his shirt, and lit up.

"Where is she?" he said at last.

Peters came to life for the first time. "Why was she there at all?"

"Just answer my question."

"She's in a cell at Bazmannaya Prison."

"You're lying."

"Why, did you think she was at Cheka headquarters?"

"What happened?"

"She was roughed up—no, wait! Not by the Cheka or the military: by the people whose idol she unsuccessfully tried to shoot."

"The ones outside the gate?"

"Human nature is a strange thing. If it hadn't been for the soldiers they'd have lynched her. She was put in a car and driven to the first place the officer in charge could think of. In other words, Bazmannaya Prison." Peters watched Grishin closely. "While everyone was concentrating on her, someone else shot Lenin."

For the first time since it had happened, Grishin relived the reality of the moment, felt the gun kick as he squeezed the trigger. For the first time it seemed important to him, though not as important as he'd thought it would, to know whether his mission had been accomplished.

"Is he dead?"

"Nobody knows for sure," Peters said irritably. "You should have been in Dzerzhinsky's office—you should have heard him trying to get some sense out of those doctors. They wouldn't commit themselves."

"How much *do* you know, Peters?"

"They dumped him in his car and drove him back to the Kremlin. Taking him to a hospital seemed too risky—they thought there might be more than one assassin, and they couldn't be sure of protecting him adequately."

"Was he still conscious?"

"Yes, but he was coughing up blood by the time they got to the Kremlin. His condition was so serious they decided to take him to a hospital after all."

"Well?"

"Everyone's completely distraught. A few details have emerged, at least. One shot hit him in the left shoulder."

"The first," Grishin said coolly.

Peters mightn't have heard. Whether or not he was aware of it, his fingertips resumed their exploration of the embroidered slipcover on the arm of his chair.

"He can't move his left hand. It's paralyzed, apparently, because the nerves have been severed. Another bullet penetrated his neck and lodged in the apex of his lung. The doctors say there's severe bleeding in the lung and the thoracic cavity—so severe that it's exerting pressure on the heart. They know they've got to do something, but they're all trying to unload the responsibility onto each other." Peters looked at Grishin. "There were three shots, weren't there?"

Grishin nodded.

"Then it must have been the third one that passed between the spinal column and the esophagus. Rozanov says it missed the carotid artery by a whisker. Those poor devils at the hospital are in a terrible quandary. Whether they operate and he dies or they don't operate and he dies because they don't, the consequences for them will be identical. Dzerzhinsky's on his way there now. He's the only person who's kept his head."

"Was that his car I saw drive off a few minutes ago?"

"You were watching, were you? Yes. Lenin may be dead by the time he gets there." The look of annoyance reappeared on Peters's face. "There's no point in telephoning. If he's dead they'll hush it up for the time being. Attempts are being made to convene the Central Committee. Trotsky and Stalin are on the Kazan front, Zinoviev's in Petrograd, pacifying the strikers there, and Sverdlov's away on a hunting trip. Kamenev's here in Moscow, but he's sitting at home in tears." Peters smiled. "Please accept my congratulations."

"I meant to kill him."

A note of cold ferocity entered Peters's voice. "Even if he doesn't bite the dust, he'll never be the man he was. That's reason enough to congratulate you. You pulled it off—not without help, admittedly, but that can remain our little secret." He paused. "What did you use? The gun, I mean—what caliber?"

Grishin shook his head. "Why, Peters? Why should you want him dead? Why did you play along? It must have suited some scheme of yours, but what was it?"

Peters's eyes went blank. His was a bloodless face, Grishin thought. He was a bloodless organism altogether, yet there was blood all around him—too much blood for Grishin not to yearn to make him pay for it with whatever ran in his own veins.

"Why must people always look for reasons, for motives?" Peters said wearily. "What good would it do you if I answered your question? We're wasting precious time. If you want me to help you—"

"Don't be so sure that's why I came!"

"Why else? No one would think you the type to let his heart rule his head, but you're here in this room, and the first thing you asked was, 'Where is she?' "

"What makes you think I'd trust you?"

"You have no choice."

Grishin reflected for a moment. He'd been guided to his objective like a blind man, first by Colvin, then by Peters. It was as if the two of them had agreed on the same plan of action—as if they were on the same side. That would explain a great deal, but he hushed the thought aside.

"Why did you kill Muranov?"

"Muranov? I had nothing to do with that." The surprise in Peter's voice sounded genuine.

"But you did kill Vera Ivanova. Why?"

"Because of you," Peters replied calmly. "If your paths had never crossed she would still be alive today."

"She knew nothing."

"She knew you, and she paid the penalty."

"Is that all you have to say? How could you have butchered the girl in that bestial way? Did you see her before? Did you like the look of her better when your men had finished with her? You make me sick!"

"What did you expect? Did you think you could come here, do your dirty work, and keep your hands clean? The Cheka was onto you. Someone in the Villa Popov had spotted the comings and goings of Vera Ivanova's mysterious visitor—someone who wanted to put himself in the Cheka's good graces. They were getting too close to you. Something had to be done to keep you alive, at least until you'd completed your business here." Peters paused. "I suppose you'd like to know about Ostrov, too."

"Yes."

"We were lucky there. Vassily Ostrov was a forger, but he was a traitor first and foremost. He concocted those forgeries for Dzerzhinsky and sold them to you at the same time."

"He was more or less coerced into it."

"Perhaps, but a traitor always has an eye to the main chance.

He decided to compound his treachery, and he came to me with the idea—to me, Comrade Peters, an influential man who might have been useful to him someday. To me, mark you! Think of the probable consequences if he'd gone to someone else!''

"Did he tell you he'd arranged to meet me at the Electra?"

"To hand over evidence of the trap, yes, and he offered to play the decoy—for a price: He would leave you to me if I left the money to him. Ostrov was as much of a threat to your survival as Vera Ivanova."

"Did you kill him yourself?"

"I hated the picture. It was so abysmally long, and besides, who wants to see all that violence and cruelty on the screen? As if there isn't enough of it in Moscow already . . ."

Grishin reached for the Mauser and rose to his feet. Picking up a velvet cushion, he held it over the muzzle and advanced on Peters.

"And then," he said, "because you were in the mood, you killed Jim Hall for good measure. Was this the gun?"

Peters didn't move. He stared at the gun with weary indifference, as if he had come to terms with the idea that Grishin was going to kill him after all. Suddenly his eyes widened and he turned his head a fraction of an inch. He was no longer looking at the cushion. Something had attracted his attention—a faint sound, perhaps. Then the moment passed. When he spoke, his voice sounded flat and drained of energy.

"Lloyd Fleming was a fool, a complete amateur. No wonder he took the bait. Your friend Hall was another kettle of fish. He was smart. He must have known it was a cleverly constructed Cheka trap—he must have, yet he let you walk right into it. He put your assignment in jeopardy. The responsibility was his—Colvin had delegated it to him. What would Colvin have done? You know the man, so tell me: What would Colvin have done to salvage your assignment?"

"You deserve a knife," Grishin said, "not a bullet."

"What do you want, revenge? Perhaps I was wrong. Perhaps I overrated you after all—perhaps that's all you're really out for, revenge."

"What happened to his body?"

"We found your note—it was yours, wasn't it? He'll be buried where you said. Row M, Plot 37, Dagmara Fyodorova . . . She was his wife, did you know?"

Grishin could find nothing to say.

"A ballerina from the Bolshoi. They got to know each other in Paris, I believe. Anyway, that was why Hall got himself posted to Moscow. They'd been married only a month when she was killed. A stray bullet got her during the street fighting last November."

It redoubled Grishin's rage and hatred that Peters should know what Hall had refrained from confiding even in him. Then it struck him: Was *he* making a mistake? Could there really be a link between Colvin and Peters? The Cheka man had spent many years in England. Had Colvin contrived to recruit him, and did he, Grishin, owe his life to that connection?

Somewhere out of his range of vision a door opened. He swung around, still holding the gun and the cushion. A girl of twelve or thirteen was standing in the doorway. She had strikingly blond, curly hair and was wearing a pale blue embroidered robe. Grishin had a lightning recollection of the International School's farewell dinner at the British Club. The girls there had looked just as precociously doll-like.

He lowered the gun, keeping it hidden behind the cushion. Peters shot him an appreciative glance and went over to the girl, who patted her curls and drew her robe more tightly around her.

"Did we wake you? I'm sorry, sweetheart."

She pouted. "Yes, you did. Who's this?"

"This?" Peters hesitated for an instant. "Just a friend."

"You've always got time for your friends."

"I'm sorry we woke you, honestly."

"You didn't come for lunch—or dinner either!"

The girl spoke Russian with a strong accent. It was obvious to Grishin that most of her life had been spent in England. Peters looked uncharacteristically sheepish.

"I know I didn't. It couldn't be helped."

"But you promised faithfully!"

"I'll make it up to you."

"That's what you always say."

"I will, really." Peters stroked her hair, bent down and kissed her on the forehead. "Off you go, Mary. We won't be long. Be a good girl and leave us now."

"I'll wait up for you to come and say good night."

"All right. We won't be much longer, I promise."

He shut the door behind her and stood listening for a moment, then turned. His face had undergone a curious transformation, Grishin noted: He was actually blushing. The color slowly ebbed, and all that remained was a vestige of the sheepish smile.

"My daughter," he said, as if an explanation was in order.

"She was brought up in England?"

The smile vanished abruptly. "Yes, someday I hope she'll lose that appalling accent." Peters made no move to sit down again. "Look, we're wasting time. Your girlfriend's still at Bazmannaya, and she's still alive. If you want her to stay that way, pray that Lenin takes a while longer to die. If the confusion persists, we may stand a chance of getting her out of there."

"Why should you worry, Peters?"

"Use your head. I took it for granted you'd urge her to leave Moscow. I even tried to speed her departure by having her phone cut off as soon as you'd called her. I thought it would frighten her enough to get her out of Moscow on the first available train."

Grishin merely nodded.

"*I* want her out of here before they start questioning her. Have you forgotten how much she knows? Have you forgotten that she passed you the vital information at *my* request? It might take time, but she'd talk in the end. If people think they've witnessed the ultimate reign of terror, they're sadly mistaken. It's immaterial to Dzerzhinsky whether Lenin lives or dies. He wants his revenge, and he'll take it." Peters paused. "Now will you listen to me?"

"You'll pay for this someday."

Peters's laugh had lost its edgy quality. "You don't like me, but you don't have to. Where do you come from, by the way—Georgia? Georgians normally prefer the knife to the gun, don't they?"

"You still haven't answered my question, Peters. Why are you doing all this?"

"Why? Why didn't Lena Valentinova leave Moscow—why did she go to the Michelson factory and take a potshot at Lenin? Why did you take on an assignment like this?"

"Did Colvin recruit you?"

Peters smiled. "I'm not for sale, not for all the gold in the Bank of England."

"So why?"

"Call it temptation. When I realized why you'd crossed the

border, I was tempted to let you go ahead and do what others had tried to do and failed. You played into my hands."

"Why?"

The gray eyes glinted with amusement. "Some things are so transparently obvious you see straight through them." He raised his mutilated hand. "Look at this claw of mine. That's the best answer I can give you."

He went to his desk, striding confidently across the room as if the Mauser in Grishin's hand no longer represented a threat, and pulled the drawer open to its fullest extent. Removing an envelope, he tossed it onto the blotter.

"Run your eye over that," he said. "Then I'll fill in the details."

Grishin joined him at the desk. Momentarily uncertain what to do with the gun, he put it down and picked up the envelope. It was unsealed, and inside were various documents including travel permits and identity cards. The first papers he examined were made out in a woman's name. The name meant nothing to him, but the photograph was of Lena.

"Don't forget she's still a Party member," Peters said, "and the Party keeps its members' records in order."

Grishin leafed through the other set of papers and was confronted by his own photograph.

"A last bequest from Vassily Ostrov. A true artist, Ostrov." Peters chuckled. "And now, listen carefully . . ."

Grishin pulled up a chair, still staring at his papers and the unfamiliar name that appeared on them. In the past, whenever Colvin had furnished him with a new identity, he had always experienced a thrill of excitement at the prospect of slipping into a new skin—always found it easy to identify with a personality that had originated in someone else's head.

But now, as Peters began to speak, a sense of infinite weariness overcame him. Tired of assumed names and fictitious personalities, he made himself a promise: If he and Lena managed to get out of Moscow alive, he would never again be anything or anyone but Grishin—Mikhail Grishin.

•26•

She had no idea what it all meant. The woman guard, tall and powerfully built as any man, thrust her through the gateway so roughly that she almost fell headlong.

"Wait there, don't move. Someone will come for you."

She heard the iron gate clang shut behind her. After the effort it had cost her to negotiate the interminable corridors and countless stone steps that lay between here and her cell, she had no strength left to wonder what was happening to her.

It only gradually dawned on her, when her cuts and abrasions began to sting with revived intensity, that rain was lashing her in the face. That, too, was when she first became aware of her surroundings: She was standing alone on the street outside Bazmannaya Prison.

The footsteps startled her. They were a man's footsteps, she could tell, and they were rapidly drawing nearer. She couldn't bring herself to turn and look.

"Put this on."

She recognized the voice at once. When she didn't react, it said impatiently, "Quick, put this coat on. We've no time to lose."

Fear and bewilderment forbade her to acknowledge that the voice belonged to Peters. Obediently, she slipped her arms into the sleeves. Although the coat was fur-lined, she started shivering.

"Well? Don't expect me to button it up for you."

The sarcasm in the voice finally convinced her: It could only belong to Peters.

"Here, take this."

It was a headscarf. She put it on, tied it under her chin, and did up the coat buttons one by one.

"And now come with me. Hurry!"

"I can't walk fast," she said, wincing as her raw tongue stumbled over the words.

He took her arm and urged her forward. She tried to resist, but he towed her along by main force.

"You're hurting me, damn you!"

"That's more like it. Lose your temper and you'll make it."

"Where are you taking me?"

"Kazan Station."

"Why there?" Again she tried to resist, but his grip was like iron.

"Save your breath. Don't talk, just walk. It isn't far."

Peters maintained his brisk pace, half dragging her along. The streets were deserted. They might have been the only living souls in a city of the dead.

Then, from one minute to the next, they were alone no longer. Turning a corner, they found themselves in a street crowded with people, all of whom appeared to be heading in the same direction with the same sense of urgency.

The street ended in a broad square. Lena made out the tall stone façade of Kazan Station on the far side. Although it was lit by arc lamps, the rain was so heavy that it blurred the building's outlines and seemed to dissolve the figures scurrying across the square. Lena, still shivering with cold, half fancied that the raindrops showering down through the glare of the arc lamps were snowflakes.

Peters shepherded her across the square. She could gauge his increasing tension from the pressure of his fingers on her arm. Once they reached the steps that led up to the station entrance, he released her. Having avoided looking him in the face so far, she found it impossible to do so even now.

"These are for you."

It was all she could do to look down at his outstretched hand.

"Personal identification, travel permits, and so on. Don't worry, they're really good. Take them." He thrust the papers into her hand. "Try not to look scared, that's all. I can't walk with you, but I'll stay close. Have you got that?"

She pocketed the papers. "What am I supposed to do with them?"

"There's a train leaving for Kazan from Platform Two."

"Kazan?" He might as well have told her to set off for Siberia on foot. She was frightened now, just frightened.

"Ready?"

Although she wasn't sure she could walk unaided, it would be a relief not to have him beside her anymore. She nodded.

"Good luck."

Lena wished he'd left the words unsaid. Coming from a man like Yury Peters, they sounded like a malediction.

She knotted the headscarf more firmly under her chin and reassured herself that the papers were still in her pocket. Then she started up the broad flight of stone steps leading to the concourse. The climb seemed endless. She would never have believed that Kazan Station possessed so many steps, or that they were so steep.

Two sentries were sheltering from the rain beneath the canopy. She was almost glad of the rest when they stopped her and asked to see her papers—in fact, she was so slow to move on when they returned them that one of the men gave her a nudge.

"You'll miss your train if you don't hurry, comrade."

"What happened to your face?" said the other. He guffawed. "Jealous husband, eh? Better get going before he turns up!"

She could still hear them laughing inside the concourse. Rain was drumming on the glass roof high overhead. Ragged children with grimy faces flitted around like flocks of sparrows, pestering travelers for kopeks.

Lena looked twice at one of the girls and stopped dead. She was so sure it was Vera that she called the name aloud, but the girl just stared at her blankly. She searched the pockets of her coat for a coin but found nothing. How, she wondered, would she manage without money on her journey into the blue? Looking around, she saw Peters a few yards away. He frowned at her to hurry. Just then a bell rang—the second bell, it occurred to her, so the train would be leaving in five minutes.

Reluctantly, she walked on. Then she noticed something. The concourse reeked of tobacco smoke, sweat, rain-sodden clothing, and the exhalations of a thousand yawning people with empty bellies. The sudden realization that her sense of smell had returned sent strength flooding back into her.

She found Platform 2 and joined the line of figures shuffling toward the entrance. There was a hole in the roof, and the rain had collected in big puddles. Her papers were checked once more at the barrier; then she was out on the platform. The air here smelled different, laden with acrid fumes from locomotive smokestacks. The Kazan train was standing on her right. The first she saw of it through the murk was the glow of its big red taillights. Then she saw the cattle cars.

The sliding doors were open, and inside each car, standing shoulder to shoulder, were scores of soldiers. They looked down at her with the same bewilderment on their youthful faces as she herself felt in her heart. Glancing back along the platform, she caught a last glimpse of Peters urgently gesturing to her to board the train.

But her legs couldn't, wouldn't carry her any farther. Her one desire was to sit down somewhere and rest. She looked around for a bench or a baggage wagon, almost reeling with fatigue. Someone steadied her by the elbows.

"Thanks," she murmured automatically. "If I could just find a place to sit down . . ."

"Can you manage another few yards?"

It was his voice, deep and calm. She thought she knew now what had happened: She was still in her cell at Bazmannaya—she was delirious like Ilya, the boy in the convent infirmary. Just as Ilya's hectic dreams had centered on his dearest possession, a knife, so she was having delusions of escape.

"Can you? Only a little farther?"

She stared at him, not knowing what to say. In the end she said, "I thought I saw Vera back there."

He gently touched the cuts and bruises on her face. She felt the pain—really felt it. *That* was no delusion at least.

"Tell me I'm not dreaming."

"Quickly, Lena."

"Quickly—that's what everyone keeps telling me. I can't . . ." She looked back, but Peters had disappeared. "How does Peters fit into this? What makes you think you can trust him?"

"Come on, there's room in a car near the front. As for trusting him, I don't. We'll leave the train as soon as possible."

"Oh, Yevgeny!" She laughed weakly. "If you think I'm capable of jumping from a moving train . . . I couldn't, honestly."

"There are stations. Besides, trains like these keep stopping in open country. Come on, it's only a few more yards."

"But where are we going?"

Grishin hesitated for a moment, as much at a loss for words as she had been.

There was no Unshaskoye on the line to Kazan, no Land of the

Five Rivers. That was what he would have liked to tell her: that they were bound for the Land of the Five Rivers.

He recalled what the Khan had said before they parted: "Other mountains, another moon, another encampment." But would she understand that? What was more, would it be the truth?

He didn't know what the truth was. He didn't even know what lie to tell. Everything was so uncertain.

He put his arm around her. "Russia's a big country," he said. It sounded awfully lame, but it seemed to satisfy her. She limped off up the platform as soon as the words were out of his mouth, so fast that he found it hard to keep pace with her.